The Urbana Free Library

To renew: call 217-367-4057
or go to "*urbanafreelibrary.org*"
and select "Renew/Request Items"

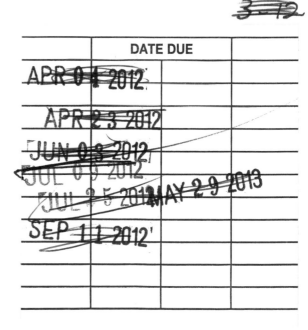

	DATE DUE	
APR 04 2012		
APR 23 2012		
JUN 08 2012		
JUL 09 2012	MAY 29 2013	
JUL 25 2012		
SEP 11 2012		

SCHMIDT STEPS BACK

Schmidt Steps Back

LOUIS BEGLEY

ALFRED A. KNOPF   NEW YORK
2012

Library of Congress Cataloging-in-Publication Data
Begley, Louis.
   Schmidt steps back / by Louis Begley.—1st ed.
      p. cm.
   Sequel to: Schmidt delivered.
ISBN 978-0-307-70065-0
   1. Schmidt, Albert (Fictitious character)—Fiction.
2. Older men—Fiction. 3. WASPs (Persons)—Fiction.
4. Retirees—Fiction. 5. Man-woman relationships—Fiction.
6. East Hampton (N.Y.)—Fiction. I. Title.
   PS3552.E373S34 2012
   813'.54—dc23   2011033751

Jacket photograph
© Christopher Campbell/the food passionates/Corbis
Jacket design by Carol Devine Carson

Manufactured in the United States of America
First Edition

For Anka, always

. . . nothing can be sole or whole
That has not been rent.

— W. B. YEATS
"Crazy Jane Talks with the Bishop"

SCHMIDT STEPS BACK

I

NEW YEAR'S EVE, eight o'clock in the morning. Sixteen more hours until the end of another shitty year of a shitty decade. What would the year ahead bring? For the nation that had—unbelievably, miraculously—overcome its history and was sending Barack Obama to the White House, Schmidt hoped it would bring redemption and cleansing. He was caught off guard by the tears that filled his eyes and wiped them away with the sleeve of his parka. Sweet tears of pride. Was there anyone, he wondered, outside Obama's family, of course, whose affection for the man was as great and as pure as Schmidt's? He dared to think there wasn't: his feelings for this extraordinary young man transcended partisan politics. They had little or nothing to do, he thought, with his having backed the Democratic ticket in national elections ever since Adlai Stevenson's second run for the presidency. The first time around, he had been too young to vote, but in 1956, realizing that Ike was going to win, he cast his vote against him out of principle and also for the fun of exasperating his father, who had adopted the reactionary convictions of his Greek shipowner clients along with their taste for custom-made shoes and suits. No, this love—why not use that word?—for

Obama existed on an altogether different level, melding with Schmidt's love for his country. Schmidt had another, more personal reason to rejoice: the hope that the curse he had laid upon himself thirteen years ago—a curse compounded of all the worst in him: jealousy and its cognate envy, blind pride, and quick unforgiving anger—had been conjured. Perhaps there was a better time ahead for him as well.

He picked up the *New York Times* at the beginning of the driveway, walked back to the house, and before going in checked the thermometer on the front porch. A chilly twenty-five degrees. With luck, by late morning it would be noticeably warmer, a good thing, inasmuch as he wanted Alice's adjustment to the caprices of Eastern Seaboard weather to be a gradual one. Four days earlier, the temperature had risen to an astonishing fifty-eight degrees, a record Schmidt had read in the *Times*. Christmas Day had been a cooler but still ludicrously balmy fifty-four degrees. According to the *Times*'s weather forecast, the pendulum would swing all the way back on the first day of 2009: low of ten, high of twenty-five. He deposited the newspaper on the kitchen table and went out again for his ritual morning inspection of the property. Sonia would be arriving in a few minutes to put his breakfast on the table. It was an unnecessary task—he was quite capable of preparing his own breakfast—but there was so little work in the house these days that, believing firmly that nothing demoralizes staff as quickly as idleness, he felt pressed to find things for her to do. The big snow—more than five inches—dumped on Bridgehampton in the space of a few hours the week before Christmas had melted in the warm weather, reviving the grass. It sparkled green as in early June. Everything else looked good too, especially the azalea and rhododendron on the far edge of the back lawn. Somehow the marauding deer had spared them, even without the usual protective black nylon netting he had instructed Gus Parrish not to use. When the gardener, taken aback, had asked why, Schmidt heard himself admit the embarrassing truth: the netting made the bushes look to him like prehistoric beasts poised to advance on the house. The sight made him uneasy. It was Schmidt's turn to be surprised when Gus acceded to the wish without the least indication of thinking his client had gone bonkers. Such discretion was cause once again for Schmidt to congratulate himself on having hired Gus's outfit to take over when Jim Bogard's nephew finally followed his uncle into retirement. All told, the Bogards had looked after the property since before it had passed to Schmidt, when it still belonged to Mary's aunt Martha, and he and Mary, his late wife, and their daughter, Charlotte, would come to spend weekends and vacations there as Martha's nearest relations and guests. Confidence is rewarded more often than mistrust. He had told Gus that he had a special reason for wanting the place to look spick-and-span on New Year's Eve, and Gus had come through. In fact, Schmidt's experience with Gus had led him to believe that when it came to reliability and finish, which at Schmidt's old law firm was quaintly called "completed staff work," Gus's people were to other gardeners in the Hamptons what Wood & King had been to the lesser breeds of New York lawyers practicing personal injury law out of offices near City Hall or Borough Hall and, ever since all restraints on advertising had broken down, touting their services in Spanish-language ads in subway cars. Gus's eye-popping bills were part and parcel of the deal, and they too recalled W & K. The name of each of the friendly Colombians who lavished care on Schmidt's lawn, edged the flower beds, and blew away fallen leaves with the infernal roar that threw into a panic Schmidt's old Siamese Sy and his new Abyssinian kitten Pi, was followed by his billing rate, a description of the services performed, and the time spent on the task. The hours, Schmidt was sure, were discreetly padded, a time-honored practice of W & K associates as well. Telephone call with Mr. Schmidt, so many tenths of an hour, revising a memo in accordance with his remarks, two hours and seven-tenths of an hour, researching at Mr. Schmidt's request points X, Y, and Z to back up the memo, eleven hours and one-tenth. Really, Mr. Schmidt would ask himself: eleven and one-tenth hours in one day? Whether the invoice was from W & K or Gus, the billable-hour entries would be followed by a list of expenses subject to reimbursement. Telephone toll calls, postage, messenger services, duplicating, late-evening meals, and taxi fare home from the office became, in the backup to Gus's bills, so many bags of eight sorts of fertilizer and weed and insect killers, and when the chattering Colombian ladies, who planted and weeded, joined the crew, also bulbs and plants and potting soil.

He heard Sonia's car on the driveway, a white Mercedes, and a fairly late model no less, the provenance of which had been puzzling him ever since the summer when she first showed up in it. Did it belong to a boyfriend? Had she won it at a church raffle or bought it with her savings? In the latter case, he was overpaying her. But how would he get the answer if he persisted in not asking the question? Time for breakfast. He greeted Sonia and sat down. The coffee was boiling hot and strong, the yogurt not half bad, the grapes excellent. Missing were the croissants and scones that he used to buy each morning at Sesame, the wonderful caterer where he still got chicken salad, cheese, and ravioli *in brodo*. The memory of those pastries, banished from his breakfast table by Dr. Tang, the Chinese-American lady who took over from his old friend and family physician, David Kendall, upon his retirement, made his mouth water. It made him wonder, too, whether he knew anyone who had not retired. Yes, of course: Gil Blackman, his college roommate and best friend, still making films; Mike Mansour, as busy as ever with his billions; and the splendid Caroline Canning and her awful husband, Joe, scribbling away.

Silly business, Schmidt thought, Dr. Tang's attention to his diet. In their own way so were the ministrations of Gus and his predecessors, continued in accordance with his orders every year since Aunt Martha died and left the house to Mary. How many years did that make? He shrugged: almost forty. How much longer would they continue? His guess was no more than ten years. He had asked Dr. Tang whether she could foresee the form in which death would come for him. You won't scare me, he had said, everyone has an appointment in Samarra, and I own a cemetery plot with a view of Peconic Bay I rather like. She laughed gaily in reply and told him that with a patient in such good health it was impossible to predict. Schmidt's simultaneous translation was Don't ask stupid questions, leave it to team death, they'll figure it out. Ever polite, he had merely laughed back. In truth, he had his own hunches: stroke or cancer, demonic diseases that don't always go for the quick kill. But whatever it might turn out to be, no one, absolutely no one, would get him to move into a nursing home. If he was compos mentis, and not yet paralyzed, he would find his own way to the exit. Otherwise, the instructions left with Gil, naming him the sole arbiter of Schmidt's life and death, should do the job, with a little friendly nudge from Gil if need be. It was no more than he would do for Gil, who had made his own arrangements giving Schmidt the power of decision. Dementia, the illness most likely to cut off the means of escape, held more terror than any other. But he had not heard of a single ancestor, going back three generations, who had been so afflicted. The other side of the coin, the agreeable side, was his overall good health. Once he got going in the morning, he was still quite limber. In truth, he doubted there was much difference between his condition thirteen years earlier, when he first called on Alice in Paris, to take an example that preoccupied him, and the way he was now. Not unless you wanted to fixate on the deep lines, running to the corners of his mouth, that had only gotten deeper or the hollow cheeks or the fold of skin sagging from his neck. Taken together, they gave him an expression so lugubrious that efforts to smile made him look like a gargoyle. The situation was less brilliant when it came to his libido and sexual performance. The grade he had given himself when last put to the test had been no higher than a pass, but as he had told Alice, he had not yet tried any of the miracle pills that old geezer-in-chief Bob Dole swore by on television. Besides, the test in question had been unfair: the lady whom he may have disappointed could not hold a candle to the incomparable Alice. Did his age and the ravages of time make it reprehensible to keep overpaying the Hampton mafia of gardeners, handymen, carpenters, and plumbers for the pleasure of having everything at his house just so? Or to pay the outrageous real estate taxes that financed town services, neatly itemized on the tax bill as though to taunt him by proving that he derived no personal benefit from them? Hell, there were lots of men unable to get a hard-on and lots of women who had faked orgasms until the blessed moment when they could finally declare that at their age they'd given the whole thing up, living comfortably in houses much grander than his. Spending more money than he! Why shouldn't he do the same? He had to live somewhere, and this was the place he liked the best. Who was there to complain about it? It was his money, his to spend or give away. He no longer had a legal heir, and his bequests would be covered by his estate many times over, leaving a handsome pile for Harvard. Unless he decided to leave the bulk of that money instead to Alice, in which case Harvard would still receive an elegant though no longer extravagant gift. Alice! Alice would be in Bridgehampton in four hours! In his house. She would be sleeping under his roof. Would he have preferred to receive her elsewhere? For instance, in some cutesy cottage in Sag Harbor with crooked floors and a permanent smell of mold? The answer was a loud and clear no: the costs be damned!

He told Sonia that he was going out to run errands, and no, she didn't need to stay to help with lunch, or to clear and do the dishes afterward, and that if his guest Mrs. Alice Verplanck called while he was out she was to say that he would be home within the hour and would call back. In fact, he didn't believe her cell phone would work in the U.S., but it was possible that she'd use the driver's. Elated and anxious, he got the Audi station wagon out of the garage, the successor to the Volvo he had traded in regretfully at the one-hundred-forty-thousand-mile mark, and drove first to Wainscott for fish chowder, then back west on Route 27 to Sesame for the bread and cheese and ravioli *in brodo* that would be their lunch on New Year's Day, as well as croissants that would be Alice's breakfast, and finally back to Bridgehampton, where the florist had prepared the small bouquets he had ordered for the kitchen table and for Alice's room. That took care of their needs through New Year's Day, when only convenience stores would be open in the Hamptons. Restaurants would be closed as well, but he didn't need to worry about dinners. They were going to Mike Mansour's New Year's Eve party, and Gil and Elaine Blackman had invited them to dinner the next day, a thoughtful gesture that had made Schmidt childishly grateful.

Alice had telephoned on Friday, the day after Christmas, and said she would take a New Year's Eve flight from Paris that was due to land at Kennedy at ten-thirty in the morning. She would have to get up before dawn, but she preferred that to the traffic on the way to the airport and the mob she would face once she got there if she took a later flight. She wouldn't hear of his meeting her at JFK; in fact she absolutely forbade it. But she accepted his offer to send a car to drive her to Bridgehampton. After they hung up, he went out on the back porch and stood there motionless, letting what she had told him sink in. Alice was really coming! He had told himself over and over that she was much too serious to change her mind and say she had decided after all that she didn't want to see him. Nonetheless, hearing her actually say I will take such and such a plane and I will be at the New York airport at such and such hour, and you can send someone to bring me to your house had the effect on him of a miracle. He had considered briefly sending Bryan, his combination handyman and house and cat sitter, who knew all the back and service roads, but in the end he concluded that the conversation of that loquacious dropout and reformed drug dealer was more than Alice should be asked to bear after eight hours in the plane. A wizened Irishman ferried Schmidt to and from JFK when Bryan was busy or Schmidt was able to put him off without giving offense. And so it was the Irishman who was sent with instructions to be early at the arrival hall beyond customs, well ahead of the flight's landing, and to hold very high and visibly the sign with Alice's name.

He looked at his watch. Eleven-thirty. She must be on the Long Island Expressway. Having checked the Air France Web site, he knew that the plane had landed fifteen minutes early. At that hour of the morning lines at immigration shouldn't be long, even on the eve of a holiday. Therefore, unless there was a hitch at the baggage claim, she would have been in the car at eleven-fifteen and therefore should be due at his house within an hour and a half to two hours. That was a conservative estimate. It took into account both the chance of bad traffic and Murphy's tendency to obey the speed limits, for which one couldn't really fault him. In a momentary regression to his days as a hard drinker, Schmidt poured himself a double bourbon, added an ice cube, and sat down in the rocking chair. The kitchen table was set with the good china and silver. The red bouquet was a nice touch. Really, there was nothing to be ashamed about in his household arrangements. He could rock in his chair and sip his whiskey in peace. At one, the telephone rang. It was Murphy reporting that they were approaching Water Mill. The man was smarter than he looked! Traffic was moving well. So they'd be arriving in fifteen minutes. His sixth sense told him when the car approached his driveway. He downed the last of his drink and rushed out to the front porch. Someone had taught Murphy to be respectful of the gravel on his clients' driveways. The car was creeping toward the house. At last it came to a halt. Schmidt opened the door. The hand that pressed his was enclosed in a long glove of dark red suede that he recognized. Alice had worn that same pair when they dined in the restaurant on rue de Bourgogne on the fourteenth of October, two and a half months ago.

Schmidt's first sight of Alice was at her marriage to Tim Verplanck, a young associate at W & K who had become his favorite. It took place at a church in Washington, Alice's father being then French ambassador to the U.S. That afternoon he danced with her at the embassy reception. She had white freesia in the coils of her hair, which was the color of dark old gold, and wore a veil of billowing ivory lace that Mary had said must have been her grandmother's. In the coming months and years there had been dinners—Mary would have remembered how many, it was the sort of thing she kept track of—at the Schmidts' apartment when, according to W & K custom, they entertained associates who worked for him, with their wives or fiancées; there had been also the annual office dinner dances for all lawyers and wives and, after Tim had been taken into the firm, much smaller dinners for partners and wives. Each time Schmidt had been taken aback, truly bowled over, by her beauty, her chic, and her bearing, so perfectly erect, her head held high, the rich mass of her hair twisted into a chignon or gathered by a clasp over the nape of her neck. She had the imperturbable good manners of a diplomat's daughter. Her vertiginously long and perfect legs had a prized place in his memory. An opportunity to inspect them had been offered to the entire firm when she came to an office function wearing a fire-engine-red miniskirt and black mesh tights, no other office wife being attired in anything remotely so eye-catching. But Schmidt was able to swear that he had not coveted her then or at any other time while Tim was alive, office liaisons, not least adulterous ones, being taboo for him and, he believed, all other decent men of his class and generation. There was another, unavowable reason: while Mary lived, all the women who had excited him had something louche about them. They were women he had picked up at hotel bars, a law student with whom he had inexcusably smoked pot while on a recruiting trip to the West Coast. The one exception would have been the half-Asian au pair who had looked after Charlotte. That shy and polite girl had offered herself to him so innocently, and yet with such explicit urgency, that prudence and principles flew out the window. But even if he had allowed himself to become aroused by Alice, he would not have dared to think of her as someone who might assent to an afternoon's copulation on her living room sofa or in a Midtown tourist hotel. It was the sort of proposal she would have repelled with scorn. She was in love with Tim, that was obvious, and even if something had gone awry between them, which he had no reason to suspect, she was too splendid, too proud—had she been a man he might have said a *chevalier sans peur et sans reproche*—for some squalid affair with Schmidt or another married partner of her husband's. Then she disappeared from Schmidt's horizon. In fact, the whole family dropped out of sight when Tim took over the direction of the firm's Paris office, Alice and the children naturally joining him. He showed up at the New York office rarely, much less frequently than his predecessors, who had all been punctilious about staying in touch, regularly attending firm meetings in New York and pacing the corridors on the lookout for open doors whereby partners signaled that a visit would not be unwelcome. It was a useful way to keep a finger on the firm's pulse and be sure nothing was brewing that would affect the Paris office.

So it happened that when he called on Alice in Paris in April 1995 to offer his condolences in person after Tim's shocking and completely unexpected death, he had not seen her for thirteen years or more likely longer. It seemed to him that she was even more beautiful: her aspect was more womanly, gentler and less haughty. The gamine had grown up. Astoundingly—in moments of subsequent bitterness he would think absurdly—he had fallen in love at once, without his lips ever having touched hers, without a single embrace. Call it late-onset puppy love; he believed it would have happened just as certainly if he had been blindfolded and had merely heard her laughter again. And now, after the hiatus of another thirteen years since that April meeting, it seemed to him that his love was intact. If there was happiness in store for him, it had to be a future shared with her.

She traveled light like a young girl, with a single smallish suitcase decorated with red decals to make it easily recognizable on airport conveyor belts and a carry-on shaped like a sausage that she hadn't bothered to zip up, so that a great number of French magazines and newspapers, and what looked like manuscripts, peeked out from it. He carried her bags upstairs and showed her the room she would stay in. It had been Charlotte's: sunny, with the bow windows looking out onto the back lawn and garden and, beyond the boundary of the property, the great saltwater pond whose population of wild geese no longer migrated. Alice exclaimed over the loveliness and said she must have a complete tour of the house and the garden. But first she would like lunch, then a bath, and then a long nap. After lunch, however, she changed her mind and said they had better look around before it got dark. When they had finished and were standing at the door to her room, he said, You like this place. You might like living here.

She didn't answer but remained motionless. Wondering whether he had guessed what she wanted, he put his arms around her. Her mouth tasted of the lunch; her hair and her clothes smelled very slightly of sweat and other odors that told the story of the hours spent in airports and on the plane. The unmediated intimacy excited him like a stolen sweet. He prolonged the kiss, but just as he felt himself harden she pulled away.

It's bath time, she said very quietly. Where will you be?

Right there, he said, pointing to his room, directly across the hall. I'll be pretending to read and listen to music.

May I come to see you?

Schmidt turned up the upstairs thermostat slightly and settled into the red armchair in his room. Ordinarily he kept the house on the cool— some would say downright cold—side, but Alice wasn't yet used to the cold of a wooden beach house pounded by North Atlantic gales. Or to sharing it with an old fellow with a lifelong habit of scrimping on heating oil. On his night table were a desperately sad novel by a Russian Jew set around the time of the battle for Stalingrad and a stack of unread issues of the *New Yorker* and the *New York Review of Books* that had been accumulating since right after Election Day, when he left on an inspection tour of Life Centers operated in Central and Eastern Europe and some states of the former Soviet Union by Mike Mansour's foundation, of which Schmidt was still the head. He was finding the novel so powerful that he had to pace himself in absorbing its terrors; he didn't think he was up to another scene of human degradation just then. Were the clean-cut, affable Ukrainians who received him at the Kiev Life Center familiar with that tale of horrors—horrors that must have engulfed their grandfathers if not their fathers? Before going to sleep the night before, he had put down the book just as an old Bolshevik, a commissar of superior rank, was being arrested for reasons he didn't understand. A much younger commissar slapped him repeatedly just to break his prisoner. For the moment, the most Schmidt could handle was to listen, while his mind wandered, to the Connecticut classical music station to which the radio was always tuned. Alice drew him to her powerfully, yes, but what he felt for her was far beyond sexual attraction. It was love, albeit an old man's love. He wanted to keep her at his side. He had offered marriage, which he devoutly wanted out of a belief, which he knew was contradicted by experience, that marriage held out a promise of stability. But he had told her he was prepared to settle for living together anyplace, on any terms she might wish. And the offer of himself was on a satisfaction-guaranteed trial basis, with assurances he would creep away quietly if she found him wanting. Was it fair, was it reasonable, to propose marriage or some other form of cohabitation with a man who had just turned seventy-eight to a woman who was sixty-three? The only honest answer was no, but he didn't want to take no for an answer and thought sincerely that arguments against his suit might be overrated. He had fully disclosed the risks, which anyway were obvious, going so far as to say that were he her father or brother he would advise against her taking them. But it was up to her. As for the wisdom of his own position, although marriage was what he ardently desired, he knew full well the penalties for entering into one that fails. In the worst case, you live with a cell mate slowly becoming your enemy and, on average, with someone more or less annoying. This was to say nothing of the physical intimacy that cohabitation made difficult to avoid. Bad enough for the woman, feeling obliged to submit to an unattractive old fellow's groping—Schmidt did not exclude himself from the thesis that all old men are intrinsically unattractive—and rather worse for the man called upon to take the initiative and accomplish repeatedly the miracle of penetration. A voice reminded Schmidt that divorce laws had fixed those problems. One could agree in advance that the unhappy husband or wife could cut and run. Perhaps his questions could be answered definitively only after the fact; it was a case of proceeding at your own risk.

Schmidt abruptly ended these ruminations. She was beautiful, fragrant, and more desirable than any woman he had known, with the sole exception of Carrie, Hecate herself, who had come to him in the form of a twenty-year-old Puerto Rican waitress. For two years indelibly marked on every nerve in his body she had been his mistress. The idyll had ended just as one would expect. She had found a blond giant gentle as a lamb and went to him with Schmidt's blessing, carrying a child whose paternity was to be uncertain. As for Alice: she may not be a magical creature of the night, but she was his type! Who is to say that the game is not worth the candle? Cowardice, he knew only too well, carried its own penalties: sour solitude and despair. Concerns about being unfair to Alice were balderdash. She was a big girl. A moment ago, she had asked whether she could come to see him after her bath. That was hardly an ambiguous gesture.

At breakfast, he had not so much as scanned the first pages of the *Times*. Now he retrieved it from the kitchen and soon

found the only piece of half-decent news: Al Franken continued to lead the deplorable Norm Coleman in the Minnesota
recount, but only by fifty votes. Recount! Schmidt had hoped
never to hear that word again, after that interlude of thug-
gery carried on all the way up to the Supreme Court that had
put W in the White House. Other than that, only tales of horror and perplexity. The day before, Hamas had fired a rocket
from Gaza that reached eighteen miles deep into Israel killing
a mother of four. According to the UN, the Israeli assault on
that wretched strip of land had already killed three hundred
seventy Palestinians, of whom sixty-two were women and
children. What did those figures prove, other than the futility
of killing large numbers of Palestinians? It had hardly broken
their will to fight. On the other hand did Hamas try to spare
Israeli women and children? That issue was not touched upon
by the *Times*. Would Hamas and Hezbollah settle for anything
less than pushing Israel into the sea? Probably not, but if they
pushed hard enough, the Israelis would drop the bomb. Just
where they would drop it was a good question to which he
was willing to bet not even Mike Mansour had an answer. And
if the Iranians too got the bomb, they would surely use it on
Tel Aviv in response, a catastrophe for the Jews on the scale
of Auschwitz, whereupon the Israelis would nuke Tehran and
Kharg Island, the latter move starting a chain reaction of
chaos for every country dependent on Iranian oil. Wouldn't
someone—Russians or Pakistanis or the Chinese, or even
North Koreans—come to the aid of their Iranian and Arab
friends? And do what? At that point Schmidt gave up. He didn't
know, and he wasn't a *Times* columnist required to pretend
that he did. With any luck he'd be dead before the answer was
revealed. Another article touched on a subject nearer his old

expertise. The SEC was sticking to its guns defending mark-to-market accounting, which required financial institutions to write down daily the assets carried on their balance sheets to whatever amount a buyer would be willing to pay that day. Schmidt adamantly believed that if the rule were suspended or abolished, the banks would rob the public blind. Anyone who had ever dealt with them had to come to the same conclusion. There was, however, a reasonable counterargument that the journalist hadn't mentioned. It held that an asset wasn't necessarily worthless just because there were no takers for it at a given time. Should such an asset then be really written down to zero on the bank's balance sheet? It would be the same as saying that your house on a shady street in Scarsdale, for which you paid two million dollars three years earlier, was suddenly worth zero just because the Dow had crashed and for the moment no buyers were to be found. Another headaching puzzle. Perhaps Mike Mansour had the right answer. When Alice and he saw Mike at dinner that evening, he might ask him. The great financier was never short of convictions or shy about pronouncing them. One could mock Mike's high-roller style, but when he opined about financial matters, it was well to pay attention. Schmidt had learned that lesson in October 2007, when Mike told him to sell shares and buy treasuries and gold.

Had he dozed off? How long had she been in his room? He became conscious of her presence only when she said, Knock knock, it's the lady from Paris. So silent when she moved, so like his cats, and his lost Carrie, Alice stood before him smiling, barefoot, toenails painted a red he found heart-rendingly gallant, clad in a beige sweat suit that he realized, when he put his arms around her, was made of a cashmere so soft it felt as if he were touching her naked body. He tried to kiss her, but she turned her head and said, Schmidtie, I've come for a serious talk. (That was the name she had discovered by which his friends called him; he disliked his given name, Albert, and its odious diminutives.)

Of course, Alice, he said, we can have a serious talk, but will you allow me an opening statement?

She nodded.

It's very simple: I love you. I've gone over everything I told you when I saw you in October. I meant it then, and I mean it now. Please give me a second chance and live with me wedded or in sin, here in this house, or in New York or Paris—or anywhere, so long as we are together and I give full satisfaction.

He wasn't sure what kind of response he expected, but he was relieved to see her smile. Schmidtie, was that the opening statement or the conclusion? What do lawyers call it? Prayer for relief?

A bit of both, he answered, but please remember that I haven't rested my case.

Then go ahead and rest it, Schmidtie. She giggled. Don't keep me waiting.

He took one long step approaching the armchair where she sat. Sinking to his knees, he put his arms around her legs and pressed his face against them.

Wait, wait, she whispered, I too have something to say. I wouldn't be here if I didn't like you, if I didn't want to be with you. But thirteen years have gone by. At our ages that is like a lifetime. Do you remember how you told me I shouldn't tie myself to an old man? Now you're even older. But I'm not afraid of that, Schmidtie. I'm more worried about what you will think of me. Now I'm old too with an old woman's body.

His notion of what the occasion demanded moved him to protest. He told her that she had not changed, that she was still the magnificent blond beauty he'd fallen in love with, that she had never been more desirable. The wonder of it, he realized, was that he was telling her the truth.

Hush, Schmidtie, she said, I know you're chivalrous. Do you also have to be silly? Have you asked yourself what you'll find when I take off my clothes?

She took his hand and guided it under her top, pressing it to her breast. Can you feel how it has changed? It's flabby. My whole body has changed. Puff and flab.

He renewed his protest, but she said: Shush! This afternoon will be all right, because it will feel new, like doing it the first time. But tonight, and then tomorrow? You've such good manners that you'll probably try to make love to me every day while I'm here. But it will feel like a chore, not because you don't love me or don't want to give me pleasure, but because we're old. What will you do? Use those pills? On the sly, of course. You're so very proper.

Oh, Alice, he whispered. No more talk.

But I told you that we must talk. How can we just forget that dreadful party in Water Mill? And then you had me come to London. For what? To berate and humiliate me. To make sure I knew that you were in a rage? And that awful loveless sex that followed. More like rape. And then all those years of silence, until you reappeared out of nowhere. Why? Because you had figured out that I'm available. Am I right?

Alice, we both know what happened thirteen years ago. I

was a fool. An idiot. I've admitted that, I've begged your pardon for it.

And I've told you I'm not angry, not anymore. I accept my share of blame. But let's make sure that this time we don't stumble. I couldn't bear it.

She had done nothing to make him take his hand away from her breast, and he had kept up the caresses, extending them to the other breast. Equal treatment. She began to moan.

Wait, wait, she said. Listen. Please, no more talk about the future. Not now. Don't make me think you are foolish. Let me propose marriage to you. When I think we are ready.

I promise, he answered. I promise.

II

ALICE WAS ASLEEP, lost in such great depths
that he was able to turn on the lamp on the dresser and collect his clothes without disturbing her. The little noise she
made in response was, he thought, a moan of contentment.
Then she buried her head under the pillows. There was nothing surprising about sleeping so soundly after a night in the
plane followed by sex that had ended in an exuberant climax,
but he couldn't help taking it as proof that he was a good host.
The thought made him feel proud even though he knew it was
childish. He too had sunk into slumber but only for a short
while. He awoke to find an arm thrown around him. Her body
was glued to his. All that ardor, her unabashed concentration,
as if she'd been straining to hear from afar some impossibly
high note that would set off the explosion of joy! That was
also how he remembered their first time. Eyes closed, body
arched, she had abandoned herself to pleasure, on her own
terms and as frankly and completely as Carrie. Certain gestures
that Carrie had taught him were now brushed away, without comment or anger. How little they mattered, whether
welcomed or banned! The protocol of making love to Alice
was in reality not unlike the one he and Mary had adhered

to during more than thirty years of a decorous and mostly affectionate marriage, but the result was profoundly different. Mary had almost never reached an orgasm. Buried somewhere inside her, he was convinced, was the fear that doing so would give him the upper hand. She'd sooner settle for adolescent pleasures of making out on the living room sofa, foreplay prolonged beyond reason, and, after the act, a clammy letdown. Probably she thought that the corollary—his feelings of guilt or humiliation—were well deserved. Shameful to make comparisons, he knew that, but could he avoid them? Alice and he would never reach the terrifying fury he had known with Carrie, but Carrie had brought him to the outer limit of his body's endurance. He didn't think that he could have followed her there much longer.

He went down to the kitchen, fed the cats, made himself a cup of tea, and drank it while he finished reading the arts section of the *Times*, which he had left downstairs. Then he washed in the guest bathroom so as not to disturb Alice and dressed for dinner. He looked at his watch. There was no hurry. Alice could sleep another half hour and still have plenty of time to get ready. Back in the kitchen, he poured himself a bourbon and cut a chunk of the Manchego he had bought for lunch. So armed, he went out on the back porch. An exquisitely drawn new moon hung over the pond. There was no wind, and the only sound was the distant rumbling of the surf. The temperature had dropped considerably, the outdoor thermometer reading only twenty degrees, and before long the cold began to get to him. He retreated to the kitchen.

The Connecticut station was playing Beethoven's Ninth. The music enveloped him, insistent, questioning, and premonitory. During an intolerable pause, the fate of every living being remained suspended, uncertain. Then, in a leap, came the exultation of the summons to joy. He responded with assent: yes, joy and gratitude. As though she too had been summoned by the triumphant crescendo, Alice appeared in the door, regal and slender in a floor-length black velvet sheath that left her shoulders bare. Some small part of Schmidt's admiration yielded to perplexity. Was it a mistake, her wearing a dress she must have bought many years ago, when she still had a young woman's skin? Would he dare suggest as much? Did she even have with her another dress she could change into? He walked toward her and opened his arms. Vast relief: Alice's shoulders were smooth and creamy. He kissed them, inhaling deeply, wanting the smell of her body to fill his lungs. Such unexpected and undeserved good fortune that she should be so beautiful, that his lips should be so welcome, that she should be smiling at him!

Schmidtie, look at me, she said, don't just stand there and nuzzle. Do you think I look all right? I want the truth: can I get away with this if I throw something over my shoulders?

"Something" was a scarf made of two lengths of silk of different colors, emerald and wine red, sewn together, that she held out at arm's length.

You're sure it's all right? she asked. I don't want to embarrass you.

He smiled and nodded.

With or without the scarf you're perfect.

He had let the Audi's engine run for ten minutes with the heater turned on. The interior would be toasty now. If only they still made front seats like those of the Nash he used to borrow for heavy dates at college, Alice would be pressed against his side, perhaps nibbling his ear. Instead, her hand was on his knee, communicating by varying degrees of pressure momentary panic at headlights that she was sure were blinding him, the menacing bulk of tailgating SUVs and pickup trucks, and, at intersections, unseen cars surging out of the night to join the flow of traffic.

We're almost there, he said to soothe her.

It's all right, really. Excuse me. What will the party be like?

As such events go, not bad. You'll get an excellent dinner. And very good wine. Mike doesn't skimp on quality or quantity.

He had noted the power of her memory. She forgot nothing—not a single telephone number or date. She would have remembered what he had told her in Paris about Mike's billions and how they continued multiplying in years when others lost money; his beginnings as an Egyptian Jew whose family had fled Nasser; as well as the work of the foundation at the head of which he had placed Schmidt. As though to prove him right, she reminded him that in Paris, when he regaled her with stories of Mike's antics, his tone had been acerbic. Had that changed? Yes, he replied. I've changed and he has changed. He has been an extraordinarily loyal, close friend. On top of that, I owe him a huge debt of gratitude. Without the foundation job I wouldn't have made that trip in ninety-five to inspect the foundation's offices and I wouldn't have seen you!

Mike has been twice married and divorced, he continued, but in all the years I've known him he hasn't had an official girlfriend. There is a lady in his life now, but it's a closely guarded secret. She's Caroline Canning, a biographer married to a novelist. She and her husband are always there, at all his parties, and even at small, intimate dinners. You'll surely see them tonight.

Is the novelist husband Joe Canning? Alice asked hesitantly.
He's one of our authors.

That's the one, replied Schmidt. I hadn't realized he was
published in France. Let's see . . . who else will be there? Gil
and Elaine.

And we are to have dinner at their house tomorrow.

Glancing at her sideways, he saw that she was biting her lip.

After a silence that seemed to him very long, she spoke
again. Schmidtie, she said, I'm so worried about all this. We
will be opening a wound that's barely healed.

No, we won't, he replied. Please don't worry. The Blackmans want my good. They want my happiness. They will
make you feel welcome. You'll see.

He took her hand, kissed it, replaced it on his knee.

He hadn't told her, and wasn't sure that he would ever tell
her, that Gil, from whom he had almost no secrets, had pleaded
with him not to be undone by the loathsome Popov, the bizarre
incident in Water Mill, and the fiasco in London—to hang on
to Alice for dear life. She was, Gil had said, his one chance
for happiness. Had he listened to him, the wound would have
healed long, long ago. But as it was she might take offense,
perhaps unconsciously, at Gil's intrusion into her privacy. He
had to be careful not to allow that to happen.

Slowing down, he turned onto Cobb Road. The rest of the
crowd, he added, is hard to predict. Mike claims this will be
a small dinner. Two tables of twelve. But Mike is always on
the lookout for new best friends. That's how he picked me up.
One might encounter anyone. He has a weird sense of humor
and not much regard for what others think, and people can't
resist his billions. It's like catnip. You'll see for yourself. And
now we're really there.

He turned left on Flying Point Road, then right into a driveway, and lowered the window on his side. A guard appeared from the darkness and called out, Good evening, Mr. Schmidt, and Happy New Year to you and the lady. Please drive up to the front door.

Same to you, Carter, Schmidt shouted back. Carter was a good man. He'd park the car so its nose pointed in the right direction for departure and relieve Schmidt of the need to back out of the long driveway, a sport Schmidt had once thought he excelled at. Now he did his best to avoid it, fearing not so much the pain he felt turning his head the necessary number of degrees as the breakdown it caused in hand-eye coordination.

A sense of great calm had descended on Schmidt. Alice was seated on Mike's right, and Gil was on her other side. That Mike had made her the guest of honor was an elegant gesture. He knew less than Gil of his and Alice's history but had been from the start in favor of the nice lady in Paris. Even more important for Schmidt, however, was that Alice and Gil were talking and laughing with great animation. Schmidt thought that he too had been treated well in the placement. He was between Elaine and Caroline, whom he had come to consider, like Mike, his true friend, at a safe distance from all three of the deeply tanned women with big white teeth and lacquered blond hairdos. He didn't know them any more than the two massive men or the third one, pale as paper and emaciated. On the contrary, those three couples—clearly they were couples even if he didn't know which woman came with which man—seemed very well acquainted. Something about them, however—the long pastel dresses? the gaily colored bow ties and cummerbunds? the Florida tans?—was eerily familiar, like the refrain of a song one remembers after the rest of the words have been forgotten. Eureka! The common denominator was the Meadow Club. Did that bastion of what the Hamptons had once been now open its gates to the occasional superrich Jew? Tsk tsk! If that was the case, Mike was giving his new toy a whirl by inviting a clutch of his fellow members. Come to think of it, while drinks were being served Schmidt had observed more Aryans than representatives of the Chosen. He could be sure only of the master of the house, Gil and Elaine, Joe Canning, if indeed Joe was present, Bruce Holbein and his chatterbox wife, and fifty percent of Alice as counterweights to the club goyim! Schmidt was convinced that Caroline was a shiksa. That and nothing else explained why she put up with Joe. She was expiating the sins of her Jew-baiting mother and father, brothers and sisters. But where was Joe? Schmidt hadn't spotted him in the living room while he was drinking his two martinis and making sure Alice was not stranded, but then he hadn't exactly been looking for him. For all he knew, Joe, true to his furtive ways, had been lurking behind a ficus plant. By now, however, he should have come out of hiding. Was anyone else missing? The chair on the other side of Caroline was vacant. He turned toward her with a questioning look.

That's Joe place, she told him, as though to forestall a question. He gets more and more uneasy dealing with groups he doesn't know, so I asked Mike to let him have his vodka in solitude in a spare room. Mike is such a good sport! He installed Joe in the study off the front hall and brought him a carafe of vodka and a bowl of caviar with his own hands!

Mike has every reason to bring Joe caviar, said Schmidt's inner voice.

I could tell Joe was pleased, Caroline continued. He'll be along in a moment. Yes, seating him next to me at dinner is another of Mike's kind indulgences. In Joe's family, and among his parents' friends, husbands and wives always sat together. He finds that to do the same makes him more comfortable.

I see, said Schmidt.

Come on, Schmidtie, don't you think it's sweet? In society, things are done this way or that way. Before you know it you have a rule no one dares to question; you just go along. Joe doesn't think he needs to conform. Anyway, we all accumulate peculiarities as we grow older. Perhaps even you, Schmidtie!

Surely, he answered.

But I bet you don't always know what they are. The thing about Joe is that he knows. He really knows! Probably it's what makes him such a good novelist. By the way, the one he's working on is terrific.

What good news! We haven't had a new Canning for at least two years.

Three, she corrected him. He says that he now enjoys writing more slowly. Also eating ice cream slowly. Before, he always tried to eat it while it was cold, before it melted. It turns out that he likes it liquid. Actually he's very busy just now. Gil and he are working on a film treatment of his first novel, the one that mirrors his grandmother's life. It cuts pretty close to the bone, so he is very touchy about it. I'm keeping my fingers crossed.

Schmidt had heard about the project from Gil and would have liked to ask her whether there was anything Joe wasn't touchy about. But before he could speak, she tapped his hand and said, Ah, here at last.

Canning was heading toward the table. One might have

said he was sauntering over if he hadn't been slightly dragging his left foot, possibly owing to a small stroke or a back problem or, as seemed more probable to Schmidt, the acting out of his reluctance to draw nearer. At last, he deposited a kiss on the top of Caroline's head and sat down looking straight through Schmidt and disregarding the hand that Schmidt had held out. This was par for the course. What a preposterous man: a lawyer doing something or other in the management of an insurance company who remakes himself into a writer, divorces a wife as unpleasant as he, and promptly marries this splendid lady, who is to boot a noted and respected biographer! He pulls off that coup even before publishing his first novel, which makes him famous, and remains as appalling ever since. Why does he have to go through some variant of this insulting routine each time we meet? He retracted his hand.

Joe, said Caroline, Schmidtie's here, he's been trying to greet you. And on the other side of him is Elaine.

Yes, yes, Canning answered peevishly, even in my diminished state—*non sum qualis eram*—he! he! I can still recognize my old acquaintance from college and law school, and also the wife of my occasional collaborator, himself a college acquaintance. I see them here often enough. Shall we say each time I set foot here? What would that be, twice a day? Or does Gil now count as a friend? I can't tell.

This could have been taken as a cue for Elaine to assure both Cannings of Gil's and her devotion, or for Schmidt to throw his glass of red wine at the novelist, if that could be managed without splashing Caroline. But Elaine said nothing, and Schmidt didn't take the bait, only saying to himself, Goddamn Canning, he has gotten under Elaine's skin, a feat hitherto thought impossible. Out of compassion for the polite and clever Caroline, he spoke to Canning: I'm very glad to see you, Joe. I've just returned from Europe. It's been quite a while since we last met.

It really doesn't matter. One doesn't pay attention to such trivia.

His voice trailed off, but he went on staring at Schmidt. Could Canning be waiting for an answer to some question he thought he had put? Schmidt had had more than enough of him, and since inexplicably neither Elaine nor Caroline seemed ready to redirect the conversation, he decided to do it, even though Caroline was left with only her husband to talk to. But that was her business. Mike and she had good reasons for indulging Canning's whims, including where he was placed at table, and for suffering the minor consequences, but Schmidt emphatically did not. You could count on Canning to make you disregard duties of friendship.

Taking advantage, therefore, of a pause in her conversation with the emaciated Meadow Club stalwart on her left, he said, Dear Elaine, I'm so glad and so grateful that you've asked Alice and me to dinner tomorrow. She was a bit nervous, but I think I've reassured her, and being able to talk to Gil tonight should make her see it will be all right. I want nothing more than for you and Gil to get to know her well—and to like her.

Of course, it will be all right, my darling Schmidtie. Elaine took his hand and squeezed it.

It was necessary to speak to her about Alice, and now it was done.

Thank you, Schmidt said, however many times I say that to you tonight it won't be enough. Let me ask you about the girls. We may not get much of a chance to talk about them tomorrow. How are they?

The girls were three in number: Lily, Elaine's daughter from a brief first marriage, and the two she'd had with Gil. Girls! That was what they used to call them twenty years earlier, and even then they were already young women. Schmidt was fond of them, his interest wasn't feigned, and getting Elaine started on that subject had an inestimable advantage: so long as he interjected the occasional "really" or "how extraordinary" or "I had no idea," she would do the rest. She would talk until something or someone obliged her to stop. The trick was to avoid saying anything that would make her feel she needed to reciprocate by speaking about his daughter, Charlotte. He managed it well: Elaine chatted away while he listened for the peals of Alice's laughter. It was a couple of minutes short of midnight when Gil rose to toast the host, as well as the president elect, and the New Year, which was bound to be happier than the one just ending. Horns were tooted by the staff, none having been provided for the guests. Then Mr. Mansour took over. He began to orate, his voice rising as he expounded his theory, which in other versions he had revealed to Schmidt more than once, to the effect that Obama's presidency, however much he personally wished it to succeed, was doomed.

The question is, he insisted, the question is can he make American politicians do his will. The last Democrat able to accomplish that was LBJ. He'd grab them by the balls— begging your pardon, Alice—and they said, Yes, Mr. President, before he'd even begun to squeeze. *Pas de problème!* But Obama is black! Black in the most racist country in the world.

Now wait, Gil interrupted, this racist country just elected him president! By a landslide!

The question is, the great financier continued, whether it knew what it was doing. I tell you that too many of those who voted for him didn't have a clear idea. Now they're saying the White House is going to be the Black House, and they didn't sign up for that. Not for having the whole picture changed! All right, Barack, Michelle—I say chapeau, she's some woman— and the cute little girls, perhaps we could give them a pass, too. But the mother-in-law, and who else, the homeless half sister, the half brothers, the whole *smaila*! How do you say it here: the whole *mishpucha*? Excuse me, Plumber Joe won't stand for it. Obama has to be such a good guy that his hands and feet are tied. You watched him debate McCain? I'll grant you that McCain is a schmuck, totally nuts, too much time in the Hanoi Hilton, too much time in the sun, whatever. You saw him smirk when- ever Obama talked? Not once, not twice, but every time. LBJ would have said, Wipe that smirk off your face or I'll tear your head off. Barack can't do that. You can't have a black man tell- ing off the Man. Please, there is no place here for angry black men! Obama has to be polite and make nice, and you know what they say about nice guys—they finish last.

In the free-for-all that followed, Gil shouted at Mike, Mike and the Meadow Club crowd shouted at Gil, while Alice laughed and laughed, and Schmidt wondered about the sound of Michelle's laughter.

What do you think of Mike's predictions, Schmidt asked Caroline.

Well, you and I have heard them before. I'm afraid he may be right about American racism. But I'm even more worried about something else: does Obama know how to manage. He and his people ran a brilliant campaign. Will they show the same talent for governing? Honestly, I'm hopeful but scared.

Of course you're scared, said Schmidt. We're standing at the edge of an abyss.

A line of guests had formed waiting to thank Mr. Mansour. Caroline had moved on, and Schmidt found himself standing next to Elaine. She had something to tell him that would explain Joe's being even more unbearable than usual.

It's awful, she said. Gil is so thrilled about the adaptation of Joe's first book, but he is also worried sick. Just this month, while you were away, Caroline took Joe to see a neurologist in the city—the best, he was Mrs. Astor's doctor. Anyway this man thinks that Joe is in the early stage of Alzheimer's.

He's always been odd as well as unpleasant, Schmidt answered. Was there something new, something out of character, that gave her the idea?

He began to have trouble writing checks. Apparently he'd always been really meticulous about his checkbook. He would never let his secretary or even Caroline get near it much less write the checks. He has to do it himself, go over the statements, reconcile deposits and payments. Then suddenly he couldn't. He'd get stuck. Unable to do the arithmetic. He noticed it himself. Not long after, he took his car to the garage they use in Springs—he's been there a thousand times—and he got lost. Absolutely lost. Going around and around in circles. Finally, he stopped at an intersection and called Caroline. He's always been forgetful about day-to-day things, but Caroline says it's never been like this, I'm terribly worried about Gil's project with Joe. Will he be able to keep the strands of the script in his head? It's driving Gil nuts.

That's really tough.

Mike and Caroline's prospects as a couple were suddenly looking a lot brighter, a fact that would not have escaped the great financier's attention. But he had better be careful not to show any sign of satisfaction. Caroline was a good woman; she would be loyal to Joe until the end. She'd nurse him as long as she could and would take very hard any hint that Mike was growing impatient.

Say good night to Mike for Gil and me, said Elaine, and give our best wishes. Gil's just coming out of the toilet. I'll take him home. He's dead tired and won't want to linger. We'll see you tomorrow evening, loved ones. At eight.

Schmidt squeezed Alice's hand. We're next, he whispered, thank you thank you and we'll be on our way!

At last the great man turned toward them. He kissed Alice's hand in his best exiled-Egyptian style, and then, patting Schmidt on the shoulder and squeezing his upper arm, offered his *félicitations*. He's one of the best, he assured Alice. My closest friend, *pas de problème*. So long as he takes my advice he will do just fine. Right now my advice is to stick to you.

They had almost reached the door when Caroline, followed by Joe two paces behind her, caught up with them.

Happy New Year and good night, Schmidtie, she called out. We must see you again soon. Lunch here? I think Mike will organize something. Until then, but aren't you going to introduce us to your Parisian friend? She turned to Alice. I'm Caroline Canning.

Alice held out her hand, and Schmidt said, I'm sorry, somehow I'm more discombobulated than usual. This is Alice Verplanck. She's an editor at Éditions du Midi, which she has just told me is Joe's French publisher.

Yes, they've published all my books, Joe piped up. Alice Verplanck, Alice Verplanck, that's right, my editor Serge Popov's girlfriend. And turning to Caroline, he asked: What is she doing here with retired lawyer Schmidt?

She's visiting me, Joe, Schmidt replied. For your information, Serge is dead, died earlier this year.

They made their way to the car in silence, but as soon as they were out of the driveway, he heard Alice stifle a sob. What an awful man! How could he!

It's all right, Schmidt told her, it's really all right. Canning is a dreadful man. But the performance this evening may have something to do with his being sick. Elaine has just told me he has Alzheimer's. Sick or well, I can't stand him.

He was on the verge of saying, Any more than I could ever stand your Popov, when she said: You know, Serge didn't like him either. He only liked his books.

Good for Popov, Schmidt thought, and good for Alice. The wound is healing, perhaps we're already there.

It was nearly one by the time they got home. Come, sweet Alice, he said to her, it's all right. We've even survived Canning. Let's have a drink.

Then he remembered. Shouldn't you call your son? he asked.

At this hour? She seemed surprised.

In Melbourne it's the afternoon.

Thank you! That's true. There was no way he could call me, she said with a giggle. He doesn't know I'm staying with a single gentleman. Thank you for this! He's surely at the beach, but I'll leave a message.

In fact, Tommy answered. Schmidt went into the kitchen, got a bottle of champagne out of the fridge, put it on a tray with two glasses, and waited in the kitchen until she had finished. Telling her to call had been a first step. From now on, if she'd only let him, he would look after her every hour and every day. They toasted the New Year and then petted, there was no other word for it, in the dark on the library sofa while a fire crackled in the fireplace and the Connecticut station brought them Glenn Gould playing the Goldberg Variations. At some point—he was past paying attention to the glow of the digital clock in the Bose—she reminded him that it was very late and they were both tired. It was time to go to bed.

My bed, he whispered.

Yes, but only to cuddle.

And then she added: You're giving good satisfaction. I think I'll keep you. Won't take you back to the store for a refund or exchange. But let's think some more about where we have been as well as where we are going. Is that a deal?

Unexpected bliss followed by a couple of hours of dreamless sleep. Wide awake and refreshed, Schmidt quietly put on his pajamas and bathrobe and went down to the kitchen. He drained the last of the champagne, put a couple of logs on the embers, and stretched out on the library sofa. She had asked him to think again about their history. Yes, he would, although he had pored over it countless times, and more intently than ever in recent months, since news reached him of the grotesque accident, a fall from one of those bicycles that any fool can rent just about everywhere in Paris, that had claimed his life. It was Gil who'd told him that Serge Popov was dead, having read the announcement in *Harvard Magazine*. Thus death had once more intruded to link Alice's life to his. First it had reaped Tim Verplanck and then, with a bizarre flourish, Popov. And as he considered Alice's history and his own, he would recall across the desert of years other stories that had enlaced them.

III

W & K's NOTICE back in February 1995 to all partners, active and retired, announcing Tim Verplanck's death had rocked Schmidt. Tim couldn't be more than fifty-four, he thought, so young and blessed with everything that should make a man happy! Including—so it had always seemed—excellent health. There's the rub, in "seemed." Schmidt knew that there are illnesses before which modern medicine is still helpless. They sneak up and kill. The memo didn't give the cause of death or the usual information about where contributions in lieu of flowers could be sent. And it said nothing about a burial or plans for a memorial service. At that time, the death of a W & K partner still rated an obituary in the *Times*, often with a photo. It wasn't yet necessary to be a former quarterback suffering from dementia or a hundred-and-two-year-old jazz musician. In fact, all it took was a telephone call from a member of the family or the presiding partner of the firm, and perhaps an offer to provide a narrative supplementing what was available in *Who's Who*. But nothing appeared in the paper, not even one of those notices that W & K would normally compose and pay for whether or not there was an obituary. Was it possible that the task had fallen between two stools because Tim had been living in Paris for so many years, and the widow was there as well, and that brute Jack DeForrest, the presiding partner, had his nose put out of joint over Tim's strange early retirement?

It seemed to Schmidt that he had last seen Tim at the Union Club during the reception that followed the funeral service for Dexter Wood at St. James, the church where that titan of the law had been a vestryman. He had spotted Tim's tall and slim silhouette right away, the mop of auburn hair, the suntanned face, and the expression of perpetual mockery standing out amid the phalanx of self-important men in navy-blue suits, white shirts, and black neckties, the uniform of W & K male partners for such occasions. They had chatted briefly. No, Alice hadn't made it to New York, her mother was ailing. But he and Alice were doing well. Exceedingly well, was what he said in fact. Why don't Schmidtie and Mary come to Paris? We'll have a nice dinner *à quatre.* Having put the question, Tim laughed, Ha! Ha! Ha! the startlingly ebullient coda to most of his pronouncements. Really happy to see you, ha! ha! ha! It took all night to get that memo ready, but here it is, ha! ha! ha! Joe Jones called to say he's sending a new transaction our way, ha! ha! ha! No, Alice and I can't make it to your dinner, we're dining with the president of Yale ha! ha! ha! Before they had progressed past "come to Paris . . . ha! ha! ha!" Lew Brenner, the New York senior partner with whom Tim had been working most closely in recent years, sidled over, and he began exchanging with Tim gossip about clients and deals that meant nothing to Schmidt. How soon after that did Tim retire? A year? Perhaps a year and a half? It would have been just before Mary's first operation. Schmidt had turned sixty and had hastily arranged to retire from the firm. He wanted to be with her during the time that she had left, time that they soon realized would be short.

But nothing, absolutely nothing, had foreshadowed Tim's decision. He was a long way from sixty, the earliest age at which the firm's plan permitted partners to retire. He was popular and hardworking. Nobody had wanted him to leave. The only explanation Jack DeForrest gave at firm lunch when he described the terms of Tim's payout was that young Verplanck wanted to write a book, whereupon one of the newly made partners raised his hand and asked why any payout was appropriate for a partner in good health who chooses to retire at fifty. DeForrest browbeat him into silence. Having made the deal, he wasn't about to have to justify it to a whippersnapper. Meanwhile a good half of the table tittered about how Verplanck had always had too much money for his own good. Why in the world would he want to work? Instant selective amnesia: by the time dessert was served the memory of the record-breaking billable hours that Tim had regularly racked up as an associate, and the volume of business he had handled as a partner, had been forgotten completely. The wolf pack could remember only his money and chic. Schmidt got back to his office in a foul mood and was about to dial DeForrest's number and ask that potentate for the real story when he realized he couldn't do it. The grudge he bore his erstwhile best friend at the firm was too deep; he wouldn't give DeForrest the satisfaction of knowing that Schmidt's cherished protégé had chosen to keep him in the dark. He put down the receiver. For the same reason, because it stung him to have had no news, no indication that there was a health problem, four years later he didn't ask DeForrest what Tim had died of, and for no reason at all, except that, having just become the head of Mike

Mansour's Life Centers, he was swamped with work, it didn't occur to him to put the question to Lew Brenner. Instead, he wrote to Alice Verplanck, pouring out all his feelings of sadness and friendship. He didn't doubt she knew, he wrote, that Tim had been his favorite associate, the young lawyer he had admired more than any he had worked with during his long career. As he happened to be going on business to Eastern and Central Europe, and would pass through Paris on his way home, would she allow him to call on her? Her answer, sent by some sort of European express mail, caught him just before his departure. It contained her telephone number, different from the one listed in the office directory, and assurances that she would be happy to see him.

It had in fact been old Dexter Wood himself, the firm's autocrat since the death of the firm's other founder, who recruited Tim. As he reminded the assembled partners at more than one firm lunch, the young man was a paragon, and it had been a coup to bring him in with the discreet help of his old friend Justice John Harlan, with whom he had played tennis and practiced law in the years gone by and for whom Tim was clerking. Quite a vote of confidence in the firm, he would intone, from the justice and from Verplanck. No disagreement was expressed. Manifestly, Tim had it all, every quality required to make him, as the younger partners put it, the complete package. Handsome, imperially slim, arrayed in discreet made-to-order suits and shirts that did not shout their Savile Row and Jermyn Street provenance, he trailed an aura of old New York money. A star as an undergraduate at Yale, he had gone on to shine just as bright at Harvard Law School, and, quite naturally, the best clerkships had followed, first on the Second Circuit in New York and then with the Supreme Court justice thought to represent the best of what the Eastern Seaboard legal establishment had to offer.

Schmidt was then a brand-new partner. The glad tidings that he had been taken into the firm had been given to him by Dexter Wood the day before Thanksgiving in 1967, a little less than a year before Tim's arrival. The old man had walked into his room, closed the door behind him, and, as Schmidt scrambled to get up, motioned him to remain seated and continue what he was doing, which was stuffing his briefcase with the documents he planned to work on in Bridgehampton during the long holiday weekend. A memorandum he had drafted and planned to submit to Mr. Wood on Monday was among the papers he had already packed. Schmidt was worried about it. He had never before worked under the old man's direct supervision or given advice on complex and, to him, unfamiliar antitrust issues, in this case the legality of the railroad tariff arrangements that Mr. Wood's favorite client, the CEO and major shareholder of which happened to be Wood's own brother-in-law, had worked out for the shipment of its product to buyers and warehouses scattered across the country. Schmidt had already delivered several preliminary memoranda on various aspects of the problem and had been interrogated by the old man in his office, the questions showing a careful scrutiny of Schmidt's work. No criticism of the work had been offered, but no praise either. Did that mean that the old man was satisfied? The fact that he hadn't required Schmidt to rewrite any of the memoranda and hadn't brought in another associate with antitrust experience to work alongside him suggested as much. But it was also possible that Mr. Wood would lower the boom only after seeing that final long memo reposing at the bottom of Schmidt's briefcase. (A hypothesis between the two was that his research and conclusions had been found acceptable as far as they went, but, at the same time, mediocre and unimaginative. He hadn't pushed his thinking far enough. He could do no better than journeyman work.)

Worries and self-doubt had plagued Schmidt since he first went to work for W & K. The ability of the partners—if one excluded three or four handling trusts and estates who may have been all right when they started but by common consent had let themselves go—and of most associates too was, like the standards set for the work, so high that only a deluded dolt would have been free of Schmidt's anxieties. This was his seventh year when, according to custom, he and other associates who had been hired with him would be either taken into the partnership or expected to leave. To be sure, not immediately or next month, a decent period of grace being allowed, but the policy of up or out was applied rigorously, so that with every week the situation of a passed-over associate who had not moved on went from uncomfortable to excruciating. Until at last he left. Left, but to do what? What became of him? Presumably he had found a job at another law firm unless, if he had remained in good graces, W & K had steered him to a position with a client. The tacit assumption was that either way it had to be a step down from W & K. The prospect of being consigned to such a purgatory, and the attendant humiliation, terrified Schmidt. How would he explain it to Mary or, even more difficult, to Aunt Martha, who seemed to hold an irrationally high opinion of her favorite niece's husband? Fortunately, he did not see his father often. But sooner or later, he would have to tell him too, and it would be wise to do so before W & K announced its new partners and he saw that his son was not among the elect. It was easy to imagine the pitying look: So this is my oh-so-fancy son who thought he was too good to come to work at my admiralty firm, the firm he could have inherited! His father wouldn't allow himself to gloat, but he wouldn't need to in order to make Schmidt squirm. Who knows? Perhaps he'd be forced to go back to his father with his tail between his legs and ask whether there might be a place for him at the firm he had as much as scorned. Schmidt was good at financings, and one-half of the work of an admiralty firm like his father's was ship mortgages and charters. The other business—for instance, how to arrest in Singapore or Panama City the SS *Boolah Boolah* or some other hapless vessel whose owners owed money to a client, and to have her sold at auction—he could learn. The conversation with Mary wouldn't be easy either, not because of anything she would say or do, but because regardless of her reaction he would have become the unsuccessful husband of a successful wife. It was not a role he had imagined. When they got married four years ago, she was an editorial assistant, at a great publishing house, to be sure, but still only a glorified secretary. But neither her pregnancy nor the arrival of Charlotte had slowed her progress. It took her only two years to become a full-fledged editor, and it seemed to Schmidt that everyone in the book business made a point of telling him that she was a powerhouse. He didn't doubt it; besides she was carried forward by the cresting tide of women's lib.

And Schmidt's own opinion of his own merit? When he allowed himself to think objectively about the partners' perception of his work, he was obliged to admit that it must be favorable. But to go from there to the conclusion that he stood higher than the five other associates, three from Harvard and two from Yale, who joined W & K the same year as he, was hubris pure and simple. At most, he could bring himself to allow that one of them, his classmate at law school, wasn't the sharpest tool in the firm's shed, and that one of the two Yalies was a slimy sneak. But could one be sure that the partners were aware of the faults of character that had earned him the contempt of his classmates? Assuming they did, though, that still left Schmidt and three others in the running, and one couldn't tell for how many openings they were competing. At firm dinners, Mr. Wood invariably babbled about how they always took in associates who had demonstrated that they deserved to be partners, those who were "breaking down the door." But no one took that seriously. You had to be needed. Was Schmidt needed? Nothing was less certain. He might well be better at financings than any other associate of his seniority, but there were excellent prospects coming up through the ranks, and perhaps the firm would wait for one of them to be ready. To top it all, now that he had gotten stuck with old man Wood's catastrophic antitrust assignment, all bets were off.

No wonder the sight of the old man sitting in the visitor's chair of his tiny office, wordless and with a wan smile on his thin lips, made Schmidt wonder whether he would faint for the first time in his life. Then the great man's lips parted. He was actually speaking, droning on about how the partners had voted—yes voted, unanimously in fact without discussion— to invite Schmidt into the partnership, and, if he accepted, they would expect great things from him. Was he disposed to accept? What a burst of affection inside Schmidt! Was there any task that Dexter, as Mr. Wood declared he was thenceforth to be called, could set that Schmidt would not be ready to accomplish? If only, for the moment, he would shut up and get out of his room! For there was only one thing that Schmidtie wanted now: to call Mary. Everything would be all right, the best private schools for Charlotte, a garage near the apartment so there'd be no more terrifying late-Sunday-night walks home after he'd unloaded the weekend gear and dropped off the car at the parking lot in East Harlem. A new station wagon to replace the ancient Buick hand-me-down from his father might be in the cards. They could afford more expert help at home, a real housekeeper. And perhaps Mary might even relent and agree to have another child.

Out of the six only he and Jack DeForrest made it. To celebrate, Jack and Dorothy joined Schmidt and Mary at the '21' Club. Martinis, shrimp cocktail, and filet mignon. After much discussion between Schmidt and DeForrest, they ordered a Pommard to go with the meat. Afterward they all went to Le Club, which was hard to get into but Jack knew someone whose name did the trick, and tried hard to go wild on the dance floor. When Schmidt and Mary got home and were in bed, she whispered, Lie back and be quiet. She took him in her mouth, and, when he came, she swallowed and swallowed and swallowed. He knew that she believed there was no better way to show that she loved him.

Then 1968 veered into disaster. At the end of January, the Vietcong had launched the Tet Offensive. Walter Cronkite, apparently no longer able to countenance the carnage, said on TV that the war was at a stalemate and had to be settled by negotiation, advice that fell on deaf ears. Horrors were heaped on horrors at home. On April 4, Martin Luther King was murdered, and race riots, arson, and pillage followed in Harlem and cities across the land. Two months later, almost to the day, Bobby Kennedy was shot in the kitchen of the Ambassador Hotel in Los Angeles; he died the next day. After protests against the war in Vietnam and loss of public support had forced LBJ to forgo seeking reelection, the Democrats nominated Hubert Humphrey at a convention that was a televised brawl both inside the hall and out, where protesters battled Chicago police. An incredible six hundred fifty demonstrators were arrested, and the city's hospitals were swamped by the hundreds of others savagely beaten by the police. In New York a student sit-in at Columbia led to a series of bloody riots when President Grayson Kirk called in the police to evict the students from administration buildings. In the resulting hubbub, the class of '68 was allowed to graduate from the college and the professional schools, including the law school, without regard to the days of classwork that had been lost. Only Harvard and Yale law school graduates were to be found among W & K partners, and in fact there were only a couple of Columbia graduates among the associates, the older partners taking considerable pride in the crimson and blue complexion of the firm. But it happened that in the fall of '68 five Columbia graduates were to become associates, and Columbia students had been working at the firm during the summer. Columbia's leniency in allowing students who hadn't really completed the year's work to graduate had now in the eyes of many devalued their degrees and academic honors. In fact the entire Columbia grading system was suspect. When the subject was discussed at W & K's firm lunch, the head of the hiring committee repeated what he had read in the *Wall Street Journal:* the law school faculty had wanted one thing only, and that was to get the class of '68 off their backs and out the door. "Anything goes" was the slogan for first- and second-year students too.

If you showed up for the exam, you got a passing grade. If you actually wrote something in the exam book, they gave you an A. We'll have to watch this carefully, announced Dexter Wood to the accompaniment of Hear! Hear! and some pounding on the table. The golden age of the university was over, and with it the sanctity of law school class ratings and elections to the law reviews; a global contagion was spreading, as those who had followed the May events in France through the periscope of the W & K Paris office were prompt to predict.

An associate of Verplanck's quality would have always been considered a feather in the firm's cap. His arrival at a time like this, however, was particularly welcome, and the older partners greeted him with an unusual outpouring of affection. He was an example of the best that the familiar and beloved system of education and selection could produce. Thus quite naturally, without a word having been uttered by Mr. Wood or any of the other firm elders, a general understanding took hold: until the happy day when—provided he didn't stumble—Tim would be taken in as a partner, he was to be put only on the most challenging projects and spared mind-numbing tasks such as updating surveys of state blue-sky laws or combing through files of a client in antitrust hot water or any work at all for members of the Racquet Club Patrol. That was how the partners doing trusts and estates work were known to W & K wags, an allusion to the midday hours they put in at that institution ingesting their daily preprandial martinis, and, unless the roof fell in and someone had remembered to tell them about it, their habit of returning to the office not more than two and a half hours before the 5:52 left Grand Central for Greenwich and New Canaan.

A first-year partner like Schmidt should have had little hope that this paragon might be assigned to help him. But Schmidt's own reputation and standing within the firm were high. The group of great insurance companies he serviced were then the firm's crown jewels, and their private placements—heavily negotiated long-term loans with intricate restrictions on dividends, investments, and borrowings—were financial sonnets in the composition of which Schmidt excelled. Even before he became a partner, the fuddy-duddies who ran those clients' legal affairs from offices in Boston, Hartford, Newark, or New York skyscrapers had frequently made a point of asking that Schmidt work on their new deals when they telephoned one of the two firm seniors, Mr. Jowett or Mr. Rhinelander, to say they were sending over some work. With his new status as a partner, Schmidt's standing as these clients' preferred lawyer became official, and when a series of proposals for very large and novel loans arrived that autumn and winter, he obtained a first call on Tim's services.

They realized from the outset that they suited each other. It wasn't only a matter of Tim's brains or superb legal training, which enabled him to see through problems clearly and rapidly. He was also possessed of common sense, without which an associate as bright as Tim might allow himself to be sidetracked by problems with little practical impact on the client's objectives just because he found them fascinating to explore. And he wrote well, an essential quality so far as Schmidt was concerned, guaranteeing the precision without which those same objectives could not be attained with a sufficient degree of certainty. It was also a matter of having fun, enjoying drafting as an art. Oh, Schmidt had never doubted that his own preoccupation with the aesthetic aspect was something that some at the firm laughed at behind his back, but Tim and he had the same understanding that their commitment to it was not only justifiable but essential. They made an exacting but seemingly pedestrian task—seeing to it that the claws of restrictions on dividends, borrowings, and investments bit down hard and prevented the borrower from diverting cash from the sacrosanct goal of paying the insurance company's interest and principal when due—become something akin to a medieval artisan's carving Passion scenes into ivory. Thus Schmidt had looked on benevolently even when he thought Tim was, well, overdoing it just a little bit, with his mania for number 2 Eagle pencils, which he sharpened just so himself rather than deposit them into his out-basket as everyone else did to be sharpened in the mailroom and returned a few hours later, or the special onionskin paper he required for pasting revised language into drafts of documents. Or his peculiar little aphorisms. For instance, when reviewing the signature copy of a document in which he detected language that had been crossed out in the course of revising a prior draft: Never allow pentimenti to show in your finished work. Or apropos of a heavily marked-up draft, Haven't we too much impasto here? Or after a conference with an inexperienced negotiator: This samurai isn't ready to wield the long sword. All that stuff was amusing and displayed nicely Tim's wide culture, but at times Schmidt feared that his protégé came across as something of a fop.

None of this detracted from his fondness for his young colleague or the gratitude he felt for his work, and when Tim became a partner in 1974, a year ahead of his classmates, there was no doubt in anyone's mind, including Tim's and Schmidt's, that he owed the promotion to his own merit but the timing of it to Schmidt. That knowledge did nothing to diminish Schmidt's dismay when Tim began, as he put it himself, to worship strange gods. In fact, in order to make sure that Schmidt got the point, he said, Ha! Ha! Ha! Adore not any strange god. The Lord his name is Jealous, He is a jealous God. Right Schmidtie? Ha! Ha! Ha! The point was that Tim had decided to move on. When in the last year of the Carter presidency the prime rate hit a stunning 21.5 percent, only fools would have borrowed long term at that rate from insurance companies, and only fools would have made cheaper money available long term to industrial borrowers. Schmidt's insurance clients were stodgy but not stupid: they switched to making short- or medium-term loans to banks and raked in interest at rates they had never imagined could be obtained. Industrial companies were starved for cash, but it would not be long before Mike Milken and his merry band at Drexel Burnham rode to the rescue and invented junk bonds. Schmidt's private placement practice never recovered from the blow, and eventually it withered. For the moment, however, there was only a slowdown sufficient to enable Tim (or was it foresight; would he have strayed even if there had been as much work to keep him busy as in the past?) to find a strange god in the person of Lew Brenner. Schmidt's junior by a couple of years, Brenner found that his practice—oil and gas deals in North Africa and the Middle East—was booming. Very quickly it became evident, to Schmidt's contained chagrin, that Tim was as valuable doing international transactions as he had been doing private placements in their heyday, that he got along just fine with Lew, and that Lew knew a good thing when it came his way. In fact, Schmidt had come to believe that bringing Tim into his orbit was part of one of Lew's carefully laid plans. That man didn't just happen to do this or that, which was Schmidt's way. All of this hurt, and hurt badly, even though he had to admit to himself that Tim was always cheerfully ready to help in emergencies and with particularly irksome problems, so that when a couple of years later Dexter Wood announced that Tim would take over the Paris office—a move backed by Lew Brenner—Schmidt shrugged and let several days pass before congratulating him or telling Mary. It was a natural-enough decision. Tim was reported to speak near-perfect French; except for occasional involvements in Schmidt's financings, which the old man described at firm lunch as part of Tim's being a good sport, all his work was international, and he had some potentially interesting business opportunities in Paris; Alice was French but having gone to Radcliffe would be completely at ease in the role of the wife of the head of W & K's Paris office; and, most important, considering the big effort of client development and public relations that would be required, Tim really wanted to take on the task.

The invitation to call on Alice when he passed through Paris was never far from Schmidt's consciousness as he traveled on his inspection tour of Life Centers in Central and Eastern Europe and certain of the new republics that had detached themselves from the Soviet Union. His last stop was Prague. On the way to dinner with his Czech colleagues he stumbled in one of the cobbled streets of Malá Strana and twisted his ankle so badly that both he and the emergency room doctor thought it was broken. X-rays showed that there was no fracture, only a bad sprain, and once the ankle had been taped he was able to go on to Paris. But not before the director of the Czech office had presented him with a carved walking stick to lean on as he hobbled around. It was thus that he found himself on a sunny April morning sitting in one of the green metal chairs near the *bassin* in the Tuileries, watching children and some elderly aficionados sail their boats. He was waiting for his only daughter, Charlotte. Parents and grandparents! His dealings with Charlotte and her husband had been odious: he was prepared for an unpleasant interview. She was in Paris, with her lawyer husband, Jon Riker, who had worked for Schmidt as an associate. Another case of a favorite guilty of betrayal: that was what Schmidt thought but didn't dare to say aloud. Tim had followed a strange god. Jon had dared to become Charlotte's live-in boyfriend and then her husband.

Those were not his only sins: among the others, his being a Jew (but Schmidt was coming to regret that he had considered Jon's being one of the Chosen a defect) and having been unfaithful to Charlotte and unscrupulous about her money weighed most heavily against him, along with the misconduct that led to his being booted out as a partner from W & K. Schmidt did not foresee a reconciliation with him. At last Charlotte appeared, beautiful and chic. She astonished him by proposing a truce, which Schmidt accepted. What else could he do? I will take you as you are, she said, and you take me as I am. We will see where that puts us. They shook hands on that, and she left to meet her husband. No embrace, just that handshake. He watched her walk toward the pyramid of the Louvre and remained in his chair for a long while. Then trying to put all his weight on the good leg, he made his way to rue St. Florentin. There were no taxis at the stand, and it didn't look to him as though there would ever be any. If he was going to see Alice, he had better walk to the address on rue St. Honoré he had written down on the memo pad he kept in his coat pocket. That is what he did, limping carefully until he reached the door of her building. He pressed the buzzer next to the brass plate that bore the initials of the Verplancks' first names: T. ET A. Someone called out scratchily *Oui?* He gave his name, and the same voice bid him in English to take the elevator to the third floor.

The apartment—large, luxurious, and silent—looked out over gardens in the back of the building. Alice led him into the library, and once he was settled in a tapestry-covered armchair that he found surprisingly comfortable, she offered him coffee. Or did he prefer a drink? It was past noon, he told her, so he would dare to ask for a whiskey. She laughed, disappeared for a moment, and returned followed by an elderly woman, whom she introduced as Madame Laure, bearing a large tray with a decanter, Perrier, and ice and what looked like a glass of tomato juice for Alice. Once he had told her how sorry he was about Tim, and she had asked about his limp, he was at a loss about what to say next and felt that she might be too, in which case he should perhaps leave. At the same time, he didn't think it was within the bounds of good manners to finish his drink and say good-bye less than thirty minutes after he had arrived. What's more he didn't want to leave: he was too content to find himself in this tranquil room in the company of a lovely and very elegant woman. A woman, it must be said, who intimidated him, although he felt certain that such was not her intention. If he wanted to stay, it was clear that he must get beyond the exchange of banalities, the sort of formulas that Emily Post probably recommended as appropriate for a conversation between a senior partner and the widow of one of his juniors, to whom he has come to pay his respects.

Alice, he blurted out finally, there is something that has

been troubling me very much about the way Tim went off the air: he didn't let me know he was planning to retire or his reasons; he didn't tell me anything. Then came the dreadful news that he was dead, but not a word from him between his retirement and that awful day. Something must have gone really wrong. We had worked together very closely from the time he came to the firm until a few years before you and he left for Paris.

He knew, of course, she answered, that you were unhappy when he started doing so much work with Lew.

Alice dear, I used to think of him as the son I would have liked to have. His working for Lew didn't change that. I hope he didn't think it did. That would be one heartbreak more.

Without any warning, she started to cry, tears streaming down her cheeks while she remained completely silent.

His gesture made awkward by the limp, he reached the sofa, sat down beside her, and spontaneously, without having formed an intention to do so, put his arm around her shoulders. Alice, he said, I am so terribly sorry, please stop, I'm sorry I asked those questions. I'll leave right now if you like, if it will make it easier for you to regain your calm.

Still sobbing, she shook her head and hurried out of the room. Schmidt returned to his armchair and waited uneasily.

There was a tremor in her voice when she reappeared, but she was no longer crying. It's such a long and sad story, she said. Are you sure you want to hear it?

He nodded.

She looked at her watch and said, In that case you must stay for lunch. Please excuse me again while I say a word to Madame Laure.

She came back, offered him another whiskey, and after a

moment of hesitation poured a much smaller one for herself. Lunch will be ready in a quarter of an hour: very simple, cold chicken and salad. I hope that's all right. Then she added, Can what I tell you remain *entre nous*? You won't feel that you need to discuss it with the firm?

He assured her that his questions had been those of a grieving friend. It would not occur to him to talk about their conversation to the firm—from which he had in any event retired—unless she specifically authorized him to do so. Thereupon she apologized, saying that she couldn't understand why she had made that request. Perhaps it was because she would be discussing for the first time certain things with someone who wasn't already aware of them. His visit was more welcome than he could imagine. It had made her realize how badly she needed to tell that story from beginning to end to someone who would listen sympathetically, who had known Tim well before Paris. And so, while they drank their whiskeys, then over lunch and afterward, when they took coffee in the library, she talked nonstop. At first he thought that he was hearing about a prolonged marriage spat, some rather selfish and high-handed behavior on the part of Tim that she badly needed to get off her chest. But as he heard more, his heart sank. The story was unlike anything he could have imagined.

She was startled, she said, when Tim decided in 1981 to go to Dexter Wood and volunteer to take the place of Billy Higgs, the partner then in charge of the Paris office who was scheduled to return to New York only twelve months later. Putting himself forward like that wasn't Tim's style. What made it even stranger, he had turned Dexter down cold four years earlier when Dexter asked him to take over from Higgs's predecessor, Sam Warren. He did that against her wishes. For many reasons she had really wanted to move to Paris at that time. He knew that, and he knew very well why. She had thought that, if the children's French heritage was to be meaningful to them, they should at some point spend a number of years in France, and the timing was ideal. Sophie was five and Tommy three; they were still in preschool, they could be moved to Paris and put into the French educational system without disrupting their schooling. Language wouldn't be a problem. She had always spoken French to them. They understood perfectly and were on the verge of speaking really well. She had also told Tim that if he was concerned about their reading and writing in English, there were ways to make sure they could: tutors, perhaps a private bilingual school with instruction in both languages. She had another personal and urgent reason to be in France, of which Tim was also completely aware. Her mother had been very recently diagnosed with amyotrophic lateral sclerosis—you know Lou Gehrig's disease—an illness for which there was no remedy or cure. The doctors thought it was an aggressive case. Some months earlier her father had at last retired from the diplomatic service, and he and her mother had decided to sell their apartment on rue du Bac and move to the house in Antibes that had come to them from her mother's family, a place that her mother loved, having spent all summer vacations there until the war. Both her parents were convinced that the Antibes climate would be good for her. It had even occurred to Alice that she and Tim could buy the rue du Bac apartment. The location was just what she wanted, there was lots of room for the children, and you couldn't ask for a better layout for entertaining. It had simply gotten to be too big for her parents.

Do you know anything about my family history? she asked abruptly.

Schmidt replied that he knew, of course, that her father had been the French ambassador in Washington. He had met both him and Alice's mother at her wedding reception. But that was all.

I am a child of the victory in Europe, she said. My father was with the Free French during the entire war. He managed to get from Bordeaux to London just as Pétain was capitulating and afterward was one of those people who were parachuted into France for special missions and then taken back to London. My mother and he met in Normandy during one of those missions. She was in the Gaullist resistance. Strangely, that's how she survived. She stopped wearing the yellow star and went underground. When my father entered Paris in August forty-four with the Division Leclerc, she was already there, and I was born twelve months later, three months after they got married. It could have been a shotgun wedding, but there was no one left on my mother's side to go after my father. My entire family ended up in Auschwitz and Bergen-Belsen, and none of them survived. They were the kind of Jews who believed that the Germans would never do to them what they were doing to the others.

Seeing a look of puzzlement on Schmidt's face, she added, Yes, my mother was Jewish. That did not put off my one hundred percent Aryan father, one of those brilliant French Protestants who come in first at every *concours*—those competitive examinations you have to take in order to go to the best schools and rise, as he did, to the top of the Quai d'Orsay. Anyway, they were older than most people when they had me, and they didn't try to have more children. My mother died in eighty-six, just short of her seventy-fifth birthday.

And your father?

For the first time that morning she laughed, making Schmidt decide that he loved the sound of her laughter. My father's very much alive, still in perfect health at ninety, sharp as a tack, and living in Antibes with my mother's best friend. Unmarried, of course—they're quite modern.

Schmidt cursed himself for having allowed her to notice that hearing that her mother was Jewish had startled him. It was a tic; he had reacted like a goddamn windup toy set off by something that was connected to a time when such things did matter to lots of people, himself included, people who now knew better and no longer told jokes about Jews, blacks, or homosexuals. Surely she didn't think he cared about it today. To apply today's sensitivities and rules to how things were thirty years earlier was unfair. A political anachronism! So he interrupted her inanely: You know, Alice, that your background—so very distinguished—was not anything that I was concerned about or that the firm took into account. I don't think anyone knew or had bothered to inquire. Look at Lew Brenner, he added. He was made a partner the year you and Tim got married, or perhaps the year before.

Alice raised her eyebrows and sighed. Wonderful never-changing anti-Semitic America, she said softly. I remember it well. But never mind. To go back to Tim, he knew how I felt and he knew about my parents when he turned Dexter down. He just told me, as though that made everything all right, You can go to France anytime you want and as often as you want. But he wasn't going to exile himself to a legal backwater. That didn't matter to Sam Warren and whoever was the partner in Paris before him because they were both lawyers without clients or any hope of ever having clients, in addition to being fundamentally lazy. Taking other partners' clients to fancy dinners when they happened to pass through Paris and making themselves useful around the American Cathedral made them happy and from the firm's point of view was probably the best use they could be put to.

Schmidt nodded. Tim was right about both of them.

I'm sure he was, and I'm also sure that he didn't mean to hurt me. He just hoped I could understand that it wasn't reasonable to ask him to do what I wished. The subtext was that my mother was going to die soon whatever I did, and he had to think about the long-term future, meaning his illustrious career. It was that simple. He didn't have anything against France. His French was very good, and he had the kind of good manners the French love. But his clients, his practice, and the firm came first. There was another unmentioned obsession, the reason we went to France together only once, on our honeymoon: his family's place on Mount Desert. He kept a big sloop at the yacht club in Bar Harbor, and his idea of heaven was to sail in those waters. So every August, or as much of every August as he could protect from clients and other partners, had to be spent in Maine. I'd go to Paris to see my parents just a few days at a time either alone or, if my parents were up to it, with the children. Naturally, I wanted my parents to know them. Otherwise, going to Paris didn't matter to me all that much: I had lost touch with all but a few of my French friends long ago. Radcliffe had done that, and before that living in Bonn, when my father was ambassador there. So the question was, what had changed his mind, why did he suddenly decide in 1981 that he wanted to move to Paris as quickly as possible? You must admit that it was strange. From the point of view of the children, the timing was awful. Sophie was at Brearley and Tommy at St. Bernard's. They were both happy and didn't want to leave their schools or their friends. The one big thing that had changed was that in 1981 Mitterrand became the president of France, with a Socialist majority in the National Assembly and the Socialist agenda of nationalizations and tax changes. In short order many rich French bourgeois decided they would play at being *émigrés* and leave Paris for New York and London—like aristocrats running away from the French Revolution. Suddenly we were meeting many interesting French people in New York. Some were old friends of my parents, who naturally looked us up, some were people my father specifically sent to Tim when he was asked whether he could recommend a lawyer in New York, some were friends of friends. That's how Bruno Chardon, a partner in a very fancy French private bank, came into our lives. He was about Tim's age, very handsome, very elegant, and very well connected. He was like another Tim, but with black hair and dark eyes, and the kind of Mediterranean skin that's slightly sallow. Tim and he got along right away. It turned out that Bruno was also a passionate sailor, so that fall Tim had his boat brought down to New York. He berthed her at City Island, and the two of them would go out most weekends, with the children if it wasn't too cold and the kids didn't have birthday parties or other things they wanted to do in the city. Occasionally, I came along too. When the weather was suitable, and Tim could get away, they'd make a weekend of it. I didn't complain because I realized that was the first time I saw Tim with a real friend. Certainly, it was the first time I had seen him be intimate with someone other than me and the children. Bruno had broken through a wall. You probably don't know that Tim and his only sister didn't speak to each other; she didn't even come to our wedding. As for those troglodytic parents, they're Ice Age cold. The deal about Maine was that we stayed out of one another's way: the sister went in July, so we went in August. The parents made no difference. Even if they showed up, they were like inanimate objects. You're a better judge of how Tim was with other lawyers at the firm. To me it seemed that he was always jovial and enthusiastic about people he worked with well— such as you and Lew Brenner—but the relationships stopped right there.

It hurt his feelings, Schmidt realized, to tell her she was right. He added, I had always hoped it was more.

You were taken in by that joviality—and those unbeatable good manners. It was the same with the law clerks he had served with in New York and D.C. and all those Yale and St. Paul's classmates. Lots of good cheer. Lots of laughter. Beyond that? Nothing. Boreal cold, like his father and mother. With Bruno he became a real person, and I was grateful for that. Bruno was also wonderful with the children and me. Completely attentive and always truly interested in what we thought, what we were doing, ready to take part in anything that was proposed. He had come to New York to reconnoiter—that was the way he put it—and told both of us that there were tremendous opportunities in advising French flight capital. People who had succeeded in getting parts of their fortunes out of France, or had great sums of money hidden outside France, all that money that was "in the shadows," needed to be invested, and the most attractive place to invest was the U.S. That created a great need not only for a banker like him but also, he claimed, for an American lawyer like Tim, provided he was based in Paris. He had to be in Paris to deal with people who were there and who wouldn't do business by telephone and to get to understand local conditions and constraints. In effect he was saying to Tim, Move to your Paris office, and I will open for you every important door in France and also in Switzerland, where most of the money is parked. I believe Bruno, Tim told me. This is an opportunity that neither the firm nor I can miss. By the way, he was quite right about what Bruno could accomplish. He introduced Tim to some amazing clients.

Schmidt nodded. He hadn't known about the source of Tim's European business, but both the quantity and the quality had been impressive and had been regularly commented on at firm lunches.

You know how Tim was, Alice continued. Once he decided to do something he couldn't be stopped. He got the firm to call Billy Higgs back early. As soon as he had Dexter's word that the office was his, he went to Paris to organize our move. Bruno showed him this apartment, which had belonged to an aunt of his who had died some months before. His two nieces wanted to sell, and Tim bought it from them without asking me to come over to look at it first. It's comfortable enough, and it worked for our purposes, but I dislike the neighborhood. My parents' apartment had already been sold, but I'm not sure that Tim would have seriously considered it even if it had been available. It hadn't been recommended by Bruno! I did put down my foot when it came to the schools. Bruno had the idea that the children should go to private schools, Sophie to one near the Trocadéro run by nuns and Tommy to the Jesuits, way over on the Left Bank. There Tim agreed with me: Catholic schools weren't for us, and besides they were too far away. So we sent them instead to a public school near here, and that worked out fine.

Schmidt had opened his mouth to put in a word for the advantages of a Jesuit education, having been sent to one of their schools on Manhattan's Upper East Side by his father, who had swallowed his anti-Catholic bile to take advantage of a first-rate education offered at a bargain-basement price, but managed to hold his tongue.

We settled into a routine. Tim worked long hours, staying at the office even later than in New York. The business that came in was often more than the office could handle. I was making sure the children were adjusting to the French system and did their homework, and I tried to run a Parisian household. My parents had a small but very pretty house—a *pavillon de chasse*—near Chantilly, just north of Paris, that they turned over to us. When the weather was agreeable, we'd drive out there on Saturday afternoon and stay until Sunday evening. There are wonderful walks to go on in the forest, which the French government keeps very clean, removing dead trees and fallen branches, clearing paths. Everyone liked it, including Bruno, who came with us regularly. It turned out that he liked to shoot, as did Tim, so during the season he and Tim would kill birds together. When the children had colds, or there were birthday parties, I stayed with them in Paris, and Tim and Bruno went to Chantilly alone. It all continued this way very serenely until the disastrous summer of 1985.

She began to cry again. They had long since left the table and returned to the library, and once again Schmidt hobbled over to the sofa and, putting his arm around her shoulders, tried to comfort her.

Thank you, she said, perhaps you don't know what happened.

He shook his head.

Sophie went to camp that summer. Camp Horned Owl, in Maine, one of those girls' camps that have been going strong for one hundred years. It was the third time, and she really looked forward to it. Her two best friends from Brearley were going as well. My mother was in very bad shape, so it was clear that I would have to skip Bar Harbor. But Tim said he would take Sophie to Horned Owl in July so that she'd be there when the camp started, return to Paris and work until August, and then make another trip to Bar Harbor with Bruno and get in his sailing. She would stay with them after camp, and they would bring her back to Paris. I was going to Antibes as soon as school let out at the beginning of July, with Tommy and our au pair. I wanted to be with my father, take turns with him talking to my mother, reading to her, changing CDs—she was listening to music a great deal—and watch the occasional TV program with her. It was more than a full-time job, because she hardly slept at night and wanted company. The physical side was taken care of by the nurses. She was by then completely paralyzed but able to breathe, chew food, and swallow, and she still spoke, but more and more feebly. It was very hard to understand her. We were waiting for the end, when she would need a tracheotomy or a breathing machine to get enough oxygen. She had decided—all three of us had decided—that we would not expose her to that torment; she said that she would stop eating and drinking, and turn her head to the wall, except that of course she couldn't turn at all, was incapable of any movement. Schmidtie, you cannot imagine how hard it is to die, how hard it is to kill even a very sick, very feeble, paralyzed old lady. Or do you know? Did you have to go through that with your parents?

No, Schmidt replied. My father died suddenly of apoplexy, and my mother in the hospital after a huge operation. There was almost nothing left in her belly when they got through.

I'm sorry, said Alice. No, I'm not, anyway not for your father. It's so much easier when they go quickly. I was reading *Emma* to my mother, one of her favorite novels, when the phone rang. It was three in the morning. Tim said, I'm at the camp, Sophie is sick, she has a high fever and seizures, I'm driving her to the hospital in Portland. I think you should come over. The au pair was a good girl, but I couldn't leave Tommy and her with my father. All three of us took the morning plane from Nice and I was at the hospital late that evening. Sophie never recognized me. She died after two terrible days. It was meningitis caused by a staphylococcus infection. Three other girls got sick, and one of them didn't make it either. The camp director had been slow to react; she called the parents instead of ambulances. You can imagine the anger and the recriminations, but I don't think you can imagine the horror of seeing the little face of a twelve-year-old contorted in pain and empty. Completely empty, somehow turned inward.

She broke off and said, I can't go on today. Would you have time to see me again?

The next day was Sunday. Where could he invite her? Brasseries would be crowded and noisy. Except for hotel restaurants, all the good and half-decent restaurants he knew would be closed. The one in his hotel was renowned for its cuisine. She agreed to meet him there at one and, as he was leaving, offered him her cheek to kiss.

IV

You're shocked, she said, I can see it in your face. I'm wearing trousers, and I'm not made up.

She did look terrible, her face pale and haggard, the pallor accentuated by her dark lipstick.

You are lovely, he replied, and why wouldn't you wear trousers to Sunday lunch unless you had been to church?

She smiled. We don't go to church much in France, except for christenings, marriages, and funerals. She bit her lip and added, There was an Episcopal service for Sophie before she was buried in the family plot at Verplanck Point. Tim is buried there too. The same priest said the mass. I'm going to be cremated. My mother didn't want it because of Auschwitz, but I don't think that's a good reason. Cremating the Jews they killed was the least of what the Germans did to them.

Schmidt was going to say something signifying agreement, but noticing his hesitation she broke in. Forgive me, she said, that's not what I wanted to talk to you about. I can't get yesterday's conversation out of my mind, but I want to. And I'm not sure I can or should go on with the story. What a splendid room this is! she added inconsequentially, looking around her.

Too much marble for my taste, but the food is good, said

Schmidt. Let's order our lunch. I have to admit, though, that I would be disappointed if you did not finish what you have begun to tell me. She nodded and said, I'll try. I'll see.

She ate and drank with frank enjoyment, and, not wanting to press her, Schmidt found himself doing most of the talking. He explained that the foundation he worked for had been founded by his country neighbor and now friend Mike Mansour, the billionaire Egyptian Jew who came to the United States with his parents as a young boy. The parents prospered making and selling curtains. Mike parlayed that small prosperity into a huge fortune and, having left Ronald Perelman behind, was ascending smoothly to the highest sphere of *Forbes*'s list of billionaires. He created the foundation to support democracy, the humanities, and capitalism in Central and Eastern Europe and former member countries of the Soviet Union.

So far I've rather liked preaching the gospel of democracy and the humanities, he continued. That of Ayn Rand and joyous market capitalism is another matter. On balance, though, I'm truly grateful to Mike. He's gotten me out of the house, I'm working again, and I'm traveling on business to places I'd never go to on my own. You probably know that I retired early, when Mary got sick with a cancer that spread pretty much everywhere. I wanted to be with her, and it was the right decision. All the same, losing both her and my life's work left me in a desert—without direction.

Oh, I didn't know that Mary was dead, she said. That's how cut off I am from the firm. I did notice, though, that there was no mention of her in your letter, and I wondered about the reason. She was so very nice. Of all those partners' wives she was the kindest to me and the funniest. I remember her making huge round eyes and rolling them when we sat across from each other listening to Mrs. Wood give a little speech at one of those firm functions for wives. I had trouble keeping a straight face.

Schmidt nodded. Making round eyes had been one of Mary's special accomplishments. She had been famous for it at Radcliffe and at the publishing house.

After a minute or so of silence he added, Alice, please go on with your story. I am eager to hear it, even if it's very painful.

All right, she said, but it is painful. More than painful—devastating. Let's see, the morning after Sophie died Tim arranged for her funeral in Verplanck Point. There was no difficulty about doing it the following day so we all drove there, behind the hearse. Five of us in a limousine, Tim, Bruno, the au pair, Tommy, and I. The drive was a nightmare, and once we arrived it was even worse. It was impossible not to stay at the big house with Tim's parents and the sister and her husband without making a public row, so in addition to all our pain and all our regret we had to face the Verplanck wall of meanness and dislike and horrid insinuations. Mrs. Verplanck actually said Tim and I were at fault. Considering the risk of infections at summer camp we shouldn't have sent her to Horned Owl. I didn't reply, but Tim flew into a rage and yelled. Have you ever heard him yell? It wasn't a nice sound. We didn't stay for the lunch after the funeral—none of us could face it—and after having a bite to eat at a mall got back into the limousine. We spent the night in some motel, and in the morning drove to Bar Harbor nonstop, except to let Tommy and Bruno—yes, Bruno too—pee at the side of the road. We were a mess when we got home, and the next day I allowed myself to sleep late and to lie down in our bedroom after lunch. Tommy and the au pair were taking a nap. I tried to go to sleep perhaps for half an hour but couldn't, and finally I got up and went to the window. It was a gorgeous, cruelly gorgeous, afternoon. The sea was so brilliant that after a moment I had to turn my eyes away from it. I looked instead down at the garden, and there, next to the gazebo, directly in my line of vision, were Tim and Bruno, absorbed in a conversation I couldn't hear over the pounding of the waves. I was about to call out to them when suddenly I realized the import of what I was seeing. They were holding hands, which in itself surprised me, because it wasn't Tim's style. I had never seen him hold hands with a man. But then Tim put his arms around Bruno and kissed him on the mouth. I mean really kissed him. They were near enough for it to be impossible to doubt that Tim's tongue was deep in Bruno's mouth. After a moment came a gesture: Bruno thrust his hand into the front of Tim's trousers and caressed him until Tim drew away and, still holding hands, they ran into the house. I thought I was going to howl, but I didn't make a sound. I wondered whether I'd ever recover the power of speech. Gasping for breath I turned in little circles in the room, fighting against the need to fall on the floor and writhe. Suddenly, I understood what I must do. I went out into the corridor. It was covered by a heavy, dark red carpet that smothered the sound of steps. But I was taking no chances and tiptoed to the big guest room where we had put Bruno. The door was closed. I still burn with shame when I remember what I did next: I put my ear to the keyhole and heard them. Fucking and moaning. Schmidtie, I knew one of them was buggering the other. What else could it be? I wanted desperately to know who was being buggered—as though that mattered—but I didn't put my eye to the keyhole. I didn't dare, I just couldn't.

She began to cry, softly and sadly. Her pocketbook was on the little taboret beside her chair. She found her handkerchief and dabbed her eyes. I'm making a spectacle, she whispered, I'm so sorry.

Her other hand was palm down on the table. Schmidt patted it. What was he to say? All he found was: I am terribly sorry. He added, Let's have some coffee, and perhaps a brandy. It will do you good.

No brandy for me, she said. I'll have a sip of yours if you have one.

The dining room emptied while they drank coffee until they were the last remaining guests.

It's a beautiful warm afternoon. If my ankle weren't in such bad shape I would suggest walking over to the Tuileries and finding a couple of chairs somewhere in the sun. But I don't think I can do it; my ankle is worse today than it was yesterday. I've got two ideas. One is that we move to the lobby or the back bar. The other, more revolutionary, is that we go up to my suite. It's one that Mike Mansour keeps all year round. It has a terrace—you can imagine the view—and a large living room if you find the air on the terrace too cool. But I don't think you will. The afternoon sun is so pleasant.

She actually laughed. I don't think it will compromise me to go to your suite. Let's try the terrace.

He had called room service and ordered coffee, and this time also a brandy. The thought had occurred to him while the waiter was busy with the tray on the terrace that she might have mentioned her apartment as a less racy alternative to his suite. He dismissed its implications. She was distraught, he was no Mike Tyson, and if his ankle was to be spared, they would have had to take a taxi and face the complications of getting him back to the hotel. No, she had made the right choice: it would have been downright foolish to forgo soaking up the sun, with a magnificent panorama of the great square, the river, and the Left Bank stretching out before them. He raised the snifter and tasted. It's good, he said, holding the glass out for her, I doubt I've drunk any that was better.

She took a big sip and then another.

I keep on saying to myself that what happened cannot be repaired, she told him, so I might as well be good to myself. You're right about the cognac, and you were right to ask me to come up here. Do you wonder why I've told you so much, and why I'm going to tell you even more?

He told the truth: no, he hadn't; he had thought his questions were ones that someone who had known Tim and liked him very much would naturally ask. And he hoped that she would go on. What he had learned thus far was horrible, but it didn't explain either Tim's retirement at such a young age or his death so soon after.

Oh, Schmidtie, you're such an adorable old-fashioned square. Let me have another sip from your glass, and I'll tell it all. I'll also tell, even though you aren't curious, why I've told you already as much as I have. I think you're nice and kind. You must have been one of those nice and very square Harvard boys I liked when I was at Radcliffe.

If I were fifteen years younger, I would have been there, said Schmidt. I certainly was square, and it's even possible that I was nice. Seeing that she gave no sign of abandoning the snifter, he called room service and asked for two more. Just in case, he told Alice.

Good planning, Alice replied. My head is turning, but

I'll try to be coherent. As you can imagine—no, you can't; I couldn't imagine it myself—I resisted the impulse to burst into that room and curse them and then wake Tommy from his nap and get into the car with him and the au pair and flee. Go somewhere we would be safe. To my father's house to be with him and my dying mother. Instead, I took a long shower, got dressed normally, and put a pad outside that bedroom door with a message: I expect to see both of you in the library. Then I told the au pair to keep Tommy busy when he got up and, when it was time for his dinner, to drive over to the luncheonette and take him to the movies after they'd eaten. I had noticed that *Star Wars* was playing when we drove through the town. After that I went into the library and tried to read the paper and keep images of Tim and Bruno out of my head. Time dragged on. Around six, I heard a car on the driveway. That was the au pair and Tommy. Perhaps a half hour later, the cook came in and said she had prepared a cold meal so she could serve it anytime. I told her to lay it out in the kitchen and take the evening off; I would put the food on the table and clean up. That's right, I was emptying the house of witnesses. Not to my crime, I could see that the roles were inverted, but to my shame. At last—it must have been past seven—I heard them on the stairs and then in the hall and then they came in the room. They too had taken showers. Anyway, their hair was wet. They sat down, and Tim spoke. They had been asleep; it wasn't a case of not wanting to face me. But they were both prostrate before me. They had been so very careful, had tried so hard to be discreet and to preserve our life together. They knew it was the worst imaginable time for me to find out, but they hoped I would understand that it was grief and despair that made them lose their heads and fall into each other's arms. At that point Bruno broke in and said the same things all over again. It was grotesque: Tweedledum and Tweedledee. Do you want to know something strange? I did believe that they had been unstrung by grief, that otherwise I might never have found out. I was so naïve, I knew so little about that side of life, but they had managed to fool even my father, who is anything but naïve! Then Tim said that although the timing was appalling it might be altogether best that I know everything. They'd been lovers almost from the first, and they really loved each other. I asked Tim whether this had always been so, whether he knew he was homosexual—I used that word because I couldn't bring myself to say "gay"—when he was taking me out, and later when he began to sleep with me and asked me to marry him, and he said no, not at that time, it had been a part of him since senior year at high school and afterward, but he took out girls too, and by the time he got to W & K he was sure that he had changed enough to be serious about me. I interrupted him there and asked whether after we had gotten together he was still going with men. He hesitated and answered very slowly and very carefully as though he were walking on eggs that it happened occasionally, there was a boy in the office with whom he'd gone to bars and to baths, and that it began to happen more often after Tommy was born, he didn't really know why. He wanted to and couldn't help himself. That was really it. I had become more distant, so completely a mother. That might have been a factor.

I felt life was draining out of me, but I couldn't cry. Perhaps it was because of Bruno. His presence seemed to me atrocious, obscene, and I said to Tim, Does he have to be sitting here? Tell him to get out.

They both began to talk at once, as though they had

rehearsed, about how all three of us were in it together, how Bruno loved Sophie and loved Tommy, and loved me too, and how Tim and he had no secrets. I was too beaten down to protest. So I asked, knowing that I was repeating myself, and that it was a stupid question anyway because there was no doubt about the answer, Do I understand that all the while you were having sex with me you were also having sex with men? How could you? Tim replied that he liked sex, and he liked me, but he really needed the other thing. The way he needed Bruno and couldn't live without him. Haven't you heard of husbands who have affairs and wives who have affairs? Do you think those husbands and wives don't have sex with each other? I nodded, which was a lie. Of course I knew they did. Yes, you do, Tim replied, just think of some of our friends. It's all the same thing. And what about Bruno, I asked, now that you're with Bruno, do you and he have sex with other men as well? Once again they both talked and talked. It boiled down to how they had realized right away that they were in love—that was Bruno's expression—and how that was all-important to them, so now they were monogamous, faithful to each other. Much later, when I was less naïve, I asked them whether they were lying to me. From what I had been told, promiscuity was the rule. I was to hear a lot on that subject from both of them, all sorts of explanations of how gay love doesn't need to be exclusive because it's a celebration of the body, and on and on. But that did not apply to a relationship such as theirs. As I said, all that was later. For the moment I felt sick, or perhaps dead, anyway more and more as if I weren't there, as if that conversation had been taking place elsewhere, which didn't prevent me from seeing and hearing, but in some other place from where I was. After a long while I interrupted and asked

Tim what we were going to do now that all this had happened.
Were he and Bruno going to leave first and let me and Tommy
and the au pair make our way to Paris or my father's house, I
hadn't yet decided which, after they had left. Or would they
let us leave first? Once again Tim and Bruno had an answer
ready to go—they were already like those married couples
who answer every question together, as though it had been
asked of both, and always say "we" instead of "I." The gist
was that we mustn't expose Tommy to a second loss and for
his sake we must all four stay together. We really can, Tim
assured me. They didn't want it to be known that they were
gay; for all sorts of reasons they weren't coming out, they
would continue to be discreet, please let's avoid a divorce
or even a separation. What about him, I asked, pointing at
Bruno. Does he have anything to say about it. He agrees, Tim
told me. You know he loves Tommy. But is he going to be
around, I insisted. The answer was Yes, couldn't we go on as
we have before, with Bruno like a part of the family? Tommy
would miss Bruno. He and Bruno love each other. At that
point, in that beautiful baritone of his, Bruno chimed in about
how much Tommy meant to him, how he admired and loved
me like a sister, and how we had achieved a rare equilibrium.
The way he put it was so elegant that I didn't begin to feel
nauseated right then. That came later. But I did say that I
wanted Tim out of my bedroom. My husband agreed with
such alacrity that even then, in my beaten-down, abject state,
I realized I had made myself ridiculous. I don't know how they
kept themselves from laughing. So we packed up, Bruno helping as though nothing had happened, and traveled together
to Paris. In retrospect I see that the loss of Sophie was a blow
that had anesthetized me. If I hadn't been so numb, I can't

imagine I would have stayed so eerily calm after finding out, just like that, one sunny afternoon, that Tim was a goddamn queer who'd been fucking Bruno and God knows how many other men before and since—and what kind of men!—and then getting into my bed. Probably fucking them even when he was making me pregnant with Sophie and Tommy.

She was crying and, it seemed to Schmidt, shivering from cold. Let's go inside, he said, the temperature has dropped. You'll be more comfortable. He led her by the hand to the sofa, closed the glass doors to the terrace, and, somewhat embarrassed to be calling room service again, ordered coffee, petits fours, and two cognacs.

You're getting me drunk, she said morosely. No, I'm getting me drunk, and yes, I don't care, and no, you don't care. I'll just keep talking. Do you think it's worse to find out your husband is sleeping around with your girlfriends, his secretary, the au pair—the mention of sleeping with the au pair stung Schmidt who had done just that and had been caught by both his wife and daughter—with call girls, and on and on, or to find out he's a pansy? Banging boys in gay baths! Getting them to fuck him! What do you think?

I don't know, he replied. I've heard it said that it's less damaging to be left by a partner who discovers he's homosexual or she's a lesbian, because you're not in competition with the person they left you for. It's more like a mutual mistake. But really I don't know. Perhaps it's different from case to case.

I don't either, but it was awful. Do you read Balzac?

He shook his head and, correcting himself, added that he had read *Eugénie Grandet* in his last year of high school French.

It must have been a good school. I'm not sure that happens today. I think *Cousine Bette* is probably his best novel. The story revolves around Baron Hulot, an incorrigible *trousseur des jupons;* someone who's always getting into women's underpants. His wife is very beautiful and *très sage*—a model of virtue and goodness. When Hulot becomes completely besotted by a horrible little woman, the wife of a glorified clerk in Hulot's ministry, and the expense of keeping her is ruining the family, Madame Hulot, who's still in love with her husband and desperate to save her family, really at wit's end, cries out, What is it that they do for men, those *filles?* I guess you'd say: "those whores." Why can't I learn it, whatever it is. I'll do it for him if only I can make him happy, if only I can keep him! She doesn't succeed, any more than I did. What should I have done for Tim? Anal sex? I did it, though I hate doing it. But now I'm convinced that what he was looking for was different, not just sticking it up some anus, and that what he needed neither I nor any other woman could give to him. He wanted a man. It's somehow different, even though the mechanics seem the same. My father, who is very worldly and wise, and never let me down during that awful time, said something that opened my eyes. He told me to stop blaming myself. He said that men who think their wife is frigid or don't like the sex they have with her for whatever other reason don't go to other men for better sex. Not unless they're homosexual. Straight men, if they're dissatisfied, go with other women, call girls if necessary.

Tim a queer! Schmidt thought. How totally unlikely. He had nothing of the pansy about him, nothing that connected with the stereotype. Were there other queers at the firm at that time? That "boy" she had mentioned, whom Tim took to gay baths, was he literally an office boy, or was he another lawyer? An associate, because at the time he surely wasn't speaking of a partner! To be astonished and shocked that such things were true twenty-five years ago, he thought, had nothing to do with W & K today: he knew of one homosexual partner (but did everyone else in the firm know?) and two or three associates. But it could be that there were many more. He had been out of touch ever since he retired. The only gossip he knew was what he picked up at the occasional firm function he attended out of a misplaced sense of duty and what he heard once in a while from Lew Brenner and, yes, also from his own son-in-law, Jon Riker, before that ornament of the bar had been forced to withdraw from the firm and deploy his legal talent elsewhere. But back then when Tim was an associate? At college, Schmidt had been dimly aware that a small group, really a handful of his classmates and other contemporaries, were the subject of jokes about being effete, limp wristed. There were a couple of tutors around whom they orbited. He hadn't precisely disliked them, but they used to make him feel awkward and uncouth. Some of them, whom he had continued to see here and there, were out of the closet, as were the homosexual writers whose books Mary had edited, the two known gays among her colleagues at the publishing house, and the shifting, ever renewed contingent of queers in occasional attendance at Mike Mansour's lunches, dinners, and parties, many of them the acolytes of a musician of genius over whom Mike happened at the time to spread his protective wing. But Tim! Old Dexter Wood must be turning over in his grave.

The waiter brought the order. Schmidt found a hundred-franc bill in his wallet and gave it to him, apologizing for driving him crazy.

They drank their coffee in silence, until it was broken by Alice. My father thought I should see a psychiatrist to have someone to talk to, and so did one of the few friends I still had in Paris. We had been at the *lycée* together, and she had also lost a child. To leukemia. She recommended a very nice woman who had her office on boulevard St. Germain. In good weather, it's a nice walk from where we live, across the Tuileries. She gave me a prescription for a tranquilizer and sleeping pills, and being able to talk to her probably helped, but nothing she said and no effort I made to be reasonable got me over the feeling that he had defiled me by doing to me the things he had either just done or was about to do with other men, with Bruno. I would lie awake in my bedroom, knowing that Tim was awake or asleep in what had been our guest room— I couldn't bring myself to tell him to move into Sophie's bedroom—and think about it. He and Bruno continued to use my house at Chantilly for weekends and they tried to have Tommy come out with them. They meant well, but it was a prospect I hated. I needed his presence. Besides, although I was certain that Tim and Bruno would be totally discreet and look after him as well as I or better, I worried about other men who I supposed joined them in the evenings. What kind of men? Fortunately, Tommy had so much homework on most weekends that he couldn't, or anyway didn't want to, go to Chantilly. When he did go, I usually went too. Can you imagine those weekends? Tim, Bruno, Tommy, and I, each of us in his or her room. Tim and I didn't share a bedroom at rue St. Honoré, but at least Bruno wasn't in the apartment; they weren't sneaking from one bedroom into the other. During school breaks and at Christmas and Easter I made it a rule, and got Tim to agree, that Tommy and I would go skiing alone or to Antibes to stay with my father. All the precautions in fact turned out to be pointless. There isn't much you can hide from a thirteen-year-old. Tommy figured out what was going on before his father got sick. How he articulated it for himself, I don't know, and we never discussed it. He made no move to do so. Probably I should have started a discussion, but I didn't know how, and for all sorts of reasons I had stopped seeing the psychiatrist and had no one to advise me. My father had been a great help at first, but after my mother's death, when he became fully aware of the loss, grief overwhelmed him. Later he became too absorbed by the relationship he was forming to be able to concentrate on Tommy and me and set me straight. Apropos of figuring things out, I finally understood why my friends had been so closemouthed from the outset when we kept on taking Bruno to their parties and inviting him to our house every time we gave a dinner. Paris is a small town, and they either knew him or knew about him. He was deep in the closet, but people less stupid than I understood what was going on in my ménage. If my parents had been living in Paris when we moved there, they would have been able to warn me.

She had finished her cognac and asked if she could have what was left in his glass.

Alice, Schmidt said, why did you stay in the ménage à trois? Why didn't you divorce?

She answered, speaking as clearly as before but more slowly. That was the subject of a great debate involving me, my father, and the psychiatrist while I was still seeing her, and of course Tim and Bruno. I thought from the first that we couldn't go on together and shouldn't try and that Tim and I should divorce. Tim was against it. It was always the same refrain. The loss of Sophie was about as much as Tommy could bear. The two children had been so very close. We shouldn't make him lose his father and his home on top of that. That was also Bruno's opinion. I know they were absolutely sincere. They both loved him. What made it easier for them to take that position was that, as I've told you, neither of them intended to come out. Bruno said it was private and cozy in the closet. He was ready to lead a march of one hundred thousand gays straight back into it. So maintaining the status quo didn't interfere with any plan of theirs. The psychiatrist told me that was all wrong, that inwardly Tommy knew the marriage was broken, even if he didn't quite know or couldn't name the reason, and that this explained some aspects of his behavior. She thought he would adjust rapidly to his father's departure. Of course, I should have listened to her. To tell you the truth, I don't know what I would have decided to do if my father had not come out strongly on the side of our staying together for the time being. It was too hard for me to go against his advice. Then I too began to prefer to maintain the façade of our marriage.

She paused and said, That's a whole other story that I'm not even going to try to tell. Tim's story becomes even more painful, but if I have enough strength to go on with it you'll get the answer to your questions. All I knew about AIDS, she continued, was what I was reading in the newspaper, and that wasn't much. I certainly noticed when Tim, who in all our years together had never been sick, not even with the flu or a cold, began to complain of sore throats, sleeplessness, headaches, and diarrhea, and that this seemed to be an unending series of ailments. I said I noticed those illnesses, which sounds cold, but I can't say honestly that they upset me. I had quit as a wife. I no longer loved him. Instead, I felt indifferent and annoyed. Slightly hostile. It's possible that, ignorant as I was, I would have read the figure in the carpet if I had still loved him and had been concerned about his well-being. I'm not sure. For one thing, I think I was fooled by Bruno, who was then and has remained perfectly healthy. It's a primitive sort of reasoning: why one and not the other? On some level, I probably suppressed such knowledge as I had or was acquiring because I didn't want to get involved or to be forced to feel sorry for Tim. So let's say that for a long time I knew nothing and suspected nothing. Then at the beginning of 1989, when Tommy and I got back to Paris from skiing during the Christmas vacation—we had gone to St. Moritz—the housekeeper, Madame Laure, whom you've met, told me that Tim was at the American Hospital with a nasty case of pneumonia. Bruno had put him there and had been looking after him. A week or so later, Tim was discharged, and Bruno brought him home. He recovered from the pneumonia, but he had no energy, he was losing weight, and he claimed that he had almost constant diarrhea. He looked like hell, but that August he went to Bar Harbor with Bruno anyway. I had refused to go; that was the second summer I had done so, and Tommy and I once again spent almost the entire summer in Antibes, this time with my father and my mother's friend, who had moved in by then. She is a wonderful woman, and all four of us got along very well. Father was able to get Tommy into a sailing club in Cap d'Antibes, and Tommy loved it. He felt like a real native.

When we got back to Paris we found that Tim was already there, having cut short his stay at Bar Harbor, and a couple of days later he and Bruno very formally asked to speak to me together and told me, for the first time, that a couple of years earlier he had tested HIV positive. The doctors put him on drugs that they said would keep the illness at bay, but as we could all see, they hadn't. He had to face the facts: the time had come for him to withdraw from the firm. He wasn't up to running the Paris office. In fact, he didn't think he was up to doing any sort of work as a lawyer. Now you know why he retired from the firm so early. Of course, I became desperately worried that he had infected me—there was no reason why he wouldn't have. I had one test for the virus, which was negative, and then two more just to make sure, and then finally the doctor convinced me that since the last time I had sex with Tim was just before Sophie died, in July 1985, there was no chance that the virus was inside me, hiding. I didn't tell Tommy about my worries. But he was extremely bright, and he saw for himself his father's condition. He too read the papers. One day after school he asked me if I thought that I too was going to come down with AIDS. Can you imagine his anguish? That's when I am afraid we made the second big mistake about Tommy. He was scheduled to start at St. Paul's that fall, but we kept him at the *lycée* in Paris. I thought—I suppose Tim did too—that it would be better for him to stay here than to throw him into that very competitive and unfamiliar environment. I was afraid it would be more than he could take.

Where is he now? asked Schmidt.

At Yale, she told him, majoring in mathematics. He did brilliantly at the *lycée*, passing his baccalaureate exam with an honorable mention and getting a gold medal in mathematics in the national contest. Now he's doing just as brilliantly at Yale. Unfortunately, he had distanced himself totally from us even before he left. A wall went up. Who can blame him? Tim, my father, and I, none of us had measured how corrosive life with Tim and me would be. In his sophomore year he came back from Yale during his winter vacation to see Tim when he was dying and stayed until the end, but that was the first time he had come to Paris since he had left for New Haven. He has spent his vacations with the Verplanck grandparents, at their place in Cold Spring, their apartment in New York, or the house in Bar Harbor. My father has tried to get him to Antibes. He turned him down cold. He prefers the monster Verplancks! They ignored Tim during his illness and didn't come to the funeral, although it was practically next door. Lew Brenner had been in touch with them, and he told me later that they rejected all suggestions that Tim was gay and had died of AIDS. So far as they're concerned, he died of a runaway metastasizing cancer, and I refused to take care of him. The sad thing is that Tommy too has adopted the line that I refused to take care of his father. But I don't know how I could have cared for him, even if I had still loved him. There was no room for me. Bruno and Tim decided he would live in Chantilly with a staff—all men, every one of them homosexual—assembled by Bruno. Bruno even offered to buy the house from me! The most I could do was to go to see Tim, which I did. It dragged on so horribly, Schmidtie, with stuff like lesions or small cancers on his skin, pneumonias, then cancer of the lungs that spread to the liver and the brain. In that house full of firearms, why neither Tim nor Bruno took a shotgun out of the gun closet and ended it I will never understand. The way he finally went was such a cheat. He had wanted badly to read and write during the time left to him after he retired, and he couldn't do either. There weren't many days when he was able to concentrate.

So Lew knew, Schmidt mused.

Yes. Nobody else at the firm. Tim asked him to tell no one.

She had been calm during that last part of her story and, it seemed to Schmidt, supernaturally lucid. Now her self-control left her. She curled up on the sofa and cried softly, like a child. Schmidt sat down beside her and stroked her hair. He didn't know what to say to comfort her. At last she stopped sobbing and asked for the bathroom. When she returned she said, You will have to forgive me, I used your toothbrush. But I washed it carefully afterward. You don't mind, do you?

He looked at her and wondered whether he had ever seen anyone so beautiful. Her pallor and eyes swollen from crying gave her face an aspect of tenderness and tragic nobility. Alice, he said, you will perhaps think I am raving, but I know I'm not: I'm falling in love with you, I want you to know it, and I don't care what happens next provided I can be with you. Always. Honest Injun, he added, feeling increasingly stupid.

Oh, Schmidtie, she said, holding out her arms, you don't really want to have me with you always. You hardly know me! But you can kiss me if you brush your teeth first. When he returned, she held her arms out again. I'm drunk, she told him, I've drunk all that remained of the cognac. I taste of cognac. Will you mind that?

He sank on the sofa beside her. She kissed imperiously, her tongue sweeping his, her arms strong and clinging with the force of wisteria. A sacred terror took hold of him, such as, it is said, possesses a novice at the doorstep of a temple where mysteries known only to the high priestess of the place are revealed. The gestures were ones he had accomplished and repeated countless times, but their meaning, he sensed, would be new and fraught with unknown dangers. She was ripe and irresistible, like a golden pear. By what right would he thrust into her? Thrust and ejaculate. Did this beautiful and tormented woman know what she was doing? His own part seemed ordained. With his arm around her waist, he led her into the bedroom.

V

HE MUST HAVE BEEN inside her when sleep descended. Was it possible that they had slept through the night? He looked at his alarm clock. Seven-fifteen. Morning or evening? It wouldn't matter to him, but what about Alice, if it were the next day? Would Madame Laure have sounded the alarm when she found that Alice hadn't slept in her bed? But no, there was nothing to worry about. The sliver of sky that showed through the bedroom window was pigeon gray and pink. An evening sky. He lay on his back, every muscle relaxed, Alice's head on his shoulder, her arm draped over his chest. Her legs held his legs prisoner. Her moist nether lips pressed against his thigh. There was no reason to wake her. From time to time she mumbled and sighed, and her embrace tightened. Once she giggled softly. Smiling, he stroked her hair and her arm and drifted off into sleep.

That was so nice, darling, I feel good all over, thank you, she whispered. Did the whispered words waken him or the feather with which she tickled his nose? Where could she have gotten the feather? Of course: occasionally they protruded from the coverlet; she had pulled one of them out.

She was sitting up, having thrown off the covers, and turned on the lamp on her side of the bed, and for the first time—he did not think that frenzy in which he had undressed her counted—he saw her entirely naked. Lustrously white skin, creamy and soft to touch, breasts so small that neither nursing nor time had deformed them, long and perfectly formed legs ending in feet direly in need of a pedicure. The triangle of hair: that was the one part of her he felt he had explored. Its aroma clung to his hands and face. He sat up too, facing her, ran his hands over her torso and back and returned to her breasts. Silently, she put her arms around him and offered her mouth, her right hand busy at his crotch, ascertaining his response. Unexpected good fortune! Afterward, while they lay side by side, exhausted and holding hands, she told him she thought she was hungry.

Are you going to take me to dinner in the nice restaurant downstairs. Or do you think I'm not dressed up enough.

At this moment you aren't, he answered, but when you put your clothes on you will be the best-dressed woman there. Alice, how did this miracle happen?

Because you got me tipsy.

His happiness turned brusquely into fear.

Is that what happened? Has this old goat taken advantage of you?

You're not an old goat, she replied. You're very nice, and I like you. But I was very tipsy. It wouldn't have happened if I had been sober. That's what makes it so wrong. I wish none of this had happened, I wish you hadn't come to see me.

He didn't point out that they had just made love again, after the effect of the cognac she had liked so much had surely worn off. Instead, barely able to speak, he called the restaurant and asked for a table and then waited while behind the closed door she took care of her toilette, and afterward while she dressed in the bedroom.

When she had finished she asked whether he was going to put on his clothes. The tone of her voice, he noted, was strangely neutral, just a degree or two above cold. Yes, he said, I will get dressed right away. My shower can wait. When he came out of the bathroom, having urinated and washed his face and hands with cold water, he found her in the living room, leafing through a *New Yorker* he had bought the day before at WHSmith's. Shall we go, he asked, his own voice hoarse. He took a sip of water from one of the glasses the waiter had disposed on the coffee table, trying to return to a manner of speaking as near as possible to what it had been when they met not so many hours ago—pleasant and courtly—and realizing that his success was far from complete.

Will you be angry with me? was her answer. It's so pleasant here and so quiet. Would it be possible to have dinner here? Something that's easy to serve and won't take long. I really hadn't intended any of this.

Certainly, he told her. To preserve his composure, he put a CD of Beethoven piano sonatas on the hotel record player, called the restaurant and canceled his reservation, and called room service and ordered a cold dinner with a bottle of a good Burgundy marked up by the hotel to a level that seemed to him unreasonable. Annoyance—with her and himself—that was what he felt. Why had she chosen to tell him Verplanck's appalling story in such grisly detail? Indeed, why tell him the ghastly truth at all? She could have turned him off with white lies, something along the line of a long fight against a cancer that first made him feel unable to go on working and then killed him. Lots of people didn't want it to be known that they had cancer of this or that. That sort of story would have been consistent with Tim's wishes: hadn't she said at some point that he specifically didn't want anyone to know that he had AIDS? And afterward, why had she led him on? She was French, and old enough to know how much cognac she could drink, not some dodo from Dubuque! The more fool he, of course, not to have turned off that stream of true confessions, to have let her drink his brandy, and to have swallowed her bait. He too was old enough to know better and not to be faced with the annoyance, really reproaches, of a woman who had led him on, rather than vice versa. In fact, the last time he'd made a fool of himself this way was as a newly hatched partner interviewing law students out on the coast, when he let an applicant draw him into smoking pot and wrestled with her half naked on a futon! But for God's sake, that was more than twenty-five years ago, and the woman wasn't the widow of one of his junior partners!

Now all that was left to them was to chew their fingernails waiting for room service. There was no telling when the order would appear. The amount of time it took one of those goddamn Arabs or Portuguese in the pantry to cut four—or would it be six?—slices of cold roast beef, put them on the plate, slap on some salad and *cornichons*, and extract the bottle of wine from the temperature-controlled closet was indecent. Or was wine kept down in the cellar? In that case, he had made a fatal mistake when he ordered a good wine! Add to that the time it would take the waiter to waddle from the pantry to his room. Rats! His annoyance was at the point of turning into cold fury. What business had she changing her mind about where they ate? There was gin and vermouth in the minibar, as well as splits of champagne. He offered her the

choice, and heard her refuse both with the simpering grace
of a senior from Miss Porter's responding to an indecent proposal. *Tant pis*, tough luck, kiddo! He made himself a martini
as solid as the Crillon, gave her the Perrier she'd asked for as
an afterthought, put a jar of macadamia nuts on the coffee
table between them, and lowered himself into the overstuffed
armchair. Legs crossed, an expression that his darling daughter referred to as "Schmidt the Hun" on his face—my goodness, where would she have gotten that sweet idea, could it
have been from her adorable mother-in-law?—he applied himself to the martini and the nuts.

His reverie was interrupted by a knock on the door followed by the waiter wheeling in the table. At last they could
eat. He tasted the wine. It was overpriced but better than
he remembered. With grim satisfaction he noted that Alice
hadn't stopped the waiter from filling her glass. Thank you,
he told the waiter, you needn't wait. We will help ourselves,
and I will call when it's time to remove the table. Turning to
Alice, his spirits revived by the martini and the wine, he said,
Alone at last!

I'm glad you're feeling better, she replied.

I'm not. I'm confused and angry at myself, he told her. I
don't like to think that I took advantage of you. The truth is
that you've overwhelmed me. I was totally sincere when I told
you I was falling in love. In fact, I did fall in love. Senile puppy
love! You can call me stupid, hotheaded, unrealistic, and anything else you like, but that's what happened. I listened to
your story, which is sadder than anything I might have been
able to imagine. Was I wrong to want to hear it? I did let you
drink my cognac—emphasis on I "let you," I certainly didn't
ply you with it—and I have offered you my affection and

admiration at a moment when you are vulnerable. Was that unfair? What am I to do now? For my part, I can't say that I wish that what happened had never taken place. Making love to you was a miracle. It put me at the pinnacle of happiness.

I liked it too, she said. Very much.

Then don't make me feel I've wronged you. Don't say again the things you've said just minutes ago. I can't help taking them very hard. They hurt! You may have a thousand reasons against allowing me to love you. My age is surely at the top of the list, but I am in very good health, and if, by another miracle, you had wanted me to, I would have done everything within a man's power to give you a good life.

Schmidtie, she said, your age doesn't scare me, and I think I would have gone to bed with you even if I had been sober, although probably not quite so fast. But don't talk about marriage, permanence, the future. Not now, not yet. That's plain silly. Let's take things as they come, one by one.

There must be something seriously the matter with me, Schmidt said to himself. In substance, this could have been his beautiful twenty-one-year-old Carrie telling him to cool it after one of his repeated offers of marriage. There, of course, the difference in age was huge: more than forty years and, even more important to Carrie, he was convinced, was the difference of class. That child of the American dream could not get over the barrier between a Puerto Rican waitress and an elderly WASP millionaire. Carrie, with her astonishing sense of caste, the beauty of a swan, innate exquisite manners, and sensitivity of a princess! But by the time he had made those speeches, Carrie and he were living together. Alice and he hardly knew each other!

Guide me, Alice, he said. Take as a given that I've fallen in love with you. Tell me how I can become yours and make you mine.

One way, she answered, is not to protest if I go home after I finish my coffee, and no, she added, you needn't take me home. The hall porter will get me a taxi. Or perhaps I'll walk—to cool my head.

And tomorrow? he asked. Can we have lunch or dinner or both? I'm not sure I've told you that I must go to New York the next day. Mr. Mansour calls. I must attend a meeting of the foundation's board of directors.

Schmidtie, she laughed, I too have a job, didn't you know? I have to be at the office tomorrow.

He hadn't known.

There is no reason that you should know.

The business lunch, she told him, was with a German author. She was an editor at a French publishing house, Alice explained quickly, her specialty being the German contemporary novel. Going to school in Bonn had made her completely comfortable in that language and in general had given her a leg up in French publishing. There was a great interest in German novelists and few editors with equal knowledge of German and bilingual in French and English. Perhaps there were none at all. But she could have dinner with him, at her place.

Then she stood up and, smiling gaily, offered him her mouth. *À demain*, she said—at eight!

VI

It was Madame Laure's day off, he learned. She spent Sunday afternoons and evenings as well as Mondays with her married daughter living in Courbevoie, a short distance from Paris, and returned to work early on Tuesday.

I've resisted the temptation to give you cold roast beef or cold chicken, Alice added, offering him a drink. Do you like cheese soufflé? You had better say you do, because that's what you're having.

He was seeing a different Alice, he thought, relaxed and cheerful—as cheerful as she had seemed when she kissed him leaving his hotel suite—and proud of her accomplishments in the kitchen. The wine she poured seemed if anything better than the wine he had chosen when they ordered from room service, but a Bordeaux, so that the comparison was of doubtful validity. Poor Tim's cellar, he thought, but she told him that particular bottle was her father's. He had laid down a great deal of wine and had given her half of his cellar when he sold the apartment on rue du Bac. But Tim balked at drinking my father's wine, she said, and had to be forced to let me serve even vintages that couldn't wait. He actually told me I should sell my wine. He was buying, and laying down, more than enough. That actually began as soon as we moved to Paris, before my father found out he was gay, but still I think it was probably his feelings of guilt. There were other ideas he had with the common theme that he didn't want to take anything from me that I can't explain otherwise. For instance the way he would sulk when I gave him a present that cost more than the price of a book or a necktie. His presents to me were extravagant. And very beautiful. For instance look at this bracelet!

The bracelet on her wrist looked like black lace.

It's iron, she said, Berlin Iron Work, made in the first decade of the nineteenth century. They're rare pieces, but Tim gave me several of them, whenever he found one. It wasn't a lie that he loved me; he was telling the truth. If only I had been able to turn myself into a man—what am I saying?—if I had been born a man!

I like you better this way, said Schmidt, horrified by his own stupidity as soon as the words left his mouth.

After dinner they moved to the library, Alice having rejected his offer to help with the dishes. We'll let Madame Laure clean up, she told him. Don't look so shocked. It would be different if I had a dog or a cat, but I don't, and she doesn't mind doing it. She comes back from her daughter's so early that she has plenty of time for it. But I was going to tell you about my job.

She had sat down on the sofa and motioned for him to take the armchair catty-corner to it.

Alice, he interrupted, I wish you would explain first how you and Tim lived together, or you, Tim, and Bruno, once you knew. Did Tim come home to dinner? Did you speak to each other? Did you entertain—I mean did you for instance invite guests to dinner? Suppose I had turned up. What would have happened?

Schmidtie, don't be silly. Everything went on as previously, except that I didn't sleep with Tim, and there was nothing other than kiss kiss on both cheeks when called for. If you had come to Paris, Tim would have invited you to dinner, and unless you had said that you particularly wanted to see us alone we would have also asked other people—from the office or perhaps the embassy. He would have decanted his best wine and made sure that I had ordered the best smoked salmon from Petrossian. Really, our arrangement was corrosive but not that unusual or unpleasant in a day-to-day sense. Don't forget those wonderful manners of Tim's. Bruno had them too, and he was more charming than any man I have known except my father. But he is almost as charming. There are many married couples living together very *comme il faut*, with the understanding that the husband or the wife or both have their sex elsewhere. Tim's being gay gave it the only touch of originality. No, I'm not turning a catastrophe into a joke, she added, seeing the pained look on his face, I'm trying to give you a clear picture.

Thank you, Schmidt replied, thank you, I do realize that such marriages exist.

But you don't like them, and knowing that they exist makes you unhappy, she chimed in. Let me cheer you up. I'll tell you about my job, which got me through the worst period. It let me keep my sanity. I was very lucky to find one at all, and so soon after that summer. It gave me a reason to get out of the house and go to the office. To be with other people. It's hard to describe how much it meant to me. For the first six months I was part-time, but I've been full-time ever since.

And it was all right with Tommy; he urged me to do it. Otherwise, I wouldn't have taken the job. He didn't get home much before me, so it was possible for me to be there most evenings to help with his homework—and just to be there. Of course, I couldn't help with the math or even supervise, and Tim couldn't either, but Tommy needed no help!

I do understand, Alice, he told her, truly I do. Apropos of work, I'm not sure I've told you that my plane leaves tomorrow late enough in the afternoon for us to have lunch. Would you like that? I was sorry not to have had lunch with you today.

I would love it, she replied, but I can't. Tomorrow I'm having lunch with my colleague who looks after contemporary American and English literature. He's more than a colleague: he got me hired! They would never have taken me if he hadn't made them. I had no work experience in publishing; in fact I had never had a real job! But he had faith in me. By the way, he went to Harvard, and he thinks he knows you. I mentioned your name today. He is Serge Popov, she said smiling.

Serge Popov! The name surfaced from the depths of time like the monster rising from Loch Ness. Yes, he remembered Popov, and remembered disliking him. Oh really, he answered.

A cloud must have passed over his face because she smiled again, this time at him, and said, Don't be like that, Schmidtie, I can't change my lunch date. Serge and I aren't having lunch alone, we're having lunch with our boss. It's important. Now stop pouting, and come here—she patted a place beside her on the sofa—and seduce me.

He limped back to the hotel through deserted streets, at the corner of rue Cambon refusing the services of a professional with spiky hair dyed green who offered them at half

price in view of the lateness of the hour. Seduction indeed!
But who had been the seducer? The awkward and rough-hewn
stranger with the beginnings of white stubble on his cheeks
or she, who had taken him into her bed and lavished on him
such tenderness? From what well did she draw it? Were there
words and gestures she had withheld, ones that she would
bestow only on a man she loved, treasures that perhaps—no,
surely—only Tim had known? In their writhing and caresses,
had it been Tim she had sought, Tim such as he had seemed
to be when he first introduced her to Schmidt? He did not
think he would ever learn the answers to his questions even
if they existed. She had accompanied him to the door and, in
their last embrace, her bare arms around his neck, her naked
body burning through his clothes, had murmured, Yes, that
would be very nice, when he told her he would return soon.
I will, I promise, he whispered. He would keep the promise.
He was certain that, however extraordinary it might seem, he
really loved her—the childish phrase pressed itself on him—
for keeps.

VII

THE OKLAHOMA CITY Federal Building had been bombed earlier in the morning. According to CBS, there were at least thirty-one dead, twelve of them children in the second-story child care center; scores were missing, possibly buried in the rubble. In the pandemonium, no one dared speculate how many of the missing might be dead or alive. But the world turns, and board meetings held in buildings left standing and unharmed must go on, so that no one was surprised when at twelve sharp Mr. Mansour called the meeting of his foundation's directors to order. At his suggestion, however, the proceedings were suspended for thirty minutes after the sandwich lunch, and before Mr. Albert Schmidt's report, during which pause the group watched the one o'clock news on CNN, wordless and transfixed by the horror of the images. No sooner had the TV been turned off, however, than a red-faced man Schmidt didn't know piped up, saying that he could see the hand of Muslim terrorists in the attack, and brought upon himself Mr. Mansour's reproof. The great financier, having been born in Egypt, and having spent his childhood and first years of adolescence in that country and in Morocco, naturally considered himself an expert on all matters touching the

Middle East. The question is, he told the unfortunate speaker, producing in his right hand, as though by magic, ivory worry beads that immediately began a *clickety-clack* staccato, the question is what you would say if *El-Ahram* tomorrow prints a story saying it sees the hand of Jews in this attack, you know, Jews trying to pin the attack on Arabs. You'll say it's nonsense. The same nonsense as what you said just now. You should be ashamed of jumping to such conclusions and speaking when you don't know what you're talking about. Having stood up to make his presentation, Schmidt sat down, expecting the chastised director to leave the room or perhaps even resign. Nothing of the sort happened. Instead, he heard Mr. Mansour calling on him to proceed with the report that they had all been waiting for.

It seemed to Schmidt after he had finished that he had been droning on far longer than was appropriate and had lost his audience. Evidently, it wasn't so. The best thing that ever happened to you, Mr. Mansour told him when the meeting broke up, the very best thing that ever happened to you was getting a chance to hang out with me. You've gotten smart. Almost like a Jew.

Thanks for the compliment, Mike, Schmidt replied. What have I done to deserve it?

That's a stupid question, Schmidtic! Are you trying to prove I'm wrong? You want to know what you've done? Let me tell you. You put on a real class act for those directors. *Pas de problème*. They were wowed. The question is: does it matter what those guys think? They're just WASPs in suits I put on the board to make the foundation look good. Holbein is something else. He's smart, and let me tell you he was impressed.

Holbein was the secretary of the foundation and so far as

Schmidt could tell the secretary or vice president of everything Mike Mansour owned, a factotum so entrenched and so
Machiavellian that Schmidt occasionally permitted himself to
wonder whether Mike himself was not under his employee's
occult control.

How did you deserve the compliment? Mr. Mansour continued. You gave a lecture on the political and economic situation in eight countries you've never been to before and the
condition of my Life Center in each. You never once looked at
your notes, and you didn't make a fool of yourself. Or of me,
because I hired you. They all believe you know what you're
talking about. Even Holbein!

Schmidt repressed the urge to ask whether Mr. Mansour
was among the believers. He had learned that the answer
would be the truth as Mike saw it, unmitigated by any trace
of tact or desire to spare his interlocutor's feelings, and once
you had heard it you had better be ready to live with it. Yes, it
was true that he had spoken without notes, but he had written
an outline of what he wanted to say on a yellow legal pad during the flight from Paris and afterward had silently rehearsed
the presentation he was going to make. That was no more and
no less than what he had done in preparation for countless
client meetings at which he had led his clients, executives of
the insurance companies and their in-house lawyers, through
the structure of an investment and the risks it entailed. But
there was a difference: during this presentation, and afterward, when he answered the directors' questions, he had been
on autopilot. His mind had been elsewhere. That had never
happened when he was in practice, however urgently personal
problems had pressed on him or how badly he was suffering
from lack of sleep or, in the sixties and early seventies, from

a hangover, the effect of those dinners Mary and he and his married contemporaries took turns giving, at which nightcaps of scotch or snifters of cognac were de rigueur and followed the ingestion of a large quantity of red wine, Chinon or Côte du Rhône, greater than he was likely to drink in a week these days. He had luxuriated, allowing his thoughts to dwell on Alice and the plan he was hatching. It was to make in May, probably mid-May, a follow-up visit to the Centers in Warsaw and in Prague. The reason? On his way home he would stop in Paris and see Alice! The secret knowledge had made his heart pound. He had already, before the meeting, obtained Mr. Mansour's approval for the project. Did he need it? Certainly not, he was perfectly able to pay his own round-trip airfare to Paris, in whatever class he chose, and his other expenses including a hotel room perhaps not quite so grand as the suite Mike put at his disposal. But a lifelong habit of traveling at clients' expense played its role—even Mary, he remembered, had liked to time their occasional trips to Europe so that they coincided with the Frankfurt Book Fair that she attended as a matter of course as one of her publishing house's representatives or some other, similar event that called for business travel. Yet another reason made Mike Mansour's blessing desirable. A quirk of Schmidt's psyche? To go to Paris on business lent structure and dignity to the Parisian escapade. He would arrive not as an old goat improbably courting his young partner's widow but as an executive—indeed the president—of an important nonprofit on his way home, having completed a valuable mission. The thought that it would be more romantic to arrive in Paris for no other reason than wanting to be with Alice had traversed his mind as well. On balance, he preferred the mission sanctioned by his friend and chairman.

Are you spending the night in the city? Mr. Mansour inquired as they were leaving the foundation's office. Schmidt looked at his watch. It was a quarter past three. By the time he had rented a car and gotten going, the traffic out to the Island would be murderous. He wasn't up to it. Yes, he answered, I'll stay at the apartment the foundation has so thoughtfully provided and head for Bridgehampton tomorrow morning.

He was truly grateful for the pied-à-terre on Park Avenue, which had not been called for by his contract with the foundation and was, instead, one more example of Mike Mansour's quirky munificence. But Schmidt had more to be grateful for that day. Speechless joy had overcome him the previous evening when he arrived from the airport at close to eleven, exhausted and feeling strangely dehydrated, although he had drunk bottle after bottle of water. A huge bunch of white and purple lilacs stood in a vase on the living room coffee table, and next to the vase was a note scribbled on a smiley Post-it. It read *These are from your garden.* It was signed *Guess Who! Carrie.* Even without the signature he wouldn't have doubted that it was she, with her unalloyed affection and natural grace, who had been responsible for that welcome. He hoped only that it had been one of Mike Mansour's security men who had driven the offering from the country, and not she. Pregnant as she was, she shouldn't be hopping into her little BMW to make the round-trip from Bridgehampton.

Another smart idea, said Mr. Mansour. You are becoming a real Jew. Is your car here?

Schmidt shook his head. I got here from Paris late yesterday evening.

Pas de problème. If you had your car here, Manuel—that was Mike's manservant—would drive it back to the beach. But this is simpler. You'll come with me in the helicopter. Manuel will pick you up. Take off at twelve, early lunch at my house, and after lunch I send you home. You know the Cannings? Joe and Caroline?

Yes, Schmidt knew them. He had been at the dinner party Elaine and Gil Blackman had given before Christmas, an event distinguished by that little prick Canning's baiting of Mike Mansour, whom he was meeting for the first time, and Mike's manifest appreciation of Caroline's looks and chic.

We're having dinner together tonight, Mr. Mansour continued. At Fabien's. You want to come as my guest? I wouldn't have asked Canning if I could have invited the wife alone, but for the time being the price of admission is having him around. For the time being—Mr. Mansour hummed an air Schmidt did not identify—for the time being.

Fabien's was a French restaurant on the Upper East Side that had risen to prominence, indeed, if one were to believe the *Times*'s inane reigning food critic, to the pinnacle of world gastronomy. Schmidt disliked it, having been obliged with some frequency to have dinner there with Mary and her star authors. Decorated in what he called Frank E. Campbell Funeral Chapel style, it managed to combine exorbitant prices with cheeky and inept service and offered a menu so complicated that Schmidt had trouble finding anything on it he wanted to eat. As for the clientele, a majority consisted of beefy men, hardly in need of a meal rich in animal fat and cream, and their bimbos, whose high-pitched voices reduced Schmidt to sulking silence. No, he was full of truly warm feelings for Mike, but the prospect of having dinner with him and the Cannings *à quatre* at that place made him want to go on a hunger strike. It was in fact astonishing that Mike's plan had been to dine with those two alone. Could he intend to slip Joe a Mickey Finn, and spirit Caroline to his penthouse? Or would someone like Holbein and wife—Holbein surely had a wife—be on hand to complete the table? No, that would not be an improvement, not from Schmidt's point of view.

I wish I felt up to it, he replied, but the old jet lag is going to hit me hard. I had better get some rest this evening. We'll catch up tomorrow.

Suit yourself.

That was Mike Mansour's favorite response when an offer of his had been turned down, and almost always it was the harbinger of a stinging reprisal. And so it was this time.

Though it's too bad. I have Enzo Errera and his girlfriend joining us; I thought you'd like them. It would have been a good occasion for you and Enzo to bond. Afterward you could see him when you liked, on your own, without waiting for an invitation from me.

How annoyingly right he was! Schmidt would have liked to have that opportunity, not only because he admired the great pianist but also because he was beginning to think that if his incredible luck held, and Alice came to live with him, or even only spent long periods of time in Bridgehampton and New York, he had better have a circle of friends and potential houseguests who might amuse her and make up for whatever she would be missing in Paris. Gil Blackman and Elaine were great, but who else was there? No one. Why did fate condemn him to look into the mouth of every horse that Mike offered, to underestimate and reject him and his gifts? The vestige of something he would have called his good manners held him back from saying, Oh, in that case, Mike, I'll take a short nap as soon as I get home and join you at the restaurant. Instead he said, I hope you'll give me a rain check, watched Mr. Mansour get into his vast black Rolls, waved good-bye to him, and walked home. Eight blocks translated into ten minutes: early enough to catch Alice before she went to bed. But there was no answer. He let the phone ring until the answering machine switched on, and left a message. Please call me at my New York number. He had written it out for her, together with his number in the country, his cell phone, and his e-mail address. To be on the safe side, he gave her the number again slowly and repeated it digit by digit. Then he undressed and got under the covers.

It was after six—midnight her time—when he woke up. She hadn't called. He made himself a cup of tea, shaved, took a bath, and waited. Seven o'clock—nothing. A quick look at the television told him the death toll in Oklahoma City was climbing. Seven-thirty, and still nothing. She had said—he couldn't remember apropos of what—that dinner parties in Paris started late and broke up very late. Often people didn't sit down at table before ten. All the same, her not answering at one-thirty in the morning seemed strange. It was close to eight by the time he was ready to go out. Could she have come home and gone to bed without checking her messages? At that late hour, it did not seem impossible; she would have felt sleepy. He knew that the telephone could not be heard in Madame Laure's room so that if he called again he wouldn't be disturbing her. If Alice was asleep, she would forgive him. He dialed the number and let it ring five, six times, and hung up. Had she perhaps gone to Antibes? There had been no mention of it, but something might have come up. Perhaps her father wasn't well. He went into the kitchen, poured himself a stiff bourbon on the rocks and drank it avidly. There were graham crackers and cashews in the cupboard and nothing else. If he wanted to have dinner—he had begun to feel hungry—and wanted to have it at his club he had better hurry. The sky had clouded over. He took his raincoat and an umbrella and rushed out of the apartment.

Contrary to habit—unless the distance was forbidding or it was raining hard, he liked walking in the city, and the thirty-five-block distance to his club was just right—Schmidt took a taxi. In fact, he needn't have hurried. His friend, the hall porter, assured him that this being a busy night the kitchen wasn't about to close; there was even time for him to have a drink at the bar. But Schmidt felt his strength flag. He was feeling the jet lag he'd used as an excuse without believing in it. Deciding to skip his predinner gin martini, he climbed the second flight of stairs to the dining room. The maître d'hôtel was also a friend and greeted him like a returning prodigal son. Yes, it was a busy night, so busy that they had put some members and their guests into the members-only dining room, but there was no one at the long table reserved for members. He suggested that Mr. Schmidt have dinner at a table for two in the main dining room. It was more animated. Although club custom, which he liked to uphold, called for members dining alone to sit at the long table even if no one else was there, because any moment another solitary member might materialize, Schmidt acquiesced. Rafael was a good man, trying to be nice. Why hurt his feelings? Besides, it had occurred to him that it would be interesting to see who—members and guests—was to be found in the main dining room, in which he hardly ever set foot. In fact, he hadn't used it since a disastrous lunch—two? three? years ago—with Charlotte's mother-in-law, Dr. Renata Riker, the dreaded shrink. The memory of that woman's duplicity and gall distracted him momentarily from his worries about Alice. Imagine inviting herself to lunch with him and during the meal handing him a copy of the tape her sneaky son Jonathan had made of a telephone conversation between him, Schmidt, and his own daughter! The daughter who was then that man's paramour but not yet his wife. He had pushed the tape away with all the indignation and scorn it merited and hadn't forgotten the outrage or forgiven Renata or Jon. As for Myron Riker, Renata's shrink husband and Jon's father, he was the only member of that awful family to have any merit: he mixed a first-rate gin martini and mostly kept his mouth shut. No, he wasn't about to breach the armistice between him and Charlotte, but the past couldn't be erased, certainly not the accusation Charlotte had hurled at him during the taped conversation, the vicious lie designed to hurt. How could she have come up with it? "Aggressive when feeling guilty" had been the bland rationalization offered by Renata the shrink. But even if accurate, that description of the mechanism of Charlotte's behavior left unexplained and incomprehensible the lie itself, the claim that in his law firm he had been known to one and all as a Jew-baiting anti-Semite. What abyss of ignominy had she dredged to concoct it?

The waiter standing at his right elbow brought him back to the present. He glanced rapidly at the menu and wrote out his order on the chit. Examining the wine list he found that none of the half bottles of red were to his taste; he shrugged and put down the number corresponding to a full bottle. Perhaps it would bring him the uninterrupted night's sleep he needed. What was left over could go into a sauce or be savored by the kitchen staff. These tasks done, he looked around the room and waved to members he knew whose eyes he was able to catch. Among them, two tables away, was Lew Brenner dining with his wife. Lew not only waved back but rose from his table and invited Schmidt to join them. They had just ordered their dinner, and there was room for Schmidtie at their table. Tina would be so happy! Advances, technological and social, never ceased to fascinate Schmidt. He had been a member of this particular club for more than twenty years, without it ever having occurred to him that Lew might want to become a member or be invited to join. His election must have happened recently. Good for Lew, who seemed entirely at ease, and, Schmidt supposed, good for the club.

I would love to join you, he told Lew. It's very kind of you to think of it.

It couldn't be helped. When two W & K partners got together, even if a wife was present, shoptalk took the place of conversation, its flow facilitated first by the bottle of Bordeaux Schmidt had ordered and then by Lew's Burgundy. Accordingly, after paying their respects briefly to the Oklahoma City victims and expressing their horror at the monstrous criminal act, they passed in review the recent missteps of Jack DeForrest, still the presiding partner, important additions to the client roster and to whom among the partners they could be attributed, the financial results of the first quarter, and the probable candidates for partnership during the election, which had been moved from the traditional year-end to June, and the candidates' chances of success. Then they drew a deep breath.

I've just been in Paris, said Schmidt. I saw something of Alice Verplanck.

It was out, and it couldn't be helped. He wanted to say her

name, to feel it form on his lips. What a hard time she's had, he added, thinking that this was the most anodyne statement he could make and yet avoid sounding brusque. It would have been easier not to have been told that Lew knew all about Tim's homosexuality and death of AIDS.

Oh yes, Lew replied, a tragedy. We followed it step by step. Tina used to say I had to get it out of my mind, but how could I? I've got to hand it to Alice. She was very decent throughout, but without Bruno. . . .

His voice trailed off, and he seemed atypically at a loss for words.

Brenner was a good man, in Schmidt's opinion, and had been a good partner. He wasn't going to play games with him. Therefore he said: Lew, I heard a good deal about what happened to Tim from Alice. She told me. I guess Tina knows all about it?

The possibility that if he said anything more he might become guilty of a gross indiscretion had suddenly crossed Schmidt's mind.

Oh, I do! He told me before he talked to Lew, Tina interjected, during a weekend when Alice and he came out to stay with us in the country. He was more at ease with me. He knew from being with me on the board of the ballet that I have lots of gay friends, guys with whom I really get along. It's a fact that gay men like nonthreatening, maternal women. So while we were on a long walk he told me how he loved Alice and the children and all that but also had this other side, which was Bruno. But I said he could talk to Lew, that Lew would understand. Later we met Bruno. What a charmer! It's too bad he plays on the wrong team.

That's right, Lew chimed in, he was worried about what I

would say, how I would react. That was, of course, after the affair with Bruno heated up and some months before they left for Paris.

Wait, said Schmidt. You mean he told you before he left for Paris, a couple of years before Alice found out, which was after their daughter, Sophie, died in the summer of eighty-five? And you knew—Alice said only you, Lew, she didn't mention Tina—and Alice during all that time remained ignorant?

That's one way to look at it, Lew answered. If you stick to the admitted facts, that's correct. He told Tina and me. We kept our mouths shut, and so did Tim and Bruno. There's never been anything like the way those two wanted to stay in the closet and keep the door shut. Then came the tragedy with Sophie, and Alice caught them at it. Is that the whole story? To be frank with you, I don't know any better than you whether it is, but I've found it difficult not to doubt it. Remember that I kept on working with Tim just as much after he moved to Paris as before, and I felt that knowing what I knew I had to watch him like a hawk to make sure that nothing happened that would spook a client. Then after he told me he'd tested HIV positive and began to have symptoms, I had to watch him like two hawks. You can imagine my concern about his emotional state, his cognitive ability, and the quality of his work. This may sound strange, considering what a great lawyer he was, and what a perfectionist! I haven't kept up with the science, but at the time there was some concern that there could be an impact on how the brain functioned. Let me tell you, except for the ability to concentrate, which was shot once those horrible illnesses piled on, his acuity was A plus—A plus to the very end.

But Lew, Schmidt interrupted, that doesn't tell me any-

thing about another way of looking at whether Alice knew
or didn't.

I was just getting to that. The other way to look at it is
that there wasn't a single social occasion from the time Bruno
arrived on the scene until Tim was so sick that they had to
move him to the hunting lodge in Chantilly when Bruno wasn't
present. By the way, that lodge is a gem. If you ever have
a chance to see it when you are in Paris, don't miss it. All right,
Bruno was and is a great guy, he was lovely with the kids, gallant with Alice, liked to sail and shoot with Tim, and on and
on, but Alice isn't dumb. And she would have had to be really
dumb not to catch on. And I'm not even mentioning Bruno's
being ever so slightly known in Paris as not being exactly a
ladies' man. That came through to me loud and clear— if you
can say that of an innuendo, ha! ha! ha!—in my dealings with
his partners at the bank and some other business relations.
So I would say to you that it is not impossible, it may even
be probable, that Alice being a very smart and very beautiful lady caught on and found it not inconvenient to let bad
enough alone. Ha! Ha! Ha!

Brenner's Ha! Ha! Ha! was getting on Schmidt's nerves.
Had he always laughed like that?

It may be even probable, as I said, Lew continued, that she
found consolations. Or one big consolation. But catching them
in flagrante delicto, kissing in the garden the day after they
had buried Sophie, was just too much, so she let them have it.

I see, said Schmidt. Do you know anything concrete about
the consolations?

No. She has never confided in me. The story about the kiss
in the garden and the horrifying funeral at Verplanck Point I
got from Tim. Let me tell you, I've been to Verplanck Point

and met the monstrous parents and the even more monstrous sister when I arranged for Tim to be buried there. How he grew up to be as normal as he did is a complete mystery. Another mystery is why in the devil's name he insisted on being buried there. Perhaps it was in order to be near Sophie. He was crazy about those children. One other word about Alice's consolations: As I told you I had been seeing them both in the period when she quote didn't know close quote, and in the period after she quote found out close quote. There was only one difference. She was truly stricken by Sophie's death. But otherwise, in the way she was with Tim and with Bruno, there was no change whatsoever.

The violent rain that had fallen while Schmidt was at table had stopped, leaving the air fresh. Schmidt walked home. It was a toss-up in the end whether Alice had guessed or hadn't, except that if she had figured it out from the start it meant she lied to him. Why should he take Lew's guess, for that was all it was, as the truth, when Tina, who seemed to have been in the thick of things, had said nothing about that? It wasn't Lew's word against Alice's; it was much less, only his opinion. Lew wouldn't be the first lawyer in Schmidt's experience to be convinced that he was capable of great psychological insight. The stuff about Alice's consolations was of the same order. Perhaps it was true. It hurt him to think it was, because of the way he felt about her, but she had not said or implied that she had been faithful to Tim all those years. If Lew was right about consolations, it still didn't make her a liar.

There was no telephone message waiting for him. Midnight, therefore six in the morning in Paris. He refused to call so early, and he was really too tired to wait another two or three hours. Even if he hadn't been, she could count. She would know how late he had stayed up to speak to her and would realize how hard he had taken not finding her at home and not having his call returned. That was not how he wanted to be perceived. It was time enough to call tomorrow, probably from his house in Bridgehampton.

VIII

HAVING DONNED THE HEADPHONES that cut out the helicopter's manic *rat tat tat*, Mr. Mansour told Schmidt he was turning off the intercom function that enabled them to speak to each other or to the pilot, and plunged immediately into studying what Schmidt recognized by its cover to be a deal book prepared by the institutional investment group of a Wall Street firm well known to Schmidt for having brought many loan proposals to his insurance company clients. A college classmate of Schmidt's ran the group, a Harvard golden boy who had divorced twice, the last time noisily, managing in the process to defy the rule according to which that precious metal doesn't tarnish. Schmidt unfolded his *Times*. There were still no suspects in the Oklahoma City bombing, but some "unnamed experts" focused on its resemblance to the 1993 World Trade Center bombing and the possible connection to Islamic militants. That gave some support to the remarks of the director Mike had brutalized at the board meeting. It was too bad the poor guy hadn't had the nerve to defend them. What were the risks he would have run? A second tongue-lashing, a hint that he resign from the board and thus forgo the honorarium fixed at a relatively modest forty thousand per year? Unless he had business pending with one of Mike's companies—in that case, he could count on Holbein, if not the great man himself, putting the kibosh on it. He folded the paper and fought off the urge to doze. They had been flying east along the Sound. The pilot changed course. Under a cloudless sky, the helicopter began to follow the Atlantic coastline. Schmidt watched intently, and it seemed to him that for all the proud houses and their swimming pools, the parking lots adjoining town beaches, and the labyrinth of roads, it was still the fresh green breast of the new world that had revealed itself first, so long ago, to Dutch sailors, overwhelming them with its wonders. The helicopter passed over Mr. Mansour's beach house and then Schmidt's, farther inland, separated from the ocean by the pond. Another few minutes and an adjustment of its course, and the little craft put down on the runway. The copilot opened the hatch and helped Mr. Mansour and Schmidt disembark. The great financier's other Rolls, a yellow convertible, was steps away. He waved the chauffeur to the backseat, took the wheel himself, and, as soon as he had confirmed that Schmidt's seat belt was buckled, drove sedately to Water Mill.

You missed a good party at Fabien's, he told Schmidt. Enzo was in great form—he always is when we're together, he knows I have his interests at heart and am doing what I can, which is considerable, to develop his career—and his girlfriend is a ten. With all due respect, big tits and a big décolleté, I wouldn't have minded sticking my hand in it. *Pas de problème*, I didn't do it. He might have tried to slug me and hurt his hand! Unless I tore off his arm first, which with the

Tae Kwon Do training I've been getting I probably could have. Either way, it wouldn't have helped his piano playing. That Canning, I don't like him. If you pardon my French, he's an asshole. But Caroline! Nice little tits, and I bet she's tight. Tight tight tight! The question is, how do I get in?

How indeed?

I'm working on it. What happens if I send him away? For instance I'm thinking of fixing him up with the studios in Hollywood so he can talk about making a movie out of one of his novels. The question is, would she necessarily go with him? Maybe not. She's writing a book. But if he goes and she stays, I can invite her to dinner here or maybe in New York. New York would be better. No question: I would show her a good time, the kind of good time she can't have with that dick.

The notion of Mike's showing Caroline a good time revived for Schmidt the unpleasant memory of just such an occasion Mike had arranged for Carrie, and the big fat pass he'd made at her, almost nipping his friendship with Schmidt in the bud. It was not a subject he wished to pursue. In truth there was no subject that held his interest just then other than what time it was in Paris. When they finally reached Mike's house it was six-fifteen in the afternoon for Alice. She'd still be at her office or on her way home. He could have asked to use the telephone before lunch was served, but it had occurred to him that it would be good to know first whether she had left a message on his answering machine in Bridgehampton. That meant delaying his call for another hour or more, but perhaps it was just as well. He'd seem less impatient. So he sat through the lunch, which he managed to notice was excellent, and drank

Mr. Mansour's champagne, cheering him on when his remarks required it and indicating surprise when that seemed appropriate, while his mind traced Alice's probable itinerary. He had consulted the weather forecast for Paris before leaving the New York apartment and knew it was a bright and sunny day. Very likely she had walked home from the office.

He perked up when Mr. Mansour put to him the question that invariably came up during their *tête-à-tête* meals: The question is, he intoned, the question is whether you're finally getting a life for yourself. You did a great job in Europe, we know that. But did anything happen that was good for Schmidtie?

He replied with greater candor than he had intended: In fact something very good happened. I met a lady I really like.

Another twenty-year-old like Carrie? Czech or Ukrainian? I hear they screw like bunnies, but if you're smart you wear a condom.

He laughed gaily and held out his hand to shake Schmidt's.

Schmidt shook the proffered hand and told Mr. Mansour he wished it were as simple as that. The lady was French, she was a real lady, and she wasn't a twentysomething. She was younger than he, but not young enough to be his daughter.

You have a photo? If you haven't bought one of those new cameras I'll give you one. It's a must-have. Manuel takes good pictures with mine. We can get someone at my office in Paris to take one of her. You want Manuel to take a picture of you? You could send it to her.

Mike, I can't thank you enough, Schmidt replied, but we mustn't get ahead of ourselves. Or rather I mustn't. But I'll keep you posted.

Pas de problème, replied Mr. Mansour. You say you like her, but you can't fool me, you're in love. The question is, how much does she like you?

I wish I knew!

The driver of the yellow Rolls deposited Schmidt at his house and told him that while Mr. Mansour and his guest traveled in the bright green helicopter, as usual enraging countless residents on the ground below them, in their houses, on their tennis courts, or beside their pools, and while they later lunched on sweet pea soup, lobster salad, and rhubarb crumble, Manuel drove the black Rolls back from the city, stopped at Schmidt's house, and carried his bags upstairs. One had to hand it to Mike. If he took charge, nothing was left to chance. The front door to Schmidt's house was open, which is how he normally left it during the day. He paused and looked around him before entering. The forsythia on both sides of the driveway had reached its peak, and so had the tulips. He liked his house and his garden. Whatever happened, he would have it as a refuge. Whom would he find at home? Carrie and Jason, the man she was going to marry, were surely still living in the pool house on the property, but at this hour on a weekday they'd be working at the marina Jason had bought. Schmidt wasn't sure whether they had already found a house or an apartment to move into. If it was a house, it would surely need renovation: a perfect project for Bryan, who had finished fixing up the living space above Schmidt's garage and created a little apartment for himself. Since the deal was that he would occupy it when he was cat sitting he was surely sleeping there, but very likely he too was at the marina. At least Sy would be at home! As Schmidt opened the screen door and let himself in, a smile broke out on his face. The little Siamese had indeed been waiting for him—there was no other explanation for his energetically wailing *meow meow*—rubbing himself against Schmidt and finally, in exasperation at Schmidt's slowness to respond, rising on his hind legs to tap Schmidt's pant leg with one graciously extended paw, making it clear he wanted to be picked up.

With Sy nestled in his arms, Schmidt went into the kitchen. There was a note on the table, but loyalty and good behavior deserve, whenever possible, instant recompense. He set a saucer of milk on the table and showed it to Sy before reading the message in Carrie's fine schoolgirl hand: *We're coming to welcome you home this evening after work, all three and seven-ninths of us, and we're bringing the dinner! Until then have a good rest.* It was signed with the capital letter *C* surrounded by arabesques in which he discerned elements of *J* and *B*. So be it! His lovely Hecate mistress, herself a wondrous child, with a baby due soon. The baby that could be his, a possibility of which Carrie had told him Jason was aware. A baby is a baby, she had told him. Jason knows about you. He loves me. So big deal. If the kid isn't his, it's mine, and he's the stepfather. Presented in that light, the situation had struck Schmidt at first as intolerable. But one makes progress, he said to himself, moral progress of sorts. He found himself ready to accept the ambiguity. Whether the little boy was red-haired with a big nose like his, or turned out to be a Nordic god like Jason, he would be at the kid's side. Discreetly, and he hoped lovingly.

There was no message waiting on his Bridgehampton answering machine, for the very good reason that the answer function of his telephone had been turned off. He didn't recall having done it, but whoever had—one of his trio of house minders or one of the Polish cleaning women—was perfectly right. Not many people called him, but, even so, it made no sense to accumulate messages over an absence of many weeks. But what about New York? Pinned to the bulletin board next to the kitchen telephone was a trove of useful information. Squeezed between the business card of the Wainscott vet who had given Sy his first vaccinations and that of the locksmith, he found the index card on which he had written the numbers he had to dial for access to his 212 voice mailbox. There was only one message—from Alice!—received that very day at 12:42 p.m., just as the helicopter was passing over Southampton.

Bonjour, *mon petit* Schmidtie, he heard her say. Shall we talk later? Kiss kiss kiss . . . She did not mention the message he had left. Forgetfulness? Had she not listened to it? Could her answering machine have malfunctioned?

His hands on the verge of trembling, he called her number, realizing that he no longer needed to look for it in his pocket calendar. It was now among the rare numbers he remembered. The line went dead, and for a moment he considered hanging up and redialing, but before he had done so, it came alive. He let it ring on and on, waiting for the invitation to speak after *le bip sonore.* Finally—he had stopped counting the rings—the line went dead again. Now there were two probable, equally infuriating explanations: one, she had turned off the answering machine, and, two, it was broken. Did he care which it was? The salient fact, as he used to put it in memoranda to clients, was that she was still out. Quarter of ten, Paris time. If she had gone out to dinner, trying to reach her before six—midnight her time—would be a frustratingly pointless exercise. Normally, after an absence, he would inspect the outside of the house and the garden, and follow up with a cruise through the interior. But his heart wasn't in it. Instead, he went upstairs and unpacked. One big advantage of the luxurious accommodations Mike had pressed on him was that he had no dirty laundry beyond what he had worn the day before and what he had on his back. The hotel laundry had done it all, far better, it pained him to admit, than Pani Basia, the member of the Polish brigade who had taken charge of his linen and everything else in the house that needed washing and ironing. His suits hung up and shirts, underpants, socks, and handkerchiefs stowed away, he put on his pajamas and lay down. He hadn't noticed how tired he was, and, fearing that if he fell asleep he wouldn't wake until the morning, he set the alarm clock for six. That is when he would try her number again. Sy materialized from nowhere. With one leap he was on the bed, pressing his purring body against Schmidt. Perhaps he knew that Schmidt needed company and affection.

I was on a sleepover, she said, when he told her that he had called repeatedly the previous evening.

Sleepover? he asked.

Yes, she replied, one of my colleagues gave a dinner at her house in St. Cloud. It was going to end too late for me to get back to Paris easily by train, I didn't want to drive, and I didn't want to get a lift home with anyone else, because there would be too much drinking. So I spent the night at Claude's and got a lift from her to the office this morning. She always brings her car.

It was hard: names he didn't know, houses he hadn't seen and would probably never see, customs he wasn't used to.

How very nice! he said.

Yes, she said, Claude is my best friend at the office. Perhaps my best friend, *tout court*. You'll like her! She works on scientific books about modern society. You'd really like her husband too. He is a very well-known lawyer, François Larbaud. A *pénaliste*. Can you say that in English? He represents defendants accused of big crimes. There is talk of his being the next *bâtonnier*. That's the president of the Paris bar.

Another glimpse of Alice's mysterious world. How would he find his way in it?

I think you'd say a criminal lawyer, he said. Perhaps white-collar-crime specialist, if it's nonviolent cases. I suppose the boys at the W & K office know him.

Immediately he wished he hadn't mentioned the firm, but she didn't seem fazed.

Tim certainly did—in part through me. They had lunch regularly.

My love, Schmidt said, sensing that the conversation was going nowhere. All the feelings I had for you have only gotten stronger. I want you, and I want to be with you. I wish you were here just now. It's so beautiful here in late April and early May. My forsythia have never looked better, the peonies are getting ready to bloom, the dogwoods and the magnolia are glorious. Couldn't you rush over for a long weekend?

Now? she asked. Now is impossible. And we've just seen each other!

That hurt, but he brushed it off.

All the more reason to rush over, answered Schmidt, but I guess we can't do what's impossible.

As he said that, he remembered from high school French that if you want to say that you'll try very hard, you say *je ferai l'impossible*, I'll do the impossible. But French class was one thing, and courting Alice another. Without missing a beat—anyway that's how he thought it came out—he continued: I've another idea. I must take another look at my Eastern European charges, especially the Polish office, which I haven't seen. How would it be if I came to Paris for the weekend of May twenty-sixth?

May twenty-sixth, May twenty-sixth, she repeated, oh but Thursday, May twenty-fifth, is Ascension Day. Everything in France shuts down from Wednesday until Monday. We call that a *pont*—a bridge—an extra goody. I've accepted an invitation from friends, in St. Tropez. I'm also going to drop in on my father in Antibes.

Oh, said Schmidt.

Wait, I need to take a look at my calendar. Yes, the following Sunday, June fourth, is Pentecost Sunday. I think the publishing house will close on Monday, June fifth. If I can swing it, I'll stay in St. Tropez through that weekend.

That was a strong dose of Catholicism for Schmidt to absorb. She was a Protestant, just like he. Why were these holidays important? Don't be a dope, because they gave an excuse to Catholics, Protestants, Muslims, and Jews alike to stay away from the office! Religion wasn't the issue: the question was, as Mr. Mansour might say, what plans one made to take advantage of it. Clearly, none of Alice's was sufficiently elastic to include him, not even in a supporting role. No, there was no use fighting city hall or shadowy friends with houses in St. Cloud or St. Tropez.

I have another idea, he said. Perhaps this one will work better. What if I came to see you around May fifteenth?

Alice's calendar was consulted once more.

That would be lovely, my darling Schmidtie. And it's sooner!

Then she asked about Oklahoma City and whether it was true it was the same Muslims who had tried to blow up the World Trade Center, and he told her that for the moment no one knew.

They brought the pizzas that Carrie liked so much and had accustomed Schmidt to like, a bowl of spinach and arugula salad, and an apple tart she said came from Sesame. Also bottled water, the name of which was new to Schmidt. He went down to the cellar and got two bottles of a Chianti. They were going to eat in the kitchen, continuing, he realized, a tradition that started with the first dinner he had had at home with Carrie. He let her set the table. It was also their custom to use the best tablecloth, napkins, silver, china, and glasses even though it wasn't the dining room. She remembered, of course, where everything was. It could have been her house, Schmidt thought.

Carrie was sticking to her mineral water, which, as a concession to Schmidt that he didn't fail to notice, she was drinking out of a glass. He poured gin and tonics for Jason and Bryan, hesitated between a gin martini and a bourbon for himself, but decided in favor of the martini, fixing it meticulously before sitting down in his rocking chair. He could not keep his eyes off Carrie. So pregnant! So beautiful! Her belly stuck out— the leotard she wore accentuating the magnificent hillock. And the other protuberances, the golden apples that were her breasts! All three men in this kitchen had made love to her, in his own case wildly, with nothing barred: her mouth, her vagina, and her anus explored with equal freedom. He had no reason to think that Bryan and Jason had been less favored. Now the three sometime tenants of Carrie's body, one still resident and two evicted, were about to eat their pizza and drink their wine peaceably and exclaim over the fruit tart. How could that be? Was a generalized decline in conventional American mores to blame for their not being at one another's throats? Schmidt was not inclined to think so; it was rather that Carrie, like a trainer of big cats, knew how to make them sit on their stools and hardly even growl.

A question addressed to him ended the reverie.

Schmidtie, Carrie was saying, wake up! Your jet lag must be something else! The doctor said yesterday that if the baby doesn't come by June twentieth, he'll induce it. What do you think of that? Are you going to be around? Jason and I would like you to be there. The other question is, can we stay on in the pool house when we bring the baby home from the hospital? We have an eye on this house out in Three Mile Harbor that's near the marina and just right, but it needs work. So if we can stay here meantime, we'll make an offer on it.

How could you doubt even for a moment, addressing both Carrie and Jason, that I want you and baby here?

He was going directly against the great financier's advice. Having heard of the plan to let Carrie and Jason use the pool house, Mr. Mansour had warned Schmidt to be sure they were out before the baby was born. Otherwise, he said, they'll never leave! Pax Mike! This was a risk he would take.

And yes, he continued, I'll make sure I'm here in June. I wouldn't want to be in one of those godforsaken places where Mike has his foundation's offices when this young man arrives.

Jason spoke up: Thank you so much! I think you'll like the

house we want to buy, and being able to leave Carrie and the baby here while Bryan and I work on it will really help.

Sure will, Albert! piped up Bryan. You've always been a great guy! The best!

Schmidt had told the little fuckup innumerable times to call him Schmidtie—unless he preferred to call him Mr. Schmidt—and it was unclear to Schmidt whether the use of "Albert" was an expression of respect or a safe way to needle him.

Carrie said nothing. Instead she got up, put her arms around Schmidt, and kissed him.

There is one more thing Carrie and I would like to know, said Jason after she sat down. We would like to name the little guy Albert. Would that be all right with you?

Yes, he said, of course, I'm happy and honored, but what will people call this poor little guy? Not Al, I hope.

We think we can make Albert stick. If not we'll settle for Bert—don't you think that's still pretty good? We can't call him Schmidtie. No one would understand!

IX

H<small>E REVISITED</small> the foundation's center in Bucharest and from there went to Warsaw for an introductory meeting with the staff. He had never been to Poland before. It existed for him only as a collage made up of Chopin played by Rubenstein or Horowitz, images drawn from John Hersey's *The Wall* and Leon Uris's *Mila 18*, the endless reverberations of Auschwitz, the destruction of Warsaw's old town during the uprising in 1944 followed by its lovingly faithful restoration, and Lech Walesa and the Solidarity movement. When the director of the Polish Life Center asked him what he would like to see in Warsaw after the second day's morning meeting at the office had concluded, leaving the rest of the day free, he said he would leave the choices up to her but thought the old town should be included in the visit. She decided they would start by having lunch there. They were seated in the back of the restaurant she had told him was the best in the old town, a long, narrow, and somber room. He let her order lunch and listened to her life story. She was born in a small town near Kraków where her parents, refugees from the eastern part of Poland that had become part of Ukraine, had settled. Of modest background—the father did carpentry, and the mother was a nurse—they had made all the needed sacrifices to enable her to attend the ancient university in Kraków, where she got her degree in modern languages. No, she hadn't studied in England or the U.S.; she learned her excellent English in high school and later at the university. She had also had to learn Russian as the principal modern language, but she and her friends had been on a mental strike against anything to do with the Soviets. They never learned it well and managed to forget what they had learned, which she now knew was a pity. The rest of her career Schmidt knew, having looked at her personnel file: a job in publishing in Warsaw, activity in the Solidarity movement that led to six months in jail, odd jobs, then, after the first free elections in postwar Poland, an editorial position in the newly founded daily that would become Poland's leading newspaper. It was from there that Mike Mansour had recruited her. That was where the file stopped, but she told him that she was married to a man she'd known since the university who taught mathematics at a high school in Warsaw and created crossword puzzles on the side. They had no children. A nice man who had long ago stopped sleeping with her. No sex! Not because he had someone else, but because he had lost interest. Can you imagine such a thing?

Schmidt answered truthfully that he couldn't, not if one lived with a woman as attractive as she.

She thanked him, and they clinked glasses. He was no longer surprised to find himself drinking vodka out of a carafe nestled in an ice bucket, rather than wine or beer. Vodka had been the principal beverage at dinners a month earlier in Ukraine and also at the previous evening's dinner. But this was lunch, and, the first carafe having been emptied, Pani Danuta summoned the waiter and ordered another. Without being prompted, she went on to say that she and her husband had considered divorce but were held back by realities of lodging: they had an apartment they liked, which she would logically be the one to keep, but how was her husband to find something affordable near enough to the high school? Such an apartment didn't exist. And then there was the more general problem of money. At the foundation, she earned more than he. That made a better life for them both. She didn't want to deprive him of that—after all, he was an old friend. Didn't Schmidt agree? He said he did and raised his glass to her. They clinked. As for sex, she added, she made do.

She proposed that after lunch they visit the Łazienki Palace and its park, which had suffered little damage during the uprising. It's mostly eighteenth-century architecture and very beautiful, she said. Feeling light-headed from the drink and the unusually warm and humid weather, Schmidt acquiesced. After a taxi ride to the park, they began their walk, which quickly seemed endless to Schmidt, as Pani Danuta kept up a learned commentary on the various royal buildings as she leaned heavily on his arm. Schmidt wondered whether the reason was habit, fatigue, or the wish to acquaint him with the heft and contour of her breast.

It was almost four when they reached the street. She got a cab instantly. When he suggested that he would drop her off at her apartment she said it was too far out of his way. They should instead go to his hotel, which was well air-conditioned, and have a drink at the bar. Later she would take the tram from there that connected to another one that took her right to her street corner. Once again, Schmidt acquiesced. As soon as they got to the hotel, she excused herself to go to the ladies' room. He visited the toilet as well and afterward waited for her on a banquette in the bar that indeed was an oasis of fresh cool air and quiet. When she returned, they settled down to a bout of vodka drinking even more serious than in the restaurant. She had ordered a liter bottle instead of a carafe and, having asked for his permission, which he granted, asked the waiter to bring canapés of smoked salmon and hard-boiled eggs and something she called head cheese, pieces of meat in a jelly. He wondered at her appetite, like that of a man accustomed to physical labor, and at her metabolism. Somehow she burned off all that food and the booze. He would have bet that there was little fat on her tall and big-boned frame. On the whole he liked her face. Plain, with even features, and blue-gray large eyes. Her hair was straight and blond. She sensed that he had inspected her and inquired: What do you think? I'm not bad? Do I pass the test?

With flying colors, he answered.

She shook her head. It's the first time you've looked at me. But that's all right. When I told you I managed to get sex, I should have told you that it's almost always with Americans or Englishmen who come to Warsaw for a few days. They don't have VD, and they don't spread gossip. What do you think about that?

I think it's very reasonable.

Then why don't you invite me to go with you upstairs?

Ensconced the next day in his seat on the afternoon airplane for Paris, Schmidt asked himself for the umpteenth time an apparently unanswerable question. What had possessed him to spend the end of the afternoon, much of the evening and the night, and Saturday morning in bed with Pani Danuta? Her take-charge attitude did not abandon her in bed, her ideas of what could be done surpassing Carrie's in their amplitude. Over dinner, she expostulated on the wretched state of Polish television—only one private channel, hopelessly vulgar and commercial, as bad as the private Czech channel—and the president of the Polish national bank who used to be the minister of finance. Sure, he knew how to say all the right things about capitalism and free market forces, but he was a Tartuffe. Both subjects were of considerable interest to Schmidt, in his official Life Center capacity; he wished she had spoken about them as interestingly at the meetings in her office.

He had planned to leave Warsaw on Sunday, taking a flight that got him to Paris at nine in the evening, after a series of weekend meetings with that hypocritical central banker, the mayor of Warsaw, and a gaggle of less important officials. However, on Saturday morning, when Danuta checked the messages at the foundation, she learned that the appointments had all been canceled on Friday, late in the afternoon, at a time when for obvious reasons she had turned off her cell phone. The excuses ranged from an unexpected summons by the president of the republic all the way to a violent attack of stomach flu. There was little doubt in Schmidt's mind that most of the cancellations were in fact due to the exceptionally beautiful weather, a belief that Danuta did little to challenge. Whatever the reason, one thing was certain: since there wouldn't be any meetings, he was leaving on the first available flight. That turned out to be one that got him to Paris that evening at seven. He had agreed with Alice that they would see each other on Monday, May 15, the date she had approved. Should he let her know that he was arriving instead on Saturday? If Danuta hadn't been in his bed, wolfing down brioches smeared with butter and honey, he would have called Alice as soon as the concierge confirmed his reservation. But Danuta's presence there could hardly be denied or overlooked; indeed, fortified by breakfast she was soon astride him. By the time they finished and had washed, it was time for lunch. How could he fail to invite her? And then he put his foot down: no they couldn't go back to his room. Over her objections and assurances that there was plenty of time before he had to leave for the airport, he put her in a taxi and gave the driver money for the fare.

Then he rushed to his room and called Alice. No answer. Wasn't that just as well? Wasn't there something monstrous and impudent about asking to see her that very evening? "See her"! What a paltry euphemism for what he was interested in! An interval, allowing for purification, was in order. But how long? Twenty-four or forty-eight hours? Should he call on Sunday morning, explain the change of schedule, and ask whether they could have lunch or dinner together later in the day? That was the twenty-four-hour solution. The more virtuous one required postponing the call until Monday morning. It was a conundrum. He solved it by leaving a message for Alice, saying he was arriving late that evening, and would explain the change of plans. Would she please call him at the hotel?

There were no messages waiting for him in Paris. This time he had remembered to write down in his pocket calendar the instructions for retrieving messages left for him in Bridgehampton and in the city. There weren't any. He unpacked, and was about to take a shower when the need to call Alice overwhelmed him. There was no answer. And she wasn't at home when he called the next morning shortly after nine or when he tried again at noon. This time he left a message. He had arrived in Paris sooner than expected, and was at the hotel.

As soon as he had hung up he realized what a stupid thing to say that was. So he called again, and said he was going out for a long walk but would call the hotel to check for messages. Could they have dinner? If not he would see her tomorrow. It was almost lunchtime, but he was too nervous and oddly impatient to sit down for a stately meal at the hotel restaurant, or order at the hotel bar. The previous time he had been in Paris his injured ankle had prevented him from taking long walks. Nothing prevented him now. He crossed Pont de la Concorde, and marched interminably first all the way to the place du Panthéon, and then, doubling back, to Montmartre. He took the cable car there to the tiny Square Nadar, got out, contemplated the white mass of the Sacré-Coeur Basilica looming to the right, and sat down on a bench. The view of the city was unbeatable, but his old nemesis, blisters, had formed where the back of the shoe rubs against the tendon. They hurt and, he supposed, they would bleed. He was asking himself whether to ask the hotel to send a radio car to pick him up when a taxi pulled up at the sidewalk. An Asian couple toting guidebooks and a camera got out. He bounded toward the still-open door, and, once inside, gave the driver the name of his hotel.

There was no message from Alice waiting at the hotel, but she called at dinnertime to say she had just returned from a weekend with friends in the country. If he was free, and hadn't eaten, they could have dinner together.

At my hotel? he asked.

Yes, the food is so good, and so are the memories.

They did not make love after dinner that Sunday as he had half hoped. Not tonight, she told him, soon after they sat down at table, we do have tomorrow, don't we, and perhaps a few more days. She had told him she was born in 1945. Therefore, she was fifty. If she had been a few years younger, he might have thought the obstacle was her period. It was too bad, but he was grateful that she had made clear right away how the evening would end. There would now be twenty-four hours of additional purification, and he did not need to spend the time they were at dinner thinking of her as a redoubt he must prepare to storm and take. She was, he was finding, as splendid as when he had discovered her one month earlier, almost to the day, when he called on her at her apartment on rue St. Honoré. Her physical beauty had never been in question, not since the day he danced with her at her wedding reception, but now he was noticing so much that had eluded his attention earlier: the enchanting grace of her every gesture, her willingness to laugh, the simplicity and ease with which she questioned the maître d'hôtel about the recipe for the cold tomato soup they were having, instantly charming that stolid functionary. He admired the way she dressed. The trousers were the ones she had worn to lunch on their first Sunday together. The top too was an old friend; she had worn it when he came to dinner at her house. But the jacket, white and summery, was new to him, perfect for the exceptionally warm day that was ending. She spent little on her clothes, that seemed clear, and he asked himself whether she had less money than one would have expected of Tim Verplanck's widow. In that case, it would be a joy to put some wind in her sails. But it was just as likely that she knew her own talent for mixing and matching, for attaining ineffable chic with small means.

But Alice's hands were the greatest discovery of the evening: almost as large as his but fine, with delicate elongated fingers, they were the hands of a mime, reminding him, as she gesticulated, which she did often when telling a story, of Jean-Louis Barrault in *Les enfants du paradis.* He imagined those fingers making shadow puppets for the delight of some child, and, at some point, he heard himself ask whether her son, Tommy, had a serious girlfriend. She seemed surprised and answered that because of the distance from her he insisted on keeping she couldn't be certain, but there was at least no sign of his being gay. Horrified at having made her feel that was the answer she needed to give, he told her he was simply imagining what a good mother she must have been and how good she would be at playing with her grandchildren. Immediately he became conscious that this too was a tactless remark, but she took it in stride, somehow intimating to him that he hadn't offended her, and said that she thought she had indeed been a good mother until the disaster with Sophie, for which she couldn't blame herself, and the derailing of her relationship with Tommy, about which she felt guilty. Grandchildren! They were a distant happy dream. Her own father had been so good with Tommy and poor little Sophie.

And what about your Charlotte? she asked in turn.

She's only thirty, he had answered, but she and her husband have been married for three years and, as they'd put it, they were together for two years before that. So it's about time. At one point the marriage was on the rocks, but they've made up. Perhaps they'll think they should celebrate by making a child. I wish I knew. My relations with Charlotte aren't easy.

As he said this, it crossed his mind that it wasn't impossible that Charlotte would accept the presence of Alice in his life and that Alice might make things better between him and his daughter, the way her mother, Mary, had when she was alive. Perhaps even between him and Charlotte's odious husband. The list of potential improvements seemed infinite. There was nothing that Alice could not make better.

She was busy at lunch on Monday, a business lunch of which there were so many. New York editors spent their lives at lunch, if Mary and her colleagues were a fair example. Apparently French editors were no different. But they had dinner together, and he spent the night with her, at her apartment. The following morning he called Mike Mansour and told him he would like to spend a few more days in Paris, for instance until Sunday, and asked whether the report on Bucharest and Warsaw could be deferred until the first board meeting in June. The great financier chuckled and said *pas de problème* if he was going to spend those days with the nice lady. Schmidt averred that such indeed was the case, whereupon he was invited, no ordered, to go on using Mike's suite.

The question is, Mike continued, the question is does she now like you as much as you like her?

I don't know for sure, Schmidt replied, but I very much hope so.

He was beginning to think that perhaps she did. During the subsequent nights she gave herself to him with such abandon that he was left incredulous and hollowed out by her hunger, a hunger somehow miraculously inseparable from a will to make sure that the pleasure was shared equally. They made love at his hotel; she preferred going home afterward to having to get him out of the way before he could encounter Madame Laure. Not that I'm fooling her as it is, she added cheerfully,

and in truth Schmidt wondered why it was easier for that esti-
mable housekeeper to note that Alice came home every night
at two or later—because most often she would fall asleep for
an hour or two, her head on his breast, before going home—
than accept his presence at breakfast. Twice they had lunch
together near her office on rue de l'Université; the other days
she had more of those business lunches. He reverted to his
student days, making the rounds of museums, going on long
walks, eating a hard-boiled egg or a sandwich at the counter
of a café.

One of the days when Alice was busy, he had lunch with the
lawyers at W & K, which had been proposed to him by Hugh
Macomber, a younger partner heading the Paris office, whom
he knew and liked. On the way back to the office after lunch
he walked with Macomber ahead of the others and found
himself asking whether the office had been able to retain
the clients brought in by Tim Verplanck. For the most part,
Macomber thought it had, which was not his doing but that of
Bud Horsey, the partner who was Tim's immediate successor
and his own predecessor. A good deal of holding on to them,
he said, appeared to depend on the goodwill of Tim's buddy
Bruno Chardon, the rather flamboyant investment banker.
Horsey had made a real effort to cultivate Chardon.

And you? asked Schmidt.

I've been somewhat remiss, Macomber replied. He's not
exactly our kind. It's too soon to tell whether there will be
defections.

What do you mean not our kind? Schmidt pursued.

Oh, you know, as I said he's got a flamboyant side. Molly—
that's my wife, I'm not sure you remember her—she doesn't
get good vibes. I think you'd understand right away what I

mean if you met him, you know, if you saw the cut of his jib. Lew Brenner knows all about it, and he's told me to do my best but not to feel obliged to go overboard. Probably even if I did it wouldn't make much difference.

I see, said Schmidt. I don't suppose you see much of Tim's widow.

Macomber shook his head. We don't really know her.

Toward the end of the week Alice announced a change in their plans. She told him that her colleague Serge Popov, who had been on a book tour with one of his authors in England, would be back on Friday and had asked whether the three of them could have lunch together that day.

Really, said Schmidt, it's his idea and not yours?

It was on the tip of his tongue to say, I can't imagine why he wants to see me any more than I want to see him, but he restrained himself.

Yes, it's his idea, she assured him, he told me your name brought back so many memories. Please say yes. It would be at one. Oh, and there is another thing. My father's lady friend is unwell, and he is feeling very anxious. I'll have to go down there on Friday afternoon, after lunch.

He told her he was doubly and triply sorry, for her father, for the lady, and for himself. He too would leave Paris on Friday, in that case, on the last plane for New York, if he could get a seat. They were having dinner in the courtyard of his hotel, the evening was beautiful, and they had just finished what she told him were the first wild strawberries of the season. It made him sad, irrationally, he supposed, to amputate Saturday and most of Sunday from his stay, and he returned to the plans he had been making. If he came back in a month, would she like that, would she be there?

She nodded. Yes, I would like that very much.

And would you come to see me in Bridgehampton during the summer? For your vacation? Anytime—and for as long as you can stay. Forever would be best!

Something like the wisp of a cloud passed over her face.

I don't know, she replied. I may have to be here to help my father and Janine. That's his friend. The other thing is that I'm hoping that Tommy will realize that his grandfather is now very old and will want to come to see him. If that happens, I will want to join them. Let's talk about all this in June, when you return. By then, everything should be much clearer.

Salve, Schmidtie! A man who had to be Popov, since he was rising from a table where he had been sitting with Alice, stepped forward and extended his arms to embrace Schmidt. How long has it been since our freshman year? Forty-five years! You haven't changed, you old thief! The same red hair and the same sourpuss expression.

Caught in a bear hug accompanied by a Slavic-sounding grunt, but ducking the proffer of Popov's cheeks or lips, however Popov's gesture was to be interpreted, Schmidt kissed Alice on her cheeks, sat down, and examined his host. He was thinner and more stooped, his hair once a brilliantine-smeared brown had gone gray and wispy, but the shiny double-breasted black suit, which, in Schmidt's opinion, cried out for the services of a dry cleaner, was a replica of the one that Popov had worn day in and day out as an undergraduate. None of this was surprising. Schmidt imagined Popov's glee at taking stock of what changes the years had wrought in him, assuming that Popov bothered to look and remember. Having ordered lunch, Popov emptied his glass of wine, refilled it, and addressed to

Alice a rapid stream of anecdotes, interrupted only by his chortles over the author he had accompanied on the book tour and a variety of literary and publishing figures to whom he referred by first name only. Schmidt didn't mind being left out of the conversation. It was not unlike the old days: chatter among Mary and her editor and agent friends. Presumably Alice hadn't seen Popov since his return the previous day and, absorbed by what Popov had to say, didn't attempt to draw Schmidt in. That too was more than all right with Schmidt. Being allowed to eat his leek salad in peace was better than what he had expected. However, as soon as his smoked haddock had been served, the respite ended.

Popov turned for the first time in his direction and announced: You have become a powerful philanthropist. Quite a step up for a lawyer!

It wasn't clear to Schmidt how this observation, which he found offensive, was meant to be taken. Never mind, he was not going to rise to the bait.

I'm not very powerful, he replied, just lucky that my country neighbor Michael Mansour recently decided to give me a job. You may not know it, but I retired from the practice of law just about three years ago, soon after my wife died.

Such a loss, cried Popov. That splendid Mary Ryan, that was her name at Radcliffe, her maiden name! Mary Ryan, Lois Witherspoon, and Ginny Burbank: three roommates, each more beautiful and intelligent than the other! I bet you didn't know that I was close to them, Schmidtie. They were three years behind us in college, but I took them out. I've always liked younger women.

Here he looked at Alice and punched her playfully on the arm.

I don't think you knew Mary at college, but I got to know her well, he continued. You, my friend Gil Blackman, my roommate Kevin, all of you left after graduation, but I stayed on, doing graduate work. When I went into publishing a number of years later, Mary and I reconnected, of course! What a powerhouse she was! Nobody in American publishing measured up to her.

That's what I've always heard, replied Schmidt.

He felt the stirring of a better feeling toward Popov. It was good to have him praise Mary in Alice's hearing.

Ach yes, and what good times we would have at the Frankfurt Fair!

Popov rolled his eyes and smacked his lips. After a short silence, he spoke again.

I had a special reason for asking Alice to bring us together. It's your neighbor and employer, Mr. Mansour. A group of us in publishing think this is the right time to establish a prestigious and important annual prize to honor the best work of fiction and the best work of poetry written in Arabic. The jury would be of very high quality. We think that given his Middle Eastern background, Mr. Mansour might be open to such a project and that you would be the right person to present it to him.

Was that the reason for this lunch? Schmidt asked himself. If it was, and if Popov and his friends had done nothing so far about approaching Mike, they must believe in the power of wishful thinking. What else would have brought about the fortuitous meeting between him and Schmidt, who just happened to have a connection to Mike, and Alice, who was Popov's colleague?

It's not impossible that he would be interested, Schmidt said. He does read a good deal, even if it isn't belles lettres. If you have a proposal, you should send it to his adviser Bruce Holbein. At Mansour Industries' main office. Since this is outside the scope of the foundation's work, Mike would anyway give it to him, and not me, to review before he looked at it himself. I'll be glad to mention to both of them that you have spoken to me.

That is very good of you, Popov said. I have another request or maybe question. Alice has told me about the foundation offices you have been visiting. Why isn't there one in Sofia? In Bulgaria? You may not know it, but I have an important connection with Bulgaria, and I consider the omission a slight.

Schmidt raised his eyebrows. One reason, he answered, is the level of corruption in Bulgaria. The foundation doesn't itself operate schools or think tanks or universities. It gives money to existing institutions and works with them. Gives advice. Finances visits by scholars and political leaders from other countries and visits by local political leaders or potential political leaders to the United States. Sometimes it organizes seminars and lectures. We fear that any money we gave to practically any institution in Bulgaria would be at high risk of being stolen.

I resent that. Popov had raised his voice.

You asked the question, said Schmidt, so I'm giving you the answer.

Popov glowered at him: You think it's worse than in Romania or Hungary, where you do have offices?

It's a matter of degree, but yes, we've been advised it's worse.

I resent that, Popov repeated.

Schmidt noticed Alice's hand on Popov's sleeve. If she meant to restrain him, she didn't succeed.

You may be ignorant of my personal saga, Popov continued.

All I know is that you were born in Bulgaria and at some point during the war or later became a refugee. A displaced person of sorts.

You are very ignorant, Popov declared. My father was the last minister of justice serving Tsar Boris III, the heroic ruler murdered by the Germans because he wouldn't let them send Bulgarian Jews to Auschwitz. My father's father was, until he died, His Majesty's court chamberlain. My grandfather died of old age in his own bed in his own palace, but my father was murdered by the Communists, along with the tsar's brother, Prince Kyril, and other members of the regency council and other high patriots. I had the good fortune to be taken into exile by Her Majesty the Tsarina. My education at boarding school and at Harvard was graciously paid for from the imperial purse. I am on terms of personal friendship with Tsar Simeon II. He is younger than I, but we have known each other since early childhood. I find your discrimination against the country of my birth intolerable.

He assumed a gloomy and superior expression that took Schmidt back to the occasions, fortunately infrequent, when Popov would unexpectedly appear in the suite that Schmidt and Gil Blackman shared at college and jump into whatever discussion of politics and modern European history happened to be taking place. The accent when he spoke English had remained almost the same: an element in it of something unidentifiable but Slavic, and now that he lived in France, and presumably spoke French much of the time, an admixture of something Gallic. The gurgling that accompanied the flights of eloquence, ire, or hilarity hadn't changed either.

That is a very grand and, of course, very sad story, replied Schmidt. I can only hope that your Bulgarian connections make it possible for you to help bring better government to your country—now that it's no longer under Communist rule.

There is more of my story that you don't know, or you would not be suggesting so blithely that I immerse myself in Bulgarian politics. That had been my hope at college and graduate school and also when I became the editor of *Currents*. I don't suppose you were a reader of that journal.

Schmidt confirmed that unfortunately he wasn't.

I'm not surprised. Then you don't know the defining effect of that seminal journal on political thought in intellectual milieus in the U.S. and Western Europe. But not long after I assumed the direction of the journal, I met my wife. She is a member of one of France's great noble families, and it was out of the question that she settle in the United States, where *Currents* was obliged to return because of funding considerations. She found the philistine and petty bourgeois mentality of ninety-nine point nine percent of your countrymen intolerable. A form of mentality, I am forced to add, that I too could tolerate less and less. So it happened that I entered the world of publishing in France, where you now find me. We were, alas, soon brought low by fate in a way that further reduced my availability for service to my country. My wife was among the last victims of a polio epidemic. Tanny LeClercq was stricken in 1956; my Solange even later, in 1959, soon after the birth of our second boy. Paralyzed from the waist down.

I am deeply sorry, said Schmidt.

Popov made a snorting noise. Yes. Of course, now that we have disagreed about Bulgaria, and you have seen how you have misjudged my position, you will be hostile to the proposal for the Middle Eastern literature prize.

Far from it, said Schmidt.

There are persistent themes in history, Popov continued, history of men and of nations. Resentments play their role. Wilhelm II. Churchill. De Gaulle. I too have been accustomed to being resented. At school and then at college. Don't try to deny it. I carried my head too high, I was too fully conscious of my real position, so far superior to what it appeared to be.

He sank into even greater gloom.

Alice, who had remained silent until then, spoke up. We must really go now.

She called the waiter and, to Schmidt's surprise, paid the check. It had been so clearly stated that it was Popov who was inviting Alice and him to lunch that he refrained from protesting.

They parted in the street, going in different directions, Schmidt first to the store on rue de l'Université in the window of which he had seen a layette that might just do as a baby present for little Albert and then to the shirtmaker on place Vendôme, where he might buy a necktie or two. For big Albert, he whispered. He had not covered more than a few yards, however, before looking back. He wanted to see Alice once more, even if it was only for a fleeting moment. He did see her. She and Popov were walking fast toward rue du Bac, with their arms around each other's waists, except that Popov's hand was actually lower. He was patting Alice on her bottom, investigating through her summer dress the valley between her buttocks. Lot's wife looked back on Sodom and was turned into a pillar of salt. Schmidt was spared that fate. But Alice, perhaps sensing his eyes upon her, turned her head in his direction. She raised her eyebrows by way of acknowledgment of his gaze and smiled comically, helplessly. He smiled back, set his teeth, and went on to run his errands.

He got to the airport at Roissy in plenty of time. Quarter of six for a seven o'clock flight. Alice's plane for Nice left from Orly at five. Perhaps that lout Popov fondled all his colleagues' behinds, male and female. What was that to Schmidt! He didn't have Alice's telephone number in Antibes, and even if he did he doubted he would dare call her at her father's house, knowing that the old gentleman's friend was ill. The thing to do was to call Alice's number in Paris and leave a message in his best French: *Je t'aime follement*. The call went through. He heard the first ring, and then the second, and then Alice's voice. Astonished, he hung up. Had she missed her plane? Had the situation in Antibes changed? How stupid he had been to hang up instead of speaking to her. He dialed again. The line was busy and continued to be busy up to the very last minute before his flight, when first-class passengers were called to embark.

As usual, he fell asleep during takeoff. It was a tic: the response of his helpless body to being strapped into a seat and carried aloft in that infantilized state. The chatter of the stewardesses offering refreshments awakened him. The plane had reached its cruising altitude, and the loudspeaker announced that passengers were free to move about the cabin. Schmidt decided that the *Herald Tribune* could wait, even though he hadn't looked at it all day. Sipping a bourbon, and devouring the mixed nuts as though he had skipped lunch, he puzzled over the failed call to Alice. No plausible explanation seemed likelier than any other. He would try to reach her the next day—Saturday afternoon her time—and leave a message explaining that taken unawares he had, like a fool, hung up instead of asking her whether anything was the matter, and trying to ring again found he couldn't get through. She'd call him back after she had listened to that message. That same day, if she was in Paris, or on Sunday, when she returned from Antibes.

Against his will, his thoughts turned to the interlude with Pani Danuta. A huge blunder. For one thing, how was he to make sure it remained an interlude? They had parted on the best of terms. Would she not expect the vodka-sodden orgy à deux to be repeated on his next visit to the Warsaw Center? How would she respond if he demurred? Would a spiteful account reach Mike Mansour? He supposed that Mike the bon vivant would laugh at his huffy WASP employee's caper, but his moods were unpredictable. In any event, Mike's shrugging off the incident did not make Schmidt's appallingly stupid behavior right or any less stupid. Here is what he should have done: directly after the stroll in the Łazienki Park take or send that sex maniac home. Beyond that, what were the larger implications of his misconduct, what did it say about him? Had he ever said no to a woman who offered herself? Yes, if the transaction involved payment of money; otherwise he could point to no opportunity he had rejected, except perhaps the flirtatious propositions of old hags in the Hamptons, widows of writers or editors or agents gone to seed. He had recoiled from the mere thought of physical contact with even the best preserved of them. But with the student he recruited on the West Coast, Corinne the babysitter, Hecate-like Carrie, Alice—indeed Alice—and now Danuta, the pattern was the same. The bugle sounds, and Schmidt jumps into the saddle. Was it because he was too unsure of himself to risk taking the first step that a woman's making herself available made him lose his head? Or was it, more simply, his unabated appetite for sex with new partners, a curiosity he hadn't outgrown. He thought it could be tamed if he lived with Alice, but not otherwise. Was there a moral distinction to be made between that "curiosity" and Tim's homosexuality that would make Schmidt's misconduct less repugnant to Alice? He wasn't sure. Did his couplings with Pani Danuta prove that his protestations of love for Alice were in bad faith? It seemed to him that such an inference was not inescapable. He was in love with Alice or as close to love as was possible at his age. Was that really true? Could his short acquaintance and still limited knowledge of her justify claim of anything more than an infatuation? He concluded it could. A lifetime of experience told him she was splendid. Another six months of knowing her would not change that judgment.

A practical problem also called into question his good faith. She was so much younger! He had been asking her in various formulations to tie her life to his. How could he ignore the disadvantages and risks inherent in that fact: the inevitable diminution of his libido and potency, incapacitating illnesses he might suffer, the near certainty that he would be the first to die? She was likely to become a widow the second time at an age when finding a suitable man to share her life would be more difficult than now. There were countervailing considerations: his interest in women that he thought was livelier than that of many men her own age; his excellent health that might postpone or fend off those illnesses and debilities; his modest but perfectly sufficient fortune that should assure a comfortable life for both of them while he lived and for her afterward. Indeed, he thought she would like the way he lived. East End of Long Island and Manhattan: not a bad combination. On the other side of the balance sheet, there was the sacrifice that moving away from Paris would entail, although he would gladly spend as much time there with her as she wished. He had tried to discuss these worries with her thoroughly and objectively. But whenever he tried to discuss their future, she would become impatient; she would sigh and say things like Schmidtie, why must we talk about that? We're having a very good time together, isn't that enough? The one time she had seemed willing to listen, she told him that all these concerns were real, but none of them would stand in her way. But that was where she stopped: in the conditional mood. They would not stand in her way, if she decided to accept his suit. But plainly she was not yet ready to do so.

He wished Gil were at his side to help him sort out this jumble.

X

THERE WAS NO MESSAGE from Alice when he got home to Bridgehampton late that Friday evening. He did, however, find one from Charlotte, recorded in the afternoon, and a note on the kitchen table from Carrie, beside a vase full of white and pink peonies from his garden, saying *Welcome, Schmidtie, we have news for you.* It was a few minutes past midnight, much too late to call Charlotte. The pool house and Bryan's apartment over the garage were dark. If Bryan had met him at the airport, he would have told him Carrie's news unless it was to be a surprise and she had sworn him to silence. But he had been picked up instead by one of Mike Mansour's chauffeurs in the security detail's huge gray SUV. The news, and the telephone calls to Alice and Charlotte, would have to wait until morning. Sy was on the kitchen table, looking at him with adoring eyes and tapping on his sleeve. This was a message Schmidt never failed to understand. It said, I want a snack, and I want it now!

He was up early, and although it was Saturday he was sure that Carrie and Jason would be up as well. Operations at the marina started at eight. His breakfast finished, he put the *New York Times* aside and was about to go over to see them when they both appeared. It was three weeks since he had last seen her. The hillock under her paisley top had become an alp. And she had become more beautiful to a degree he thought was supernatural. When had she been a waitress at O'Henry's, the local steak and hamburger joint? Almost four years ago? O'Henry's, the joint where she would serve him his meal, and when she was tired late in the evening remind him of Picasso's *Woman Ironing.* Picasso had never painted a Madonna. If he had, before the need to push his art forward led him to decompose faces and bodies, the result might have been a likeness of Carrie as she was now. Or if Bellini had fallen in love with an olive-skinned, languorous working girl, perhaps a street urchin bearing a child of an unknown father, whom he had invited to pose in his studio. Jason beaming beside her, the blond mountain—whose paintbrush had painted him? Of course, Norman Rockwell! Portrait of a young line repairman, in his overalls, setting out for a day's work after a hurricane.

Hey Schmidtie, she cried after embracing him, big news! Jay and I are lawfully wedded! We went to Riverhead last Friday morning and did it! Isn't that something? Bryan and one of the girls from O'Henry's were the witnesses.

It is big and wonderful news; I'm so happy for you. He embraced Carrie again and once again vigorously shook Jason's hand. I only wish I could have given a wedding lunch for you!

We didn't want you to, Carrie said, it's a hassle. That's why we were sneaky and got it done while you were away.

Carrie's extraordinary tact: in truth Schmidt had been turning over in his mind what he would do when those two finally got married. A reception on the lawn following a morning ceremony? Something in the house or under a tent if it was in the evening? Should he have a band or a DJ or no music at all? And above all, who would be the guests? Carrie's parents, Mr. Gorchuck, the Board of Education employee, and Mrs. Gorchuck, the Puerto Rican cook with swollen limbs, Mr. and Mrs. McMullen, Jason's Nova Scotia father and mother, Mike Mansour and Gil and Elaine Blackman, Mike's staff, at least those whose services at Mike's house could be temporarily dispensed with, the boys and girls from O'Henry's, and who else? Perhaps Jason's pals from the New York police force, if he had kept up with them. A strange group and a strange social occasion! Now he would be spared this trial. That left little Albert's christening. He was to be the godfather! Would he be expected to give a reception, presumably for the same group?

Dear Carrie and Jason, he replied, I would have so much liked to do it here, on the lawn.

That half lie took him right back to Charlotte's wedding, to her cruel—in his opinion—and stupid choice of a restaurant in Tribeca as the setting, rather than the house in which she had been brought up. He took a moment to collect himself.

It's too early in the morning to talk about such things, but I want to give you a handsome wedding present. Jason, you listen to me. You're the practical one in the family. You figure out what would be best and tell me. The sky is the limit.

In that at least he was 100 percent sincere.

Gee, thanks, Schmidtie, was Jason's response.

He might have said more, but Carrie took over. Say it with cash, Schmidtie, she told him, the new house, little Albert, the marina, it's like a drain. Money goes out, and very little comes in.

Consider it done, Schmidt said.

Hey, we have more news. Little Albert! The doctor wants him to come out on June fifteenth. He's so huge and well developed he thinks I may have made a mistake figuring out his due date. She laughed and nudged Schmidt with her elbow.

Another overwhelming wave of feeling. Because the baby was almost there, because the earlier it had been conceived the less certain was the paternity of the blond Viking nodding and wiping tears on his sleeve. In which case—no, he wasn't going to think about it yet. Let the baby come, let his features tell the tale. But for the record he told them: I'm so glad I'm back and that I'm not going anywhere until sometime in June. Hooray for Albert, Mama and Papa, and the doctor!

Schmidtie, that's not all! Carrie replied. We've signed the contract on the house in East Hampton. The closing is in eight weeks to give the people living there time to move out, and the guys are going to get to work on it right away. We'll be out of your hair before Labor Day!

Out of my hair! Never, never. The door will be always open; when you're here, you're at home.

They said it was about time they headed for the marina, and he accompanied them to the front door. Holding it open, he watched them get into Jason's pickup. His elected family: Carrie, his young mistress; the blond giant who virtuously and rightly had taken her away from him; and the mysterious child about to be brought into the world.

Nine o'clock. In a half hour he could safely call Charlotte. He poured himself another mug of coffee and began to go through the stack of mail. Ninety percent was junk. The rest was bills that he set aside along with his bank statement and communications from his two investment advisers, who seemed to be sending more and more bulletins on the state of the economy and its future. Out of a sense of duty, he skimmed them. What a waste of paper! Every reader of the *Times* knew that George H. W. Bush had bequeathed to Clinton a mess that the Republicans seemed bent on making worse, but the investment advisers found it in themselves to see the good in their shenanigans. Of course, their clientele wasn't all mavericks like Schmidtie, disloyal to their social and economic class. The poor guys had to play to their public. The country really had deserved better than that silly man with his silly preppy personality and habits. It must be easier to fool the country than your high school classmates. Schmidt knew people older than himself who had been to Andover with Bush and were ready to certify that even then he was a creep. All the same, Schmidt was taken aback by his own rush to judge and condemn. Silly Bush. Appalling Popov. Why exactly had Popov been so appalling at college and ever after?

Clearly, Popov's being a Bulgarian didn't help. Knowing nothing about Bulgarians, Schmidt didn't like them. They were a backward nation, he believed, steeped in Eastern Orthodox religion, using the Cyrillic alphabet, and teeming with bearded and unwashed married priests. Could anything be more unattractive? Popov fit right in. There was something unwashed about him as well, then and now. That black suit, for instance, that he had worn at a time when practically no one at Harvard College wore a suit unless going to a funeral or a wedding, and, even then, nothing like that black double-breasted number plus a shirt of dubious whiteness, a frayed necktie narrow like a ribbon, and an outrageous red pocket square. Did any of that really matter? No, it didn't, but it managed to make Schmidt uncomfortable. The two or three men who wore suits whom Schmidt liked and respected were golden-haired boys born with gold or silver spoons in their mouths. Was it then Popov's seeming poverty that made him

repellent? No, it really was more the pasty white face and evident want of personal hygiene. All right, Popov was a slob,
and a slob whose roommate Bill, also Gil's friend, was an even
bigger one. Yes, but who was Schmidt? A dress-code enforcer
or a housemother inspecting her little charges' fingernails?
No, there was more to it. Popov had made him uncomfortable, talking over his head, pulling rank as a sophisticated
European—a European born into a powerful family, a fact that
was not then unknown to Schmidt—taking advantage of
an American who wouldn't get to Europe until the summer
after his sophomore year, for whom the ballet and the opera
were terra incognita, and, worse yet, so far as Popov and his
actor roommate were concerned, who believed that Truman
had been right to go to war over Korea and didn't consider
Eisenhower a moron. Gil, the wonder-boy Jew from Brooklyn,
already held the full set of requisite liberal ideas—including
an unshakable conviction of Alger Hiss's innocence—played
the piano, had brought a record player and a stack of opera
LPs with him to Cambridge, and had been to Europe twice.
Gil's father was a surgeon and his mother a dress designer, and
so Brooklyn wasn't somewhere in East New York but a brownstone in Brooklyn Heights. It was obvious to Schmidt why
he wasn't meanly envious of Gil, why he didn't resent him:
he had had a late-blooming schoolboy's crush on him that in
some form still endured. One thing was certain: Schmidt's dislike for Popov would not have taken on so sharp and invidious
an edge without its lining of resentment and guilty curiosity.

Half past nine. He called Charlotte. After three rings, a sort
of milestone of promptness in his telephone communications
with her, she answered.

Dad, where were you?

You mean yesterday?

Yes, I called three times and finally left a message.

Actually I was on a plane returning from Paris. I made another short trip. But I sent you a letter before leaving, with my itinerary and all that.

Jon or I must have tossed it. We had such a stack of junk mail when we got back.

Of course, thought Schmidt, who would bother noticing his return address on the envelope?

I'm sorry, he told her. I didn't change the message on my telephone because people now say that if your message announces that you are away you're inviting burglars. There have been a couple of burglaries around here. Did you have a good time?

Are you near a chair? Yes, then sit down. Dad, I am pregnant. The baby is due in September! And we know it's a boy! I haven't told anyone except Jon's parents until now. I wanted to be sure he'd stick around. We're calling him Myron. Jews can't name a child for a living parent, but Renata has an uncle whose name is also Myron, so that's all right. We're in the clear.

He wished she hadn't told him about that name just yet, but really it didn't matter, not at all. With great effort he managed to speak: Sweetie, sweetie how absolutely marvelous, I'm so happy. How I wish your mother were alive! She would have been over the moon. Is Jon there? I would like to congratulate him.

That would have been the first time he had spoken to his son-in-law in a long while, longer than he cared to remember, and he was relieved to learn that it was not to be. Jon was at the gym and afterward would be heading straight to

the office. She would transmit Schmidt's congratulations. He
decided he would put the question—perhaps, given the truce
they had declared, it was not out of order and wouldn't bring
her wrath on his head. Was there any chance of luring her and
Jon to Bridgehampton—for instance, over the Memorial Day
weekend?

Guessed wrong.

Dad, she replied, the syllable stretched into Daaaad, we
just can't, I'm taking a maternity leave from my office—it will
have to be unpaid, of course, they only pay for one month—
and moving up to Claverack.

Claverack was where she and Jon had bought a house in
order to be closer to the senior Rikers' property, refusing the
gift he had offered to make her of his interest in the house in
Bridgehampton, the house where she had been brought up.

And what if I scooted up to the city? he asked.

Really, Dad, can you just stop and imagine what's involved
in the move? I haven't got one moment free.

He noted that she wasn't inviting him to Claverack.

Yes, she continued, Renata thinks it would be best for me
and the baby if I got out of the heat and hassle in the city, and
I think she's right. Jon will come up every weekend, and then
he'll take what's left of his vacation.

Oh, said Schmidt, and then you'll come back to have the
baby in New York?

I don't think so. There is a very nice modern hospital in
Hudson, just about seven miles away. Low stress, no hassle.
They encourage midwives and breast-feeding, which is what I
want. You can come to see the baby when we bring him home.

I see, said Schmidt. Very well, thank you for telling me.
Good luck. Stay in touch.

Then he did sit down and wished it were later in the day, that the sun were over the yardarm. He needed a drink. Reflecting on his need and the time of day, and the absence of anyone on the premises who might reprove him, he got out the bottle of bourbon from the liquor closet and the quart of milk from the refrigerator and made himself a very tall drink, one-half milk and one-half booze. He allowed it to soothe him. It was too early to call Gil Blackman. He let another half hour pass before trying Gil's New York office and was told by the secretary that Mr. Blackman was at his country house in Wainscott. She would connect Mr. Schmidt.

The familiar voice cried, Schmidtie, how terrific! Are you in Bridgehampton or are you speaking from Kharkov? If you're here, would you like to have lunch? The usual? At one?

That's what I had hoped, Schmidt replied. I'll see you at one.

The Polish cleaning women were making a racket in the house, running the vacuum cleaner, shouting to one another. Schmidt took a sweater, just in case, and headed for the beach. As often happens in May, when the moon is in the last quarter, the ocean was like a lake, lapping the shore lackadaisically. There was no one else in sight, no footprints on the brilliantly white sand. Schmidt walked fast as far as Gibson Lane, checked his watch, and turned back. He was home by twelve.

The blinking light told him there was a message on the answering machine. Jon Riker's voice, asking Schmidt to call him at the office. He repeated the telephone number. Quite possibly, Jon was on a peacemaking mission, not a bad idea from any point of view, and, as a practical matter, necessary now that there was going to be a grandchild. Riker came to the telephone at once and said nothing. At a loss for words himself, Schmidt offered his congratulations. Since Riker

remained silent, Schmidt told him it was too bad that he had·
to spend a beautiful May Saturday at the office rather than
with his pregnant wife.

That elicited an answer: Can't be helped, times are bad for
the legal profession right now, so we all have to hustle. You
should be grateful this doesn't apply to you; it wouldn't fit
with your established habits.

A stupid and malicious thing to say, Schmidt thought, but
he wasn't about to allow himself to be riled. He said nothing.
The silence sank in, and Riker spoke again.

There was a reason for my call, Al. It's your grandson. What
are you going to do for him?

Riker knew very well that Schmidt loathed being called Al.
Why was he doing it, and what was it that he wanted? He
replied calmly: Can you explain what you mean?

Al, you must know what I mean. Are you going to set up a
trust so the kid can sail on his own bottom?

So that's what it was. The man was a swine.

I see, said Schmidt, and what do you mean by little Myron's
being able to "sail on his own bottom"? Being able to pay his
bills? You're going to charge him room and board and make
him pay for his visits to the pediatrician? I hadn't realized you
were broke.

Jesus, Al, don't play dumb. I'm not talking about room
and board or visits to the pediatrician. Have you heard how
much nannies cost or preschool or kindergarten or elementary
school and high school? I'm not even talking about college and
law school or medical school!

I will make myself clearer. Do you earn so little, are you so
broke, that you can't take care of your own family?

Are you trying to be funny? You do know that my parents

are hard up. My mother has said that she told you. So I'm helping them. Doing what's needed.

A hideous weight of fatigue had descended on Schmidt.

Look here, he said, I can't help wondering which one of you thought up this request—if that's what it is—your father, your mother, you, or Charlotte, and I guess I don't much care. You tire me. There is no end to the trouble you make.

Jesus, Al, you're off the reservation!

Oh yeah? thought Schmidt, where had Jon learned that expression, the favorite locution of the same W & K presiding partner who had booted Jon out of the firm.

Shut up, he told Jon. I'm telling you the truth. Now listen carefully, and if you like make a tape of what I'm saying. One, Charlotte is my daughter and my natural heir. Unless she drives me up the wall—I don't really care what you and your parents do or say—she will inherit money on my death. I'm not saying all my money; she's already had a lot. Two, Charlotte's children will be the natural object of my generosity. I mean just that: natural object of my generosity. I don't exclude—depending on how you and Charlotte are fixed financially—helping pay for your children's preschools, schools, and so forth. You forgot to mention summer camps: yes, I'd help even with summer camps. But I won't be badgered by you or Charlotte into making gifts to little unborn Myron or any other kid you may have that aren't currently needed and that under the tax laws are murderously expensive. Have you heard about the gift tax? Or the generation-skipping tax? Why should I throw my money out the window to pay unnecessary taxes? When the time comes, I will be generous, but that time isn't now. As for your helping your parents, that will be part of your financial circumstances I will consider. I am truly sorry about their difficulties. Being a psychoanalyst today and not getting paid can't be fun.

Thereupon Schmidt hung up. It was the first time he had hung up on a member of his family and one of the exceedingly rare times he had hung up on anyone other than a salesman making cold calls.

"The usual" was O'Henry's, where at one time Schmidt had felt obliged to evade the attentions of superannuated and misshapen literary widows who regularly lunched there, and where he and Mr. Blackman had accustomed themselves to meeting because the hamburgers and steaks were good and the wine, if they overpaid, met Mr. Blackman's exacting standards. The great filmmaker was already there, at the table to which his worldwide fame, assisted by Schmidt's standing as Carrie's former sugar daddy, entitled them. As though their greeting had been choreographed, each opened his arms to embrace the other. They had not seen each other since before Schmidt's first April visit to Paris. Mr. Blackman had been filming a television miniseries based on *The Scarlet Letter*, to be released in the fall. Great to see you!, spoken by them in unison, resonated in the half-empty restaurant. They ordered rapidly.

How did it go? asked Schmidt.

The filming? I'm pleased. I've got little Kyra Sedgwick playing Hester. She's marvelous. Chaste as new snow atop a volcano of passion.

Fabulous! And Dimmesdale?

Sam Waterston. He's perfect. Great actor and the contrast between him and Kyra is perfect too—it leaves me speechless. I'll just say it's exactly what I had hoped for. But that's not what I wanted to talk about. Elaine is on a tear about the amount of time I'm spending in L.A. Of course she knows what I'm doing is important and brings in big bucks; of course I've told her that she is welcome to join me there, but *entre nous* that's a disingenuous offer. I know she hates Southern California and wouldn't stay more than a week. The truth is that she has a very good sense of smell. She knows I'm not spending all my days on the lot and my evenings planning the next day's shoot. Her solution is to make my life miserable when I'm there by calling every fifteen minutes in the evening and, when she gets me, by complaining. She says she's going to invite the Mummy to come and stay!

The Mummy was Gil's sobriquet for Elaine's aged, rich, and, to hear him tell it, prodigiously mean mother.

How are you really spending your evenings, you old rascal?

Remember my old flame Katerina?

How could I forget?

Katerina had been Gil's secretary, a Greek beauty of the sort Cole Porter must have had in mind when he wrote of a two-timing husband that his *business is the business that he gives his secretary,* who had left Gil for a stockbroker and fellow Greek she met over a holiday in Jamaica.

I can't either, replied Mr. Blackman, every time I do it with my new girl I think of her. She's the same type, half Greek and half Italian—a dynamite combination! Guess what her name is!

Venus.

Wrong! Aphrodite. The Greeks carried the day.

And you call her Aphro?

Guess again. No, you'll never get it: DT.

By Jove! Pardon me, by Zeus!

You wouldn't believe, she's so great, and not just in the sack. She has ideas and a point of view, she can talk, and she's talented, really talented.

A starlet?

No, she's in production. The plain fact is that I can help her, I can make her career, and she knows it. It will keep her on the straight and narrow. She wants to move to New York, so we can be together more easily once I've finished editing.

Is that a good idea? With Elaine's acute sense of smell? And anyway hadn't you told me after Katerina that you were going to bury your staff certain fathoms in the earth?

True, true. I am a repeat offender. I love Elaine, and when I don't give her reasons to get on her high horse she is the best of wives, but when I'm with DT, when I touch her skin, when I have her breasts in my hands, it's so good that my head spins. What can I tell you? I want her. Every inch of me wants her.

I understand that. And you think you can keep her on a string because of her career? Aren't you setting yourself up for real trouble?

Mr. Blackman reflected. Real trouble? I don't think so, because I'm not going to give her a job in my organization. Anyway my organization doesn't amount to a hill of beans. I'll help her get in with other people. That may not be very nice, but at least it's not illegal. The bigger picture? Let's be realistic. Why would a girl like DT let herself be banged on demand by an old schnook like me? It's not for my pretty teeth or beautiful eyes or abs of steel. One gives what one has. And what about you?

What's left at the bottom of this bottle won't last us while my tale unfolds.

They ordered another bottle of wine, and Schmidt told

his story. The story of the first meeting with Alice in Paris and being smitten and having almost at once hit a home run. He withheld what she had told him about Tim Verplanck. It had no bearing on his feelings for her. He continued with the events of the second visit to Paris, and confessed the escapade with Danuta. The rape of Schmidt by an oversexed Pole!

Schmidtie, my dear Schmidtie, heaven is smiling on you! Alice seems made to order. Court her, humor her, don't crowd her with commitments. She's got a job she likes, she lives in a fabulous city, don't ask her to move to your château in Bridgehampton and give up the world. That's like taking holy orders! She can come here—especially if you pay the airfare—and you can pop over to Paris. You'll have fun! I'm so happy for you, and I can't wait to tell Elaine.

Thank you, said Schmidt, that's exactly the kind of advice I needed. I will follow it. I think I can do it. And what about Danuta? You don't think that episode means that I'm not really serious about Alice?

My dear old pal, you and I have been made to want to screw. What was it you told me? That you think there will be no Danutas if you get to live with Alice? I think that's exactly right. But even if some enchanted evening you succumbed to the charms of Danuta's little sister, it wouldn't be the end of the world. Not if you were very discreet about it and Alice didn't find out. Do you remember the film I made of *Rigoletto* years ago?

Of course, great film.

Not half bad. Well, I'm thinking of going back to filming operas. My next project will be *Così fan tutte*!

They had gotten around to dessert, and since it was late it

seemed right to follow the waitress's recommendation: rhubarb pie. Coffee later.

It's time for comic relief, said Schmidt. I had a bizarre lunch
with Alice and your old pal Popov.

Gil listened to Schmidt's account and said, Popov, Popov,
you've always had a thing about him. Such a surprise in the
case of the broad-minded, unprejudiced, thoroughly rational Albert Schmidt, Esquire! What have you got against him
except that he doesn't bathe or change his underwear?

That's only a part of it: you forgot pompous and full of
himself. Also: Having Alice set that lunch up on my last day in
Paris, when I had hoped to be with her alone, and letting Alice
pay for it. And the stuff about having married a member of
the high aristocracy! As the kids in the W & K mailroom used
to say, give me a break!

Poor Popov! That's part of the problem: he is poor. The
wife—Chantal? Ghislaine? Isabeau? one of those funny
names—is the daughter of a duke.

Solange.

That's right: Solange. She's the daughter of a duke who is
poor and a duchess who has bags of money. It's lucky that
Popov can tap into the money because the care of Solange
costs a mint. Of course I'm sure he enjoys having a huge
apartment on rue de Lille in the ducal palace and vacations he
can spend at the ducal château, and so on, but he's really hard
up. That's why he and Solange are still together. Money and
real estate: that's what keeps marriages intact, not children.
Not that I feel too sorry for him. The last time I saw him, four
or five years ago, he told me that he had somebody on the side.
Didn't tell me who, but someone he thinks is pretty great.

And the young duchess? She has no objections?

Who knows? She was paralyzed right after those boys were born. Is it possible to have sex with someone paralyzed from the waist down? I've no idea. Maybe it's fantastic. I'd assume that she thinks it natural that Popov find relief elsewhere.

You're probably right as always. Now some family news: Charlotte informed me this morning that she's pregnant, and it's a boy! He's due in September!

Fantastic. Congratulations! Wait till I tell Elaine. This news on top of Alice—she's going to dance a jig.

You are my best and dearest friends. Schmidt's voice broke. The little boy's name will be Myron. Same as Jon's father. That's OK with me. But let me tell you about my conversation with Jon. Please don't mention it to Elaine. You understand. I'm stuck with that guy. One day he and Charlotte may start coming here again.

Mr. Blackman listened to the account of the telephone conversation, nodding his head.

It's awful, he said. Jon is a prick. Come and have dinner with us tonight.

It was close to four by the time Schmidt got home. He tried Alice's number, on the off chance. There was no answer. Evidently she was in Antibes. Sy wanted to play, and afterward he made it clear he needed a treat.

So did Mr. Schmidt. He was going to take a nap before dinner with Gil and Elaine.

XI

SIX HOURS' DIFFERENCE. Noon eastern daylight saving time equals GMT + 1:00; noon in Bridgehampton, six in the afternoon in Paris. Schmidt was growing to loathe this calculation, of late repeated too many times each day. He made a log to keep track of his calls. Saturday afternoon around four, therefore ten in the evening in Paris, Alice doesn't answer. Sunday morning at ten, therefore four in the afternoon, still no answer. So she hasn't returned from Antibes. The same result at one in the afternoon (an effort to catch her before dinner in case she had returned but was going out) and also at midnight. He didn't dare to call any later, although she had told him that if she is awakened by the telephone and talks to someone, she has no trouble going right back to sleep. That's the sort of thing people say; it's not necessarily the truth. The next call was at nine on Monday morning, three in the afternoon Paris time. Partial success. The housekeeper answered and informed Schmidt that Madame was *au bureau*. At least now he knew that she had returned to Paris and was alive. At noon, six o'clock her time, he called again. No answer. Of course, she was at the office or between the office and Lord knows where.

This exasperating activity could have gone on much longer had it not been for the call of duty. Mike's invitation to lunch at one had been faxed to Mr. Schmidt while he was at the hotel in Paris and confirmed by the great financier's secretary by phone that morning, but Mr. Schmidt had not yet shaved, bathed, or otherwise prepared himself. He attended to those tasks and, resisting the temptation to sneak in one more call to Alice, got into his car.

We'll talk about the Bucharest and Warsaw offices at the board meeting tomorrow, said Mr. Mansour, unless there is something you want to tell me privately or something you want me to think about before the meeting. By the way, I suggest you go up with me by helicopter. Take off at five. I can't invite you to dinner because I'm having dinner with the governor. The guy's brain is the size of a pea. He's the governor of New York, and he likes to eat early! So you're coming with me?

Schmidt nodded.

First rate. You should stay in the city Tuesday night too and go with me to the ballet. We'll have dinner afterward with Wendy Whelan. She's really something. And what a dancer! You're on?

Of course, with great pleasure.

The arrival of Manuel the houseman, ready to serve lunch, cut off the possibility of continued effusions on the subject of Mike's thoughtfulness. In most circumstances, Mike believed that food comes first and talk later, and Manuel was serving his employer's favorite dish, lobster salad, which the latter wolfed down with dollops of additional mayonnaise. You had to hand it to Mike's chef. The lobster was, as Mary had used to say, sinfully good. So was the wine. The first hunger assuaged, Mr. Mansour wiped his mouth and spoke.

Actually, he said, I wanted to find out about you. That nice lady in Paris, have you seen her again?

Schmidt nodded.

And she was the reason you wanted to spend some more days in Paris. So you still like her?

Schmidt nodded again. He had taken a second helping of the lobster salad and once more had his mouth full.

And has she decided that she likes you?

That is the question.

Mr. Mansour laughed and said, Yes, as the bard said, that is the question!

That's about it.

When are you going to see her again?

I hope in June, mid-June. Oh and I don't expect that to be a foundation trip. I'll just go over and stay a few days.

Mr. Mansour asked Manuel to bring his PalmPilot, and having consulted it, he said, I'm going to Paris on June eighth. You can come with me on my plane. If you stay until June thirteenth, you can come back with me.

That would be perfect.

Fine. We'll be in good shape. I'd like to meet this lady. Maybe we can bring her back to New York with us. Ha! Ha! Ha! Did you get a picture of her?

No, said Schmidt sheepishly.

In fact, why hadn't he? Not to show Mike but to put on his desk or on his dresser.

We'll take care of it next month. Unless you can ask her to send one in the meantime. On another subject, Mr. Mansour continued. Jason and Carrie: she's having the baby induced on June fifteenth. I assume that's why you like the idea of coming home on the thirteenth? Am I right? Or am I not?

You are right. And you certainly stay informed.

It's the security guys. They talk to Jason. Don't forget he was their boss. They told me. The question is: who is the father? What is your opinion?

Mr. Mansour's eyes were little slits. He was smiling beatifically.

Why of course Jason, answered Schmidt. Does he think otherwise?

Ha! Ha! He's not saying he isn't, that's for sure. He's behaving very well.

He's a very good fellow. You do know they've gotten married?

Yes, yes, I've given them a handsome present. Here Mr. Mansour made a little gesture with the thumb and index finger of his right hand, which in vast areas of the planet denotes counting rapidly a wad of banknotes.

You see, replied Schmidt, great minds think alike—or if you prefer I'm learning from you. That's the kind of present I gave them too.

You have gotten a lot smarter. And if you're really smart you'll stick to the story that the kid's dad is Jason, no matter what the little fellow looks like. I suppose he'll be called Jason Junior.

As a matter of fact, they're calling him Albert. I think they want me to be the godfather.

Very interesting, very interesting, said Mr. Mansour as he began working the ivory worry beads that he had set aside while he was busy with the lobster salad.

Are you interested in my own family news?

Other than that you want to marry the nice lady in Paris?

Yes! I'm going to be a grandfather. My daughter says the baby is due in September.

Mazel tov! cried Mr. Mansour and pressed an invisible button that summoned Manuel. Our friend Mr. Schmidtie is going to be a grandfather. Please get some of my very special occasion champagne.

One could only admire and envy the preparedness of the Mansour household. The champagne arrived instantly, delicious and perfectly chilled. They clinked. This must be, thought Schmidt, how the Strategic Air Command functions. Some little light blinks—perhaps once perhaps twice—sirens begin to wail, fifty figures in flight suits, helmets, and goggles slide down a chute and rush to bombers that other shadowy figures have towed to the runway, the figures in flight suits mount, canopies open and shut, *vroom vroom*, and the H-bombs are on the way. *We'll be over, we're coming over, and we won't be back till it's over over there!*

Mike, he told Mr. Mansour, if everybody were as ready as you for all occasions, just think: there wouldn't have been an Anschluss or a Pearl Harbor!

Pas de problème. And no Yom Kippur War either.

They should put you at the head of the Joint Chiefs of Staff!

They could do a lot worse.

A moment of silence ensued, and then Mike spoke again. Your daughter, Charlotte *n'est-ce pas*, is still married to that Jewish boy, Jon Riker.

Indeed.

And he's still with the Grausam firm?

To the best of my knowledge.

I've kept an eye on him. Not all the time. That firm is all right, but it hasn't taken off as it should. They're high-caliber lawyers, but they haven't caught the right wave. Not yet. Take bankruptcy: it's their important specialty, but they aren't in any of the big cases. I'm just telling you that so you'll know that his income isn't what you'd expect for a partner his age in a firm like your old firm. It's something to keep in mind.

The clicking of the worry beads accelerated.

Schmidt tried Alice's number as soon as he got home, a little after nine in the evening her time. To his surprise, Madame Laure answered. *Madame est sortie dîner*, she has gone out to dinner. Was there a message? The question threw Schmidt for a loop. He didn't want to ask her to call him in Bridgehampton, since by the time she called he might be on his way to New York, and, not knowing when he might be reachable there, he didn't want to leave the New York number. He left the stupidest of messages: he would call again. As though she could have any doubt about that!

He reached her the next day, which was Tuesday, from New York. She had just come back from the office, she told him, and wasn't planning to go out. Madame Laure had prepared a simple dinner, and afterward she was going to bed. Antibes had been exhausting, her father feeling anxious and Janine really not well at all. Some sort of pulmonary *saleté*—infection—not quite a pneumonia, more like a bad bronchitis. The coughing tired her terribly and, of course, kept her father awake.

Have they engaged a nurse?

They hadn't, not until I arrived. I found two, one for the day and one for the night. That still leaves some hours uncovered, but my father refused to do more. He's worried about money—it's the way he is—even though most of the cost is covered by insurance, and anyway money is not a problem for her or for him. Schmidtie, it was so sad. Being at a sickbed is so tiring, and so depressing.

He told her that he had called from the airport on Friday afternoon, when she was leaving for Antibes and he was on his way to New York, to leave a bunch of kisses on her answering machine, but in fact she had come to the telephone, which startled him so that he hung up. He tried her number again, almost immediately, to apologize, but it was busy and remained so for almost an hour. Oh yes, she told him, I was on the phone with Air France for more than an hour, more like an eternity, trying to get a place on a plane on Saturday morning. So was probably everybody else booked on the flight they canceled. Then I went out to dinner with Serge and one of his British authors. He'd been trying to talk me into it all afternoon. In a way I was glad the flight I thought I was on didn't leave. We had a really amusing time, and I had one less night of being the head nurse.

Goddamn Popov, thought Schmidt.

I have dates to propose for our June rendezvous, darling, he told Alice. What would you say if I arrived on Thursday, June eighth, and left on Tuesday, the thirteenth?

I'll be waiting for you, she whispered. I may even buy a new frock.

He had barely hung up with Alice when his telephone rang: an unusual occurrence in his pied-à-terre. So few people telephoned him anyway, and practically no one knew his New York City number. He picked up the receiver and listened warily. It was a voice he recognized and, next to Popov's, the last voice he wanted to hear. Renata Riker, Charlotte's busy-body grasping and evil mother-in-law. The thought that the poor deluded girl believed she had found in Renata the mother she lost when Mary died was unbearable.

Schmidtie, spoke the voice, this is Renata. I hope I find you well. You and I need to talk about our children and our grandson.

Schmidt said nothing.

Schmidtie, are you there or have we been cut off? Will you please say something.

Clearly she wished to avoid the less dignified hypothesis, that he had hung up on her.

I'm here, he replied.

Schmidtie, you are acting out your resentment of Jon. That you resented him when you found he was living with Charlotte, and when they got married, we both know that very well. Now he has committed the greatest crime of all. He has impregnated her; she has conceived and will bear his child! Not yours. His! He has usurped the role you and so many other fathers unconsciously reserve for themselves. These are feelings that should be examined and worked through before they do more harm.

What twaddle, said Schmidt. Do people pay you to hear it? No wonder you say there are fewer and fewer of them.

You can't get rid of me with insults, Renata replied. I know you're in New York, and I want to see you this afternoon or evening or just about anytime tomorrow.

You do have a lot of free time!

He knew it was cruel to laugh, but he couldn't help himself. The effect was immediate. Renata began to cry. For a moment he thought it was a trick, but no, those sobs were real and wrenching. It was his doing, and he had better calm her. But he wasn't going to let himself in for a lunch at his club or a restaurant. They had tried that before.

I have to leave my apartment at seven. If you like, come over for a drink at six. Please bring Myron if he is free.

I will see you at six, replied Renata. Charlotte has given me the address.

It was a fine May evening, and Schmidt was amused to see that Renata's collection of Chanel suits or Chanel knock-offs was equal to the occasion. This one was white. Even if it was true that she and Myron had fallen on hard times, she had not lowered her standards in other aspects of her ward-robe either. She wore signature Chanel beige pumps with black patent-leather toes and beige stockings. Her pocket-book matched the outfit. But none of these things was new, a fact that enabled Schmidt to calculate the cost of the whole get-up: in the years before Mary fell sick with the illness that would kill her he would occasionally buy for her one of those suits or some accessories, and so he knew what such things used to cost. If you kept buying them, pretty soon you were talking about real money. There must have been other extrava-gances as well. No wonder that the Rikers' savings were being depleted. In other respects, she had changed. When he saw her last, the previous autumn, at his favorite Northern Ital-ian restaurant over lunch to which she had invited herself, he had noticed that she had aged more quickly than one would have expected, her once-jet-black hair gathered in a tight bun at the back of her head having turned completely gray. Since then she had cut her hair into a pageboy and had not bothered to dye it. Her eyes looked even more tired; the bags of yellow had darkened and were perhaps larger. He found it difficult to believe that the first time they met he had made a pass at her and that, when he was sick with a violent flu, she had reciprocated with an unexpected deep kiss. Less than three years had passed since then, but now his gestures and hers seemed equally ridiculous, in fact grotesque.

She looked around her, peeked into the bedroom and the kitchen, and, returning from her tour, nodded. This is quite a little flat, she told him, and in one of the best buildings on Park Avenue. You're a favorite of fortune, Schmidtie!

It's a company apartment, picked out and decorated by the company. I use it when I'm in New York on business.

The company is your billionaire friend's foundation, unless I'm mistaken. That's what Jon has told me.

Schmidt replied that her son was well informed and offered her a drink.

Nothing alcoholic, she told him. Any sort of juice or water.

He gave her V8, which he kept in the refrigerator, hesitated between a bourbon and a martini, and settled on a martini because while he fixed it the clock would be running. He might shave three or four minutes off the interview.

She was on to his game and followed him into the kitchen. I've come here to talk to you, Schmidtie. When you called Jon, why did you first tear his head off and then hang up on him? What was the capital offense? Asking his very rich father-in-law to make a secure financial arrangement for his first grandchild?

Schmidt had finished measuring out the gin, added a drop of vermouth and several ice cubes, and shook vigorously. An olive jar was open. He took one olive, washed it under the kitchen faucet, dried it with a paper towel, laid it carefully in a glass, and poured out the contents of the shaker. Having taken a sip, he turned toward Renata.

You know, he said, when I hear you talk I begin to wish I were a Jew. It must be nice to have a Jewish mother wiping your nose and your behind even when you get to be a grown man and running interference for you. As I told your grown son, I've had my fill of you Rikers, *mère, père, et fils,* of you and your money grubbing.

Money grubbing! cried Renata.

Yes. I've given Charlotte a pile of money. First, when she decided she didn't want the house I lived in, her aunt's and her mother's house, the house she was brought up in. That money was supposed to pay for the property she wanted to buy near your place in Claverack, or the apartment in New York, or both. Frankly, I get lost in the Riker finances. All I know is the result: the property was bought in both their names. Then Jon slapped a mortgage on the apartment or on the house or both even though with the money I had given no debt should have been needed. And then, when they split over the revolting affair he was conducting with one of the firm's paralegals, he refused to give back to Charlotte what was hers! How slimy can you get?

How dare you say such things!

It's easy; no trouble at all. I've always given Charlotte money freely, even if she could never bring herself to ask for it nicely or to thank me nicely. What she and your son have done with it I honestly don't know. And then your son has the gall to ask me to provide for the unborn Myron!

Well, Schmidtie, Renata said slowly, you're certainly less inhibited than when I first met you. You were so WASP polite you could hardly bring yourself to speak. And now, just listen to you! Is it your Puerto Rican waitress girlfriend who has loosened your tongue? That girl should be a therapist.

She had drunk her V8. After a look at her wristwatch she said, I see we have thirty-five minutes left. Could I have a glass of whatever it is you are drinking? A martini, I suppose. Poor Myron has had to give them up.

Schmidt remembered Myron's excellent martinis and having let himself get suddenly and stupidly tipsy on them, but he was not interested in bittersweet reminiscences. He poured Renata's drink, refilled his own glass, and sat down. If she wanted to talk on he would listen. For another thirty-two minutes.

Are you angry because they're going to call the baby Myron, rather than, for example, Albert?

He answered truthfully that he wasn't. The name wasn't one he liked. He did not mention the coincidence that a baby due to be born before little Myron would indeed be called Albert. Perhaps one Albert at a time was enough.

You say that, but residual hostility may still be there. You should know that Myron hasn't been well, he's got heart problems, and they're aggravated by worries about his practice. He's still doing group therapy in the city, but there may be a possibility of a hospital position up in Columbia County, near Claverack. If that pans out, he may commute to that job from the city, or perhaps I will commute the other way around. The point of all this is that they were looking for a way to boost his morale.

Schmidt nodded.

You should also realize that Jon is not earning as much as he had hoped or deserves. His firm is not as profitable as it should be. That's a worry. You already know that he is helping us. I'm not proud of that, but I'm not ashamed either. Myron and I, and Jon as well, on top of everything else, we have all had considerable investment losses. Are you aware of that?

You mean the losses? It's the first time I've heard about them. Charlotte hasn't mentioned them, and she certainly hasn't asked for advice.

That is because you intimidate them.

Balls!

The beneficial effects of the second large martini were spreading pleasantly through Schmidt's body. Balls, he repeated. It was such a fine expression, preferable to both "twaddle" and "humbug."

Your army basic training talk doesn't scare me, replied Renata. I will tell you something else you may not know. Charlotte and Jon are deeply anxious about the financial implications—maybe I should say consequences of your liaison with that waitress. Given that concern, they think it's only natural to ask you to do what's right in order to protect your daughter's and grandchildren's future.

I have news for you, Renata, said Schmidt. Under the laws of this great state of New York, my daughter and my grandchildren, born and unborn, have no interests in my property except such as I choose to give them. I have no intention of disinheriting my daughter, but if you and the other Rikers persist in insulting me I may just change my mind. Or leave my daughter something that she and Jon will doubtless think is a pittance. So watch out, and tell them to watch out. And now your time is up.

That wasn't strictly speaking true, and she knew it. Schmidtie, she said, aren't you even planning to see your pregnant daughter?

Schmidt shrugged. That is pretty funny, he said. I have asked her to come to see me in the country, and I have offered to see her in New York. She turned me down.

He was momentarily too proud to mention that she hadn't invited him to Claverack.

Don't you think you could manage to drive out to their place? Claverack isn't such a hard drive from Bridgehampton. You can also take the train from the city to Hudson. They'll pick you up there.

There is a small detail, he replied. They've given me no reason to think that they want me there. And now you really must go.

XII

THE LONG YEARS Renata had spent listening with her third ear to supine patients had not been wasted. She saw right through Schmidt: he yearned to see Charlotte but would not go to Claverack unless he was invited, and he wasn't about to fish for an invitation. This was a problem she could solve. As though by chance, Charlotte called Schmidt the very next day.

Dad, she announced, you should come to visit in the country before the baby's born. That way you'll also get to see the house, I mean our house, and also the Rikers' house, if you like. They're both great. Renata thinks it's a good idea. You'll understand why Jon and I like Claverack and hate the Hamptons. There is just one thing: next weekend is Memorial Day weekend, and we have some people Jon works with staying with us here, so we can't have you. Is there another weekend that suits you?

Why that's considerate of Renata, replied Schmidt, wondering what had happened to Charlotte's intelligence of which he used to be so proud. I'd be very happy to see you, but I'd rather come during the week. I'd arrive in the morning, we'd have lunch, and after lunch I would leave. A light and airy visit!

Maybe that's best, she replied. On weekends Jon is so bushed that he needs to relax. He wants to see friends and his family. Absolutely no one else.

Schmidt made no reply.

Well, can you tell me when to expect you? She made no effort to conceal her irritation.

What about a week from tomorrow? Schmidt asked. I could be there at noon.

That's fine, she replied. You know how to get to Claverack, don't you? I'll send you directions so you can find the house.

Click. She hung up.

It wasn't long before the telephone rang again. It was Renata.

You were right to say you wouldn't spend the night, she told him. Twenty-four hours of exposure to your pent-up hostility might have been too hard on Charlotte. As it is, she's making a big effort to work through it. She deserves to be rewarded!

Thank you, Renata, he answered. I am certain that you will find something suitable.

As this was obviously only the beginning of her attempted family therapy, he told her: I really can't talk now. You caught me as I was going out the door.

We'll talk again soon, she replied, after your visit.

He decided to spend the night in the city before driving out to Claverack. Lew Brenner was free. He arranged to have dinner with him at the club. When they met, Lew apologized for his wife. Tina would have been so happy to see Schmidtie, but she was spending the week in the country.

They drank their martinis at the bar and then moved upstairs to the dining room. After they had decided what they would eat and what wine they would drink, Lew told Schmidtie he wanted to give him a heads-up. After the election of new partners in June, Jack DeForrest will come under strong pressure. The young Turks are up in arms about him.

I wonder how you feel about this, Schmidtie, Lew continued. You and he were so close when we were all associates, but I've had the impression that after he became the presiding partner there was tension between you, more tension than one assumes will always be present in dealings with *el supremo*.

That's a difficult subject, Schmidt said, but you've got it pretty much right. Tell me the sins of which Jack stands accused and who is likely to succeed him.

If only it were so simple! But that is a difficult subject too. There is no specific charge. You know the general situation just as well as I: the Dow has been moving in the right direction, the unemployment figures too, but there aren't enough big deals. That makes the kiddies nervous. They go around saying things like I'd kill for a deal. Thank goodness that's not the picture in my neck of the woods. I have big transactions going, and everyone working with me is very, very busy. But the picture in the rest of the firm isn't that positive, and Jack, instead of being a cheerleader for the firm, acts like Mr. Gloom and Doom. He's fixated on numbers: are the billable hours up or down and by what percentage? Same with receivables, and all those per partner and per lawyer statistics. He should be talking about our tradition of service to clients, the fun of working together, and so forth. All that morale-building stuff that old Dexter Wood was so good at. So even though Jack has two years to go in his term as presiding partner, chances are that he will be pushed to step down.

Well, Lew, you've always had interesting work, and lots of it.

As he said that, Schmidt realized that W & K's office politics and personalities had receded far enough from his mind to make it possible for him to feel only a trace of the former envy of Lew and his with-one-hand-tied-behind-my-back prowess and successes.

I'm lucky, Lew said, that's all. And I've had good help. Just like you. Take someone like Tim Verplanck! They will probably want to reach far down, into the younger ranks. If you have any suggestions you should let me know.

Ruminating, they sipped their wine.

Apropos of Tim Verplanck, Schmidt said, I went back to Paris and had lunch with Hugh Macomber and the rest of the gang.

Good man, young Macomber!

He told me he wasn't any too sure of hanging on to the clients brought in by Tim—the ones who are still there. As you know, there have been defections. He mentioned some sort of problem with that friend of Tim's, Bruno.

Yes, there is a problem. A real problem. Both Macombers—his wife, Molly, even more than he—are wonderful people, but basically they're American provincials. There's no other word for it. If you say "investment banker," the picture that comes up before their eyes is that of any one of Hugh's Princeton classmates who's now a partner at Morgan Stanley or equivalent, married to a wife just like Molly, with two kids, one at

Chapin and the other at Buckley. So when they come face-to-face with Bruno, it's the wrong picture, and all they see is that he's queer. There's no wife, there aren't any kids, so what kind of an investment banker is he? An aberration. He makes them uncomfortable. He'd fit into their conception of life if he were a painter. Or a society hairdresser! What they forget or don't see is that there are many Princeton graduates who were members of the same eating club as Hugh who are now bankers at Morgan Stanley and similar firms and are just as gay as Bruno. Or Jewish like me!

He paused, apparently expecting Schmidt to say something. Seeing that Schmidt was going to remain silent, Lew continued: The point is that what you do in bed doesn't make you any better or worse at mergers and acquisitions.

Yes, said Schmidt, only it's too bad for the Paris office.

I'm trying to pitch in, Lew said. Bruno's very sophisticated. He sees through Hugh and doesn't hold against him the way he has reacted. He knows it's cultural, involuntary. The problem is with referral of clients and encouraging clients to stay even though Tim is gone. All that would be easier, and come more naturally, and Bruno would do it gladly, if he and Hugh had a warmer relationship.

Of course, said Schmidt. By the way while I was in Paris I saw Alice again.

He'd said it! Schmidt's sole purpose in talking about young Macomber had been to lay the groundwork. He didn't want her name to come out of the blue.

You could put your time to much worse use, said Lew, and raised his glass to Schmidt. She's a lovely woman.

Yes.

If she's free, she'd be perfect for you, Schmidtie. She'd

understand you; she'd fit in. She's someone you could be proud of.

I'm fifteen years older!

If you say so. I haven't done the arithmetic, but I don't think it matters. You're in good health, you don't look your age, and you've got a nice life—especially now that you're running Mike Mansour's foundation. I'd give it some real thought provided, as I said, she's free.

There's no indication she isn't, but how would I know! I do hope to see her again, though, when I'm in Paris next month.

Great idea, replied Lew. Tina and I will be there for a week. If we overlap, the four of us should have dinner together.

The route to Claverack was distantly familiar. Before Charlotte was born, Mary and he went up to concerts at Tanglewood on occasional weekends, staying either with a Radcliffe friend of Mary's married to an architect who had a house in Hillsdale, just west of the Massachusetts line and about twenty miles from Lenox, or a W & K partner, a litigator for whom Schmidt had written a series of memos, whose house was in Great Barrington. They had less fun staying with the litigator, but the drive from his house to Tanglewood was only half an hour, instead of the hour it took to get there from Hillsdale, and staying with the litigator was probably good for Schmidt's career. Having served as FDR's envoy in Lend-Lease negotiations, the litigator was convinced of the indispensable value of government service for bright young lawyers. Evidently he thought that Schmidt was one and expounded to him and Mary the need for Schmidt to shake himself free of the shackles of W & K for a couple of years, perhaps four, and work for the good of the country. He must do it, he would say,

if only for the sake of his *New York Times* obituary! It was easy
for the litigator to talk: he had a rich wife. Schmidt didn't; in
fact Mary had just gotten her editorial assistant's job, which
paid next to nothing. In Hillsdale no one preached to them:
Mary's friend was a great cook; the other houseguests, like the
hosts, were all roughly Schmidt's contemporaries; and on Saturday, because there was no afternoon concert, they all flew
elaborate kites provided by the architect in the beautiful field
behind the house, which, standing on the brow of a hill, was
favored with a breeze even on sultry summer days. The litigator died two years after Schmidt became a partner and had
a celebrity's treatment in the press; the expert cook and the
architect divorced. The house in Hillsdale was sold, and
Schmidt and Mary never saw the architect again. They continued to see the expert cook until she remarried, moved to
Oregon, where she opened a restaurant, and died of cancer
like Mary, only some years earlier.

Wrung out by memories of old friendships and death,
unbearably excited at the thought that in two hours he would
see his daughter, so beloved and so alienated from him, he
found his way through the new and renamed roads that finally
put him on the Taconic and stepped on the gas. The Volvo
was incomparably more powerful than his old Beetle. It shot
forward as if outraged. Conscientiously, he slowed down to
sixty-five, which he thought unlikely to irk any of the cops
lurking on the richly planted shoulder or median, turned on
the radio, and to his surprise found that he was still within
the reach of WQXR's signal. That, on top of the Volvo, was a
distinct improvement over the old days.

The house, a two-story white clapboard affair with black
shutters, stood in a field, in the fenced portion of which grazed

Aberdeen cattle belonging, as he found out later, to the nearby farmer who had sold the property to Charlotte and Jon. Charlotte met him at the front door. Less than two months had gone by since he last saw her, in the Tuileries. That chic and svelte young woman had undergone a transformation. Here she was, in a blue-and-white-striped gingham dress that was not designed to conceal the huge belly. Would the baby be huge, too? She was actually smiling. He kissed her on both cheeks and then once again, for good measure.

I am so very happy, he told her.

When they sat down in the kitchen after the tour of the house, she asked him what he thought.

It's lovely, he answered, very well renovated, in the best taste, exactly what I would expect from you. And I think the baby's room is just right. He will like it.

Actually, she said, Renata deserves ninety percent of the credit. She has a good eye and knows how to deal with workers.

I'm not surprised, Schmidt answered. I recall that their apartment on Fifty-Seventh Street is very handsome, very well done.

You've only been there once!

He wasn't sure whether that was to be taken as a taunt or an expression of regret. It was better not to inquire. Instead he asked whether he could have a drink: a bourbon or a gin and tonic. There was no bourbon, but the gin and Schweppes tonic water were produced. Since she told him to help himself, he made it strong. By the time he got back on the road, it and whatever else she gave him to drink at lunch would have been metabolized, and if not he would pull over to the side of the Taconic and take a short nap.

There is something I would like to ask you, she said, and I hope it won't make you fly off the handle.

Go ahead. I'll try to control myself.

I'd like to hire a live-in combination baby nurse and housekeeper. Someone flexible and experienced, who could help me out now just with coping and would be good with the baby when he comes. I've got someone with good references, who I think would be right. I wonder if you would pay her salary and social security and the rest of that stuff.

I think it could probably be managed.

Then he added, he really couldn't help it: Did you get her through Renata?

If you must know, yes. She called the agency in New York she has always used. I suppose that nixes it. I mean if something has to do with Renata or Jon, it's immediately verboten.

Not necessarily, he answered, it depends on what they're up to. What salary does Mary Poppins command?

Live in, both here and in the city, six thousand. She gets one month of vacation, so I'll need someone to cover.

I think I can swing it, said Schmidt, both her and the substitute. Provided, of course, she is also selected by Renata. When can Poppins start?

Next Tuesday, right after Memorial Day, if I let her know today.

Go ahead and tell her she's on. I'll give you a check for the first month's salary right now.

He drew his wallet out of his pocket. There were always two blank checks in it, evidently just for this sort of occasion. His head felt just a bit light: effect of the second gin and tonic he was working on, or of check writing? No, it came from the exquisite clarity of the situation. First, Jon makes the big grab: Listen up Albert, it's time to set up a trust for little Myron. That tanks, so master tactician Renata decides to go for the smaller stuff: a mere six thousand per month! That's just the first step. But he would give twice as much, with good grace, if Charlotte explained her and Jon's mysterious finances, if she asked him nicely, if the Rikers could keep their mitts off his dealings with his daughter. He handed her the check. While she examined it, he felt in his coat pocket the present he had for her: a turn-of-the-century French pendant in the shape of a butterfly, suspended on a chain. Give it to her right now? He decided to wait. There was no telling how the visit would end.

After what seemed like a long silence, she said, Thanks! I will tell Renata to call this woman. Do you mind if I call her?

He shook his head.

There must be a special number for Charlotte's personal use that rings in Renata's consultation room. At twelve-thirty, she should be in the middle of some patient's fifty-minute hour. But she picked up at once. Schmidt heard her say, Hello sweetie! How is it going? OK, his daughter replied, he's given me the check. You can call Yolanda when you get a chance. Yes. Love yah!

"Love yah" indeed, Schmidt remarked silently. The high intelligence, its mysterious disappearance has already been noted. And the good manners, so carefully instilled by Mary, by Aunt Martha, and even, believe it or not, by him! Where had they gone? It would be hard to say that some sort of street smarts had taken their place, because a truly street-smart girl would know better moves than this dropout from the upper classes.

You want to eat? she asked.

Yes, he replied, but perhaps it would be easier if I took you out. Some place in Claverack or Hudson?

I've got some food ready.

She put dishes, glasses, and forks and knives on the table, leaving it to him to organize them, brought from the pantry a half-empty bottle of a California red, and from the fridge a bowl of Niçoise salad. There was bread on the sideboard, and she put it on the table as well.

Charlotte, said Schmidt, audibly choked up, this was your mother's favorite summer dish, and you've followed her recipe. Thank you!

You're welcome. I suppose you thought I'd order in a pizza. Of course, I'm not nearly as good a cook as your girlfriend Carrie.

Ah, that meal Carrie prepared so generously the one time they met has stuck in her craw, mused Schmidt. How too damn bad.

I don't know, he answered, I haven't tasted enough food that you've prepared. But I do see that you haven't kept up with developments. Carrie has married a lovely guy who runs a marina in East Hampton, and she expects a baby next month.

That must have burned you up!

Not really. As I said, he's a lovely guy, he's the right age for her, and I think they'll have a good life together.

That's a new generosity, Dad. Wow! I haven't noticed your being so broad-minded and kindly about Jon's and my marriage.

Goodness, replied Schmidt.

What was he to do? Talk about Jon's cheating on her and his unethical or, if not unethical, then surely reckless behavior that led to his expulsion from W & K, not to mention his disgraceful refusal to return her rightful property when they broke up? Remind her that Jon, who owed to Schmidt's support his partnership at W & K, never passed up an opportunity to needle the old man? Talk about how, in a grotesque replay of the story of Ruth, she had ostentatiously turned away from him to follow her mother-in-law? Or her and Jon's truly remarkable lack of gratitude for the tons of money she had already received from him? What use would any of that be?

Goodness, he said once again. We mustn't have a debate about that while I'm eating your delicious salad. I don't suppose you drink coffee these days?

She shook her head.

If you don't mind making it, I'll have some. Very strong, and at least one big cup.

Soon afterward he left, the gold and lapis lazuli butterfly still in his pocket. His mind was made up: he would give it to her, but only when he came to see his grandson for the first time.

It was after six when he reached Bridgehampton. Sy was in the house, which was as it should be; he had recommended that Bryan shut the kitty door so that he couldn't go out when Bryan wasn't there to answer cries of distress. The enthusiasm of Sy's welcome, however, was at such a high pitch that Schmidt sensed that something had gone awry. Indeed, the kitty litter box, on the cleanliness of which Bryan prided himself, had not been changed, and without question Sy was starved. First things first: he picked up the cat and assured him of his devotion, fed him, and took care of the litter. Recompensed by grateful purring, he opened the kitty door and watched Sy's infinitely prudent exit into the garden.

Only then did he check the telephone messages. The red light was blinking. He pressed the play button. Jason's instantly recognizable Boy Scout troop–leader voice told him that Carrie's water had broken early that morning while she was still in bed; contractions began a couple of hours later; he had taken her to the Southampton hospital. The message had been left at twelve-twenty, while he was in Charlotte's kitchen, drinking his gin and tonic. He's probably still at the hospital, thought Schmidt. Jason's cell phone number was posted on the kitchen bulletin board. No answer. Schmidt tried Bryan next. Carrie's in the room where they keep them while they're in labor, Bryan told him. She's been there since noon. Jason is mostly with her. She's doing real well. He had to go back to the marina to help out the two other guys but was now going to keep Jason company.

Schmidt reflected. Have you and Jason eaten?

The answer was yes; he had brought a pizza and some beers, and they ate on the back of the truck.

I wonder whether I should head over, he said. Jason will want to stay until the baby is born, but you should call me, at any hour, if there is something new to report, or you have to go back to the marina. A first child can take very long to come out. So be sure you call me. I'm not going anywhere, and I don't mind—I really don't mind—if you wake me up. So, anything new, or if you or Jason need to be relieved, you call me. All right?

It had slowly become clear to Schmidt that he must not step out of his present role. And what was that? Carrie's former lover—but so was Bryan—and her and Jason's friend and

benefactor. That was all. The fact that he had given Carrie
a handsome dowry changed nothing. No, most certainly he
wasn't her father. The paradox was that he now had a father's
love for her. The memory of the sex between them—the
ecstasy that had lifted him so high that he felt he had been
transformed by it—was as vivid as ever, and he thought it
would never wane. At the same time, he was convinced, he
knew, that if he were alone with her, and she signaled, in one
of the numberless ways that were her secret, that she wanted
him, he would recoil from violating the taboo. It came down
to this: he would now no more sleep with her than with
Charlotte. His love for his Hecate had become paternal. The
heartbreaking other side of the paradox: he foresaw that this
sallow-skinned enchantress, whose body he had so passion-
ately and lovingly explored, would be a better daughter to
him than Charlotte, just as he might be a better father to her.
Yes, there was a place for Bryan at the hospital as Jason's best
friend and business partner, and none at all for Schmidt. It was
time for him to step back. Unless something terrible came up:
some change in Carrie's condition or a problem with the baby.
Later, when he called Bryan again, there had been no developments; Jason was still with Carrie. I might go out, Schmidt
told him. If I don't answer at home, would you please call me
on my cell.

He made himself a martini and drank it slowly. The *New
York Times* lay on the kitchen table. It didn't interest him.
There might or might not be enough food in the fridge for
his supper. He didn't look and he didn't care. The waves of
emotion washing over him were too strong for the solitude
of his kitchen. He whistled for Sy. The kitten, dignified and
unhurried, came in through the screen door that Schmidt held

open and received his award. Half a slice of Oscar Mayer ham, cut in little pieces. That transaction concluded, Schmidt shut the kitty door for the night, shaved, took a bath, put on fresh clothes, and drove to O'Henry's. It had crossed his mind that he could call Gil Blackman and see whether he was in Wainscott and happened to be free. If Elaine had made good on her threat to install the Mummy in the house, there would probably be nothing in the world he'd like better. It was also possible that Elaine or Gil might think of asking him to have dinner with them. No, calling Gil was a bad idea. He didn't want to relate his visit to Claverack: not yet, anyway. And he didn't see how he could share with Gil his feelings about Carrie. They were too tender, too important. And how to keep them from becoming conflated with Gil's Sturm und Drang over DT?

He hesitated about ordering a martini—what if he had to rush to the hospital?—but with a shrug he ordered one anyway and drank it too fast, waiting for his steak. A compromise was called for. One glass of wine with his meal would have to do.

Mary had been in labor for almost thirty hours with Charlotte. He couldn't understand how she bore it, and he had pleaded with the obstetrician for a cesarean. The brute— Schmidt still remembered his name, Dr. Bubis—refused. Finally Bubis got the baby out with forceps. No injury to the baby or to Mary, thank God. It was pure luck. Schmidt couldn't bring himself to believe that any skill had entered into it. There were many explanations for Mary's not wanting another child, but that long agony must have been a major one. Who could blame her, especially as Bubis had talked her into the Lamaze technique and administered an epidural only a couple of hours before the forceps? Schmidt hadn't asked who was delivering little Albert. Now he wished he had. He might have had him or her checked out. Too late for that. But probably it was just as well not to rock the boat. She was young, and in the best of health.

The call came just after three in the morning. It was Jason. Do you want to speak to Carrie? he asked. She's right here.

Schmidtie, she whispered, he's an ugly big bruiser with red hair. I think you'll like him. I love him already.

XIII

Dıes ırae.

Mike Mansour's plane touched down at Le Bourget, the airport north of Paris where almost all private aircraft bound for Paris land, on Wednesday evening, a few minutes after seven. Alice was expecting Schmidt at her apartment at nine-thirty. Passport and customs control at Le Bourget was almost nonexistent, and Mr. Mansour's Paris Rolls was waiting on the tarmac. Even if they hit heavy traffic going into Paris there would be plenty of time to shower and change before going to Alice's; he might even call and ask to come early. Having slept through most of the eight-hour trip, he felt rested. He would see her in two hours! His body tingled from excitement.

The question is, are you inviting me to dinner tonight with your nice lady, or do I have to eat alone? Mike Mansour had asked.

Oh Mike, Schmidt had replied, I wish I could, but I'm having dinner at her house. Another time, let's do it another time.

Pas de problème, was the great financier's answer, and, benevolence personified, he announced that he was taking Schmidt and Alice out on Saturday evening. It would be his treat. He might even have a surprise guest.

The ground crew had already put their suitcases in the trunk of the car; Mr. Mansour and Schmidt had finished shaking hands with the captain, the copilot, and the stewards; the chauffeur, cap in hand, stood at the open passenger door of the Rolls, when a small white car approached at breakneck speed. A man wearing some sort of uniform got out, greeted Mr. Mansour, and asked to speak to Mr. Albert Schmidt. This gentleman here, Mike said pointing, whereupon the airport official handed Schmidt an envelope.

Go ahead and open it, said Mike.

Schmidt nodded. It was a fax from Myron Riker. He read it aloud, his knees about to buckle: *Charlotte was injured in an accident. She's at the hospital in Hudson. Please call me, and meet us there.*

The cell phone number appeared at the bottom of the page.

I've got to call him, Schmidt said to no one in particular, and I've got to get there. It surprised him that he was able to speak.

Hold it, said Mr. Mansour. The question is how you can get there, and if you call before you know that, you're nowhere. *Pas question!*

Archie, he continued speaking to the captain. Please get on the phone—he handed him the cell phone—and find out how quickly your people can have a crew here to take the plane back to New York—no, not New York, to Albany.

You mustn't, said Schmidt.

Let me put it to you this way, replied Mr. Mansour, the last commercial flight from Paris to the U.S.—he looked at his watch—will leave in a few minutes. You can't catch it. I want to get you where you need to go, and the plane needs to go back anyway. I don't want it sitting here while these guys—

his wagging index pointed at the crew—live it up at the Lido! *Pas question!*

Mr. Mansour, said Archie, you're in luck. There's a crew at the Sofitel in Roissy waiting to fly commercial that can get here in less than an hour. Shall I tell them to come?

Yes. *Prestissimo!* And tell your people to get a landing slot in Albany, whatever it takes. Schmidtie, now you can make your call. Was that Riker's father writing to you? You can tell him you'll be in Albany around eleven this evening his time and will get to that hospital from there. No need for him to worry how. One of the security boys will meet the plane and drive you there.

I don't know how to thank you. He realized he had tears in his eyes.

You're a fucking idiot. Let me tell you this: if you're like me, and have a lot of money, really a lot of money, you have the right to spend a little of it on your friends. You may not know it, but you're my best friend. *Pas de problème.* Even if your best friend is Gil Blackman! Ha! Ha! Ha!

Schmidt shook the proffered hand and stepped out of Mr. Mansour's embrace to make the call he dreaded.

Schmidtie, Myron answered on the first ring, she fell; she'd climbed on the windowsill to fix a blind that had gotten stuck. She was holding on to it to steady herself, it slipped out of the socket, and she fell backward. Probably she passed out. Yolanda—that's the baby nurse she hired—found her. She was bleeding heavily, so Yolanda called the ambulance. They're still working on her in the operating room. There is the problem of the concussion too, but it doesn't seem serious. It's good that you're coming.

Will she be all right?

I'm sure of it. Of course, she's lost the baby.

Oh, so long as she's all right they'll make another one, replied Schmidt, instantly realizing that for some reason his remark was grossly stupid.

Myron made no direct response. Instead he said that probably Schmidt wouldn't get to Hudson before midnight, and by that time it was likely they—Renata, Jon, and he—would have been obliged to leave the hospital, and he certainly wouldn't be allowed to see Charlotte. The best thing for Schmidt would be to call Myron after he landed in Albany. He would give him the news.

That conversation ended, he called Alice. Her voice: hearing it he began to wish shamefully that Mike Mansour had not taken matters in hand. Without his plane, he would have been obliged to spend the night in Paris, and he would have spent it with Alice. Miscarriages happen all the time, he thought, the Rikers have overreacted. Once they have dragged me there, that awful trio will do everything to shove me aside. These were thoughts he kept to himself. To Alice he said that he could to return to Paris in ten days' or two weeks' time. Would she like that?

Hush, Schmidtie, she replied. Don't make plans to visit me now. First see Charlotte and make sure she's all right. Be with her. Help her. Let me know how she is.

The plane made better time than the captain first estimated, landing in Albany shortly after ten. Once again, Myron answered at once.

It was a huge hemorrhage, he said, and it went on too long. The time that passed before Yolanda found Charlotte, the wait for the ambulance, the ride to Hudson. They transfused her right away and tried a D & C. It didn't work, Schmidtie, it didn't work! So they did a hysterectomy to save her life. It's all right now. She'll be in the recovery room until tomorrow morning. Schmidtie, listen to me. She's out of danger. Let's meet at the hospital at ten. No visitors are allowed earlier.

Stony faces of the mother and son Riker. Only Myron held out his hand for Schmidt to shake. We'll be able to see her starting in about a half hour, but only two by two. Why don't we let Jon and Renata go first. You and I will take the second shift.

Schmidt had in the meantime talked to his new doctor, Dr. Tang. Hysterectomy after a miscarriage? she asked, sounding nonplussed. Well, that is late in the term. Every case is different, but usually the hemorrhage can be stopped with a D & C. You say they tried it? Perhaps the uterus ruptured. I am truly sorry for you and your daughter and for your entire family.

While they sat in the waiting room, he repeated the conversation to Myron. Yes, said Myron, that's what I would have thought too. I've asked to see Charlotte's obstetrician, but he's at a medical meeting in New Orleans. The other obstetrician is also away; they didn't tell me where. The emergency room physician—a reasonable and calm man—did try the D & C and was getting nowhere, so they got in the general surgeon who was on call. You can't second-guess people in these situations. Even with the transfusions they were afraid of losing her.

After what had seemed like a long time, mother and son Riker returned.

Charlotte wants to see Myron first and then her father, said Renata. She's exhausted. These should be short visits.

An age ago, when Charlotte was still a schoolgirl, he had waited with other parents on the sidewalk for the bus bringing the Brearley girls back from a school excursion. Suddenly, when they were getting off, he experienced a moment of panic. He wasn't sure that he would recognize his daughter. The panic returned, twisted into a new shape as he stood in the door of the hospital room looking at the woman lying in the bed. Yes, this was his poor daughter, there could be no doubt; the nurse had opened the door for him, indicating that this was the room. Face lifeless and white, eyes closed, perhaps she was asleep. He went in on tiptoe. She opened her eyes, and her expression changed. Charlotte was trying to smile.

My darling, he said, you're all right. You're going to be all right.

He took her hand and kissed it.

Hi, Dad, she said. I'm glad you made it here. I thought you were in Paris.

Someone very intelligent—so far he hadn't asked who it had been—called the house or the foundation, figured out that a fax could be gotten to me, and I rushed back. I had just landed, and I was able to turn right around.

Myron sent you the fax. He told me before the operation.

I see. He is very intelligent.

There was a chair next to the bed. He sat down and kissed her hand again.

I don't want to tire you, he said. It's such a happiness to see you. I was so scared on the plane. I thought we'd never get across the Atlantic and, once we were over the St. Lawrence Seaway, that we'd never make it to Albany.

Dad, I'm not going to be able to have children. They took

my womb out. I so wanted to have that little boy! Now Jon's going to leave me. What's the use of a wife who can't have children? What's the use of marriage?

No, he won't, sweetie, there are lots of happy childless marriages. You'll see.

Sure. We can have a dog. Or two dogs. Or a dog and a cat. We can adopt!

Many people do adopt and love their adopted children so much it doesn't make any difference. This is not the time to start thinking about it. This is the time to get well enough to leave the hospital and get all your strength back.

Sure, Dad.

She began to cry. He quieted her as best he could, calling her all the childhood names.

Dad, she said after a while, do you think you could stay until Friday afternoon? Jon has to go back to the city—he's on trial and it's a big case—and Renata and Myron have to get back to their patients.

Nothing could make me happier. I'll be back in the afternoon. You get some good rest. The nurse is making all sorts of signs to get me out of here.

That day, and the morning of the day that followed, which was Friday, were the happiest time he had known with Charlotte since Mary died. He read aloud news from the *Times*. They started *The Warden*, which he had put into his suitcase. They talked about incidents from the old days, which she remembered more accurately than he, all involving Mary, that testified to the harmony of their household; she told him Radcliffe dormitory gossip that made him laugh although he had long forgotten the names of the girls who had figured most prominently in her stories. In that mood of easy intimacy they agreed that he would go back to Bridgehampton for the weekend, leaving before the Rikers arrived so as to escape the worst of the Friday afternoon and evening traffic, and would return on Monday and stay until she was discharged. The surgeon thought that if she kept making good progress a Wednesday release was likely. At that point, either he and Yolanda or one or more of the Rikers would take her home.

They were close to finishing a game of Scrabble around noon on Friday when Renata called. Although Charlotte had said nothing and had made no sign to suggest it, he went out into the corridor so that she could speak more freely. It was a long talk. Finally, he heard her put down the receiver and went back into the room to ask what she would like to have for their farewell lunch. She was allowed to eat soups brought in from the outside and plain meats such as roast chicken. There was a nearby grocery-cum-delicatessen Schmidt had found that sold precisely that kind of fare.

She stared at him blankly and announced: They will be here by three, that is, Renata and Myron. Jon can't get away until late. He may not even get here this evening.

That's too bad, Schmidt replied. Have you thought what you might like for lunch? Chicken soup and cold chicken? It's twice the same thing, but they're both good. Vanilla ice cream for dessert?

It doesn't make any difference. Whatever you like.

There was a dark look about her, so he asked, Darling what is the matter?

Oh, not much. I'm just facing what I have become.

He hurried with his purchases, stopped at the florist's to

have white and pink peonies arranged in a vase, and so encum-
bered arrived at Charlotte's room. He could see that she had
been crying.

They ate their lunch in almost complete silence. She had
looked at the flowers but had not said a word about them.
After clearing the plates and throwing away the paper napkins
and the rest of the disposable junk that without fail accom-
panies a takeout order, he asked again what had happened to
make her so sad.

Nothing, she said. Renata told me that the grandparents are
really disappointed. When Leah—that was Renata's mother—
heard I could never have children she cried so hard that Ron
had to tear her away from the phone.

Ron, Schmidt recalled, was Jon Riker's grandfather.

I'm so sorry, he said. It's new to them. They'll adjust. We
all will. Don't take that sort of thing so to heart.

You know that Seth—that was Renata's younger brother—
is gay.

I didn't.

Well, that's the fact. He won't have any children. I have
no womb. Renata and Myron won't have a grandchild from
me, Jon won't have a son, and I can get a dog. A nice standard
poodle. Do you recommend honey color or black?

Darling, I'm so very sorry.

No, you aren't. Or maybe you are. It doesn't matter. But
you sure were right. You knew how to call it. You knew not to
set up a trust for little Myron. You knew he wouldn't need it!
You put a hex on us!

Darling, this is crazy talk. Stop thinking and saying such
things. How can you!

I'm telling you the truth, that's how I can! You hate Jon, you hated the idea of having a Jewish grandson, and you showed your colors! I'll never forgive you!

Darling Charlotte, I beg you, stop!

Don't darling me. I know what I'm talking about. And I'm not alone to think so. Renata thinks the same! Anyway, it all figures. That Puerto Rican floozy has just had your kid. Right? Jon checked up on it. A little boy called Albert. Isn't that cute!

Instead of responding, he murmured good-bye and leaned over to kiss her. She pushed him away so vehemently that the IV tube was wrenched out from the port in her forearm. Schmidt called the nurse and, while she busied herself repairing the damage and scolding her patient, crept away.

XIV

THE THOUGHT crossed his mind that he should assure Charlotte once more that he would come back after the weekend and stay with her until she was discharged, but as he was leaving her room he instantaneously decided to say nothing. Whatever he said was almost certain to provoke another salvo of insults, one that might make impossibly difficult all future dealings, as well as, most immediate among them, his return to her bedside. Indeed as he was driven back to Bridgehampton by Mike Mansour's security man, he asked himself over and over: had so much damage been done already that he couldn't bring himself to do it, that he wouldn't be able to return? The answer that came to him uniformly each time was that he had no choice. The blow that Charlotte had suffered was so cruel that he must do everything in his power to help her. He must do nothing to make the hurt worse. Like all the countless other tantrums that had marked her rebellious adolescence, this odious outburst had to be disregarded. Forgiven. Certainly, but the great difference was that then they had been two, Mary and he, to sift through the barrages of wild accusations and demands, to laugh and to commiserate with each other. They were a family. Now he was quite alone.

Charlotte had chosen another family, one that, with the possible exception of Myron, was hostile to him. There was no one to whom he could repeat Charlotte's tirade, no one whose advice he could seek, no one to whom he could turn for reassurance and consolation. About the miscarriage and the hysterectomy, he had already told Alice, and he would tell Gil Blackman as soon as he could see him and Mike Mansour upon his return from Paris. But Charlotte's tantrum, the horrible accusation, could never be mentioned. They made him feel ashamed; he did not want anyone else's thoughts about Charlotte to be stained by them.

But it was essential that, one way or another, Charlotte and the Rikers be told that in spite of her behavior he would return. He ruled out calling her or Jon or Renata, but fortunately he still had Myron's cell phone number. He called him from the car, thinking he would leave a message detailed enough to obviate the need for a conversation. But no, Myron picked up at the first ring, surely the only member of the New York Psychoanalytic Institute to answer the phone with such alacrity.

Look, Myron, he said, I was about to have lunch with Charlotte when Renata called. I went out of the room to give them privacy. Before that conversation, Charlotte and I had been having a good time together. From the moment she hung up, she was a changed woman. I can only suppose that the conversation did it. Charlotte then said to me some extraordinarily unpleasant things. I'm telling you this by way of background, not to complain about Renata. The reason for my call is this: Prior to her outburst, Charlotte and I agreed that I would come back to Hudson on Monday and stay until she's discharged. I said I'd take her back to the house and help Yolanda to settle her in. Of course, if one of you is there that won't be necessary. I am also planning to engage a night nurse to be with her for the first few nights. What I am asking of you is that you find a way to assure Charlotte that so far as I am concerned that deal stands, and I intend to show up on Monday and do exactly what I said I'd do.

Years of practice had not been lost on Myron either. He thought before he spoke. At last, after a weighty silence, he said: Mmmm. I see. In Charlotte's situation such feelings and expressions of hostility might be expected. I will deliver your message. Personally I am grateful for it.

That was done. Unless Myron or some other Riker made a move to stop him, he would go to Hudson. He had established the routine of being at the foundation's New York office from Tuesday through Thursday. There was really no other efficient way to get the work done, and the arrangement brought with it a huge benefit he had not enjoyed since retiring from W & K: the undivided attention of a first-rate secretary. Since he had planned to be in Paris, he was not expected in the New York office. All the same, out of a lawyer's long-ingrained habit of keeping in touch with his secretary, he called Shirley, told her about Charlotte's condition, and said that during the day he would be at the hospital, where there was no cell phone reception, but he would check his messages, and if there was anything urgent, he would call her back. She said she was sorry with such apparent sincerity that momentarily his mood lifted.

When Mary and he built the pool house in their garden, their intention had been to make sure that they wouldn't be disturbed by Charlotte's noisy young friends lodged there or by her even noisier parties. That had proved to be the case, but neither the soundproof walls nor the wall hangings installed as additional protection were equal to the force of young Albert's lungs. His heart beating hard, Schmidt caressed Sy, who had been waiting for him on the front steps, and, accompanied by the cat, he crossed the lawn. He was about to see the baby again, but this time, alas, through the prism of Charlotte's catastrophe. The door leading to the pool-house apartment was open. He knocked on the frame and went in. Carrie was in the kitchen nursing the baby and called for Schmidt to sit down. Isn't he something? she asked. He sure likes his milk, and he sure likes where it comes from! You don't need to turn your head, Schmidtie, don't be a dope, you've seen my tits often enough before! Indeed he had. She had taken off her top and her bra so that they were on full view. A longing came over Schmidt, not for her body, of the sort to make him harden, but instead a sweeter longing for the time they had together, a happy time that now irrationally seemed so simple and innocent.

What a good boy, he said, and what a good mommy! I think he's grown since the time I saw him at the hospital.

Of course, he's grown, dopey! He's eating his head off. Have you taken a good look at him?

Shifting the baby from one breast to the other she held him up, his face close to Schmidt's.

Who do you think he looks like?

Winston Churchill.

Try again!

George Washington.

Wrong! Think of a distinguished New York jurist!

Carrie, what are you saying?

Just what you think!

I think I'm not going to think. Sometimes too much think-ing leads to mischief.

Schmidtie, it's just you, me, and Albert Jr. who are here. We can talk.

I think I'll sit down, he said. I've just been on a long drive from upstate. Is there some whiskey or gin anywhere?

She pointed him to the liquor cabinet. Mistrustful of a bourbon he didn't know, he made a gin and tonic and looked around until he found some crackers.

Do you love Jason? he asked.

She smiled at him and whispered: He's my god.

That's what I hoped to hear. And, Carrie, do you remember the lunch at my club when you told me you were pregnant?

How could I forget? That was right after we went to your office and you gave me one million American dollars because I didn't let Mike Mansour lay me.

Exactly so. And do you remember how you told me that a kid is a kid, and Jason didn't care about this sort of stuff. You said something like: "Jason knows about you and me and it's no big deal. If the kid isn't his it's still mine, I'm the mother, and he's the stepfather."

Boy, you have a good memory!

I do! I thank the Lord for it every day! The last thing I want is to start losing my marbles. Let's go back to being serious. How has Jason been with young Albert so far?

He's crazy about him.

I hope that never changes. You know, of course, that there are ways of finding out with certainty who is who.

She nodded.

Tell me if you think I'm wrong. I believe we shouldn't try

to find out. If you love Jason, the best thing for you and Albert and Jason is for Albert to be Jason's son. You mustn't allow any talk that puts that in doubt. How do you feel about that?

I think you're right, and I think I'm right to love you.

Shush, said Schmidt. I love you too, but I love you now like a father.

Then take the baby, Pops, and let me get dressed.

It had been so long since he had held a baby that he was sure he had forgotten how, and then he remembered about putting a diaper over his shoulder and burping him. It was a long while before Carrie returned from the bathroom, but Albert didn't seem to mind.

It's time for his nap, she said.

The crib was in the bedroom. She rocked it and very quickly Albert was asleep.

He's a good baby, she said.

I can see that. Now look. A kid is a kid so far as I'm concerned as well. Just like Jason, I'm going to love him because he's yours, and I'm going to act accordingly. I'm thinking of such things as kindergarten, schools, summer camps, college, and so forth. But I want to be discreet about it, for his sake and yours. Understood?

She nodded.

When will Jason be home?

It's Friday, so the marina's busy. Not before eight. Bryan's coming with him to eat. You want to eat with us?

I'm bushed, Schmidt told her, so please feed me another time. But if I may I'll come over for a drink. Give me a ring or send Bryan to tell me when it's a good time.

The lapis lazuli butterfly lay in his bedroom wall safe. He knew he would never be able to give it to Charlotte. The dealer from whom he bought it was likely to take it back or allow him to exchange it. What would he give as a reason? The truth? He didn't think he could do that. That the lady for whom it had been intended didn't like it? The dealer would know he was lying. Alice. He could give it to Alice. That too felt wrong. A crazy symmetry required that the butterfly go to Carrie. He took it out of the safe to have it ready when he went over to the pool house later.

He figured it would take a good three hours to get to Hudson in Monday morning traffic. Full of foreboding he set out before nine. He had said he'd be at the hospital around twelve; he might as well be on time. The dreaded call from Renata came, as he had supposed it might, on Sunday evening. He resisted the urge to hang up.

Schmidtie, she told him, it's very constructive on your part to have offered to go to Hudson.

She paused here, and Schmidt wondered whether she would tell him not to bother coming, that she or Myron or Jon would be there or—why not?—the grandparents or the gay brother. Schmidt remembered something about his being a photographer. If so, his schedule should be flexible; he could undertake to look after his niece-in-law. But no, such was not Dr. Riker's intention. She might have been simply waiting for him to say something.

I hope you will be careful not to challenge Charlotte's view of your actions and your intentions. You may have found listening to her analysis of them painful, and it's possible that Charlotte in her fragile condition did not articulate her insights as precisely as she should have, but you must face the truth. The insights are valid. Your own emotional equilibrium will benefit from that kind of introspection—really a serious self-examination.

Why was she on the telephone, why wasn't she right there in the room with Schmidtie? His emotional equilibrium! Nothing would enhance it as much as punching Renata in the face very hard, hard enough to break her nose and knock out a few of those big white front teeth. He would go for the nearest equivalent that the circumstances allowed.

Very slowly, very distinctly, enunciating perfectly, he said: Fuck you, Renata! Fuck you!

Thereupon he hung up, not slamming down the receiver but putting it down with the utmost delicacy.

There was no question in his mind that this exchange with her mother-in-law had been reported to Charlotte. She looked at him stonily when he arrived, gave a monosyllabic answer to his question about what she would like for lunch, and went back to reading a book. He stole a look at the cover: Stephen King, *Insomnia*. He shrugged, ate his lunch in her silent company, took away the debris, and checked with the head nurse on Charlotte's progress. She's doing just beautifully, he was informed. The doctor would decide on when she will go home during his morning rounds. Could be tomorrow, could be Wednesday. And what time were the daily rounds? Eight o'clock, he was told. If he was there at eight-thirty, he should be able to catch him. Next he went to the business office and inquired about night nurses. Yes, such persons were available for hire. It would suffice to request one the morning of his daughter's release.

All that was good. But there was still the matter of what to do with himself for the time being. He returned to Charlotte's room and found she was sleeping. He had his own book with him, *The Way We Live Now*. It was guaranteed to absorb him.

Later that afternoon it was time for Charlotte's walk up and down the corridor. The nurse asked Schmidt whether he would like to accompany his daughter, but before he could answer Charlotte told the nurse, I'd rather go with you. When they returned, he left the room while the nurse was busy with Charlotte behind the closed door and came back in after the nurse had left.

I don't know why you're here, she said to him.

You said that you would like it, that you didn't want to be alone.

That was before, she interrupted.

Before what? Before you insulted me?

That's right, she replied, before I told you the truth you didn't want to hear.

I see, said Schmidt.

He said that not because any truth had suddenly been revealed to him but to give himself time to draw a deep breath.

If you would rather not have me around I will, if you like, get a private day nurse to be with you until you go home. I can come to see to your discharge from here and to take you home. I intended, by the way, unless you object, to get a night nurse to be with you at home, at least until the weekend, when I assume Jon will join you, or longer, if you prefer. By the way, you needn't worry about the expense. I'll pay for all of it.

You can pay for as many nurses as you like, she said with a sneer, it's still cheaper than doing the right thing by little Myron. Yolanda can check me out of this place. Perhaps you can just take care of any payment not covered by insurance. I really want you out of here.

Being spoken to in this manner was without precedent in his experience; he wasn't sure he had heard of any father having been addressed by a child with such bile. Goneril? Regan? What would be next?

I will see whether that can be done, he answered.

Fortunately, the business office hadn't closed. Yes, Charlotte Riker's housekeeper could take her home when she was discharged; yes, the day nurse and the night nurse could be arranged; he could pay by credit card for the private room and hospital extras; the nurses, however, had to be paid by check. With some difficulty, a blank check made payable to the nurses' agency was accepted. He walked heavily up the stairs to the third floor.

Good-bye, Charlotte, I have arranged it all and paid for it all, and now I'll yield to your wishes and leave. At one point, not so long ago—a little more than three months—you suggested a truce. It makes me unhappy to see it broken.

She made no answer.

There was one more thing that had to be done before the return drive to Bridgehampton. He called Myron Riker. This time he reached only a recording. The message he left was dispassionate and detailed. If there was any question or complication concerning the arrangements he had made, Myron could reach him on his cell phone while he was en route and later in Bridgehampton.

He got home too late to call Alice, and perhaps he would not have called her even if he had arrived much earlier. He felt soiled. Bryan was in the kitchen, feeding Sy. Schmidt explained that the situation had changed and that he wouldn't be going to New York. He'd take care of Sy himself. Really,

the humiliation had been extreme. He felt unable even to
cross the lawn to visit little Albert and his parents. He had a
drink and let its calming effect penetrate his body before dial-
ing Gil Blackman's number. Miracles never cease. Gil himself
answered, not Elaine or the Chinese cook. Another miracle:
Gil hadn't had dinner and had no dinner plans. He would like
nothing better than to have dinner with Schmidt at O'Henry's.

To what do I owe my luck? Schmidt asked after they'd sat
down at table. Where is Elaine?

In San Francisco with the Mummy. The Mummy isn't feeling well, and Elaine is suddenly worried about the Mummy's
gold being bestowed on a cat and dog hospital rather than her.
Hence the paroxysm of filial attentiveness.

I see. How wise she is! The temptation to disinherit can be
powerful.

You're preaching to the converted, Schmidtie. Napoléon's
worst crime was to write into his code children's rights of
inheritance.

And why are you here? Is *The Scarlet Letter* now a miniseries?

Unfortunately, yes. Now I've got to figure out how to get
DT moved to New York. I'm working on it.

Gil, said Schmidt, I've gotten you here on false pretenses. I
would have liked to have a jolly dinner, and perhaps in the end
we will have one, but first I must tell you about Charlotte. He
recounted the disastrous failure of the emergency room doctor to stop the bleeding, the D & C that hadn't worked, the
hysterectomy.

Physical gestures of affection between Mr. Blackman and
Schmidt were rare. This time, however, he got up and gave
Schmidt a hug.

Taking his seat again, he said, you know, these days it's very common that couples for one reason or another are unable to have children. They adjust. Charlotte and Jon are young. Money isn't a problem. Probably they'll adopt.

I'm sure you're right, answered Schmidt. Thank you! But that isn't all. His resolve didn't hold; once again, he couldn't help himself. He told Gil about the scenes Charlotte had made and the slurs and insults, omitting only the bits related to little Albert. The implications for the baby, and for Carrie and her marriage, were too grave. He couldn't take the risk. But he recounted the horrid conversations with Jon Riker and his mother. They're monsters, he said, dangerous evil monsters.

Mr. Blackman remained silent for a long time. Finally, having emptied his wineglass and motioned for the waitress to bring another bottle, he shook his head and said, Yes, they are manipulative monsters, and Charlotte is weaker than I would have imagined. I think that's how you had better think of her: weak and easily influenced. If she weren't under their thumb, she would realize that no one is more generous with money than you. She'd also see that her husband has a double agenda: he wants to get your money or very strong assurances that it will be coming his way eventually, but that's not enough. He also needs to force you to give it; the money alone isn't enough: he wants to humiliate you. Of course, you've played into their hands, my poor dear friend, by letting the Rikers see that you're a closet anti-Semite.

How can you Gil! Schmidt cried out.

I can because it's true.

Hearing those words rocked Schmidt. A clear echo of Charlotte's rebuke. Were they all in league?

Have you forgotten, Mr. Blackman continued, how awful

you felt about having Jon the Jew become your son-in-law? If you think it didn't show, you're wrong. Jon wouldn't have missed the signals. Or the song and dance about your going to a Thanksgiving meal at the parents' house? I can assure you they haven't forgotten. And those are only the two examples I remember. There must have been others. A kind of leitmotif.

I had my reasons to be unhappy about having Jon first live with my daughter and then marry her that had nothing to do with his being Jewish. Among them was my hope that she would find someone quite simply better, more gentle, and with broader interests. How silly that seems today! Unfortunately, subsequent events have shown that I was right about him. He has behaved disgracefully. His relentless attempts to antagonize and humiliate me are the least of it. You yourself just put your finger on that charming proclivity of his!

That's all true. But you gave them a little opening through which they have driven one truck after another! Forget—no, don't forget—what I've told you about anti-Semitism. Just don't let yourself get tripped up by it again. I know you're harmless, and your heart is in the right place, but I've known you practically all my life, and you're like a brother to me. But it suits those people to cast you as a bigot. Don't give them more ammunition, and leave them alone. All the Rikers, Charlotte included. Life has countless surprises in store for each of us, some bad or worse, and some good. One of them could work a change in your favor. Charlotte may yet come back and start acting more or less like a daughter.

You're right, said Schmidt. Anyway, I don't see what else I can do.

Apropos of nothing, said Mr. Blackman, or possibly apropos of DT, I am thinking of doing something—a feature film—based on Joe Canning's new book, *The Serpent*. Have you read it?

Schmidt shook his head.

I thought you wouldn't have. So I brought a copy for you. Read it if you have a chance.

The next morning Schmidt telephoned Alice, at the office. The need to speak with her was almost physical; it prevented him from concentrating on the simplest routine tasks. She was at her desk, the operator told him. A moment later, she was on the line.

Alice, he said, this sad business at the hospital has been stabilized. Charlotte will be discharged tomorrow. She's going home. I want and need to see you. I can be in Paris the day after tomorrow. I can stay the whole weekend, until Monday morning. We can drive to some nice place in the country if you'd like to get away from Paris. Or if you'd rather we could meet somewhere else—in London or Madrid. I have to be in the office most of next week. So if this weekend doesn't suit you I could come the weekend after, the weekend of the twenty-third. Please say yes to one or the other or better yet to both!

There was a silence. He supposed that she was looking at her pocket calendar. When she spoke, she said that there were so many complications, too many to enumerate, some involving her father and some connected with the office. Could she call him back? At one o'clock his time? Or later, for instance at six in the evening? She was going out to dinner, but she'd go home first to change.

At one please, said Schmidt. I am hungry and thirsty for you.

It was half past one when she called. Something had come

up. She was sorry, neither the coming weekend nor the weekend after was possible. Again she cited the complications, all sorts of complications, too boring to discuss. But in the offing there was planned a business trip to the United States that might or might not come off.

Really! Schmidt exclaimed, then come to see me!

Schmidtie, I adore you, she said. Try to remember how hard Mary had to work at her job, and she had such a track record, so much clout! I have to prove myself at every step. If the trip does take place, it will be all business. I can't imagine being able to get away, but if it turns out that I can, I will. You will be there anyway, won't you?

This is awful, thought Schmidt. If I were still at college, and she some Radcliffe girl I was pursuing, I would have to say that she's giving me the runaround. But we're grown-ups! We have made love. She shrieked when she came, with such abandon, her face wild and joyful. How can this be?

Alice, he told her, every day I am more convinced that what I feel for you is love. Not puppy love, but a man's love, a grown man's love: the real thing. I've been going through a very tough time. I need to be in your arms. Please find some days—what am I saying, one day!—when you can see me, and I will meet you wherever you like.

Schmidtie, I adore you, she repeated. It's not so simple. Let's talk, but not now. You'll be around, won't you? All I can do now is send you kisses, bushels and bushels.

There was some Gruyère in the refrigerator, as well as a baguette left over from the past weekend. He ate them voraciously, bread in one hand, cheese in the other. Still hungry, he found a chunk of Hungarian salami and ate that too, not bothering to peel the skin. Making coffee was a bother. He washed his face and hands, brushed his teeth, and went outside. All was quiet in the pool house, but Carrie's little convertible was in the driveway. She was almost certainly at home.

May I come in? he cried softly so as not to wake the baby.

Just as softly, she answered, Yes.

She was at the kitchen table, the *New York Times* spread out before her.

Hi, he said. How's young Albert?

Sleeping, she whispered. It's about time! He drank me dry.

Smart kid, Schmidt whispered back. It's such a gorgeous afternoon. Wouldn't you like to take a dip? Afterward you can run your errands. I'll stay here and babysit my namesake.

XV

IT WAS TEENAGE BEHAVIOR, really, but the next morning he decided that he wouldn't call Alice. She had said, Let's talk, but not now; she had his telephone number; she knew he had an answering machine and listened to messages; and anyway he would be home most of the day. Let her call. He too could play hard to get. He didn't ask himself how long the game was to go on, but the probable answer, as long as he could hold out, meant this was likely to be a short match. Soon after breakfast he did receive a call from Paris, but it was Mr. Mansour, in an excellent mood. Have lunch with me, he said. Just the two of us. Is Friday good? I'm getting in the evening before. And come to dinner on Sunday night. I'm inviting the beautiful Caroline Canning, her funny husband, and the Blackmans. What do you think? I think it's a good program.

What was Schmidt to say? As Alice had put it, he'd be around. And so he acquiesced.

The next call was from Myron Riker.

Schmidtie, he said, I thought you'd like to know that Charlotte is at home. I appreciated your smoothing the way for Yolanda to handle the discharge process, but in the end I canceled my patients and drove up there. I also appreciate more than I can say the arrangements with the nurses. Charlotte says that both of them, the day nurse and the night nurse, are very competent and very nice. Of course I am most grateful for your overwhelming generosity, paying those thousands and thousands of dollars. Round-the-clock care is so very expensive!

Don't mention it, replied Schmidt. I'm glad that all is well.

Myron made an *umm* sound, and continued: Actually I don't think that all is well. From what I hear, Charlotte has behaved very badly. I don't know how to speak about it. But I want you to know that in my opinion, for what it's worth, you have behaved like a good father and a gentleman. I can imagine how you must feel, and I want you to know I'm sorry.

It's my turn to thank you, said Schmidt. It's the first kind word from—what shall I call it?—your side. Poor Charlotte isn't herself. I guess anything can be forgiven her. But look, I'm going to be very frank. I don't believe Charlotte would say the things she says if Renata didn't put her up to it. That's something I don't understand. What is your opinion? Why does she do it? What do you think is going on?

Another *umm* sound. Then speaking very slowly, Myron said, Renata has been through a very rough time too, for reasons that pertain to her and reasons that pertain to Jon. It sometimes happens even to good and experienced analysts like her that they confuse their private lives with their profession. They step out of their role. They find themselves suggesting certain constructs to impressionable people. I think that's what happened here.

You're not telling me that Renata is treating Charlotte?

Of course not. But she's become so involved with her that

there is almost the same transference and the same impressionability on Charlotte's part.

And what should be done?

I hope that Jon will find his footing. That would help. Charlotte will soon feel better physically. That will help too. I am going to try to get Renata to put more distance between herself and Charlotte and Jon and their marriage. Let's talk again, but first let's allow some time to pass.

Lunch was served on the deck, the table set under two Roman umbrellas. The ocean was flat, the beach empty, the sun at its zenith, and Mr. Mansour resplendent in a navy-blue silk shirt and yellow silk trousers. The shirtsleeves were rolled up, for comfort and perhaps also to show off the great financier's powerful forearms and the wafer-thin Piaget watch on his left wrist. The right wrist was encircled by a copper band. Why did all rich people—at least the ones Schmidt knew—believe in the magic power of those bracelets? He was barefoot. The worry beads were out, doing a brisk business.

No shoes, he said, noticing Schmidt's downward glance. It's just the two of us. The feel of teak is good for your feet. Go ahead and take off those ridiculous L.L. Bean things.

Schmidt obliged. It was exactly what he had wanted but hadn't dared to do.

That's better, Mr. Mansour continued. If you give me your shoe size, I'll get you some better moccasins; you know, suitable for your age. You've got average feet. The man I have in Paris will build them for you.

I like these shoes, Schmidt protested.

That's because you don't know any better! You should have been with me in Paris. Sorry, of course I know you had to get back. You haven't told me: is your daughter out of the hospital?

Schmidt nodded.

You should go to see her on Sunday. Emil—that was the name of the security man who had driven Schmidt from Albany to Hudson and then back to Bridgehampton—will take you out there and bring you back. No use spending the night over there; you'd wear her out.

Thank you, Mike! said Schmidt. It's what I would like to do, but this weekend is too soon.

He had decided not to tell Mr. Mansour about any aspect of the quarrel with Charlotte and Jon. Since it touched in part on money, Mike would consider it a problem he was uniquely qualified to solve. He would offer to step in to mediate, a prospect even more horrifying for Schmidt than the dismal current situation.

This weekend I'll stay here, he continued, and I look forward to your dinner. You've been so thoughtful and kind about everything that I'm overwhelmed by gratitude.

Pas de problème, pas de problème.

I've got one more thing to say. You've told me that you're my friend. Now I really know it's true. And I am yours.

Clickety-clack, clickety-clack. Mr. Mansour smiled. You're getting smarter all the time. There's no telling how it will end! What was I saying? You should've been in Paris. You didn't know it, but Caroline and Joe Canning were there as well. I didn't take them with us on the plane, but I brought them back. Another thing you didn't know: I got Canning into a writers' retreat at Royaumont. Do you know about Royaumont? It's a medieval abbey north of Paris that used to belong to a rich family called Gouin. Rich, rich, let's say they thought they were rich. They fixed it up and gave it to a foundation. *Clickety-clack clickety-clack.* I'm a member of a committee of leading businessmen that runs business programs there. As you can imagine, I'm influential. The foundation also has important cultural programs, and that's where Canning comes in. He jumped at the chance to participate with five or six other well-known writers. Very prestigious! Ha! Guess why I arranged it!

Because you're a good guy.

Wrong. Because you can't bring your wife or your husband! For this retreat only the participants are allowed to stay at the abbey! No husbands and no wives! So I told the Cannings they could have a weekend in Paris, at no expense, organized by me, as my treat. While Joe is at his retreat, I take care of Caroline. After the retreat is over, I bring them both back to New York with me. *Pas de problème.* It all worked out! Joe had his seminar, and I had Caroline.

You're a devil, said Schmidt. You should be ashamed of yourself. They're a good married couple.

Who says they aren't? But does Caroline have a life with that schmuck? I tell you she doesn't. She likes the books he writes. All right. He likes the books she writes. All right. He gives it to her maybe once a month for old times' sake. That's all right too. She likes it—somewhat. What choice does she have, who can she compare him with? No choice and no comparison. Here is where I come in: I show her a really good time—the best restaurants, the best hotel suite—and then we do it like she's never had it before. No comparison! A woman I've laid never forgets it, never gets it out of her mind!

That was not Gil Blackman's theory, as Schmidt remembered; Gil was convinced Mike was a one-night-stand artist and even on that schedule was hardly able to get it up.

What's your secret, Casanova? asked Schmidt.

Size. And I like doing it. *Pas de problème*. Oh, and I'm rich. Ha! Ha! Ha!

Wonderful formula, said Schmidt. No wonder I haven't had your successes. And what happens later? I mean, if she can't get you out of her mind?

Nothing. She's smart. If she wants a refresher course, a couple of hours here, a couple of hours there, that can be arranged. Where's the harm, I ask you? I haven't taken anything from that silly schmuck. She's still with him, just as beautiful, just as intelligent. What more can he ask? If she's learned a new trick or two, maybe she'll show him. He comes out ahead. I'll tell you something else. She's clean! And she smells good!

You're atrocious, said Schmidt.

Sure—who's disagreeing with you?

Dessert had been served. Key lime pie. Mr. Mansour helped himself to two pieces right away and asked for a third. It's the best, he announced. Let's talk about you. What about this Riker guy? Have you seen him? Do you want me to send him some work? I'm looking at buying a public company out of Chapter Eleven. It could be right up his alley.

Mike, Schmidt replied, you're atrocious but also very kind. Sure, I'd like to send him some work. He'll do a first-rate job. But please do it so that there is no mention of me, our friendship, and so forth. You know what I mean. The way things have shaped up, I need to be out of the picture.

Pas de problème. I'll tell you how it goes.

What is it about me, Schmidt asked himself, as he was
getting dressed to go to dinner at Mr. Mansour's, that makes
me such a square? He liked Caroline and disliked Canning.
Why should he begrudge her a good time? Why should it get
his dander up that Mike has slept with her? Envy? He had
never thought of Caroline that way. A stupid sort of conform-
ism, wanting people to behave correctly? Painful though it
was to admit, he thought the more likely answer was envy.
Not envy of this particular exploit of Mike's, but envy of
people who are lighthearted, who can break rules without suffering his kind of sour remorse. One thing was certain: when
they met at dinner, he would see Caroline and Joe, and indeed
Mr. Mansour, through new lenses, ones ground to the great
financier's prescription. This dazzlingly serious and learned
woman had succumbed to Mike's blandishments, had been
hypnotized by his billionaire tricks, and had experienced the
wonders of size! Good heavens, if that was possible, then the
sky was the limit for conjugal misbehavior! Did she also have
sex with Joe—Mike had said she did, but how would he know?
Schmidtie, you dodo, replied an inner voice, he knows because
he asked her, and she told him during an interlude between
one orgasm and another. And if Joe and she do sleep together,
once a month or once a week, for old times' sake, as the Egyptian fiend had reported, does she smile from ear to ear through
the ordeal thinking of the Egyptian and his outsize tool? He
had to give Mike credit: without question, he could have—
perhaps he had!—a lifetime supply of hot and cold running
starlets and models eager for the cornucopia of good things he
could offer. But no, he had gone for a woman in her fifties, only
a few years younger than he; he had gone for class, Caroline's

intellect and charm as well as her fine body and lovely face. Or was this instead Mr. Mansour's kinky side: his need to see whether he could cuckold the celebrated novelist and seduce the noted biographer, a desire for a richer-than-usual taste, such as connoisseurs seek in Auslese wines or in well-hung grouse? And Joe! For all his touted penetration of the secrets of the heart, he had left Caroline in Mansour's care just so he could shoot the breeze with a roomful of French intellectuals. He had earned his horns.

After the main course had been cleared, Mr. Mansour proposed a toast to the success of the new project: Gil had moved beyond thinking about a film based on Joe's new novel to a full commitment. He was going to make the film! Right, Gil?

Gil nodded. Subject to the usual outs. I look forward to it, if it can be done.

If I back a project, there is no way it can't be done, announced Mr. Mansour, wagging the right index at Mr. Blackman. Or am I wrong?

Gil smiled and said nothing.

Canning, who until then had uttered only his usual mono-syllables, suddenly piped up: Speak for yourselves! I haven't moved beyond thinking. I wouldn't know how.

Touché! Mr. Mansour laughed. Of course, I'll be deeply involved, I've already shared insights with Gil, and I'm going to share them with you, Joe. I see the screenplay as a collabo-ration between a great novelist and a great filmmaker—with my input. I don't think I exaggerate when I say that they will be essential. You have *Chocolate Kisses* and its huge success as an example. It's Gil's and my joint effort.

That was one of Mr. Mansour's claims that Gil rejected vehemently, though not in his presence.

The worry beads had been inactive. Now they went *clickety-clack* at their accustomed speed.

Joe and Gil, Mr. Mansour continued, listen up slowly. One issue we have to visit is how we lighten the mood of Joe's book. You know, so that it will play in Peoria! The question is, Joe, the question is, why are people in your books so disagreeable?

Could it be because that's how people are, Canning replied, or because that's how I see them? Perhaps both.

Touché again, conceded Mr. Mansour.

Caroline, what do you think?

That Joe is the best!

Thank you, *chère amie*! Caroline and I got to be great friends in Paris, but that doesn't mean she has to agree with me every time. I'll call the next witness. Schmidtie, what do you think?

Whatever it was that ailed Mr. Canning must have been contagious. Schmidt answered: Think about what?

The book, cried Elaine, the book, *The Serpent*!

I found it gripping, said Schmidt. Gil gave it to me, and I read it straight through.

That's no kind of testimony, Elaine broke in. I'm an investor in this film, and I'm with Mike! Something has got to be done to the plot! Listen slowly, like Mike said: A widowed father—a distinguished lawyer like you, Schmidtie, but living in North Dakota—tells his son who has just graduated from law school that he can live rent free with his great-aunt in her brownstone in Brooklyn while he is clerking for a judge in New York. What Joe could possibly know about North Dakota is another question. Who even cares about North Dakota anyway? I'd move the father to the Hamptons. Anyway, the kid agrees; the great-aunt is thrilled. He lives with her for five years, until she dies. The father is the executor of her estate. Practically everything is to go to the American Red Cross. But the father does the executor thing and discovers there is no money, practically nothing left at all. His son had been robbing the old woman blind ever since he moved in. It gets worse. He had terrorized her! I think she was on to him but didn't dare to protest or seek help. I got lost in the legal stuff about whether the father was absolutely required to turn the kid in to the police. I don't know if it matters. The point is that the father makes it clear to the kid that he has figured it all out, and no sooner has he done so than he realizes his own son will try to kill him. Do I have it right so far, Joe?

Silence.

All right, it's your book, but it's going to be our movie, continued Elaine, and I have to tell you the plot made my flesh crawl. Besides, how can you have a major film without some major romantic interest?

But, Elaine, Schmidt interrupted, there is a major romantic interest, though maybe not a role for Julia Roberts. The romantic interest is Vincent the anthropologist, the expert on cannibals!

Well, well, said Canning, we've quite a team here. Elaine has got the plot right, and Schmidt has figured out the romantic interest. What do we do now, Mike and Gil? Do we ask them to rewrite my novel, Mike, or are you going to do it yourself?

Back at home after Mr. Mansour's dinner, Schmidt wondered why Canning bothered to write those novels. It couldn't be for money: Schmidt had a pretty good idea that a midlist novelist's royalties, even combined with what Caroline earned, couldn't pay for the way they lived. They lived off his insurance company pension and savings. It must be that he wrote in order to people a small corner of the earth with characters as repulsive as himself. Then a more interesting question entered Schmidt's mind: Could Mr. Mansour have designs on Elaine too, and, if he got Gil out of the way, if he sent him to L.A. or North Dakota, would she be his for the asking? *Pas de problème!* Look at Caroline! There she was, cool as a cucumber, on best terms with the Egyptian fiend and all the while listening indulgently to her schmuck of a husband.

Under the influence of these thoughts, which had awakened his sexual hunger, Schmidt found his resolve had weakened. It no longer seemed possible to wait placidly for Alice to call. He had to take action. It took the form of a short fax he sent to her home: *June seems difficult for you, but July is almost upon us. Can we see each other then? Weekdays, weekends, anytime at all and anyplace will do.* What astonishment and joy the next morning when he found on the fax machine in his kitchen Alice's reply: *Darling Schmidtie, July 14, Bastille Day, is on a Friday. Take me away from the frenzied French! Let's meet in London on the thirteenth and remain through the following Monday. I'll bring a little black dress, in case you decide to take me to the theater. Yours in every way, Alice.* Facsimile suddenly became his medium of choice. He wrote back: *I'm already in seventh heaven. Rendezvous on the thirteenth at the Connaught.*

Why was he so sure of finding an accommodation in that sought-after hotel? He had come to have faith in Mr. Mansour's secretary. There would be room at the inn for Alice and him even if all the world came to London to be taxed.

XVI

THREE AND A HALF WEEKS until the rendez-
vous in London! Schmidt had never been so lonely, so starved
for affection, not even in the weeks following Mary's death.
Then he had been numbed by the long vigil at her sickbed and
stupidly busy with the myriad tasks required for the settle-
ment of even a straightforward estate like hers. Trivia took
time, time that would otherwise have been spent wallowing
in booze and despair. Besides, Charlotte and Jon were at the
house every weekend. Together with Charlotte, Schmidt had
slogged through the most painful task of all: clearing out
Mary's closets. Except for the few things that either Charlotte
wanted or could be given to the brigade of Polish ladies who
cleaned the house, all her poor forlorn clothes—dresses, coats,
shoes, the inventory of intimate possessions went on and on—
were carted off to the East Hampton thrift shop. They burned
Mary's underpants, having been told by the thrift shop that
it wouldn't take them. Then there was Mary's Toyota. First
Charlotte wanted it, and then she didn't. After what seemed
like days of waiting at the Motor Vehicle Department office
in Riverhead, Schmidt managed to transfer it into his own
name. Then he put it in the garage, never to be used. The real

solitude began when all those tasks had been accomplished, when Charlotte returned to her weekend routine of running on the beach and spending what remained of the day with Jon, behind closed doors. They were never at home for meals other than breakfast. Otherwise, they ate out, alone or with friends from the city. Invitations to join them were rare and ungracious. Then came the first quarrels: over the boorish manner in which Riker announced to Schmidt their engagement, Schmidt's failure to accept the Riker parents' invitation to Thanksgiving with sufficient alacrity, Charlotte's rejection of the gift he proposed to make to her of his life estate in the house, and, worst of all, her refusal to wear Mary's bridal dress or to have her wedding reception at the house in Bridgehampton. Quarrels begat quarrels: he could expect from Charlotte heartache; never company or solace.

Meanwhile it was becoming clearer than ever to Schmidt that there was no place for him in the world in which Mary and he had lived so pleasantly during their weekends and vacations. It was a world of powerful editors and literary agents and writers successful enough to own or rent a house in the Hamptons. Large parties, given in honor of publication of books and visits by authors deserving to be so fêted, alternated with intimate dinners nicely calibrated to ensure that peers of the realm dined in the company of peers. Of that realm, Mary had been a natural denizen, a duchess by virtue of her charm, talent, and power. Schmidt had been tolerated as her consort. With her gone, invitations to the little dinners had stopped abruptly. Those to lawn parties, at which marginal agents, junior editors, and midlist writers hoped to rub elbows with their betters, turned into a slow trickle, and then they too stopped. Schmidt knew that in part he was to blame.

His prickliness, his professed dislike of small talk, his inability to move graciously from one group of guests to another, were fatal flaws that were not counterbalanced by wealth or success in the law sufficiently well publicized to impress even laymen. He was a retired lawyer and nothing more, a husk. A former partner, to be sure, in a great firm whose name these sophisticated agents, editors, and writers recognized as a center of power, but what kind of a lawyer had he been? Private financings! No hostile takeovers or defenses against the same to his credit? Absent from great First Amendment battles? Nothing could be more boring. He had thought that Lew Brenner, for instance, thrown into this pitiless milieu, would do just fine. He could talk about Arab sheikhs, Russian oligarchs, and barbaric Texans, deals in which billions of dollars and the policies of sovereign states were balanced on the edge of a knife. What could Schmidt talk about? The newest fashions in leveraged leases, the insurance company lawyers he had known, the vast ethical problems raised when he had been called on to opine whether a sale was a true sale or a disguised loan? He reeked of ennui and knew it. On top of that, he would accept invitations, then fail to show or show without having accepted, both venal sins when committed by a peer of the realm, mortal in his already marginal case.

The apparition of Carrie in his life had moved him into another sphere of existence, the sphere of bliss. Bliss that he had known would vanish like a mirage, even when awkwardly, clumsily he ventured to propose marriage, showed himself ready to be nothing more than a doormat under her feet, or perhaps a stepping-stone to some subsequent more appropriate marriage and higher station. Bliss came to an end as it must, leaving in its wake the mystery of little Albert.

And, inevitably, his short-lived happiness had been added to the monstrous inventory of Charlotte's resentments. There was no doubt: the ever-deeper—he was beginning to fear permanent—estrangement from his daughter was his life's principal liability. On the asset side of his balance sheet he put seeing Carrie and little Albert daily and babysitting with Albert whenever he wasn't in Jason's and Bryan's way, but that was a rapidly depreciating asset. They would be leaving his pool house in the early fall. Without a word having been spoken, he had reached an understanding with Carrie. Its gist: keep it low-key. Let Jason stop by Schmidt's kitchen to talk about how the marina was doing—better than Jason had expected—and progress in refurbishing the house, into which all too soon the young family would be moving. But Schmidt needn't reciprocate and make his way to the pool-house kitchen to drink a Coors with Jason. The implications of that understanding for the future saddened Schmidt. But the future was still only around the corner. He need not try to deal with it now. And apart from that? He could claim Gil and Elaine Blackman's friendship and, of course, Mike Mansour's. How often could he let it be known to the Blackmans that he was available for a meal? And were there limits even to Mr. Mansour's patience and hospitality? Of late it seemed to Schmidt that there were none. He marveled at his good fortune.

The major new asset on his balance sheet was the work he was doing for the foundation in New York, on Tuesdays, Wednesdays, and Thursdays. He thought that in the fall he would add Monday afternoon, although with Shirley's help he was already carrying a full week's workload. You've got the moxie of a young W & K partner, Mike Mansour had told him, not a broken-down retiree. Had he been Sy, Schmidt would have purred to hear this compliment. He had not forgotten Carrie's report of what Mr. Mansour had said after Schmidt had accepted the foundation job: Schmidtie can do it, but maybe he's gotten used to not working. He might quit or something. That piece of gossip had come to her, of course, from Jason and had made Schmidt wonder whether he had not set himself up for yet another failure by taking the job Mike had offered apparently in spite of those doubts. While he was at his foundation office, talking on the phone to the heads of the Life Centers and translating their eccentric English into his own, attending to correspondence, even being grilled by Mike's vizier Holbein, he would naturally forget his loneliness. For lunch, he would have a sandwich in the foundation's cafeteria or at his desk or, more often, walk over to the club and sit at the members' table. The chitchat there almost invariably concerned things and people he knew nothing about. He would have liked, he told himself, to get to know the swarm of young people employed by Mansour Industries in the building where the foundation had its office, but he had concluded it was a lost cause. When in contact with them, for instance standing in line for his sandwich or venturing to share their table in the cafeteria, he couldn't help being conscious of their lack of interest in him, and the unspoken question: Who is this relic? It was equally true that, having looked at them closely, he was just as glad to leave things as they were. To keep his distance. These traders and accountants, Mike Mansour's bean counters—managers and engineers employed by companies in the Mansour Industries group were tucked away in the provinces of the empire and seldom made an appearance at headquarters—were young men (their female colleagues apparently ate at their desks) uniformly coatless, ballpoint pens protruding from the pockets of their white shirts, excessively wide neckties fastened at midpoint to those shirts by gold pins, their cell phones holstered at the belt and sometimes connected to the ear by a variety of gizmos, with loud voices and accents of neither Syosset nor Oyster Bay but boroughs and towns less frequented by Schmidt. Aha! triumphed Schmidt's conscience. Why don't you come out and say it, say they're Jews! Immediately Schmidt rose for the defense: Objection! Schmidtie is no anti-Semite. They're unattractive wonks, there is no reason that Schmidtie should like them! And so perhaps they were, but Schmidt doubted whether, with Mr. Blackman sitting in judgment, the accused would be acquitted or let off with a warning.

City evenings were lonely as well. The only W & K partner with whom he was still on easy terms was Lew Brenner, to whom paradoxically he had not been close before. The guests Mary and he had entertained at home in the city—it seemed to him they had been legion—were not much use either. For they too had been Mary's professional friends. The others, college and law school classmates, executives of client companies, he felt no urge to call them, to listen to surprised greetings, to announce, Hey, it's me, Schmidtie, I'm back, back from the dead! Instead, he went to the movies across the street from Lincoln Center or to the ballet and afterward ate a hamburger at O'Neal's. A production of *Lohengrin* closed the season at the opera. He had felt lucky to have caught it and, in obeisance to his and Mary's former habits, had dinner during the intermission at the opera's fancy restaurant.

He was therefore astonished and initially pleased, too pleased for his taste, when, upon returning to Bridgehampton late one Thursday evening, he saw in the neatly sorted and stacked mail on the kitchen table an invitation to the Fourth of July party to be given on July 3, the fourth itself being a Tuesday, and so logically the evening when the multitudes would be rushing back to the city. Bill Gibson, a literary superagent famous for wresting seven-figure advances from publishers in the U.S., and smaller but still eye-popping ones in Europe, for books that didn't always earn them out, was the host. Schmidt remembered that he had once had a sort of personal connection with Gibson. In those days when they were still likely to meet regularly at literary gatherings, the agent, instead of looking through him or avoiding his eye, would spontaneously engage him in conversation. The reason? High finance and financial combinations interested Gibson; he was under the impression that Schmidt was the designer of devilishly complex schemes, not merely an artisan skilled in giving them contractual expression, which was closer to the truth. But at least two years had passed since he had seen Gibson, certainly since they had talked, and he couldn't remember having been invited to his Fourth of July party since the summer after Mary died. This invitation had obviously been sent by mistake; a secretary had used an old list, compiled before Schmidt had been dropped. An envelope addressed to *Mr. and Mrs.* would be the dead giveaway. He fished it out of the wastebasket and was puzzled to find it addressed to him alone. Too bad, he would send his regrets. That was what he told Mr. Blackman the next day when they met for lunch at O'Henry's, putting what he thought was a humorous spin on it: the automatism of secretaries in this day of computer-generated lists and so forth.

You're nuts, replied Mr. Blackman, a case of incipient paranoia. Nowadays it can be treated with low doses of medication. I saw Bill the other day, and he told me spontaneously and specifically that he hopes you will come! He realizes you haven't been in touch and wants to catch up. Elaine and I are going. Do you want us to take you?

That suggestion was unprecedented in the long history of their friendship, a sign of solicitude that made Schmidt wonder whether Gil really thought he wasn't well. But no, that was nonsense. He accepted the offer, managing to sound almost as grateful as he really was.

Good, said Gil. You're on our way to his place. We'll pick you up. Let's say at six.

It was pleasant to arrive at the party with Gil and Elaine. If the number or the average price of the cars parked along the road on both sides of the stone gateposts flanking the driveway, or the black-clad security guards, with wires sticking out of their ears, who checked names of arrivals against a list, or the presence of not one but three village cops directing traffic was a guide, Mr. Gibson's fête could already be pronounced, at least for the literati of the Hamptons, the social climax of the long holiday weekend. Schmidt knew from experience that, had he come alone, he would have trudged, a solitary figure, along the road from his car to the gate and up the long driveway to the house, too shy and too ill at ease to tag along with any of the couples ahead of or behind him, even those he knew and greeted. What was he to say to them? Through too long a silence he had lost the power of speech. But the Blackmans' protection had worked a magic change. It had transformed a sad figure, easily mistaken for an intruder, for a minor houseguest of one of Bill Gibson's friends, a transient doomed to disappear the next day and never to be seen again, into someone possibly worth meeting or at least greeting with more than a semblance of warmth.

Postadolescent boys and girls in black trousers, white shirts, and black bow ties were circulating with trays of white wine, red wine, and sparkling water; canapés of foie gras or broiled tuna; miniature spring rolls; tiny frankfurters; and assortments of crudités. Elaine took a glass of white wine, and Gil expertly parked her with a group that had formed around a perorating novelist.

Let's go to the bar and get a grown-up drink, he said to Schmidt. I have something to tell you, he added when he judged the distance from Elaine to be sufficient. I've got a studio for DT on East Sixty-Sixth Street, just a hop, skip, and jump from my office. Of course I'm giving her a job too. That's why I'm going ahead with Canning's book, even though he's an asshole and Mike will be on my back to make the movie more salable. I'm all for that, of course, especially as I am thinking I might put some of my own money in it. Make that Elaine's money. God knows she's loaded!

Here's an idea, said Schmidt. Perhaps it's crazy, and perhaps Canning would tear your head off if you proposed it. How about a sex change? Why not make Vincent the cannibal anthropologist into a girl, and get Julia Roberts to play her? Canning isn't gay. I think he made Vincent a queer only to be chic. It has no bearing on the story.

They had reached the bar and ordered double bourbons on the rocks.

Schmidtie, you rascal, that is inspired! the great filmmaker replied very slowly. Why didn't I think of it? I spend too much time thinking about DT. I don't believe Mike is here—by the

way we should introduce him to Gibson. If he comes onboard
with it, which I'm sure he will, I'll give Canning a call and say
this is how it's going to be. You know what? I think he'll say
yes if I sweeten ever so slightly the price I'm paying for the
rights. It's going to be a whole new ballgame. I think you've
just improved our gross by fifty to eighty million in the U.S.
alone. *Cin cin!* To *The Serpent*! I'll list you in the credits as literary adviser to the producer. Wait till Elaine hears this!

Apropos of what Elaine hears, Schmidt said, don't you
think you should be more careful about DT? I don't think
you've ever before set up a mistress in an apartment. It sounds
to me like two households, a double life. You didn't do that
even with Katerina. You're playing with fire.

I am, old friend, but I don't know how to stop. All she wants
to do when we're together is fuck, and she fucks like a whirling
dervish. She's taken it to a new level. I can't let go.

Schmidt patted him on the back. Be careful.

I'm trying, replied Mr. Blackman, believe me. Let's find
Elaine and rescue her.

With that they turned to find themselves face-to-face with
Alice and Popov. Her arm was under his left arm; he held her
hand; her breasts pressed against him.

Popov, you old devil, what are you doing here? roared Mr.
Blackman. You've crossed the ocean, found your way to Water
Mill, and haven't bothered to announce your presence! Shame
on you!

Schmidt heard himself say, in a funny neutral voice, Hello,
Alice, hello Serge!

I'm doing the same thing as you, bellowed back Popov,
drinking Tovarich Gibson's booze and celebrating Indepen-
dence Eve. Had I known I'd be anywhere near Wainscott, I

would have taken the liberty of disturbing the great cineaste to bring greetings from Tovarich Godard. But this young lady and I—Alice Verplanck, may I present to you the famous Gil Blackman—we are staying with Jeremy at his *Schloss* on the North Fork, and nothing had led us to believe that we would twice cross the waters of Peconic Bay, glittering like a bejeweled diadem in the midsummer calm, to make landfall at Tovarich Gibson's fête champêtre. As you can imagine, Jeremy, rich in oxen and milk-white asses, is Comrade Gibson's star author! Ours as well.

You're forgiven, but just barely, said Mr. Blackman.

A change in the tone of Gil's voice told Schmidt that he had grasped the enormity of the encounter.

Well, enjoy the *fête champêtre*, he added, while we look for my beautiful Elaine. Come on, Schmidtie. Time and tide, you know how that goes.

One second, said Schmidt. Alice, may I have a word with you?

She nodded and followed him a few steps away.

I am sorry, she told him. This is a total surprise.

For me too, replied Schmidt. In more ways than one.

I know, she said. We have a date in London in ten days, don't we? I'll explain then, if you will let me.

All right. He nodded. Rendezvous in London.

That was rather strange, said Mr. Blackman when they were all back in his car. Let's drop you off at your house. You can visit the loo and join us for dinner—Elaine, what shall we say, at eight? Eight it is! Schmidtie, has the Popov got your tongue? You are joining us?

Later during drinks, while Elaine was busy in the kitchen, Gil said: What ho? Were you aware of this?

Schmidt shook his head.

That was really something.

Schmidt nodded.

On the other hand, perhaps it's nothing, Gil continued. Professional colleagues doing the necessary care and maintenance of an author who must account for a nice chunk of their publishing house's profits. Judging by what you've told me about what's gone on between you and Alice—by the way, she's a knockout—that's the likely explanation.

Unless she's making a fool of me. Perhaps for Popov's amusement.

Why would she bother? She's an adult; you're an adult. Why would she let you get all wound up about her if it was just—what shall we say—an escapade?

Why indeed, answered Schmidt. I wish I knew. But I'm going to find out in London. I told you, didn't I, we have agreed to meet there over the July fourteenth holiday.

Mr. Blackman nodded.

Well, she just told me she expects to be there. As previously arranged. Do you think I'm crazy to go along?

You mean to keep the date in London? No, said Mr. Blackman. It's not crazy; it's the only thing to do. I don't see what you've got to lose.

Perhaps my dignity?

Nonsense. Have fun. Have as much sex with her as you like and she'll let you, and give her a chance to tell you what's really going on with Popov.

Schmidt found a telephone message when he got home. It was from Myron Riker, asking him to call back before ten that same evening or first thing on the Fourth of July. "First thing," he specified, was after nine but preferably before ten. He would have his cell phone turned on and would await Schmidtie's call.

Schmidt called at nine sharp.

Thank you for calling back.

Schmidt could tell that Myron was searching for words.

Let me put it simply, Myron said at last, it's not surprising, but it's a cause for concern. Charlotte is suffering from depression. Some—Renata and the first psychiatrist Charlotte consulted—would call it severe depression. My own judgment is that she's somewhere midway on the spectrum from mild to severe. But that's only terminology. The point is that she is suffering a great deal. She's moved back to the New York apartment, but it doesn't really matter whether it's Claverack or Manhattan, the fact is that she isn't fit to go back to work, and staying at the apartment alone while Jon is at the office, with nothing to do all day except see her psychiatrist, is not a situation that's conducive to good management of her condition. So to make a long story short, the psychiatrist she is now working with has recommended an institutional setting. Her medication would be monitored, and the psychiatrist—no reason you shouldn't know his name, Alan K. Townsend—is a senior consultant there, which means he sees patients twice a week. He'd continue to treat Charlotte.

It was Schmidt's turn to be at a loss for words.

Myron, do you think this is a good idea, medication, institutional setting, all of that. What room is there for therapy in all this? Oh, my poor Charlotte.

Yes, Schmidtie, yes, I do think it's a good idea. I can assure you that I put nothing, I mean nothing, ahead of Charlotte's welfare. Treatment of depression has changed. Very few people still attempt to deal with it exclusively or even principally by analysis or other talk therapies. The new medications—I'm sure you've heard of Prozac, but there are other, more subtle drugs as well—if administered expertly and combined with psychotherapy are really very effective. We know now that the cause is principally physiological and the treatment has to be aggressive. I mean very aggressive, because otherwise serious, perhaps irreversible, harm can be done to cognitive functions. Trust me please. This is as good a solution as can be found.

Where does this take place? I mean the institutional setting? And when?

The transfer to Sunset Hill? Optimally next week. Sunset Hill is in western Connecticut, and it's a very good environment.

And what can I do?

Myron once more seemed to have difficulty expressing himself. Schmidtie, he said, I hate to say it, but the most important thing you could do is to pay for Sunset Hill and Dr. Townsend. Insurance will pay a bit, but I'm afraid that what I'm asking you to pay will be quite a lot. I am so sorry. I would have thought Jon could pay for it, but he has shown me that he can't.

All right, said Schmidt, as the Riker family knows, I'm good at paying bills.

Immediately he was shocked at what he had said. Please forgive me, Myron, I'm just flailing about. Of course, I'll pay. Do what's needed and direct the bills to me. If insurance does pay something, the checks can be endorsed over to me.

Understood, Myron answered. Thank you.

But I meant what can I do for Charlotte? Can I see her? Will she see me? Now? At this place, Sunset Hill? Will Dr. Townsend talk to me?

Schmidtie, I doubt she will want to see you now. She tends to be unresponsive. Later, in Connecticut, I should think so. Townsend won't talk to you without Charlotte's permission. If I were you, I would write to Charlotte. A short letter, very affectionate and very supportive, asking for nothing, wishing her luck.

Schmidt thought this over. He was going to say, You're a good man, Myron Riker, but he stopped himself. Instead he told Myron he was genuinely grateful and counted on him to give him news, tell him if he could help in any other way.

Five minutes later he called Myron again and said he had two questions he should have put before: Was it all right to allude in his letter to her illness and to Sunset Hill? And why had his daughter, his only child, set her face against him?

These are good questions, Myron replied. I think you can, as you say, allude to her situation, but don't carry on about it. Mention it, if you can do such a thing, in passing. As for the second question? I don't know the answer. Perhaps Alan Townsend will find out. All I can say is that, as a general rule, it is more likely than not that something will go seriously wrong between a parent and a child. It's such a fraught relationship.

The conversation having concluded, Schmidt made a second pot of coffee and drank a big cup, to which, contrary to habit, he added sugar and milk. Should he type or write by hand? Type, he decided. Charlotte knew that the only letters he didn't type were letters of condolence.

Dearie, he wrote,

You are never far from my thoughts. Everything in this house speaks to me of you. I walked east on the beach the other day, all the way to the Sagaponack cut, and remembered how you liked to wade in the pond, and the times, when the cut was open, you practiced bodysurfing on your little Styrofoam board. You were so brave!

I hope you go on being brave. You've been through so much, like being hit by a truck. Now it's time to rest and heal, and, as you used to say, get all better. Please remember that near or far I am always at your side, always ready to help, always adoring you.

Your Dad

He reread the letter. It wasn't much, but he didn't think he was capable of doing better. Later that morning he mailed it to Charlotte's New York address. He supposed that, if it arrived after she had been moved to Sunset Hill, Jon Riker would have the decency to forward it. On second thought, there was no reason to credit him with any fine feelings. If Charlotte didn't answer within a reasonable period of time—what would that be? two weeks? longer?—he would ask Myron to try to find out whether the letter had reached her. And if it turned out that Myron couldn't obtain or supply that information? Stop, Schmidtie, he told himself, you can't go on like that. If she doesn't answer, you will write to her again, at Sunset Hill, and send your letter by FedEx, specifying that someone must sign for it.

XVII

THERE WAS NO LETTER from Charlotte in Schmidt's mail when he picked it up at the post office on the day of his departure for London. Only bills, including a whopper from Dr. Townsend and a request by Sunset Hill for a deposit against charges to be incurred by Mrs. Jonathan Riker. He wasn't surprised that Charlotte hadn't written, and it would have been difficult to say without fibbing that he was disappointed. The letter, if it came, would almost certainly bring insults and bad news. Myron had told him over the telephone that what he called the slow healing process had begun. In addition to sessions with Dr. Townsend, there was group therapy and arts and crafts—the latter, according to Myron, being a form of occupational therapy. Of course, thought Schmidt, sedated patients sit in a circle cross-legged on the floor and dump on their parents and spouses before having a go at macramé or finger painting. Nevertheless, the thought that a letter—whatever its content—might sit on his kitchen table unread while he was disporting himself with Alice Verplanck was intolerable. That is why, having turned the problem over in his mind dozens of times, he asked Carrie, who sorted the mail that Bryan picked up during Schmidt's absence, to watch for anything that looked like a letter from Charlotte. If one arrived, she was to read it to him over the telephone. It was apt to be unpleasant, he warned her. She nodded. It wasn't a big deal. In the days when she and Schmidt had lived together she'd been treated more than once to Charlotte's scenes and understood without further explanation the sort of shock he dreaded. That was one thing he had done right: there was no one else to whom this task could have been better entrusted, no one possessed of as much discretion or tact. She'd read the letter to him and never mention it again, unless it was to offer consolation.

The tryst in London had taken on such incalculable importance, had filled him with such contradictory emotions—excitement, hope, but also foreboding—that he decided to arrive a day early and allow himself twenty-four hours in which to regain his equilibrium after the overnight flight. Calm was what he needed, and serenity. But as he went through the motions of looking at those paintings in the National Gallery that he considered old friends, walked in Hyde Park, had dinner alone at a club near Covent Garden with which his New York City club was affiliated, and the next morning, on the spur of the moment, got a haircut and manicure, he understood less and less why he had listened to Gil and kept the appointment with Alice, why he had allowed himself to think that he had nothing to lose thereby. Or rather, he understood too well; fundamentally, tacitly, he had adopted Gil's underlying cynical advice: have sex with her and have fun. Yes, he wanted Alice, wanted her urgently. A nonstop slide show of their embraces was in progress, and he had no wish to avert his eyes from it. If only their Paris trysts had been on that footing, the present excitement he felt, the eagerness of his body, would have been uncomplicatedly joyous. He would have asked the concierge to have a summery flower arrangement placed in the room. He might now be on his way to Heathrow to meet her plane. If only he had not told her right away—far too prematurely and foolishly, he now realized—that he wanted her to be with him always, had talked of marriage. To give Alice her due, she had demurred, but so sweetly and gently that he had allowed himself to take what he thought was her coyness for modest and timid acquiescence. The more fool he, he now thought.

The Jesuit high school teachers had eschewed poetry other than big chunks of the *Aeneid*, and his quondam enthusiasm for Latin led him to catch up in college. He had read and reread Catullus, and now lines from one of the poet's diatribes against his mistress Lesbia supplied the captions for the slideshow: Now that I know you I burn even hotter, / but you seem lighter and cheaper. / You ask how can that be? Such injuries / force a lover to love more, and also to wish well less. What injury had Catullus suffered? That Lesbia was unfaithful. Wasn't that true of Alice as well, a comical difference being that Popov, as the lover with clearly the more ancient title, had more to complain of than he!

Her plane was due at two. If there was no delay, she'd be at the hotel around four. The sparkling sunny day was perfect for another walk in Hyde Park. On his way out, he stopped at the porter's desk to make a reservation for a late lunch for one at the hotel and ordered that summery flower arrangement. For heaven's sake, he loved her! He had been pining for her! The little devil wont to whisper in his ear tittered. You're hedging your bets, my boy, are these flowers really an homage of love or a private joke, a sneer! Well, which is it? Shut up, Schmidt replied, I don't know. Restaurants generally gave Schmidt reason to believe in the inevitable decline not only of the West but of every corner of the planet. No wonder then that to find the dining room so charming and the maître d'hôtel a paragon of practiced courtesy improved his disposition. A decision ripened as he consumed his excellent lunch. Alice had told him at Bill Gibson's party that she would explain in London. Well, let her. There were three full days for her to do so, and he was in no hurry. If it so happened that in the interim he treated her like a tramp, that was too bad. They were in Evelyn Waugh country. As a character in *Vile Bodies* might put it, hard cheese on Alice.

In fact, as soon as the bellhop who brought her suitcase into the bedroom had disappeared—the magical powers of Mr. Mansour's secretary had transformed the double Schmidt had asked for into a suite—Alice opened her arms and said, Here I am, Schmidtie, do with me what you will. On the plane I touched myself under the blanket just thinking about it. You made me come.

Let's get undressed, he whispered in reply.

The bed was very wide and very long—some sort of oversize king—larger than the one at home and built for sleepers of greater girth and weight than he and Alice, and the bedroom, although it gave on Carlos Place, was wonderfully silent. He had worried that he would not be equal to the demands of this tryst, but to his astonishment he was. A combination, he supposed, of sexual hunger unappeased for more than six weeks, the relative novelty of making love to Alice, a certain humility of Alice's he was discovering that made welcome certain gestures and demands she had previously resisted, and of course the account of her masturbating on the plane. Crucial new facts were disclosed after the first frenetic embrace. Lying back against the pillows, the covers thrown off, her hands on her breasts teasing the nipples, she told him that she had brought herself to a climax twice before falling asleep, her hand still in her underpants. So the stewardess found her when, upon the announcement that the plane was entering a zone of turbulence, she lifted Alice's blanket to make sure that her seat belt was fastened. Suddenly awake, feeling her face turn red, she saw the stewardess wink and burst out laughing. Her neighbor in the window seat, an old British battle-ax who would not have been amused, fortunately had remained fast asleep. The salaciousness of this account of Alice's arousal, and her accepting as perfectly natural that thinking about him should arouse her, aroused Schmidt in turn, with a force that reminded him of his prime. He wanted to take her over and over and to drive into her with all his strength. But he was careful. Even in the heat of their transport, he avoided saying he loved her or speaking of a shared future. He told her only that she was making him unimaginably happy, to which she, panting, would reply, I want to, I want to. And it was she who murmured more than once Schmidtie, I love you.

The days passed more quickly than Schmidt had expected, great chunks of each day spent in bed. It was already Monday. The next day she was to take an early morning plane to Paris; he was going home in the afternoon. But by the time they sat down to dinner on Monday evening, she had not mentioned Popov's name or given the promised explanation. His resolve to let her take the initiative had held. More than once it crossed his mind that being in this sort of no-man's-land was not disagreeable, that perhaps saying good-bye without anything having been explained or settled was the best outcome, provided he could keep her. But could he? Wasn't that the rub right there? And on what terms? At the cost of repeated humiliations, such as on Bill Gibson's lawn? Was he ready for some French version of polyandry? Sharing her body with the odious Popov?

Schmidtie, she said after the wine steward had filled their glasses, I have promised you an explanation. I'd prefer not to give it, but I think you expect it.

He almost said, Don't, let's remain as we are. I am not ready for the scaffold. But he couldn't pull it off and felt his head nodding, as if of its own accord.

It's really quite simple, she continued. I know you've figured out most of it. I'll just add some history. You'll understand me better. Perhaps you'll judge me less harshly. Yes, Serge and I have a relationship. It's a very old one. It began the summer before I went to Radcliffe. He was working for a publishing house in Paris—Flammarion at that time, not the one where we both work now—and he'd come to Washington to talk to my father about General de Gaulle. Someone, a well-known political figure, was planning a book about his wartime years, and before signing it up Flammarion dispatched Serge to do some fact finding, to gather from my father whether de Gaulle had been portrayed fairly. My father invited Serge to dinner at the embassy, and that's how we met. I thought he was very serious and sophisticated. After that it all happened very quickly. He was the first man I slept with. Then Serge went back to Paris, and in the fall I went to Radcliffe. Serge was already married to Solange; she was already paralyzed; they had their children; he couldn't have afforded visits to

Cambridge to see me even if he had thought of such a thing; and nothing was ever said about a divorce. I guess I knew it was out of the question. Even if he hadn't gone back to Paris, if we had lived in the same place, I don't know that I would have been willing to go on with a married man. I was heartbroken. Afterward there were Harvard boys I went out with, but none of it was very serious. Then I met Tim in Washington, and before long we were engaged and married. You know all that.

He nodded and said, Alice dear, eat your soup. It's supposed to be eaten hot.

The remark was so stupid that they both burst out laughing.

You know, she continued, that Solange's parents are very *mondains*—very social. At the time when Tim and I moved to Paris, they entertained on a grand scale at their place on rue de Lille. There is a big garden in the back—more like a small park—and in the summer season, in Paris it's June, they always give a famous garden party. *Le tout Paris*, everyone who counts in Paris, is there. Anyway, because of my parents, Tim and I found ourselves on their list, and the first time we went I naturally ran into Serge. It's awful, isn't it? I hadn't seen him since Washington, and I hadn't thought about him for years. He has never said that he had thought about me. But he invited me to lunch. I was already quite unhappy in my marriage. His marriage, ever since Solange fell sick, had been reduced to taking care of her and bringing up the boys. Right after lunch we picked up where we had left off. It didn't take very long at all before it became a regular thing! I didn't want to meet in hotels—I was much more proper then!—so he rented a studio apartment near the publishing house. Now he owns it. He has been very good to me, Schmidtie. Helping me get my job is just one example. I would never have gotten it without him. But it was the emotional support that really mattered. I wouldn't have been able to get through those awful years with Tim and Bruno if I hadn't had Serge to turn to.

I see, said Schmidt. I take it this began before that awful summer of eighty-five, before you found out that Tim was gay.

She hesitated.

Yes, she answered. Tim was neglecting me. We were hardly ever together. I mean he hardly ever made any effort to sleep with me. It was hateful.

She wiped a tear from each eye.

But were you already suspecting that he was in fact gay?

Yes and no. Serge told me that Bruno had that reputation, and I began to connect Tim's lack of interest in me with that, but I had no proof until that time. This will seem odd to you, but until then I had never met anyone who I knew was homosexual!

Old Lew Brenner is still batting a thousand, thought Schmidt, but in reality what difference does it make when she found out? It's all so stupid.

Schmidtie, please try to imagine how badly I needed someone to lean on!

I do understand that, I do understand that very well.

That was the truth. He had moved on to a more important question and decided to put it.

Alice, he said, what I don't understand is, where do I come in? You're still with Popov. That is clear to me, and you don't deny it. Why did you sleep with me when I came to Paris the first time? Why did you sleep with me the second time? Why did you sit there and let me say I love you and I want to marry you—I did use those words—why did you let me carry on like that? And why did you invite me to that preposterous lunch with Popov? Why didn't you tell me you were coming to the U.S. with that man? For that matter, why are you here?

She wiped more tears and then answered: Schmidtie, that's really quite simple! I wanted to. I wanted to get in bed with you. You said you fell in love with me in Paris at first sight. Can't you see that something like that happened to me too? I'm not used to talking about being in love. But in my own way I am! I want you! Please don't send me away.

Oh, Alice, he said, that's the last thing I want. You're my dream of happiness. My only dream. But what about Popov? Does he know about me?

No, she said, looking sadder than when she was crying. I've not told him. He thinks I'm visiting a friend who is married to a don at Oxford. Those times we had in Paris he was away.

Yes, said Schmidt. That part, I mean his being away, had crossed my mind. But I want to be sure that I really understand: you are not thinking of telling Popov about us. Let me put it more simply, you don't intend to put an end to that relationship. Is that right?

She nodded.

But you also intend to continue to see me?

Oh yes, she said, so very much!

But why, Alice, why? Why do you want to deceive Popov? Please forgive me for using that word, but that is the right word. Why do you want to sleep with two men? What is there about me to make you do it?

Schmidtie, you don't understand. Serge isn't like you. He has never been like you. We make love so very rarely! He likes it to be known among his friends that we are together; he likes to be seen with me; he likes to lie in bed with me and talk. It's always been like that. Very little of the real thing, of what I do with you. Now we hardly ever do it. Please understand. The thing with Serge is like an old marriage. If I left, I would be destroying him. I can't do that. You wouldn't do it if you were in my place.

They had finished the main course and the bottle of wine.

Let's have a good dessert, Schmidt said, something to go with champagne.

So it's all right? she cried. You understand, and it's all right.

He didn't answer for a long time, not while he ordered the champagne, which arrived at the table with great speed, not while they decided on a soufflé, not until the waiter had filled their glasses.

This is terribly, terribly sad, he told her. That's really all I can say now.

That was the truth. He wanted to tell her that it was all right but did not think he could live with the answer she wanted. Or with the answer he feared was the only one he could give.

Schmidtie, don't you see, can't you feel that we are happy together? Why do you want to give up our happiness?

He drew a long breath. All right, he said, I'll try to explain. It's a case of having started out on the wrong foot, a case of mistaken assumptions. I didn't think I was having a fling with you—I use the word "fling" because it's the mildest term I can think of—I wouldn't have dared to think that you'd want such a thing. I really and truly fell in love, with all the sincerity and seriousness I'm capable of. There is surely something very wrong with the way I think and respond, but I can't go into reverse and say all that serious stuff about love was a silly mistake, Popov stays in the picture, but Alice and I can meet when he's away or otherwise engaged and have a grand old time. I just can't. I can't eat the crumbs that fall from Popov's table. So I suggest we finish our soufflé, finish our champagne, have coffee and a brandy as good as the one we had in Paris. And after all that let's go back to the hotel and have a great night in the sack! Isn't that in a nutshell what you propose?

I don't think I deserve that, she said. Or perhaps I do. Perhaps it's exactly what I was asking for. Let's do it that way. A night in the sack and then good-bye. But I hope you will remember what I'm about to tell you: you're making a horrible cruel mistake. One that you'll never stop regretting.

When her alarm clock rang in the morning, he reached for the telephone to order breakfast. She stopped him, shaking her head angrily but saying nothing. She locked herself in the bathroom afterward. When she emerged she was dressed. Her little suitcase was ready—she had packed it before they went to bed. She swooped it up and walked out, slamming the door behind her. In the meantime he had pleaded for forgiveness, begged her to speak, asked for another chance. She ignored him.

The champagne, most of which he had drunk? Fury at her and Popov? At himself? No sooner had she told him that he was making a mistake that he would regret than he realized that she was right. But how to recant? Then once they were in the sack—those words, those awful words—he made love to her without uttering a loving word, without tenderness, transforming each caress into an assault. He turned into exactions gestures she had accepted before, indeed had seemed to welcome: the finger exploring her anus, the fellatio demanded and received, the endless cunnilingus. The cunnilingus he drew out until she screamed in one more paroxysm, after which he treated her to a triumphant recitation of those qualities of her cunt that made him appreciate it more than any other he had known. After they had finished, he came to his senses, and he begged her to forgive him. But it was her turn to be silent. She said nothing, not another word. As though he had stifled her. A great night in the sack! Those words, he feared, were destined to resound endlessly, unto his doom. He looked at himself in the bathroom mirror after she left. His face was white, bloodless. He was a ruin.

XVIII

Of course, there was no letter from Charlotte waiting for him. He wrote again, a shortened version of the first letter, and sent it Express Mail, together with a long-sleeved shirt of blue and white stripes, of the kind she used to like, bought when passing through Jermyn Street on his first day in London. He'd wait ten days for her to answer or call; in his letter he reminded her that she could call him collect at home, at the office, or at the New York apartment. If he didn't hear from her by then, he would ask Myron's advice. Should he get in touch with the director of Sunset Hill or Dr. Townsend to see about arranging a visit? Did Myron have a different idea? Or was he condemned to waiting for some word from Charlotte, some indication of an improvement? Work, concentration on the foundation, in the meanwhile, was the prescription for him. That and avoiding ill-considered or impulsive actions.

He had arrived in Bridgehampton late in the evening. The next morning, before he had brushed his teeth, before his first cup of coffee, he called Mr. Mansour's preferred florist in Paris and ordered a mauve orchid to be delivered to Alice. Judging by the price, it was an orchid tree. Just as well. He wanted something that would shout "contrition." What would the card say? He understood the question the salesclerk asked in French and tried to dictate the reply in English: *I behaved like a lout. Please forgive me. Signed, Schmidtie.* The florist's employee got stuck on the word "lout," stubbornly, insisting it should be "louse." That was perhaps an improvement, but not one he was ready to adopt. There was also trouble over "Schmidtie." She insisted on "Schmidt." Merde, he said in English, and settled for a message in baby French he knew for sure was grammatically correct: *S demande pardon.* Hard cheese on Schmidtie. Some hours later, while he was eating his lunch of sardines and Gruyère, the florist called. The same young woman. Madame Verplanck had refused to accept the delivery. His credit card would be credited with the price of the plant, minus the cost of delivery. Shame, burning shame, overwhelmed him. What was he apologizing for? The harsh, unloving sex and the lecture on the quality of her cunt? Definitely. Was it a vaster apology, encompassing a withdrawal of his preposterous claim to her fidelity? He had made no such claim. What he had demanded from her was honesty. She should have told him about Popov. Had she done so, the question of fidelity would have never arisen. He would not have accepted a time-share. The refusal sprang from something buried deep inside him that could not be reached or altered.

Such was his frame of mind when he met Gil Blackman for lunch in the city at the Four Seasons Grill in the Seagram Building, a restaurant that sleek New Yorkers like Mr. Blackman treated as their club, the headwaiters and the owners having memorized or entered into the computer their idiosyncrasies, whether concerning dietary preferences or the table at which they felt most self-importantly happy.

Triumph? cried Mr. Blackman.

Defeat.

I can't believe it. You went to London and blew it. Why? How?

And so Schmidt attempted to explain. Since all he could say about his last night with Alice was that he had treated her badly, without any tenderness, even though she had as much as apologized and said she loved him, the explanation seemed absurd even to him. The look of incredulity on Gil's face knocked out what little wind remained in his sails.

Good grief, Mr. Blackman said at last, the lady explains to you that she has an old thing going with Popov, something that the way you tell it sounds as though it were more about friendship and sympathy with his situation than sex, and you get up on your high horse and gallop away! If you don't want a time-share, as you put it, why not take her away from Serge? Give her a better time in bed and out than he can. How can you be jealous of her past with him? Or did you think she was a virgin?

No, he didn't. Yes, he was a fool. And no, there was nothing he could do about it. There was no prying her from Popov, and he couldn't share with Popov of all people, couldn't be a party to cheating him. That was the gist of Schmidt's answer.

Mr. Blackman nodded and ordered another gin martini. You want one? he asked.

Schmidt shook his head. Not if he was going to get any work done in the afternoon.

Bizarrely, it occurred to him that if his poor late Mary had heard him she would have rolled her eyes, a gift that not even Mr. Blackman possessed.

You'll live to regret it, Mr. Blackman continued, not the

martini but once again cutting off your nose to spite your face. It's really a habit, isn't it, beginning with letting that brute DeForrest stiff you into not making a run to lead your firm, your early retirement, the prima donna act that almost cost you your job with Mike's foundation. The idea that when he offered you the job you had the gall—no plain stupidity—to tell him that you were hesitating, that working for him might interfere with your friendship! What a self-defeating asshole you can be. Then I pulled you back off the window ledge. Probably I should have gone to London with you. You're too dumb to be allowed to run around unattended.

Stop, said Schmidt, please stop. I'm wretched enough as it is. I haven't even told you about Charlotte.

Mr. Blackman listened intently and remained silent for a while after Schmidt had finished. Holy Moses, he said finally. I have an idea. Do you know Elaine's cousin Jerry?

Schmidt shook his head.

He's like the pope of New York psychoanalysts. Most of them he's trained personally. Suppose I asked him to have a shrink-to-shrink talk with this fellow Townsend and find out what's really going on from his perspective? Whether that works or not, making it clear to Townsend that he should pay close attention to this case can't hurt.

Schmidt nodded. Please do.

All right. Now I'll tell you some cheerful news. Believe it or not, Canning has bought into the sex change. We now have a female lead. Your screen credit is secure.

That's great, said Schmidt. Are you getting Julia Roberts?

She's too pretty. We need someone with more edge. I think we'll get Sigourney Weaver.

As they said good-bye—their partings, Schmidt noted,

were becoming increasingly emotional—Mr. Blackman said: Schmidtie, you're as stubborn as a mule. I know that. But please do yourself a favor and climb out of the hole you've dug for yourself. Hop on the plane. Go to Canossa—I mean Paris. Woo her, get her back in bed, let time take care of the rest.

Schmidt nodded, shook Gil's hand once more, and went his way uptown on Park Avenue. It seemed to him he was staggering, although in fact his gait was perfectly steady. The sun was blindingly bright. He crossed over to the west side of the avenue in search of patches of shade and continued north. Gil was right: being an idiot about DT, Katerina, and their predecessors had not impaired his judgment in the affairs of others. Why not take the advice of his best friend, an artist who had shown in film after film how well he understood women? Why? Because he didn't trust Alice. That's what was at the heart of his preposterous stubbornness. She had lied, tricked him into sharing her with Popov, made a fool of him. He had attempted an apology—flowers ordered by telephone, the message dictated to a salesclerk—the sort of thing that would have sufficed if he had forgotten her birthday. Too bad. Begging her pardon in sackcloth, on his knees, was beyond his power.

Whether owing to cousin Jerry's intervention, a discreet nudge from Myron, or the passage of time, proving once again that ripeness is all, Schmidt received at his office a telephone call from Dr. Townsend's medical assistant. Repressing the urge to ask medical what, he listened attentively and respectfully. The young woman, of Russian extraction he was willing to bet, told him that the doctor was aware of the letters he had written to his daughter, Charlotte, and of the fact that she had not answered. If Mr. Schmidt was interested in having a consultation with Dr. Townsend about Mrs. Riker's condition, the doctor would clear it with her and schedule an appointment. Mr. Schmidt should understand that the fee for the consultation would be one hundred fifty percent of the doctor's usual fee for a treatment session and would not be reimbursed in whole or in part by insurance. Mr. Schmidt acquiesced. Two days later, the same young woman called again. The consultation could take place the following day. I'm in luck, thought Schmidt, remembering that in the past New York psychoanalysts disappeared from the city on the first of August and didn't reappear until after Labor Day. He must have managed to get through to Charlotte's shrink just as he was going out the door.

It was a singularly impersonal office: not a diploma or a photograph of wife, children, horses, or sailboats to be seen. In their place, lithographs of old New York, before the heart of the city moved uptown, and, above the indispensable brown leather couch, an ecumenical group of photographer's studio portraits. Schmidt identified Freud and Jung. The others, Dr. Townsend told him, were New York greats: Abraham Brill and Lawrence Kubic and, in a category of his own, Wilhelm Reich, a much misunderstood and underappreciated man. Having been disposed to distrust him, Schmidt found this young man—he supposed that he was in his early forties—attractive and direct as soon as he began to speak. Even without the diplomas, he had no doubt that Townsend was the product of one of three or four boarding schools and then Harvard, Yale, or Princeton and that he had spent his boyhood summers in Maine or on Long Island. It didn't hurt to have interviewed dozens upon dozens of bright young fellows applying for jobs at W & K. The thought of those years of practicing law, of the company of young people he had admired, of all those loyalties, abruptly filled Schmidt with nostalgia.

Look, Mr. Schmidt, said Dr. Townsend, I don't do family therapy, and I'm not going to try to improve your rapport with Charlotte. My purpose is to get some information from you that may help me treat her and to respond to your perfectly natural and legitimate desire to have a better understanding of her situation. Is that all right with you? Please bear in mind that I may or may not tell Charlotte what you say to me and that I may or may not believe what you say. All right?

Schmidt nodded.

First, can you tell me what you think have been the principal traumas in Charlotte's life? No need to go into the accident, I mean before the miscarriage and the hysterectomy.

Schmidt nodded again. Really, he said, there was little, or rather I can't identify much. There was a frightful row when she was eleven or twelve, and I put my foot down and said we couldn't afford to board her horse in New York. So frightful that the memory is still very vivid. It must have been the first time I refused to give her something important she really wanted. By the way, my wife, Mary, and I presented a united front on the subject of that horse. Then there was my own misbehavior. During a very difficult summer—difficult because Mary, who was suffering from what was diagnosed as a depression, treated me with considerable hostility—I allowed myself to sleep with Charlotte's babysitter. It came out much later, only about three years ago, that Charlotte had understood, however imprecisely, what was going on. How she realized it I don't know, the girl and I were extraordinarily careful, and neither of us detected any sign of snooping or any lessening of Charlotte's affection for her or for me. It was Mary who caught us, because of a stain on the sheets, and she fired the girl. But then Mary improved and resumed tranquil relations with me, including sexual intercourse. Perhaps the mere fact of the girl's being fired, perhaps something that she blurted out, had allowed Charlotte to figure out what had happened either then or in hindsight. I can't tell. Is that enough? Do you need more detail?

Townsend shook his head. Not for the moment.

All right. His gorge rising, Schmidt plunged into an account of his complicated—for he insisted that it was such—aversion to Charlotte's marriage to Jon Riker; his decision to give his life estate in the Bridgehampton house to Charlotte as a wedding present and to move out of the house, a decision he duly acknowledged as being motivated by his distaste for living with Charlotte and Jon in a house of which he was not the master, a decision that for rock solid tax reasons turned into his buying Charlotte's remainder interest; his dismay at Charlotte's decision to be married by a rabbi in a Soho restaurant instead of his house.

He stopped for breath and said, I have realized something. I am giving you a version that has benefited from Renata Riker's raking me over the coals about what she claimed to recognize as my deep-seated anti-Semitism. I have come to realize that there was in fact a thread of anti-Semitism running through my relations with Jon Riker and his family. I am indebted for this insight to Dr. Riker and also to my best friend, who happens to be a Jew. That's a fact and I'm not going to deny it, but I want you to know that I have done my best to purge myself of my anti-Semitism, and I think I have succeeded. And I would like you to accept my assurance that my animus against

Jews, such as it was, never involved my harming a Jew in any way whatsoever. For example, Jon Riker owed his partnership in my old law firm almost entirely to my advocacy. Not that his work wasn't excellent. He just needed a little push to get him over the top on time, without what might have been a humiliating delay. You might say that I've been an anti-Semite only on aesthetic grounds! He laughed nervously, conscious of Townsend's blank stare.

I see, said Dr. Townsend.

Yes, said Schmidt, you too find my fig leaf too small. All right. Let's go on to subsequent traumas Charlotte may have suffered. I suppose I have to include my liaison with a very young—twenty years old—and very beautiful half–Puerto Rican waitress that started after the blowup with Charlotte over the house or just around that time and lasted more than two years. I know Charlotte resented it. Whether it was a trauma I can't tell. I mention it for the sake of completeness. Other traumas: Jon Riker's affair with some sort of paralegal at the law firm and a huge unrelated indiscretion or perhaps something worse that led to his being booted out of the firm. Charlotte's own affair with a colleague at the public relations firm she worked for—that too ended badly. She was going to start a new business with him, using my money, because he hadn't any, when all of a sudden he dropped her and went back to the wife he had divorced or was divorcing. I can't remember which. Charlotte and Jon got back together, but I would imagine the bloom was off the rose for them. The firm with which he is now can't hold a candle to Wood & King, my old firm, where he would have been set for life. And the Riker parents—I may be telling tales out of school—seem much less prosperous than they once were, and all of this has precipitated what I can only call a raid on Charlotte's money. Then, curiously enough, in April of this year, Charlotte extended an olive branch to me. A truce that ended with another attempted money grab by Jon. He had the chutzpah—perhaps I shouldn't use that word—to try to get me to set up some sort of trust for the unborn child who would have been my grandson. As though anything in my history with Charlotte justified their not trusting me to be generous!

He paused before continuing. And that brings us to the miscarriage. I do want, though, to say one word more. Renata Riker's role in all this has been nefarious; her conduct has been inexcusable.

Mr. Schmidt, Dr. Townsend said mildly, I don't mind your blowing off steam about Renata Riker or anyone else, but it's Charlotte's traumas I asked you to describe. Thank you for the information you have given me. I have to say that you have a remarkably well-organized mind. Now I will tell you what I can about your daughter.

Reading from notes, he told Schmidt that Charlotte's depression was a notch or two below severe. Like Myron Riker, he disliked the taxonomy. She was beginning to respond to medication but resented the inevitable side effects: fatigue, listlessness (themselves akin to symptoms of depression), and, of course, some weight gain. Not significant, but still there; in due course she will shed those pounds. There was initially marked hostility toward what she called his ur-WASP side. That had dissipated, and he was observing in its place positive transference. Charlotte's ego, her sense of herself, appears to be surprisingly fragile. Staggers under a weight of guilt and insecurities—that is, Dr. Townsend said, what he had written down, verbatim. In all cases of significant depression, suicide is the greatest danger, and a reason for concern. In Charlotte's case, however, his worry was mitigated by the institutional setting, and he believed that by the time she left Sunset Hill that risk would have been very substantially diminished. Prognosis: on the whole good. In a while—he couldn't quantify what that meant—he would gradually reduce the doses of medication with a goal of eventually, after she had been discharged, weaning her entirely. He expected that he would be prepared to recommend sending her home before Christmas. But that was no more than a guess; getting to that point might take significantly longer. From that point on the regime he would recommend was therapy and monitoring—specifically two sessions a week—with him or another psychiatrist qualified to administer medication as well as therapy. Return to work, something that is on Charlotte's mind, was very much recommended but shouldn't be rushed.

Listening to this nice, rational, attractive man, Schmidt wondered about his parents. There must be parents somewhere; he didn't look or sound like a foundling or someone who had from the start been in foster care. Parents or the equivalent are always lurking somewhere, like cockroaches. Had this nice even-tempered man been inoculated at birth against parent poison? Or was he on meds himself, carefully monitored by a Townsend look-alike sent by central casting, lest this nice Townsend erupt in his nice Carnegie Hill duplex, assault his nice can-do wife, batter his nice kiddies as they get home from Chapin and Buckley, and then hang himself with his own suspenders—Schmidt was ready to swear the embroidered braces were from Turnbull & Asser and were guaranteed to support the one hundred seventy pounds of bone and

muscle Dr. Townsend seemed to be carrying. Yes, that is how
he would do it: tie the end of the suspenders that's not looped
around his neck to the banister, ease himself over the side, and
poof. All the air has gone out of Dr. Townsend!

I am truly grateful to you, he told the doctor, for this explanation and for everything you are doing for my daughter. An
obvious question: could I see Charlotte?

I'll ask her when I see her this afternoon. If she is receptive
to the suggestion, I'll make the arrangements at Sunset Hill.
Are you generally available?

Yes, Schmidt said. I can be there any day, at any time.

Good. My medical assistant or I will call you. I have to warn
you, though, a visit may turn out not to be as pleasant for
you or Charlotte as you and she—in her normal condition—
would like. If you would like to let me know how it went, here
is my summer telephone number. I'm about to leave on a short
vacation.

The appointment at Sunset Hill was at one on Saturday. Schmidt foresaw summer beach traffic in every direction: a trip that should take two or two and a half hours could
easily take four. Having slept badly the night before, he ate
his breakfast in a hurry and while shaving noticed an uncon-
trollable twitch in his left cheek. Was this some sort of little
stroke? His mouth was so dry his tongue stuck to his palate.
Just to see whether he could, he tried to say *miserere mihi* and
found the words escaping his lips as feeble squeaks. Fear death
by water, but ferries it would be: the first one from Sag Harbor
to Shelter Island, the second from the other side of that island
to Greenport on the North Fork, and the third from Orient

Point at the tip of the North Fork to New London. New London! The roost of Admiral Hyman G. Rickover, father of the nuclear submarine. Count on an anti-Semitic aesthete to find the Jewish angle! There was a mob at the ferry canteen, but Schmidt elbowed his way to the counter. Two hot dogs with mustard and relish: a delicacy he could swear he hadn't tasted since the Red Sox game to which he took Charlotte, along with a clutch of underbred classmates, in the spring term of her senior year. The home team actually won! They had beer too, the boys and girls having all turned twenty-one, but even if they hadn't no one was going to card them. Schmidt would have liked a beer to go with the ferry dogs, but prudence counseled against that and even coffee with milk and sugar—where would he go to pee once back on land? By the side of the road? The last time he tried that, on the Long Island Expressway, a cruiser pulled up behind him, and the pimply Irish cop who got out said he'd write him up for indecent exposure. Come on, you're kidding, retorted Albert Schmidt, Esq. That went over big: You think I'm kidding? I'll run you in. There are women and children driving by, and you stand here waving your dick in the air. There was nothing like the prospect of being run in to calm Mr. Schmidt, and once calmed he was such a model of sweetness and reason that the cop couldn't resist calling him sir. Have a nice day, sir, and get home safe!

He was at the reception desk of Sunset Hill at a quarter of one, having fully recovered the power of speech, the voice that had held spellbound a thousand cops and a thousand insurance company lawyers. Mr. Schmidt, he heard it say, Mr. Schmidt to see Mrs. Riker. Dr. Townsend's patient, the doctor set up the appointment.

The receptionist scrolled down a column on her computer screen and greeted him: Hi, Albert, take a seat in the waiting room back there. The doors to the toilets are marked. I'll send someone to get her and to take you to the interview parlor.

He did as he was told, both with regard to peeing and to sitting down. He was alone in the waiting room. On the coffee table before him were old issues of *New York*, *U.S. News & World Report*, *Men's Health*, and *Golf Digest*. He plunged into a muckraking exposé of plastic surgeons' obscene fees in New York. One o'clock. One-fifteen. He was summoned to the reception desk. A handsome woman of a certain age in white introduced herself as Mrs. Riley.

Mrs. Riker won't have visitors today, she said. I'm sorry you have come all this way from . . .

Long Island, Schmidt volunteered.

Yes, Long Island. As I said, we're sorry.

Schmidt shook his head. How can this be? he asked. Dr. Townsend set this up.

I understand, but the patient isn't up to receiving visitors.

And does she know I'm here? What did she say when you or one of your colleagues told her?

Mrs. Riley shook her head. We know this is very difficult. You're her father, aren't you?

Schmidt nodded.

Mr. Schmidt, you look like a nice man. I'm going to tell you something I'm not supposed to. When your daughter heard you were here she got into the clothes closet in her room and has refused to get out. Don't take it too hard. I've got a difficult daughter too. These are bad, bad kids. It isn't always our fault.

He thanked her—there didn't seem anything else he could do. When he got home he called Dr. Townsend and told him that Charlotte refused to see him, leaving out the part about the closet. He didn't want to get the nurse in trouble. It was a test for Charlotte, the doctor told him, and a test for you. You seem to have fared better.

He made the trip to Sunset Hill again in early October. When, standing in the door of the interview parlor to which he had been ushered, he saw her, sprawled in a chintz-covered armchair, his first absurd impression, dissipated immediately, was that he had been brought to the wrong room, that the woman with the expressionless face that seemed to have been flattened, like the pale faces of certain chimpanzees, was someone else's problem. But no, this was Charlotte, looking through him with red-rimmed mocking eyes. Her legs stretched out before her were unshaved. She had on a housedress of the sort his mother had worn almost constantly during her long last illness, a garment so vile that he thought if it belonged on anyone it would have to be one of the women who clean toilets in office buildings, and brown leather sandals that displayed dirty feet and toenails that surely hadn't been clipped since the accident. The housedress made it difficult to judge whether she only seemed pudgy or had in fact put on weight. She didn't rise when he entered the room or respond to his greeting of Hello, Charlotte dear, I am so very happy to be able to see you! He realized that he didn't dare to bend down and kiss her.

Repressing an incipient shrug, he sat down in the other armchair, facing her across a low table, and said, I've brought some books I thought you might like, a radio and CD player, and some CDs. I've been told you're allowed to have music in your room.

She nodded, and a moment later said, You can take the books back. I'm not reading anything. Thanks for the CDs. I suppose they're all Mozart.

She hefted the tote, not condescending to look inside.

No, said Schmidt, only two. It's an eclectic mix. You've even got Michael Jackson and the Grateful Dead. Something to please every taste.

Oh yeah? It's that girl. The one you've got a child with. You sent her shopping for me.

I think you mean Carrie, replied Schmidt.

Charlotte rolled her eyes and said, Whatever.

As a matter of fact, she had nothing to do with those CDs. A kid at the foundation where I work suggested some of them. The classical jazz and ragtime I picked myself, including some Jelly Roll Morton that I think you'll like. And by the way, Jason is the father of Carrie's child. Life is hard enough without adding imaginary problems.

Sure.

The people working here—at the reception, and the nurse who brought me here—all seem very pleasant, and I saw that there is a nice big garden.

I don't go in it. I don't like to see the other freaks. It's bad enough to see myself.

I'm so very sorry.

He searched for something else to say and failed. It was all too stupid.

Look, Dad, she said after a while, I'm sick. I'm not as sick as I was, but I'm still plenty sick. You've seen Alan Townsend, so you know. It's no use kidding yourself or me. I've got big worries. Will I get out of here? When will I get out? Will Jon want me back? What will that bitch Renata tell him to do? Will I be able to work? What's going to become of me?

She began to cry and pushed him away angrily when he came over to pat her head and tried to hold her.

No, I don't want your handkerchief; no, I don't want you kissing me. I've got big problems and you can't help me. There is too much bad stuff between us. So please go away. I let you come so you could see for yourself. And now go away.

All right, he said. I don't want to tire you out. Please let me know if you decide you'd like to see me. Or if I can help. In case there is anything I can do.

XIX

THE LORD BLESSED the end of Job's life better than the beginning. He gave him thousands of sheep, camels, oxen and she-asses, seven sons, and also three daughters as fair as any in the land. Job lived to see his sons' sons and his sons' sons' sons—no fewer than four generations. Hideous sadism, thought Schmidt, followed by a revoltingly crude payoff. The Lord could keep his cattle. No accretion of worldly goods would restore Charlotte's womb. There would be no generations of sons or daughters, no little Myron, Albert, Renata, or Mary (the Virgin's name in any event was surely anathema to Charlotte and her husband). Instead, she was afflicted by acedia, angst, and confusion, refusing life's beauty and joys! Cowering in a closet! Turned into a mean, acid-tongued frump! His insides twisted like a rope at the thought of the calamity. Yes, he would hope for her cure or, failing that, a long remission. Dr. Townsend had told him that both results were possible. That was also the view of an author whose work he had consulted on Dr. Townsend's recommendation. He would also hope that Jon Riker would treat her well, that her fears were ungrounded. Yes, treat her well until the day she left him, an outcome Schmidt was taking a vow not to wish for. He'd made too many wishes over the years: they had boomeranged to hit him in the teeth. If Charlotte and Jon did remain together, they might want to adopt. But even that might prove impossible. Charlotte had been branded by Sunset Hill.

As for him, his earlier losses—Mary's devastating illness and death; his consequent decision to retire early and give up his beloved profession; Carrie's leaving him, heartbreaking though necessary and natural; the abject attempt, ending in humiliation, to join his existence to that of a woman he had fallen in love with and had mistakenly believed worthy—those were pinpricks compared with the latest catastrophe. What was left for him to do? He must love her and, no matter how frequent and how harsh her rejections, stand ready to help. Beyond that, scaled-down expectations and modest goals: do good work for the foundation, protect young Albert, avoid doing harm, and escape whipping.

On a Saturday, when the heavy nor'easter had blown itself out, and the presence at the marina of both Jason and Bryan was no longer required, Schmidt invited Carrie, Jason, and little Albert to lunch. It was time, he thought, to make official, by repeating it in Jason's hearing, the promise he had made to Carrie. The baby in his portable playpen was so placed that he had a good view of him. That big nose that had alarmed and moved him when Carrie brought him home from the hospital no longer seemed so aggressively large. Since it couldn't have shrunk, little Albert's face must have filled out enough to deprive that organ of its telltale pretensions. He was going to be a fine boy, most likely with his mother's sallow complexion and with her dark eyes. The Puerto Rican team was ahead, and he was rooting for it.

Over coffee, he told Jason about Charlotte's accident and how she would never be able to have children. Most of what he had to say Carrie had already heard. Then, smiling at the baby, pleased to see how contentedly he kicked and gurgled, he made his speech.

Perhaps one day, after Charlotte has gotten completely well, she and Jon will want to adopt, he told them. It's possible, but I'm not sure that it's likely. If they do adopt one child, they may want to adopt another one, or perhaps more, so as to have a larger family. I mention these possibilities only because I want you to know that I've thought about them and have taken them fully into account. Whatever Charlotte and Jon do in this respect will have no effect on what I'd like to do for little Albert here. Or other children who for one reason or another come into my life and become dear to me. If you'll permit it, if you agree, I will pay for the education of Albert and any brothers and sisters of his—tuition, tutoring, living expenses away from home, and so forth—from preschool through graduate work. Summer camps are included. The works. Will that be all right with you? Obviously, if the marina makes you so rich that you want to bear those expenses yourselves, you won't be obliged to accept my money. I'll set it aside instead as a nest egg for the kids.

Carrie let out a whoop and ran around the table to hug him. What kind of dopey question was that? Hey, Albert, send Schmidtie a kiss! You just got yourself a pretty good deal. Schmidtie, this is so generous I can't believe it.

Jason too had stood up and with great seriousness shook Schmidt's hand.

Sit down, sit down, Schmidt said, and raised his hand as a signal to cease further effusions.

Well, that's good, he said. But I want you to understand that my question wasn't all that dopey. What I'm going to do will lead me from time to time—for instance, when you're choosing a school or a camp or when decisions have to be made about going to a boarding school or staying at home or about college—to stick my big nose into your affairs.

He couldn't help it. He winked at Albert.

If that's really all right with you, he continued, you've made me very happy. I'm a lonely old man. I need to think I can make myself useful.

That was as brave and as sincere a speech as Schmidt was capable of making. But a little green-hatted devil whose proboscis resembled Schmidt's, perching on his left shoulder, took a cynical view. Congratulations, chum! he whispered in Schmidt's ear. Including the siblings in your largesse was one smart move. You hadn't told me that part. It will sure spare young Albert some grief. But watch your step anyway. Don't forget: we never forgive our benefactors, and no good deed goes unpunished. Leave lots of air between that little family and you. Don't crowd them.

Shopping for sufficiently fine and clever wooden toys for young Albert took up a good deal of Schmidt's free time when he traveled and obliged him to carry an empty suitcase, which was filled gradually as he visited one capital after another. Central and Eastern Europeans were still carving, and putting carts and wagons together without nails or glue. The search continued when he was at home in Bridgehampton or New York. He had become an avid reader of FAO Schwarz catalogs, which disappointed him more and more, and as time he spent staring at the screen of his computer increased, he became an habitué of online outlets, as well as eBay, where he hunted for antique toys in mint condition. The kid, as he referred to little Albert in his thoughts, seemed to like him, the way, Schmidt supposed, he would have liked Mr. and Mrs. Gorchuck, Carrie's elusive parents resident in Canarsie—Schmidt still had not encountered them, and for all he knew they had not yet set foot in Carrie and Jason's house in East Hampton, in which case perhaps Carrie took Albert to visit them at their home. Schmidt hadn't undertaken to inquire, remembering from the time when he and Carrie lived together that Carrie strongly preferred to keep distinct parts of her life in separate compartments. Or the way Albert would have liked Jason's parents, had they lived somewhere closer to Long Island than Nova Scotia. It all went to show, he thought, how good it is to have money: if your children want to see you, you can hop into your car or on a train or plane and go to where they are. Or vice versa. You send the tickets or a check. And how shitty it is to have none or too little. No, being treated like a sort of grandfather, or anyway allowing himself to believe that was how he was treated, suited Schmidt just fine. Wasn't that all he had hoped for when he could still take for granted that one day Charlotte would have children? Nor was he only attentive, as a virtual grandfather, to keeping Albert supplied with trucks, puzzles, and games. Schmidt had taken on as well the responsibility for the kid's religious and spiritual education. It was Jason's elder married sister, living in Nova Scotia like the rest of the family, who stood up with him at the font, and not, as he had feared, one of O'Henry's waitresses, Carrie's former colleagues. Let there be, however, no mistake: Schmidt's democratic principles were intact. He liked those very young women, their welcoming bosoms, and the occa-

sional whiffs of barely suppressed body odor, knew their first
names, and left generous, sometimes extravagantly generous,
tips. But ever since the nature of his connection with Carrie
had moved on to a Sunday-best bourgeois respectability, he
preferred to see them only in their professional setting.

Schmidt had taken to heart the advice of the little
fellow with the big nose and the green hat: he was doing
enough for young Albert—and therefore Carrie—to vent a
tiny part of the affection dammed up within him to the point
of overflowing. He hoped he was not doing too much, that
he was not in the way. Experience proves that being a good
grandfather—whether de facto or de jure—is not a full-time
job, unless you live in the seclusion of the Alps and are lucky
enough to take into your house and your rough heart Heidi,
your little granddaughter. Or to find yourself in some analo-
gous case. Therefore, although Schmidt thought of Albert
often, always feeling a happy warmth in his heart, and when
in Bridgehampton saw the boy and his parents as often as he
thought was prudent, being Albert's Albo—a sobriquet suggested by Schmidt fearful that the kid would mispronounce
Schmidtie—was not even a part-time job. It did little to fill
the void of his days and nights.

Running the foundation was the more effective remedy. Old
habits persist. Schmidt had always worked hard as a lawyer
and had been capable of an eerie concentration that sheltered
him from noise, interruptions, discomfort, and, he well knew,
thoughts unconnected with his work. That detachment, that
absolute fixation on tasks at hand, had it not been the subtext of Charlotte's reproaches in the first quarrels she picked
with him after her engagement to Jon? She had berated him

for having had his old trusted secretary transmit messages to her, make travel reservations, arrange for the time during the workday when they could speak on the telephone. That same concentration was now saving his sanity.

To his surprise, and subsequent amusement, Schmidt discovered that his foundation job opened the door to a social life in a milieu where he would be lionized. It consisted of so-called fine arts or cultural trustees or cultural affairs executives—the inventiveness of the nomenclature used to tart up fundraisers and public relations operatives was stunning—who had recently joined his club. Dazzled by Mike Mansour's fortune, they saw in Schmidt the vade mecum to the Mansour billions. The fact that the foundation operated only overseas and didn't make grants to U.S. institutions didn't discourage them, a separate deal or a new charitable initiative being always imaginable. Some of them probably, on a smaller and personal scale, salivated at the thought of the lectures they could deliver, and seminars they could lead, in Prague, Warsaw, Budapest, and even in other less romantic destinations, all compensated by honoraria and reimbursement of every travel expense, including first-class airfares. Schmidt had no moral objection to such calculations, understanding all too well that those nicely turned out ladies and gentlemen had apartments and houses to maintain and their own and perhaps other mouths to feed. Only, as the perennial aesthete, he found offensive, like a stain on a carpet, both the nomenclature and the hunt at the club for business and personal advancement. These were sins against the established order and civility.

Ever since *The New York Review of Books* began publication, he had been a faithful reader of its personal announcements, not because he was looking for a restored fifteenth-century farm in Umbria or a studio with exposed bricks and ceiling beams on Île St. Louis or wanted to enter into a progressively intimate relationship with a Boston divorcée or female Jewish academic ready to travel, but because they amused him as stylistically perfected communications, shot like an arrow into the air with the hope of lodging it in the heart of a kindred soul on the Upper West Side.

His circumstances had changed. He found himself sending terse, though he hoped well-turned, replies to divorced and single females—he avoided widows—with their love of music, travel, Italian and French food, and interest in financially independent gentlemen between sixty-two and seventy-two. That bracket, he found, was the most sought after among the aforementioned females. He enclosed a photograph taken of him for the foundation's annual report: the least stuffy and off-putting he possessed. Three of these shafts hit a target. The images he received in return, however, did not incite him to proceed. Somewhat discouraged, he kept on reading, and one day came upon an announcement, in a genre he had seen before and distrusted, the scent of which now drew him. Its author claimed she was a married woman of fifty, residing in Bedford Hills—the *ne plus ultra* of Westchester respectability—seeking afternoon meetings in Manhattan with an equivalent gent. Discretion guaranteed. How should he parse "equivalent gent"? Schmidt took the approach that had been taught to him by Paul Freund when the Harvard Law School was still worthy of its name: It's a constitution, gentlemen, we are interpreting, we must look at the problem being addressed and find reasonable solutions. Soon enough he came to an interpretation that was not unfavorable. The lady couldn't be thought to insist on a married man, unless she was seeking the spice of double adultery or had determined to avoid anyone who might seek permanency. Even if those desiderata were in her mind, he could probably allay her concerns by delicate advocacy. That left the question of age, but he doubted that she was unwilling to consider candidates who did not claim they were her own age or younger. Biology being what it is, fifty-year-old male seekers of adventure were likely to prefer ladies who were significantly younger. In the end, he decided not to push his luck by confessing that he was a widower. He wrote to her, enclosing the photo he had used in previous correspondence with fellow readers of the *NYRB*, avowing his age and also his continuing vigor. As an aside, he told her that in Manhattan he lived alone and unencumbered.

The color photo he received by return mail showed the lady in a see-through blouse, her breasts small enough to fit in the palm of his hand, the nipples rouged. She had large black eyes, a large and slightly hooked nose, a wide mouth, and black hair. He concluded she was of Italian extraction. She wasted no time, proposing to meet him the following week on whatever day and in whichever bar near his place he would specify, though not too late in the afternoon. She wanted to be able to catch the 9:22 to Katonah. All things weighed, he proposed the Carlyle at 5:00—why be rushed by the train schedule?—on Tuesday. She was better than he expected: not just fine breasts but a good figure and decent legs, and she struck him right away as clean. That had been a worry. He had planned to get her to bathe or shower with him before getting down to business, but it was better to have her be clean to start with. Judging by the size of her pocketbook, she had with her all she needed to repair her makeup, mascara and all.

Vera was her name, and once more she wasted no time. Her scotch on the rocks drunk, she said, You don't look like Mr. Goodbar, let's go.

She was also in favor of washing and had brought a toothbrush and toothpaste, and in the tub, which she preferred and in which she asked him to join her, she washed his T & T (tool and testicles, she explained) and invited him to reciprocate. There was no foreplay. She lay down, raised her knees, and said clearly but nicely, Eat me, in the process coming with a good deal of noise. He had thought that she would return the favor, but she shook her head. Let's screw first. You won't last sixty seconds if I go down on you. Later I'll give you head to raise you from the dead! She was right. When he proposed dinner afterward, in a trattoria on Third Avenue, she looked at the alarm clock—it was past eight—and asked if he had anything in the fridge. Just some cheese and scotch. That's fine, she'd have a snack and be ready to hop on her train. You want to meet again? she asked. You're OK. Just kinky enough. If I see you again, and if you're still nice, we'll do anal.

Over the years—she would say good-bye to him on her sixtieth birthday, allowing that she and her husband were moving the following week to Fort Lauderdale—he learned very little about her. The husband was a podiatrist with a practice in the rich suburbs successful enough to pay for the house in Bedford Hills and the second one on a Floridian canal, as well as putting a son through Cornell's hotel management school and a daughter through Iona College—she's a dope, Vera explained, she takes after him. Schmidt assumed that "him" was the husband. She never volunteered, and he never asked, why she wanted him to service her weekly, complaining when he was out of the country but assuring him that she hadn't replaced him during his absences. It was an arrangement that he would have understood better if she had asked for money or expected presents, but no, when after two unsolicited "anals" he tried to show his appreciation in the form of an Hermès silk square decorated with a Greek motif, with good humor she pushed away the shopping bag containing the scarf in its box and said, Hey, your wife will like that. Save it for her. Come on, let's fuck! We're wasting time.

This form of friendly, unalloyed carnality was new to Schmidt, but he grew to look forward to it, the way, before Mary had forced him to resign from the Bridgehampton Country Club because it would not brook Jewish members, he had looked forward to his weekly Saturday and Sunday morning singles game with the local surgeon who beat him more often than not, thus spurring him to play better than he would have with a weaker opponent. An absurd detail: he appreciated Vera's punctuality and, on those occasions when she agreed to have dinner afterward, her no-nonsense unvarying regimen: *caprese*, veal cutlet Milanese, and two cappuccinos. It was the same with wine: she never failed to drink her half of the bottle or deviated from her preference for the Piedmontese. If he allowed himself a personal question unrelated to the business at hand in bed, he was rebuffed. For instance, when he asked her if her family was Italian, she told him, It's none of your business.

How right she was. Schmidt continued to read the personal ads in the *NYRB* after Vera's retirement, but he never again launched himself into the adventure of connecting with a lady seeking companionship. He'd been so brilliantly lucky once; it was better to quit while he was ahead. Besides, the hunger that had made him restless and willing to execute his repertoire of well-worn, hardly varied, mostly grotesque moves with any woman whose body did not repel him had at last abated. Had Vera left him sated, a condition that would prove temporary? Or had he aged? It was difficult to be sure; during his tours of Life Centers it seemed inevitable that some sufficiently attractive woman—a researcher, Center employee of one grade or another, a professor lecturing under the aegis of the foundation—would give the unmistakable signal of availability. In such cases he responded and performed. Schmidt, it must be said, had progressed in savoir faire since his first couplings with Danuta. He no longer felt that a vodka or slivovitz binge was the price he had to pay for climbing on top of those ladies or letting them ride him, and he learned to bring down the curtain on sessions with them early enough to allow himself a good night's sleep. It occurred to him that he had at last grown up.

XX

At lunch *en tête-à-tête* in Water Mill, some months after the disastrous second visit to Sunset Hill, Schmidt heard Mr. Mansour say he'd felt for a while they should have a talk.

You've been busting your chops at the foundation, he told Schmidt at the end of their long review of new initiatives. Holbein says so too. Whether you know it or not, he thought it was a mistake to hand the foundation over to you. Now he says he was wrong.

That's good to hear, replied Schmidt.

It was interesting to learn that the foundation had been handed over to him; he'd always had the impression that Holbein was spying on him and that Mike was looking over his shoulder.

So I've told Holbein to give you a raise and a bonus. Don't tell me you don't need it. You just think you have a lot of money. Let me tell you you're wrong. You definitely need it. *Pas question!* I'm also putting you on the board of Mansour Industries. That's a big job and an honor that comes with an honorarium. Ha! Ha! Ha! Don't tell me you don't accept. I'm telling you that you do.

Of course I accept, Mike. It's an honor and an amazing show of confidence.

Yes. You can say that again. But that's not really what I want to talk about. I have some other news.

Coffee had been served. Schmidt nodded when Mr. Mansour's houseman Manuel offered to refill his cup, and it being a cold Saturday afternoon with sheets of rain obscuring the swollen surf beyond the plate glass windows, he nodded again when Manuel showed him the label of the bottle of Bas-Armagnac. 1965. The year of Charlotte's birth, he told Mr. Mansour.

Santé! Mazel tov!

They clicked, Schmidt straining to control a tremor in his hand and lip.

When we both went to Paris, and you had to go back, but I stayed, Caroline and I spent some time together. I told you that. You remember?

Schmidt nodded. He didn't think he'd forget that week if he were condemned to drag out his days as long as Job.

But here is something I haven't told you. I've bought a little house in Sagaponack. I wanted to get closer to you!

Mr. Mansour began to cough and choke on his own joke, until Manuel, appearing behind him without having been summoned, as though rising from a trapdoor, hit him hard twice between the shoulder blades and offered him a glass of water.

Yes, said Mr. Mansour once he had recovered. That wasn't part of the program, but that's how it is. We've gone on seeing each other. A lot when I'm here, sometimes every day. No one knows, not even Holbein, except Freitag, the T and E lawyer at the law firm, because if anything happens to me I'm leaving money to Caroline. And now you know too. I'm telling you,

you WASP schmuck, because I love you. She said it was OK to tell you. So what do you say?

Goodness, Mike, replied Schmidt, so many things. I'm honored that you chose to tell me, I'm astonished, I ask myself how in the world can she get away with seeing you here. She's got Joe right in the house!

Pas de problème. He spends all day in his office with the door closed. She doesn't think he knows or cares whether she's in the house or out, so long as she's put his lunch in the refrigerator in his room. Always the same: tuna salad on white bread, three celery sticks, an apple, and bottled water. That's all. She works on her own stuff in the morning, but in the afternoon she can drop in, and she does. She does, she does, she does!

Mr. Mansour left his chair and did a little tap dance as he pronounced those last words.

But she doesn't like having my guys see her go in and out. Anyway, with the traffic back and forth between here and where they are in Sagaponack sometimes we lose close to an hour! That's why I bought the little house. She crosses Route Twenty-Seven, drives half a mile, and I'm there waiting for her. *Et voilà!* The housekeeper comes in the morning and so never sees her. Nobody sees her! *Pas de problème!* Except guess who.

Mr. Mansour jabbed himself in the chest repeatedly with his index finger.

And when I'm in the city, he continued, sometimes she says she's going to the opera or the ballet. He doesn't care if she goes alone.

Mr. Mansour laughed some more before continuing: He's such a schlemiel; he's never once said, I'm coming with you, not once since she and I have been together. So what do you think?

Love in the afternoon squared! I think you're very lucky. Thank you!

And what happens next?

Schmidt didn't need to ask why Caroline was unfaithful to her husband with the great financier. Mike's boast about his unique tool and sexual prowess was still fresh in his memory, and perhaps it wasn't a boast; perhaps he was telling the unvarnished truth. Schmidt could think of at least two more reasons: Canning was a dreary pill. Mike could be weirdly amusing, possessed of the sort of omnipotence that before the era of billionaires had been the attribute of monarchs reigning by divine right, if not Zeus himself. Showers of gold were de rigueur for kings and could be used inventively by a god, but there were so many other tricks. Had he come to her as a swan? Imprisoned her in a cow that he mounted like a bull? One could put nothing past him. But Canning was hardly more of a pill and a turkey than when she married him—there was nothing new there. She had been attracted by something— God knows what, probably his talent, which had not yet been recognized. That talent, to believe *NYT* critics—Schmidt didn't—was still there, in full bloom. But *pas de problème*! as the man with the golden dick would say. He sleeps with her in the afternoon, and at night she opens her legs, or however they do it, for Canning. Nice!

And what happens next? repeated Mr. Mansour, working the worry beads. What should happen?

I mean you're single—divorced—she's a very serious woman, very gifted, very much respected. Do you go on getting together in the afternoon and so forth in your new little house or wherever you do it in the city?

If she'd only leave the schlemiel, I'd marry her tomorrow,

answered Mr. Mansour. I said to her I'll give him money, lots of money, to get him to move on. Out of our lives! She won't let me. He needs her! That's what she says. He won't be able to write! Big deal. *Entre nous*, if he never wrote another word it wouldn't be a big loss. You know why I'm financing that stupid novel of his? One, I like Gil and I like what he does. Two, it gives me some control over the schlemiel. A slam dunk! Joe, you're needed on location in Brooklyn or out in the Midwest, wherever that stupid book starts. Joe, we need you to present the project to distributors! *Pas de problème*. Caroline and I are doing our best. One more thing strictly *entre nous*: he's got all sorts of things wrong with him, blood pressure, cholesterol in the stratosphere, on and on. He might do himself and me a big favor and die. I'm saying this to you on the Q.T. Right?

That was the first time Mr. Mansour had ever asked him to keep something to himself. It must happen from time to time, he thought, when he's about to buy or dump a public company. But in private conversation this had to be a first.

Then you'll just go on happily and hope Joe won't figure it out.

Schmidtie, said Mr. Mansour. I want her with me all the time. I invite them every time I have someone coming to dinner or lunch unless it's with you or Gil and I don't want him to fuck it up, or Holbein when we talk about money. You know why? So I can look at her and hear her laugh. Dinner with them *à trois*, without another guest or two, I can't do it. So I wait. So I wait!

Another first. Two big tears escaped Mr. Mansour and ran down his cheeks before he could wipe them with a yellow silk handkerchief he produced from the pocket of his black cardigan.

Enough about me, he continued. I wanted you to know. That's all. The question is: have you got a life yet? You haven't told me what happened last summer with the nice lady in Paris, but don't bother. I've figured it out, with just a couple of hints from the great filmmaker. Don't get upset: it was just a hint or two. He didn't tell me anything he shouldn't. The question is, can you get on my plane tonight—I'll come with you or you can go alone, but you'd be better off if I came with you. We'll go to Paris, you pick up two dozen red roses, and what else? A nice pin at Buccellati, something simple, with a nice diamond and maybe some sapphires, and you'll ask her to forgive you. She will. I guarantee it.

It won't work, Mike. She won't have me, not after the way I screwed it up, and at this point I don't want her. Not on her terms. It can't be. It was a beautiful dream, but that's all it was. It's over.

You give up too easy. I don't, but I've had a different life. I had to fight. Fight every inch of the way. Now I don't. I just raise my pinkie. So the question is, have you got a life? What do you do when you're not at the office or visiting Carrie and little Albert? By the way, smart move taking care of all the kids; that is what I would have told you to do.

How the hell do you know about that?

Pas de problème. I've told you already. My guys and Jason talk.

I see, said Schmidt. Tell me, is there any way to get rid of you and your guys?

Click click. There isn't. Once you're my friend I never drop you. Especially when you're in trouble.

All right. Can I have some more of this Armagnac?

Be my guest! But first answer the question.

It took Schmidt a moment to bring himself to speak.

All right, Mike, he said. I haven't got a life. It's true I work
hard at the foundation. I'm glad Holbein has noticed. Since
you know everything, you surely know that next week I'm
going on one of those tours of your Life Centers. Then I'll
come back, and my nonlife will go on. At some point, something will break. The perpetual motion machine will stop. Are
you satisfied now?

No, I'm not, because I'm the best friend you'll ever have.
Let's move over there, Mr. Mansour said, gesturing toward a
group of armchairs. He must have pressed a button, because
Manuel arrived to pull out his chair and strike a match to light
the wood in the fireplace.

Mr. Mansour thought longer than usual before speaking
again. Charlotte is still bad? he inquired. The question is,
how bad?

Ever since Schmidt could remember, ever since he was a
little boy living in the shadow of his huge and competent
father, and the mother who'd robbed Schmidt's life of color
and taste, he had held his tongue. He allowed Gil Blackman to
know much of what he didn't tell anyone else, not even Mary.
With her, he had never entirely let down his guard. There was
no reason to do so. He told her all she needed to know about
his standing at the firm, his money—what he earned and what
he spent and at the very beginning what little he owed—
his thoughts about Charlotte's education. But beyond that?
About what he might have called his feelings? Had anyone
asked—had she asked—he might have said, There is nothing
to tell, it's easy to see, I wear my heart on my sleeve. And now
this strange man with worry beads and private jets wanted to
know about Charlotte. That he wouldn't be satisfied until he
had been told everything was clear to Schmidt. And that he

could tell when something was being held back was clear too. Mike had forced his friendship on him but, after the one outrage that perhaps had taught them both something, had been a true friend. One who, for all the ocean of differences that separated them, understood him. Schmidt drained his glass and began to feel very tired. He hadn't told Gil, he hadn't had the heart to inflict on him this great sorrow, but someday soon he would have to.

Manuel was lurking in a far-off part of the huge living room that Mr. Mansour used for lunch and dinner when he was alone or with only a guest or two. Schmidt raised his hand with the empty glass, waited for Manuel to fill it, and asked for a glass of water. His lips were parched.

Click click.

He looked carefully at Mr. Mansour. For the second time that afternoon he wasn't smiling. All right, Mike, he said. Here is what's been happening.

In April of the following year, some months after that conversation, Charlotte telephoned Schmidt at his office. Mrs. Riker on line one, said his secretary. Aha! Mrs. Riker, therefore his daughter, not Renata, not Dr. Riker.

Dearest Charlotte, he started.

Dad, she cut him off, I need to talk to you. Not on the telephone. Can you get over here?

Certainly, he answered, when would you like me to be there?

How about tomorrow? Can you be here in the morning?

I'll be there by eleven, he answered. *Click.* She had hung up.

He had spoken with Dr. Townsend several times, calling him before he left for Europe, then when he returned, just before Christmas, and twice more, in early January and in Feb-

ruary. Each time the news was: She's making slow progress.
No, at this point he couldn't predict when she would leave
Sunset Hill; it was up to her. When would he be able to see his
daughter, he kept asking. Let's leave the initiative to her was
the regular reply. The last time he had insisted. Mr. Schmidt,
the doctor said, your last visit was not a success. Do you really
want more of the same? She is making progress, and I think
that in time she will have things to share. She'll reach out
to you!

"Things to share"! "Reach out to you"! Where had this
nice overgrown preppy picked up those expressions? Quiet,
Schmidtie, Schmidt said to himself, he got them from his wife,
his children, his patients, the preacher at whatever loosey-
goosey church he attends.

Dr. Townsend, he said, obviously I don't want a bad visit,
and I don't want to force anyone's hand. Even if I did, I don't
think I can. Would you at least tell me something more about
her condition? Is she as medicated as before? How does she
look? Is she reading the newspaper? Books?

If Townsend was irritated, he didn't let it be heard in his
voice.

Let's see, he said. Medication: the doses are smaller, considerably smaller. She's pale, which is normal at this time of
the year since she's mostly indoors. She doesn't pay much
attention to her appearance. A hairdresser is available at Sunset Hill. She hasn't taken advantage of his services, although
urged to. I don't have the impression that she's reading books,
but she clearly reads the paper or watches news on television
in the common room. I can tell you she's really worked up
about Newt Gingrich. Oh yes, she enjoys the arts and crafts
shop. That seems to be a new interest.

I see, said Schmidt, I suppose that does sound like progress. Do you think that means I'll be able to visit soon?

Mr. Schmidt—a note of irritation could now be heard—let's leave it to your daughter. If there is no movement from her side by the summer, please call me. We'll discuss what might be done.

As soon as Charlotte had hung up, he called Dr. Townsend. He was with a patient. Schmidt left a message: he was going to see Charlotte the next morning. She had called and asked him to come!

Mrs. Riley, the sympathetic nurse he had met during his first aborted visit to Sunset Hill, greeted him at the reception desk. She's ready for you, she said, good luck! and led him to the interview parlor. Charlotte in blue jeans, and a man's shirt, not Schmidt's, perhaps Jon's, perhaps no one's, hair too long but washed, face less puffy than the last time, and perhaps not puffy at all, began to get up from the sofa and quickly sat down, suppressing what must have been an involuntary gesture.

Hello, sweetie, he said, I am so glad to see you.

Definitely, Charlotte had no use for preliminaries or small talk. Dad, she announced, I'm getting out of here. Townsend has me on two drugs, both low doses. I can handle it if I see him in the city. He says he has openings on Tuesday and Friday, and he may be able to squeeze me in on Thursday.

That's great, replied Schmidt, I couldn't be happier.

Have you been paying for all this, I mean this dump—she made a vague circular gesture with her right hand—plus Townsend, or is it Jon?

It's me.

Figures. Well, it'll be a relief not to make out any more checks to Sunset Hill. What a name!

Paying for it is the least of my worries.

As soon as the words were out, Schmidt regretted them. It was perhaps a mistake to interrupt her. It turned out not to matter.

Don't worry, you'll have lots else to pay for. I'm not going back to Jon, she continued. I don't know whether I'm through with him or not, but I know I don't want to go back to the apartment. I need a chance to think this through and work with Townsend without having him and that bitch Renata on my back.

Schmidt nodded.

You do understand that I have no money? I checked on my accounts at Chase, regular and savings. He's cleaned them out. I don't know about my investment account. That was also a joint account. I bet that's been cleaned out too. I haven't got a cent.

I see, said Schmidt.

Dad, I'm not asking whether you see or don't see. I want to know whether you will pay for an apartment as well as the shrink and give me enough money to live on. Can you give me a straight answer? This isn't going to be forever. I'll go back to work as soon as I can. That's if anybody will take me.

Dearie, said Schmidt, of course I'll give you money to live on, including the rent and the doctor and everything else. How can there be any question about it? Would you like me to help you find a place? I'll be glad to. Just give me an idea of the neighborhood. Uptown? Downtown? East or west? And of course I'll help you get out of here. I mean checking you out, getting you from here to the city, to your new place, if we can find a nice one in time, or to a hotel, and I'll give you cash and whatever else you need. You could also use my apartment in the city while you look. I can go to a hotel or find some other solution. Oh, and I'd like you to open a checking account in your name only.

OK.

There was a pause before she continued.

Moving into your apartment would be just more than I can take. Dad, get one thing straight: I need you to help, but I don't want you on my case.

I do understand, Schmidt replied. May I ask a question? You've twice referred to Renata Riker as a bitch. The last time I saw you and today. That's a big change in your feelings. Can you tell me what has happened?

Something like a cloak of lead descended on Charlotte. She scrunched down, hugging her knees. Yeah, I was dumb. I didn't get it. She's an evil, manipulative bitch. You know what she's telling Jon? That not having grandchildren will break her heart. Break her fucking heart. You can see what that means. If you don't want to break your mommy's fucking heart get rid of the shiksa, get rid of the damaged goods!

She began to sob but kept talking.

I just know that she put it in his head to take the money. I can hear it: If you don't take it Schmidt will figure out a way to block those accounts. She really does hate you!

So I've noticed. Is there a particular reason? I can't think of anything I've done to her other than saying no to a couple of outrageous requests. Including one that I lobby W & K to take Jon back into the partnership! That was two, three years ago? While you and he were split.

You really don't know?

He shook his head.

Think hard. You still don't know? I'll help you. That time, after the Thanksgiving lunch, you made a pass at her and didn't follow through. Then when we all came to Bridgehampton, and you got sick, she stayed behind to make sure you weren't alone when Jon, that asshole Myron, and I went for a walk. What a crock! So you were in bed, and she French-kissed you and grabbed your dick. And you? Still nothing. Not then, and not later. It made her go nuts! She even told you she had some guy screwing her, and Myron knew all about it, so you'd understand the coast was clear. So how dumb can you be?

Good grief! She is nuts. That's pure nonsense. And why tell you? Why does that make her hate me? Some kind of hell-has-no-fury-like-a-woman-scorned idea?

I guess you could put it that way. She didn't tell me right away, not when it happened. She saved it for when she wanted me to move back in with Jon and you had gone ballistic about getting Jon out of the apartment and trying to have the place, plus the house in Claverack, transferred into my name. That really burned them both, mother and son. So the idea was to explain to me that you were always trying to stab Jon in the back because he's Jewish. That, and on top of it your guilt about having come on to her, and how those guilt feelings turned into aggression. I didn't get it until later, when she started the shit about grandchildren, that she had the stuff about guilt feelings ass backwards. It was her fucking guilt and her aggression.

XXI

THAT CHARLOTTE'S PROGRESS remained steady and then accelerated over the balance of the year, Schmidt could judge not so much from face-to-face meetings, of which there were but few, Charlotte having continued to insist that he "stay off her case," as from telephone conversations in which she expressed her wishes, really demands, for money and assistance in the war against Jon Riker. It didn't take long—perhaps two or three weeks after he had installed her in a sunlit one-bedroom apartment on a chic block in the West Village—for her to decide that she wasn't going to go back to him this time. Some days later she called to announce she wanted a divorce. No she wouldn't sit still for any chitchat with that bastard or that bitch, no bullshit about reconciliation. She'd heard that song before. Divorce, and the return of her property, were her unconditional demands: suddenly, the proposition Schmidt had in the past tried without success to have her accept, that property bought with funds from her father was rightfully hers, had acquired the dazzling force of revealed truth. Yes, she was willing to take sole responsibility for the mortgage she and John had put on the Claverack property, as well as for the unpaid balance of the loan they had taken out jointly to finance the shortfall of the purchase price of the apartment—especially if Schmidt gave her the money to pay off the mortgage and the loan—but apart from that no quarter was to be given. Schmidt advised her to seek once again the help of Joe Black, the divorce lawyer he had recommended when she and Jon had split the first time. Black knew her, and he knew the Rikers. It wouldn't take long to bring him up to speed. The trouble was, as both Black and Schmidt separately explained to her, that New York was still the last state in the Union without a no-fault divorce law; proof of adultery, abandonment, or cruel and inhuman treatment was still required. The last time around, it was clear that Jon had committed adultery and she had not condoned his misconduct. She did not have such proof this time. One could perhaps obtain it; there were discreet investigators specializing in such matters. Otherwise, the standard way to proceed would be for her and Jon to enter into a separation agreement and file it with the court. One year later, a decree of divorce would be granted at either party's request. Unfortunately, Jon was not likely to accept a separation agreement unless he thought it was financially advantageous for him. That pointed to the need to consider various ways of making his life difficult. For instance, Charlotte could move back into the apartment and start using the Claverack property, hoping to provoke some form of behavior that might give Black grounds to seek a court order that would, in effect, evict Jon. No way, was Charlotte's response. Black had checked up on the status of the mortgage and cooperative apartment loans. Jon had been making payments on both, but not on time. It was an interesting question whether he would continue to make them now that Charlotte was no longer at Sunset Hill. That other shoe dropped almost immediately in the form of a letter from Jon to Charlotte demanding that she reimburse him for one-half of the payments he had made entirely from his own funds during her hospitalization and that she start contributing to subsequent payments as they came due. The letter also asserted a claim that Black said must be taken seriously, that Charlotte, by having originally put the apartment and Claverack in both their names, had made to Jon under New York law a completed gift of a spouse's "moiety," meaning a conjugal one-half stake in both those properties. Nothing in the law compelled the return of such gifts. A call by Black to Jon, asking whether he was represented by counsel, elicited the answer Black had expected. It was once again Cacciatore, well-known in the divorce bar for his scorched-earth tactics. Firmness and patience, firmness and patience, Black counseled Charlotte, they'll be your best friends.

Joe Black isn't getting anywhere with Jon's lawyer. Do you think he's tough enough to deal with that shyster? Charlotte asked Schmidt in October of that year. She had said she wanted to see him, and they were having lunch near her apartment. Can't you find me a real shark? Joe says they won't deal unless Jon gets some part of what I'm paid for the apartment and Claverack. He's figured out that I'd be putting them on the market. I guess that was a no-brainer.

I'm told that Joe Black is plenty tough, Schmidt replied, but I can certainly look for someone else. I'll ask Mike Mansour who handled his last divorce.

OK, do that. Dad, I'm tired of being on an allowance. My

boss says they'll take me back, but not before they start a new campaign, and that's six or seven months away. I need to get my life back together before that. It would sure help to have that money.

Schmidt nodded. He was learning that it was better not to interrupt. Just let her talk, so he didn't state the obvious, that even if Jon suddenly became reasonable and agreed to a separation agreement that gave her title to her property it would probably take longer than six or seven months to sell the real estate.

There's this guy I met in Sunset Hill, she continued. It would help to have the divorce.

Schmidt nodded again.

Don't worry. He wasn't one of the inmates; he taught art. He's a good painter. He sculpts too. He's widowed. His wife died a year and a half ago. Anyway, I like him.

That's wonderful! said Schmidt, unable to restrain himself.

Yeah, anyway. He's got a kid, a girl, twelve years old. She goes to Friends Seminary. He lives on Perry Street.

Good school, interjected Schmidt.

She's a good kid.

Can you tell me something about this young man? You know, his name and what kind of art he does?

She snickered. Josh White, and no, Dad, he isn't Jewish. I know that'll be one load off your mind.

Very carefully Schmidt did not rise to the bait. Was this possibly one of the Box Hill Whites? he asked himself. There are so many artists among them.

He's an abstract artist. His gallery is in Chelsea. It's well-known. He's well-known too. Yeah, and he teaches at Cooper Union, not only Sunset Hill.

I'm very glad for you, said Schmidt. I hope I can meet Josh sometime soon.

Dad, don't push. Just find me some divorce lawyer who'll know how to get back my property and get me out of that marriage.

The very next day, Schmidt lunched with Mr. Mansour, not at Schmidt's club, for which he was thinking he might propose his friend, but at the Four Seasons Grill, which Mike, like Gil, used as a substitute for all the even more exclusive institutions to which he did not yet belong. Schmidt came to the point directly, asking who had represented Mike in his two divorces. I need someone, he said, who can break knees, elbows, the works.

Pas de problème, said Mr. Mansour, I've had two, one for divorce number one and the other for number two. Both are killers, but I think number one has retired. Who's the happy couple? Let me guess. Charlotte wants to leave that guy Riker. *L'chaim!*

He raised his glass to Schmidt and continued: Tell your Jewish uncle the details. The details! *Pas de blagues!*

Having heard Schmidt out—Schmidt had resigned himself to no longer censoring the accounts of his travails with Charlotte—Mr. Mansour turned pensive and said, It's no good. There isn't a divorce lawyer alive who can blast him out of that apartment or that house upstate. Not anytime soon. She wants to marry this painter?

Schmidt nodded. She hasn't said so, but I think that's probably the idea.

So she had better get divorced and get the marriage license before the guy changes his mind, replied Mr. Mansour.

He reached into his coat pocket and brought out the worry beads. *Click click. Click.*

I have an idea, he said. I know about Riker's firm. I had it checked out when you told me he went to work there. They do good work. The senior guy is Irv Grausam. He's a litiga tor, doing a lot of environmental litigation. Superfund cases, and so on. We have a company in Mississippi that's in a big mess. They're being sued for discharging all sorts of dreck into some stream. It's all bullshit, and we could settle, but I have a rule against settlements. I say make those plaintiffs and their lawyers fight: make them spend money and fight every inch of the way. Once you start settling, you're roadkill. I'm going to call Irv in and say we'll retain him to litigate this big mess for us—and when I say a big mess I mean it—but on condition he makes this character Jon give back her property to the daughter of my best friend. It's a free country! If he doesn't want the retainer, doesn't want the fees, that's fine with me. There are lots of other lawyers who'd die to work for me. But if he wants the job, he's got to straighten out his boy Riker. I want him to give back to his wife her property and sign the separation agreement. The whole deal. *Pas de problème!* Now tell me, am I a good friend?

Mike, you're the best. But let me think for a moment. I don't want you to get in trouble.

You mean I'm threatening Irv? I'm not. Don't ask me to clear it with Holbein. I'm not going to. Leave it to me!

Schmidt heard first from Renata. She called the New York apartment. You are a bastard, Schmidtie. First you let those awful men at W & K wreck Jon's career. And now you sic your attack dogs on him at Grausam & Trafficante. God will punish you. She did not ask him to call back.

So it worked, Schmidt said to himself.

The call from Jon Riker came a few days later, on a Saturday. Schmidt was at home in Bridgehampton.

Al, said his son-in-law, is there anything you won't sink to? Getting that Egyptian of yours to call Irv Grausam so that he'll pressure me? On a matter that had no connection with the Egyptian or with my law firm? Only one purpose: to fuck me. You've always been a prick and you'll always be one so let me tell you my bottom line. I won't transfer the apartment or the house to your lovely daughter until and unless I'm fully reimbursed, with interest, for every cent I spent fixing them up and every cent I paid on the mortgage and the apartment loan. I know she has no money, so you will have to pony up. Did you get that?

Yes. You can tell your lawyer that as soon as you transfer the properties to Charlotte and sign a separation agreement that Joe Black approves you'll get that money.

Charlotte called two weeks or so later. Schmidt was at his office.

Dad, Joe Black says the papers are ready to give me back the apartment and Claverack. The separation agreement is ready too, but Jon won't sign unless he gets reimbursed for what he had put in. Why should that asshole get anything? He lived in the apartment and in Claverack, didn't he?

The reason to pay him is to get this done, to get Jon to go away. Isn't that what you and Mr. White want? asked Schmidt.

Yeah, but he should be paying me. Are you going to give me the money for this?

Yes.

She said, I guess then it's OK, I guess I'm grateful to you, and hung up.

That the separation agreement had been signed Schmidt inferred in the course of a telephone call from Charlotte, in which she asked for the name of a broker to handle the sale of her apartment. He gave her the name of the young woman who had handled the sale of his Fifth Avenue apartment after he retired. She had obtained what seemed at the time to be a spectacular price. When he asked Charlotte whether she needed a broker for Claverack, she said she already knew someone in Hudson. Schmidt had not yet met Josh White, the response to a couple of requests that all three of them get together having been a particularly elongated rendition of the word "Dad." Translation according to Schmidt: *Get off my back.* He was in the meantime dutifully paying Dr. Townsend's bills, which now came to him directly, as well as Charlotte's allowance, rent for her apartment, and the extortionate premiums on her individual health insurance policy. That she had not bothered to thank her father beyond her one grudging "I guess I'm grateful to you" was a sort of harshness he had come to expect. Her failure to thank Mike Mansour, without whose help the stalemate in the war of the Rikers would have doubtless continued, was another matter. Each time he remembered it, he felt the sting of shame.

The letters he had written to Charlotte since Mary died, typically at times when his exasperation needle had entered the red zone, had not been a success if improvement in her behavior was the right measure. They did, however, make him feel better. It was with eyes wide open that he wrote:

Dear Charlotte,

I am very happy that you have been able to recover your property and are on your way to becoming a single woman. You wouldn't have gotten there without Mike Mansour. I have told you what he did. It was entirely his idea. He deserves your gratitude and a letter from you expressing it. Incidentally, the reason I am certain that you haven't written is that, given the interest he takes in your welfare, he would have told me if you had.

As you can imagine, I continue to wish to make Josh White's acquaintance. Please think about how this might be arranged. Anything, going from a cup of coffee down in the Village, to dinner in any restaurant you and he like, all the way to a short or long weekend in Bridge-hampton, would be fine with me.

Your loving father

It was not one of his finer efforts. Nevertheless he mailed it. Some six months later the broker he had recommended to Charlotte called him and announced that she had a buyer with good credit, who would have no difficulty passing the co-op board and was willing to pay Charlotte's asking price. She had also referred Charlotte to a lawyer who would handle the closing. Incorrigible, knowing that his advice wasn't wanted, Schmidt nonetheless asked whether his daughter knew that she could perhaps avoid paying a capital gains tax on the sale if she bought another apartment within a year. The broker told him that both she and the lawyer had discussed that possibility with Charlotte, but it appeared that Charlotte preferred to keep the cash and stay in her present apartment or move in with a man she was seeing. That was interesting.

Schmidt wondered whether there would be a wedding and, if so, whether he would be invited or left to learn about it from the announcement in the *Times* or some printed card sent after the fact. Some weeks later, during the weekend, the telephone rang in his kitchen, and a conversation commenced preceded by a *Daad* of medium duration.

I bet Gwen told you I've sold the apartment.

Schmidt acquiesced.

So I've got all this cash I need to invest. Will the man who looks after your money take me as a client? I mean it's chicken shit compared with what you have.

He'll be happy to take you, and I think he'll give you a break on his fees. He'll calculate them on the basis that you and I are members of a family group.

That's good.

Have you got his number?

Somewhere. You think you can send it to me?

Certainly.

I'm starting again at my old firm. Three days a week.

Schmidt remained silent longer than usual to see whether anything more would be said on this subject. Nothing was.

That's great, he said, that will give you a chance to get your sea legs before you start working full-time.

Oh yeah? I think they're jerking me around. They'll never take me back full-time. Anyway, I won't need my allowance once my money is invested. But can you go on paying the doctor and the rent? The rent, that's just for the time being.

She couldn't see him, so Schmidt shrugged and made a face.

Certainly, he replied. Let me know when you want me to stop the allowance.

Yeah, I will. Oh, and can you pay the health insurance?

I already have. I've paid the first year's premium in advance.

OK. That's good. See you!

Before she managed to hang up, he said—cried out might be closer to the truth—Charlotte, don't you think I could meet your friend Josh?

Daad, she replied, will you lay off? I don't want to spoil it with him. He'll think it's pressure or something.

With that she got off the phone.

Little Albert's third birthday came and went without Schmidt's having met Josh White. Fortunately, there was a different treat in store for him: Carrie asked him to take the kid for his first haircut. They went to the barber in Sag Harbor whom Schmidt used when it was inconvenient to get his hair cut in the city. The old fellow was ready for his new customer and went to work in accordance with Schmidt's instructions: just a trim and completely natural. We want to give his hair shape, but we don't want him looking as though he'd just been to the barber. Through it all, Albert maintained perfect poise, sucking on one of the big green lollipops reserved for good little boys. As the locks of hair fell—Albert's hair was now the color of Carrie's and promised to become as heavy and lustrous—Schmidt felt a pang of regret. He took one of the locks from the white apron with which the kid was covered, asked for a tissue, wrapped the hair in it, and tucked it into the watch pocket of his trousers. If he had kept his father's huge gold watch, which the old man had worn on a chain, he could perhaps have had some ingenious jeweler alter the cover so that it would hold the hair like a locket, and he could see it whenever he opened it to expose the face. The other solution might be to put the hair in a frame, something like those boxes used to display butterfly specimens. He would ask Carrie for advice.

That's a fine grandson you have, Mr. Schmidt, said the barber when Schmidt pressed the tip at last into his hand. I hope he will be a regular customer.

Thanks! He really is a good boy, Schmidt replied.

He took Albert back to East Hampton, watched him blow out three candles on his cake, and for about an hour looked on while the boy and his friends from the nursery school played some of the games that Schmidt found he remembered from Charlotte's birthdays.

Then he went home, put the lock of hair in his desk drawer, and forgot about it until a lunch with Gil Blackman at O'Henry's a couple of weeks later. So far as he was concerned *The Serpent* was ready, Gil told Schmidt. It had been a long haul, much too long. Working with Canning hadn't been a picnic, and they had been forced to wait until Sigourney's schedule opened up. But now that it was done, he was pleased. There would be a screening of the director's cut for Mike, Joe and Caroline Canning, the indispensable Holbein, top studio executives, and, to Schmidt's delight, Schmidt.

I'm inviting DT too, said Gil, though I can't figure out where I will seat her at the dinner afterward. If she isn't at my table, she'll be unhappy. But if she is, I had better have a good story ready for Elaine. I haven't worked all that out yet. The good news is that, as you'll see, the film is great. Even better news is that I've got Canning out of my life! That really rates this joint's best bottle. It's my treat. We'll drink to my liberation.

Are you serious about having DT at the dinner with Elaine?

I can't help it. She'd scratch my eyes out if I didn't. She's got a terrible temper. I'll explain that she's been working on the project since the start, but behind the scenes, as it were—that's pretty funny, you've got to admit—and just couldn't be excluded. Besides, you've just given me a great idea. I have to have her at my table because both you and Mike will come alone. That way there will be only one extra man.

Gil, you're playing with fire.

What's new about that? Mr. Blackman said, his face darkening. But let's talk about something else. For example you. How are you, old pal?

Schmidt had been having lunch with Gil, or dinner with him and Elaine, so regularly that there was nothing, literally nothing, he could think of that he was doing or not doing that might amuse Gil. It was like the good old days—or bad, depending on your point of view—when Schmidt kept his nose to the financing grindstone at W & K. What exciting happenings did he then have stored up to relate to his glamorous friend? That the loan to Podunk Cement Company had closed, and he had another one in the works, with Dumboville Power Company as the borrower? That he had felt left out of the conversations and overwhelmed by the company at the National Book Awards dinner, at which Mary had naturally taken a table, and had been ready to dance on it because her author won? But yes, there was one anecdote, and, even if somewhat sentimental, it was pleasant.

You'll laugh at me, he said. Ten days ago, I took little Albert for his first haircut, on his third birthday. I wish Norman Rockwell had been there to paint us. I got so broken up that I picked up a lock of his hair, wrapped it in a Kleenex, and took it home.

And you still have it? asked Mr. Blackman.

Of course.

Schmidtie, this is your chance. Your chance to get the answer to the big question. One that has to be answered or your life will become more and more difficult. Are you that boy's father or not? I think you need to know. Not so that you can tell Carrie, or God forbid Jason, or even me. But for your own stability. I happen to know of a lab that does DNA testing. It's a reliable outfit. Do it, old pal! You mustn't go through the rest of your life not knowing where you stand.

I don't know, said Schmidt. I'm not at all sure I want to know. Suppose I'm not his father, am I supposed to love him less? I don't want that. Suppose I am his father, what would I do beyond what I'm doing now? Carrie's pregnant. When that baby comes, do I care for it less or more depending on the result in little Albert's case? I think I know the answer. Whatever I learn, I will always love Albert best. For a crazy reason: he came so soon after Carrie left me. He's swathed in my love for her. And that won't change even if it turns out I'm not his father. So what would be the point?

Putting your house in order.

That was something Schmidt understood instinctively—perhaps craved, even though it went against the advice he had given Carrie soon after the kid was born.

I'll do it, he said. I hope I won't live to regret it.

XXII

Y CHROMOSOMES DON'T LIE, Mr. Schmidt, the technician at the SureDNA laboratory told him. Normally I don't touch cut hair, there just isn't enough DNA there, but this sample was productive. Here, look at the slides. You can see for yourself. There is no way this individual and you are related.

Schmidt thanked the man, got into his car, found the Long Island Expressway entrance, and headed west back to the city. Well, now he knew. The oracle had spoken. Was that the answer he had wanted? Not entirely: in some part of his besotted brain had dwelled a half-formulated, timid, guilty wish to be told that the beautiful little boy was his child. It had coexisted with the certitude that, lest he unhinge Carrie's marriage and thereby visit untold harm upon little Albert, any knowledge he thus gained must go with him to the grave, and that, indeed, he must do everything in his power to affirm Jason's paternity. Carrie's adorable Age of Aquarius notion that it didn't matter who was the boy's father, to think that Jason, even if he knew that it wasn't he, would be a good stepfather and love the kid because Carrie was its mother, was great, so far as it went. It might work just fine for Jason and would certainly be the best result possible if the real father were dead. And the effect of such knowledge on Albert Schmidt, Esq., still very much alive and residing a few miles up the road? Unspeakable torment: forced to stand by and watch stoically while Jason reaps the best of the boy's love and Jason, or Jason and Carrie, take decisions concerning the boy with which he, Schmidt, disagrees, and to accept being excluded—as by the force of circumstances would inevitably happen—in many moments of crisis or joy. None of this vision implied suspicions of future bad faith or ill will. Far from it. It was just the way it would happen, and unlike divorced fathers who haven't custody of their children, he would not be able to assert any right to be heard. Of course, he would continue in his role of honorary uncle or grandfather, his wallet always open, melting from happiness each time the kid smiled at him. But at some point, when the little boy notices that Albo's or Uncle Schmidtie's largesse somehow diminishes his dad, won't he turn against Uncle Checkbook?

You consult oracles at your own risk and almost always to your harm, the knowledge they impart being laced with poison. It had been a narrow escape, but he had indeed set his house in order. He would love little Albert as Carrie's son, a child who could have been his but wasn't, and he would be able to look Jason straight in the eye. He had not been a party to slipping a stranger's egg into his nest. The blond giant was raising his own son and working for his own son's future. A virtuous example for Schmidt to follow, a reminder to concentrate his efforts on the well-being of his only issue, his own Charlotte.

Opportunities to do so had begun to present themselves, at first hesitantly. Almost exactly a year earlier, the day after Timothy McVeigh was sentenced to die for the Oklahoma City bombing, Charlotte telephoned. It being mid-August, Schmidt was in Bridgehampton, on vacation, reading the account in the *Times*, remembering how the news of the carnage at the Federal Building had intersected the board of directors' meeting to which he had rushed from the arms of Alice. Dad, said Charlotte, for once pronouncing the word normally, I thought you'd like to know I've finally sold the house in Claverack. You can stop making the mortgage payments.

Congratulations, Schmidt replied, were you able to get a good price?

Pretty good. I'm going to look for a house in Connecticut, somewhere near Sunset Hill. It would be convenient for Josh. He teaches there Mondays, Tuesdays, and Wednesdays. I hope what I got for Claverack will be sufficient.

Now this is good news, thought Schmidt. She's talking to me as though I were a human being, she's still with this guy White, and she's actually made a plan, a sensible plan.

He replied: What a good idea.

Oh yeah, and I'm going to be full-time at the agency, starting in September.

That is simply wonderful. Congratulations!

And one other thing: Alan Townsend and I agreed that it's enough if I see him twice a month starting when he gets back from vacation. He's also going to take me off medications, but he wants to be there when he does it.

I'm thrilled.

Got to go, said Charlotte. See you!

Schmidt felt his jaw drop. Was this Charlotte or a particularly able impersonator? On the supposition that he had in fact been talking to his daughter, he called the florist in the city and sent her a large white orchid plant with a card reading *Congratulations and love from your dad.* As he was placing the order, he remembered his failed attempt to apologize to Alice, a memory that still burned like a hot wire and could have sufficed to keep him from ever saying anything with flowers again. In fact, he came close to canceling this order but didn't, deciding—in his opinion reasonably—that the fault then had lain not with the orchid but with his own behavior. His astonishment grew when Charlotte thanked him, sending a Hallmark card with a kitten in a basket on the outside, and inside it the words *Thank you* in red script. It was a first, and he wished he could have chuckled over it with her mother. She had, however, signed it. Until then, the only ready-made thank-you notes he had received had been from elevator men, garage attendants, delivery boys at various establishments, and mailmen to whom he gave cash presents at Christmas, and retired cleaning ladies to whom he sent annual checks. But then it occurred to him that Charlotte must know—but how? had he told her?—of his love affair with Sy and was very gently teasing him. That seemed to him a clear sign of returning health.

The next call came on Friday after the Labor Day weekend. Mother Teresa had died that day, and after reminding Schmidt that she was going back to work "like a real person"—a statement that wrung his heart—she expressed her admiration for the saintly nun. Schmidt was momentarily at a loss for words, remembering vaguely that she had received the Nobel Peace

Prize many years back, as had such worthies as de Klerk and Arafat (each being paired with his better to share the distinction). He had had no prior inkling of Charlotte's interest in India's poorest.

Still, he recovered in time to say: Yes, it's sad. She did have a very long life, and I suppose she was very tired.

Eighty-seven is not so old, replied Charlotte. She could have gone on with her work. And poor Diana! It's so sad, so tragic!

It seemed to Schmidt that she was crying very softly. The accident in which the Princess of Wales died had been five days earlier, the previous Sunday, and while Schmidt was aware of the outpouring of national grief in England, the depth of Charlotte's feeling once again surprised him. He hadn't known her to be an Anglophile, and he had certainly never seen her display any interest in the follies of the British royals. But sensing again that he stood at the edge of a minefield, he remained perfectly still.

Yes, that was very sad too, he said. How old was she? Forty-one, forty-two? She had two sons, didn't she?

Dad—the word had edged toward Daad—she was thirty-six! Only four years older than I! It's so dreadful, so terribly dreadful, to be so unhappy and never get a chance to make up for it!

Now she was really crying, and not bothering to hide it.

Sweetie, said Schmidt, I'm so sorry about her, I'm so dreadfully sorry you feel so bad.

She blew her nose and continued: Can you imagine, yesterday at the office this jerk Olson—Schmidt remembered vaguely that one of the managing directors of the firm went by that name—called her a little slut? Said he couldn't understand what all the fuss was about? If I didn't want so badly to go back to work, I would have thrown something at him—I don't know what, maybe the trash basket. It was full of half-empty coffee cups. Would have served him right.

Oh my, said Schmidt, people are so unfeeling.

He realized that he would have been capable of making a similar if probably less harsh remark.

Jenny has a photograph of Lady Di on her desk and has a candle burning in front of it. Sort of like the people outside Buckingham Palace she saw on TV.

Schmidt remembered that Jenny was Josh White's daughter and hoped she wasn't going to set the apartment on fire.

How old is she now, he inquired, is she still at Friends?

Thirteen. She's a great kid. Yeah, she's still at Friends. Dad, she continued, the reason I'm calling is that we found this amazing house in Kent. It would be just perfect; it has an artist's studio that's now being used as a sort of super guest room and an artificial pond. We're going to look at it again tomorrow. The money I got for Claverack isn't quite enough. Will you help me buy it? I don't want a mortgage if I can help it because I haven't got enough money coming in to carry one. So if I can, I'd rather buy it free and clear.

Certainly, replied Schmidt, I'll help you. Are you going to have to do much by way of repairs? Remodeling?

Nothing. Just a coat of paint. Josh says he'll slap it on himself. I guess that's what you do if you're a painter!

She actually laughed.

Schmidt wondered how much capital would be required to "help" but decided not to ask. Whatever it was, he would find it. To hell with worries about the gift tax and tax efficiency. There was enough money to fulfill his promise to Carrie and

Jason about the kids' education and enough for him to live on if he tightened his belt. He wasn't going to spoil this moment for Charlotte.

That sounds fine, he said. Let me know how it goes and how much you need. And do get a competent lawyer. If you need a recommendation, I can ask around.

It's OK, Josh has someone. A Sunset Hill graduate like me, who practices out there. I guess we Sunset alums got to stick together.

She laughed again before saying, Got to go—her current sign off, which did not get Schmidt's goat—and was gone.

Sy had climbed into his lap during the phone call and was purring vigorously. That meant that he wanted to be fed and found it politic to make himself agreeable, an approach whose obvious merits Schmidt thought he could highly recommend to anyone who wanted his money. Charlotte hadn't exactly purred, but, given her vast talent for making herself odious, she was doing pretty well at the capture of benevolence. The chief virtue of the house seemed to be that it suited the still-unknown Mr. White! About to shrug, he restrained himself: Sy, who detested sneezes and other loud noises and ill-considered gestures, might have been spooked. It occurred to Schmidt that Sy had taught him a lesson he could apply in his dealings with Charlotte: be patient and let her take the initiative. She would produce her Josh, and his Jenny too, but in her own good time.

A world gone mad. With scary consistency, Charlotte's calls were intertwined with news of disasters and disgrace. Before the end of the year, in a Manhattan federal court, a jury convicted the terrorists who had exploded a truck bomb in the public garage under the World Trade Center in 1993, while in

Egypt other terrorists killed more than sixty tourists who had hoped to visit Luxor. The White House reeked of trailer trash sexual scandals, the tempo of repugnant revelations accelerating until a year later no one in the nation—perhaps no one on earth in reach of a television signal—could be ignorant of the nice chubby Jewish girl who had spat the presidential ejaculate out on her blue dress, the liquid that dozens upon dozens of porn queens and princesses would have lapped to the last drop, and threw the dress into her closet instead of sending it out to be cleaned. In the closing days of the year, the president was impeached, but not before he had ordered air strikes against Iraq to enforce the no-fly zones. Other events, pregnant with menace and resonant, had preceded that premonitory act: India and Pakistan each conducted tests to show the other that it had the bomb; other murderous terrorists attacked U.S. embassies in Dar es Salaam and Nairobi, leaving hundreds dead and thousands injured; U.S. missiles rained on terrorist bases in Sudan and Afghanistan. Outside of Laramie, Wyoming, a gentle, waiflike gay student was tortured and beaten to death. Frequently Charlotte called to commiserate with Schmidt about these and other catastrophes. He took those conversations, her knowledge of current events, and her eagerness to discuss them with him as nothing short of miraculous. He still hadn't met Josh—and she had given no sign that she thought an introduction was in order. But she had sent Schmidt photographs of the house in Kent and actually thanked him for the hefty contribution he had made to paying for it. He hoped that she'd had the sense to keep the title to the house in her name, but he didn't dare to ask. In the old days one could have presumed as much, since to the best of Schmidt's knowledge Charlotte and Josh weren't married, but times had changed. Even stranger than not knowing Josh was the fact that he had seen Charlotte only three or four times since his second visit to Sunset Hill, briefly over coffee or a sandwich. He risked her ire by making a crack: now that he had pictures of the house, wouldn't it be a good idea to send him one of her?

Relax, Dad, she said, I look all right. Better than when you last saw me. I've even got a nice haircut.

Well, that's good, thought Schmidt, I'll keep my fingers crossed. Aren't her words and general liveliness sufficient reassurance? If seeing her father and being fussed over by him, perhaps even being hugged by the old man, were on her wish list she'd meet him in the city or Bridgehampton, returning to the house and beach that had been her childhood vacation universe. That she knew how to get what she wanted he was certain without reciting all the recent examples. Recent examples? Don't bother to count them. Be modest and grateful that your daughter is a functioning young woman again, that she has found a man she likes and managed to stay with him for two years. As for you, Schmidtie, get on with your life—such as it is.

He did his best. Leaving for Europe, he swept through the Life Centers, which were now nine in number. Afterward, he visited archeological sites in Anatolia with a group organized by the Fogg Museum, returning home in time to see the president admit to the nation on television that he had lied about his relationship with the obliging White House intern. He had called Charlotte's numbers in the city and in Kent to tell her that he had returned and was on his back porch, reading about the imminent economic collapse of Russia, when his own telephone rang. It was Charlotte.

Dad, she said, I guess you're home. Josh has been talking about how he'd like to meet you. I guess he's like you. Is anyone living in the pool house?

No, no one, replied Schmidt, reminding himself to let her lead.

In that case, do you think Josh and Jenny and I could come and stay there over Labor Day weekend? That's in two weeks. Jenny's fifteen now. You won't mind her.

Nothing could give me greater pleasure, you know that. I only wish it could be sooner. How will you get here, by train or the Jitney or by car?

By car. We'll be coming from Kent. We're all on vacation here.

That's great, said Schmidt, that's the best coming-home present I could have hoped for. Just let me know whether to expect you for lunch or for dinner.

Lunch. So we don't get stuck in the Friday before Labor Day rush hour traffic.

Very wise. Oh yes, he added, I'm just looking at the calendar and I see that on that Sunday Mike Mansour is giving his annual Labor Day lunch. I know he'd very much like to meet you and Josh, and of course Jenny. It would be nice if you came. As you may remember, he was very helpful.

Daaad, please don't start organizing me so far in advance. I'll talk to Josh and send you an e-mail. Got to go now. Good-bye.

She hung up before he had a chance to say another word, but Schmidt thought that her adding good-bye to the usual "got to go" sign off was something of a breakthrough. It was enough to take the sting out of Daaad at almost full bore. In truth, he could imagine nothing she might have said that would have diminished by an iota his joy. She was coming for

a long weekend, it was her idea, and she was bringing the man
he was beginning to think of as her husband and the girl who
would be her stepdaughter. He had intended to call Gil, but
had not gotten around to it. The receiver still in his hand, he
dialed his number. Gil was there and saw no reason he and
Schmidtie couldn't have one of their soul-baring lunches at
O'Henry's. When he returned he found an e-mail from Charlotte on his computer screen:

> Thanks, Dad! Josh says we'd all three like to go to Mr.
> Mansour's lunch. C.

Jenny turned out to be a somewhat smaller than life-
size portrait of her father: lanky, slightly stooped, big hands
and big feet, plain but pleasant and cheerful face framed by
blond hair that both the daughter and the father wore in a pony-
tail. Blue eyes behind round glasses looked at the world and
its inhabitants with what seemed like constant surprise. She
wore a short denim skirt, a white Mostly Mozart T-shirt, and
running shoes. Josh was dressed in neatly pressed khaki trousers, a blue work shirt familiar to Schmidt from the L.L. Bean
catalog, and a loose white cotton jacket. The father and the
daughter were each carrying a small L.L. Bean duffel bag. In
addition, Josh carried what Schmidt thought had to be Charlotte's overnight suitcase. And his daughter? Schmidt thought
she hadn't looked so well since before she had married Riker:
erect, lithe, and radiant. And turned out in linen and khaki, as
though she had been shopping with Mary. He stepped toward
her, remembering to let her make the first move. Miraculously,
she kissed him! Dizzy from happiness and gratitude, he shook

Josh's hand, kissed Jenny on both cheeks, saying to himself
how perfectly fine they were these two Whites, it's as though
I had known them forever, as though they had always been
coming here. I have nothing to worry about.

Charlotte, he said, Please take Josh and Jenny to the pool
house. I strongly advise a dip. Whenever you're ready, come on
over to lunch. I have some lobsters in the kitchen that are very
eager to make your acquaintance.

When he recalled later the events of that weekend, poring
again and again over each scene as though he were viewing
a home movie in slow motion, he would savor the images of
Charlotte—he had been so proud of her!—and of their Monday morning at the beach. Under a cloudless sky, the beach
was almost deserted, most renters too busy vacating their
houses and loading their possessions into station wagons for
the long drive home to take advantage of the sand that the
receding tide had washed clean of footprints and left so brilliantly white and packed hard, or the long and regular September waves. It was warm, in the mideighties, but a gentle
onshore breeze made the air feel light and fresh. They had
all jumped in, and while Charlotte, Jenny, and Josh remained
close to shore, bobbing up and down in the surf, Schmidt set
out for a swim along the shore, allowing himself to be carried
east by the current, repeating to himself an incantation that
buoyed him, gave him strength, he thought, to swim as far as
Montauk: I am happy, I am grateful, everything is as it should
be. But he wasn't going to Montauk, his little family—why
shouldn't he call them that?—had probably climbed out of
the water and was wondering what to do about the errant old
codger. To test his new strength, he swam against the cur-

rent, battling it with huge strokes, caught a wave that like a conveyor belt carried him to the shore. Here I am, he cried!

It turned out that the girls—that's how he had started to refer to Charlotte and Jenny—wanted to lie on their towels right up near the dune and read. He glanced at the covers of their books. Charlotte was reading *The Hours*, and Jenny *Ethan Frome*, a summer assignment, she told him, that included writing a report. That too filled Schmidt with pride. His daughter, the ace literature student, was reading a first-rate book, and so was this kid whom he was eager to welcome officially into his family and home. He had warmed up from the swim and suggested to Josh that they take a walk together. Schmidt's future son-in-law turned out to be a fast walker, just as fast as he, and they congratulated each other on the excellence of the sand. Josh had been telling Schmidt about his parents— the father a professor of American history at the University of Virginia, the mother a pediatrician—and his only sibling, a younger brother who was also a doctor, still unmarried, when he stopped in midsentence and came to a halt.

Schmidtie, he said, I've been beating about the bush. I want to tell you something much more personal. But we can keep walking. First, my late wife. It was a long agony. She had ovarian cancer, which was removed together with her uterus but nevertheless metastasized, altogether it took her six years to die. Jenny was by then nine. She was expecting a little brother. The cancer wasn't discovered until Pam—that was my wife's name—began to hemorrhage. She was in her sixth month, but the baby couldn't be saved. Considering what followed, the years of chemo, radiation, and surgery, it was surely just as well. You can imagine that having lived through this I was immediately sympathetic to Charlotte's case.

Yes, said Schmidt, of course. He would have said more, but it was clear that Josh wanted to go on talking.

It would have been much worse if I hadn't had Jenny. You've had a chance to observe her. She's a good girl, really intelligent, and brave. I can talk to her like an adult. She's better than most adults, actually.

Schmidt nodded in the brief pause. He was beginning to worry about the direction of Josh's story.

I should tell you that I fell in love with Charlotte very soon after we met. Perhaps two weeks later. She was the most gifted of her group. I was glad to stay after class and talk to her. It took her much longer, naturally, since she wasn't well. But as she began to feel better she began to like me too. Schmidtie, she has made me incredibly happy.

Why, Josh, I am so happy to hear that!

But you must wonder why we aren't married, why we are still living apart—I mean in the city. Of course, we are all staying at Charlotte's house in Kent. Let me explain. I don't believe that Charlotte has kept you as informed as you'd probably want to be.

The words That's an understatement! were on the tip of his tongue. He did not say them, contenting himself with a nod.

I realize that, and I realize that this has been hard on you, but somehow it's been a part of her getting better. Let me explain. Jenny means everything to me. She is my great treasure. Very frankly I was afraid of proposing marriage to Charlotte, or even asking her to move in with us, until I became very sure that Charlotte has really become solid. You know what I mean. I could not risk Charlotte's having another incident—becoming very depressed—after Jenny had become dependent on her. As she would, because Charlotte is irresist-ible. But now it's all right.

So you think Charlotte has become solid? I don't need to tell you how important that is to me.

Yes, Josh replied, I do. I also think that Jenny has become mature enough to handle any difficulty that may come. But it won't. I won't let it. The long and the short of it, Schmidtie, is that I have come to ask for your daughter's hand.

Schmidt felt his knees buckle. Hell, at his age, after the swim and the walk, why shouldn't he do it? He sat down on the sand and motioned for Josh to sit down beside him. It was Charlotte who had told him that she and Jon Riker had decided to get married. He thought then that announcement spelled the end of a bearable existence slowly reconstituted after the loss of Mary that he might be able to sustain, so strong was his resentment of that man. Then Riker, in his own kitchen— they were staying with Schmidt in Bridgehampton—had had the gall to say that he hoped Schmidt approved of his making Charlotte an honest woman! How different, how unexpected, and how fitting seemed to him Josh White's proposal.

I am more deeply moved, Josh, he replied, than I know how to tell. Has Charlotte said yes? Because, if she has, I give you my consent with the greatest joy.

She has, she has! They stood up and embraced.

As they walked back toward the girls, Schmidt remember-ing what it is to walk on air, Josh explained that between his teaching jobs and sales of his work he made ends meet. Jenny had a scholarship at Friends, he owned his studio and the apartment, left to him by his late wife who had owned it, and there was a trust for Jenny set up under his wife's will that would pay for Jenny's college and give her a small income. A good new development was that his gallery dealer had proposed a contract under which he would be paid a monthly advance against future sales.

So as you see, Charlotte won't be coming into opulence, but our situation could be a great deal worse.

The children—that was his new term for them—wanted to leave for Kent directly after lunch, Josh having to teach at Sunset Hill the next day. Schmidt felt it was providential that first thing in the morning he had assembled a meal intended to be festive. He had a moment alone with Charlotte later, while Josh was putting their things in the car.

You are doing a very good thing, he told her, you will be a happy family.

I know, she answered, I plan to do my best.

The news came some three and a half hours later. Schmidt had done laps for precisely thirty minutes, the daily goal he had set; he had taken a shower and dressed and, aiming to continue the festivities, had made himself a gin martini. The Blackmans had invited him for dinner at eight, Gil saying it would be the usual suspects: Mike Mansour and Joe and Caroline Canning. When the telephone rang, Schmidt picked up the receiver eagerly, thinking that it was surely Charlotte or Josh calling to say that they had arrived and to thank him. But it was the police. There had been an accident. Would Schmidt be able to get to Patchogue? Yes, Patchogue, Brookhaven Memorial Hospital? Could the officer tell Schmidt what happened? It would all be explained when he arrived. Did he need directions? Schmidt wrote them down, his hand trembling, obliged to have them repeated twice before he was sure he had them straight. Then he called the Blackmans, told them where he was going, and got into his car.

The accident had happened on the Long Island Expressway, and it was huge. In traffic going at least sixty-five miles an hour, an eight-wheel rig carrying a load of steel I beams braked suddenly just ahead of Josh's station wagon. One of the beams was sent flying, crashed through the windshield, decapitated Charlotte in the passenger seat, continued on its way, and crushed the skull of Jenny, who was right behind her. Under the impact of the blow, Josh turned left sharply—or perhaps he was no longer in control of the car—and an SUV in the far left lane slammed full force into the side of the station wagon, with maximum impact at the driver's door. He died on the way to the hospital. They found Schmidt because the directions to his house, with his name and telephone number, lay in the glove compartment, together with the car's papers.

Yes, Schmidt could identify the bodies, and thanks to the conversation with Josh on the beach he could tell the police lieutenant that the father and daughter's next of kin could be found in Charlottesville. There were papers to be signed.

Then, supported by the police officer who saw that Schmidt was unsteady, he had a cup of black coffee, went to the toilet to urinate, and, seeing himself in the mirror afterward, while he washed his hands, asked himself aloud: Why should this man be alive?

XXIII

THE ANSWER to that vast question seemed quite simple to Schmidt. There was no reason that he should go on living other than his imperturbably good health—if he were to die in an accident, which seemed a likelier end than illness, he hoped his death would be as instantaneous as Charlotte's—and his lack of desire to kill himself. He had thought of suicide after Mary died and had inventoried the means: wading into heavy surf fully clothed and swimming out as far as he was able, a gambit guaranteed to drown even a strong swimmer; leftover pills that had been prescribed for Mary, including those that, as it turned out, had not been needed to put her over the top. What had stopped him then? Loss of nerve, disguised as pity for his own body, unprepared for the rolling and scraping against the ocean floor, and when the availability of pills, which involved no violence or superhuman effort, became clear, a high-minded pretext he had found, according to which he mustn't leave it up to Charlotte to clean up after both mother and father, that it was up to him to settle Mary's affairs. Evidently, he was still not a candidate for drowning. He knew he couldn't do it. He thought he knew equally well that if it were really necessary in order to escape a greater

evil, if the alternative were great suffering that could be alle-
viated only by procedures that turned his body into a bag of
flesh fitted with tubes for intake and evacuation, or if he were
threatened with imbecility, he would wash down those little
buggers with whatever he then fancied most—vodka, bourbon, gin, or even cognac, which of late he avoided because it
seemed to keep him awake. But at that point at least insomnia
would no longer be one of his concerns. And he couldn't care
less who cleaned up after him, whether the job was dispos-
ing of the body by having it buried next to Mary's dissolved
bones at the Sag Harbor cemetery or emptying his closets and
delivering the contents to the East Hampton charity thrift
shop or liquidating his assets and, after paying some small
bequests and funding the trusts for Carrie's children and Carrie, because surely he would leave money to her, delivering
the rest to the Treasury of the United States, the New York
State Finance Bureau, and Harvard University. Hell, he knew
who would do it: that clown Murphy, his former trusts and
estates partner, who had in his safe his last will and testament
and was designated therein to serve as Schmidt's executor.
No, it was no longer fear or some cockeyed notion of noblesse
oblige that kept him away from those itsy-bitsy pills. It came
down to this: he chose not to kill himself because, being well
housed, well fed, and well clothed, he was not averse to being
alive. Yes, alive in the arid plane of granite on which Charlotte
alone had flowered. In other words, he was a swine.

A swine who read the newspaper and occasionally watched
television and now sounded off about current events at Mike
Mansour's table free of the accustomed Schmidtian con-
straint, surprising himself and those who knew him best, to
wit Gil and Mike. Schmidt had observed the neat intertwin-

ing of public disasters with what he now thought had been Charlotte's stations of the cross. He continued his catalog, noting how each new horror ricocheted off his carapace of swinish indifference. The murderous pacification of Chechnya and the atrocities in Kosovo: how far away they seemed to the head of Mike Mansour's Life Centers! He bet against the success of peace talks in the Middle East and in Ireland, unwilling to grant that good sense could prevail over bloodlust and hatred. The slaughter in Timor, that was more like it. The stabilization of the economies in Asia disappointed him: wasn't it about time for all those little people to be taught a lesson, to realize that better fifty years of Europe than a cycle of Cathay? Might not the Y2K calamities cut everyone down to size, the yellow dwarfs included? He read Coetzee's *Disgrace*. The rape of Lurie's daughter, her acceptance of her fate, made him cry as if he were still capable of pity or compassion. The following year, schadenfreude had him rubbing his hands as he watched the dot-com bubble burst. Heeding Mike Mansour's advice, he had eschewed Internet technology investments. Schadenfreude likewise made him nod knowingly when he read about the intifada: the last Israeli leader he had admired had been Yitzhak Rabin, whom the Jews themselves had killed. It served them right to have as their statesman Ariel Sharon. But even the swine he had become refused to scoff at the bombing of the USS *Cole*; Schmidt mourned the seventeen sailors who met their end in the Gulf of Aden. Had their shrouded bodies been entrusted to the sea, he wondered, had that old custom survived? What was there to admire in the last year of the millennium? he asked himself on the climactic last day of the Democratic National Convention as he watched the incumbent president in a dark suit of Italian cut, confident and fit, his meaty nose turned up in greeting, emerge from an endlessly long white tunnel and walk toward the television cameras. The scenery suggested powerfully some as yet unrealized and triumphal segment of the *Star Wars* saga, the departing president's buoyant stroll into the future, the long and treacherous journey from his mother's trailer to the Oval Office having been accomplished. A fittingly meretricious capstone for eight years of tawdriness that had led, Schmidt thought, straight to the ascent of W and Cheney and eight years of the darkest misrule in American history. Yup, the carryings-on of a narcissistic man with a taste for sluttish women and fast food had done as much as the machinations of Karl Rove, or Anthony Kennedy's shamefully joining the four Supreme Court Neanderthals in the decision, signed by none of them, that allowed that duo to squeak into office.

Tuesday, September 11, 2001. Perfect blue sky, perfect late-summer temperature. If it hadn't been for the foundation's board meeting, Schmidt would have stayed in Bridgehampton. As it was, he had driven in the evening before, got to the office early to prepare for the meeting, which was to start at ten. His secretary, Shirley, walked into his room shortly after nine to say good morning and ask whether he wanted coffee.

By the way, she added, one of those pesky little private planes has plowed into one of the World Trade Center towers. There's smoke coming out the building where it hit. If you come to reception you'll have a good view.

Schmidt glanced at his papers. For all practical purposes he was ready. He walked down the corridor to where a large number of Mansour Industries employees already assembled in the forty-eighth-floor reception area were looking toward the southern tip of Manhattan, staring at the smoking tower, when the second plane hit. No one thought any longer that some neophyte aboard his Piper or Cessna was to blame. The traders who occupied two-thirds of the floor and had been glued to Madrid's *El Mundo* on their computers, unable to reach other sites, dashed in with the news; someone brought in a television set and connected to a German station. On the screen tiny-seeming figures, some of them holding hands, could be seen jumping from the vast height of the wounded buildings. Someone shouted, Look! Look! Schmidt turned away from the screen to look south, and before his eyes one tower crumbled and, not a half hour later, the second. Then came news of another plane that had hit the Pentagon and another still that had crashed in a field in Pennsylvania. And the passengers in those planes, men, women, children their seat belts buckled—waiting for the moment of impact, knowing that they were to die in flames of burning jet fuel. Schmidt found that he could not detach his thoughts from them, as though it were his own nightmare from which he was unable to awake. Were they praying? Strangers embracing strangers next to whom they sat across armrests? Recollecting quickly all that had been good and beloved in their lives? Some of the children must have understood, but the others? The infants? Did the sound of their wailing fill the planes' cabins? Did it soften the murderers' hearts or was it their foretaste of paradise?

Force of habit? Some other form of automatism? Schmidt went down to the boardroom. Mr. Mansour was there along with Holbein, who worked in the building, and three other directors who said they were stranded. They had arrived for the meeting around the time it happened—the pronoun was already becoming a shibboleth—and now? It was not clear what one was to do now. Mike left the room briefly and returned followed by a dining room employee carrying a tray with bottles of whiskey, glasses, and ice. Drinks were poured, and then Mike went around the room embracing his directors one after another. Suddenly, incongruously, they were all hugging, patting one another on the shoulders. The question is, said Mr. Mansour, what to do next. Should we have lunch here? I don't think so. I'm letting everyone in the building go home if they can. If they can't, I'm telling them to check into a hotel at the company's expense or sleep here. Meals are at the company's expense too. The chief of security has checked. You can move around Manhattan, except downtown, but you can't get out of the city. The bridges are closed, and the subways aren't running. You can telephone but not to all exchanges. Cell phones don't seem to be working. Schmidtie, he said, taking him aside, let's you and I go out to the Island together as soon we can. Probably it will be tomorrow. Make sure I can find you.

That was good of Mike, Schmidt thought. If they found they had to jump out of some window they too could hold hands.

He returned to an empty office. Shirley had left. He checked his telephone. It worked. But he had absolutely no one to call. Carrie? She was not the kind to worry; he did not need to reassure her. To talk to her about "it"? That was beyond his present capacity for speech. As he collected papers to put in his briefcase—but for what purpose?—a thought crossed his mind. Wasn't Jon Riker's firm in one of those towers? He remembered the firm's name, and his hands trembled as he turned the pages of the telephone directory. They must have moved. The published address was that of a building at the bottom of Broadway, one of those huge old buildings; he had attended meetings there in the past. No, there was no one to call and no place to go to. He supposed his club might be open, but who would be there? Other wrecks like himself? His kind of misery doesn't like company. He decided to go home. Home to his company flat. It had become a beautiful afternoon, except for the cloud of smoke and soot rising from the pyre to the south, the sort of afternoon that should have made one feel happy, glad to be enjoying the quiet reminiscent of a holiday, so empty of traffic were the streets, so many fathers, whose offices had closed, were walking hand in hand with children or pushing them ahead in baby carriages. Why stop when he reached his building and sit in his living room drinking himself into a stupor? He continued uptown until he reached a line stretching for two or three blocks of people waiting to give blood at the Lenox Hill Hospital.

All ages and classes were represented, all manner of clothes and demeanor, waiting with such infinite goodwill to do their duty as citizens, as humans. Totally unshaken: some, particularly prescient, had brought folding chairs and tables, but the line moved so slowly that they rarely needed to shift their improvised quarters. Companionably, they were playing cards. Gin rummy seemed to be the favorite, but Schmidt also noted games of bridge and poker. One or two groups of yuppies, in their office-casual Friday attire now worn all week, were sitting cross-legged on the sidewalk, their cards spread before them. He took his place in line. Perhaps an hour later, there was a vacant chair at one of the tables; someone had given up waiting. Whether because of his age, which betokened someone who knew how to play bridge, or some other reason, a young woman got up and asked Schmidt whether he would like to take the dummy's hand. He thanked her and sat down. A large black man in a doorman's uniform told him not to worry; he'd hold his place on line. How kind that was! Schmidt embraced him. At one time Mary and he had played regularly, and memories of Culbertson's conventions still rattled in his head. He found himself pulling out trump and making his bid. Then the word was passed that the blood center was closing: no additional donations would be accepted. The reason became apparent in the following days. There had been almost no wounded in need of transfusions, and there was more than enough plasma on hand for the few burn victims who had survived.

That evening he had dinner at Mike Mansour's triplex with him and Caroline Canning. When Mike called, and had ascertained that Schmidt was free, he said, Dinner won't be just you and me; Caroline will be with us. She came in yesterday evening to see *The Producers* with me—by the way, it's a great show, almost impossible to get tickets, but if you want I can get them for you, *pas de problème*. I recommend it. She was planning to go home this morning, but she's stuck! Just like you and me! Let me put her on. She'd like you to come.

Indeed: without alluding to what Schmidt knew she made it clear that she trusted his discretion. They were cozy, like an old married couple, she and Mike. So these were the joys of adultery that the stubborn fool he was had high-handedly refused. One week earlier he had returned from Europe on a direct flight from Warsaw. Had he been smarter, he could have stopped off in Paris, used the little apartment on the place du Palais Bourbon that Mike Mansour had decided was a better perch for Schmidt than the hotel on the place de la Concorde, and introduced Alice to its beautifully maintained Empire furniture, including the *lit bateau* that was actually big enough for two.

The country will not recover from this anytime soon, said Caroline. Muslim terrorists, a foreign plot! It's food for Know Nothing xenophobia and racial prejudice of the worst kind. And for the persecution complex of American crazies: like Tim McVeigh, like the Branch Davidians, like the Birchers, and the militias in the Northwest. You'll see.

Pas de problème. The question is, added Mike Mansour, nodding, what will Bush do. His government is weak. He'll do what all weak governments do. He'll start a war!

They were between courses, and Mr. Mansour's fist was at rest on the table. Caroline put her hand over it and caressed it, in agreement.

What do you think should be done, asked Schmidt.

Pas de problème. Send the CIA and whoever else you need, borrow some Mossad agents, find the bastards who were behind this, cut off their balls, stuff them in their mouths, and then slit their throats. Posting photographs of the corpses on the Web would be a nice touch. Ha! Ha! Ha! But this government is too dumb and too weak to do that. *Pas de problème!* They'll go for another Gulf War! Look for an easy triumph on the cheap!

Do you agree, Caroline, asked Schmidt, as a historian, as someone who has written about the Red Scare in the twenties?

She drew a deep breath and continued to fondle Mike's hand.

Mike's right about weak governments in general, and this is a weak government. Wilson was unable to function, he was out of it, when his attorney general, Mitchell Palmer, launched his raids. Would Wilson have let him do it if his mind had remained unclouded? I doubt it. Bush, the people around him, right now they're in shock. When they realize that this is a golden opportunity to kick some butt, they'll have no trouble selling him on the idea.

You're so astute, Caroline, Schmidt blurted out, I am so glad you allowed me to join you tonight, I'm so grateful to you and to Mike.

Hush, Schmidtie, she said, you've already had a couple of rough years, and now this! We have to endure it, you have to endure it, we didn't want you to be alone. Who can say what sorrows your daughter has been spared?

The swine in Schmidt began a retreat, it seemed to Schmidt, the beginning of which dated from the unexpected and weird concern he had suddenly felt for the odious Jon Riker. No, it hadn't been a moment of weakness. To have wished that Riker had been asphyxiated or burned alive in the tower where his office had once been would have meant he had gone mad. He had avoided folly. One thing leads to another. Myron Riker had appeared out of the blue at Charlotte's funeral, standing among the handful of other mourners: the Blackmans, Mike Mansour, Caroline (without Joe), Jason and Carrie, and Bryan. Myron had read about the accident, he told Schmidt and, having murmured a few words of condolence, disappeared instead of following the others to Schmidt's house for the baked funeral meats. And so, some days after he, Mike, and Caroline had returned to the Island, Schmidt remembered Myron's gesture. He still had the cell phone number. He called Myron and told him about verifying Jon's address. Yes, Myron replied, thank you, they only moved a year ago. Otherwise, with Jon's habit of always being at the office before eight . . . He didn't finish.

The quality of his grieving for Charlotte, the outrage that had been like a long shriek, gradually was transformed into a ritual of remembrance. When he was at home, he would look at the albums Mary had put together recording Charlotte's childhood and adolescence and go over and over incidents that they recalled. The pictorial record stopped there, that fact offering a reminder of a different sort, attesting to how early she had grown away from them, even while Mary was still alive, well before the onset of open hostility after she and Jon decided to get married. When he was traveling, he carried a frame holding four photographs of her at different ages, always setting it on the nightstand, and he would think back, proceeding year by year but leaving out the bad times, until it seemed that her ghost had been appeased. Yes, Charlotte had been spared a lot. Inevitable disappointments in a new marriage, the ravage wrought by passing years, the constant menace of a return of her depression, illnesses, and pain. Doctors he had asked about sudden decapitation were unanimous: there would have been no anxiety, no possibility of conscious sensation. She had likewise been spared the knowledge of the Dark Age engulfing the country and the shame that Schmidt like many other Americans felt when going abroad, whether he went to Europe on foundation business or to South America or Asia on museum tours, for which he had resumed signing up.

After the disgrace of Abu Ghraib and the still open sewer of Guantánamo, hope for his country began to stir in

Schmidt with the first signs of strength in Barack Obama's candidacy. He read hastily his autobiography, wondered whether anyone so angry at American racism could be the president of white as well as of black Americans, and decided to trust this skinny and brilliant young man, a man married to a girl who, in a simpler time, had she been white and single, would have been America's sweetheart.

It was in mid-September, after Obama had secured the Democratic nomination, that Schmidt and Gil Blackman met at Schmidt's club for their first lunch in town that fall. The subjects of their conversations had changed little over the years, except that now Mr. Blackman avoided mention of his daughters and stepdaughter or Charlotte, a tactful omission for which Schmidt did not fail to be grateful. Another difference was that Gil no longer mentioned DT. The film business Aphrodite had decamped, pocketing a million dollars she had extracted from Mr. Blackman as the price of not telling Elaine about her abortion. It was money well earned and well spent, was Mr. Blackman's stated opinion, with which Schmidt agreed, although he knew that behind the façade of his friend's Olympian calm lay a lake of fury and resentment. The show must go on, and Mr. Blackman, not having had a hit since *The Serpent*, was thinking about another cooperation with the unbearable Joe Canning. One that would be truly difficult: the idea was to make a film based on Joe's first book, the novel that had made him instantly famous.

It will be hell, said Mr. Blackman. The story is about a woman called Magda, who, like Joe's grandmother, emigrates with her parents from Belorussia. The family settles in Minnesota, but Magda leaves to lead her own life in South Dakota.

From there on, the stories of the two women are very much alike, the only interesting difference being that the grandmother was Jewish and Magda is a shiksa. Joe's line has always been that Magda's story is fiction, and not the story of his grandmother. He claims it only follows the grandmother's story in outline. You can imagine how this sort of hairsplitting goes over with journalists and other interviewers who are convinced he has written a barely disguised true story of the grandmother. True or not, it's clear that there are things Magda does that Joe would have trouble admitting had been done by his beloved grandmother. On the other hand, if they are invented, that bastard is even sicker than we imagine. If they are true, he is a monster of indiscretion. Adding to the complications of fact versus fiction, there is the question of Joe's surname. Canning doesn't have much to do with the name of his Belorussian shtetl forebears on his father's side, and none of his cousins has adopted it. There is no telling what his siblings might have done. He doesn't have any. I have to hand it to him, though. After being badgered more often and far longer than he liked with questions about whether the book is a fictionalized biography of his grandmother, and about his Anglo-Saxon name, he finally came up with a reply that rings true: he said he doesn't want to be thought of solely as a Jewish novelist. That's fair enough. Who would want to stand in the shadow of Bellow and Roth?

The die is cast, Mr. Blackman concluded. I've spoken to Mike, and he's crazy about the project. Hot to trot. No turning back now.

That's wonderful, said Schmidt. I hope it does as well as The Snake!

You and me both. Now I have some other news for you. Fasten your seat belt and open your mind. I don't suppose you read *Harvard Magazine*. Do you?

Schmidt shook his head. Can't stand it, he said. Ever since they changed the format.

That was a hundred years ago. Well, I read it, mainly for the class notes. Guess what I read about our class?

Once again, Schmidt shook his head.

Serge Popov is dead. Died last June. In Paris. Fell off his bicycle. No helmet. Boom boom: he's dead.

Goodness, said Schmidt.

Schmidtie, please stick you know where your "my goodness" and "my my" and "good heavens." That's not the response I was hoping for. It's your last chance, you old fart. You owe it to yourself to find out whether Alice is free, whether you still like her, and whether she can stand you.

Gil, thanks for this news. But stop looking for a Hollywood ending. You do recall that Alice and I did not part on a good note. You're asking me to make an even bigger fool of myself. Sending me to offer her an old fart with whom she can have the pleasure of living out the last ten years of his life? That's one offer I bet she can resist.

Why ten? What's to stop you from living till you're ninety-five?

That would only make it worse.

XXIV

ARE YOU A VULTURE, or one of those *pauvres types*, losers, who can't resist a funeral? I mean any funeral? Alice asked Schmidt when he finally reached her at home. Her voice was as harsh as her words. He had been trying her number for several days, without leaving a message. You heard that Tim was dead so you showed up. Now poor Serge is dead, and right away it's you again. What kind of man are you?

A desperately sad man. A man who fell in love with you many years ago and now wants a second chance. Please give it to me. Please agree to see me.

I don't see why.

I want to come to Paris to explain to you why. Please let me. What possible harm would that do?

It would upset me. I'm sad enough as it is. I don't see why I should give you a chance to make it worse.

He heard her stifling a sob.

Alice, trust me, please! I won't upset you. You'll do us both a great injustice if you refuse to see me. Please think about it overnight, or longer—but not too long please! When may I call you again?

All right, she said. Tomorrow, a little earlier. Call me at eight. Good-bye.

That would be two in the afternoon, Schmidt's time. He would be in New York, which was a good thing because work would keep his mind off the call he was to make. He ate a sandwich in the cafeteria, wished that he still smoked, and at quarter of two was at his desk, a triple espresso laced with hot milk before him. She answered on the first ring.

Dear Alice, he said, please give me a favorable answer.

There is no favorable answer. Anyway, I don't know what it would be. If you do come to Paris, I suppose I can have dinner with you. When will you be here?

The day after tomorrow, he said, this coming Thursday. October fourteenth.

Very well. Call me at the office.

It was close to noon by the time the plane landed. He could hardly contain himself waiting for the announcement that cell phones could be switched on. If it took much longer, she'd have gone to lunch, and there was no telling when she'd get back. He'd been an idiot not to agree with her where and at what time they would have dinner. At last! She answered at once; he did not have to speak first to the secretary. Alice, we've just landed. I'm still in the airplane. I am so eager to see you, so happy that it will be in a few hours, I can hardly wait for this evening!

Are you staying at that hotel? she asked.

No, in an apartment the foundation rents on place du Palais Bourbon.

What's the number there?

He gave it to her, slowly, and then also his cell phone number, asking her to read them both back and to try the landline first when she called.

Look, Schmidtie, she said, the fact is you pressured me. I'm not at all sure that agreeing to see you was a good idea. I'm having lunch with a friend whose advice I trust. If after talking to her I decide to see you I'll call. Otherwise, I won't. Please don't argue with me. In the worst case you will have a very good dinner somewhere alone. I hadn't thought about you in a long time, and now that you've reminded me that you exist I'm furious.

She hung up.

Somehow he got off the plane, collected his suitcase, and took a taxi to his apartment. Would she call? He thought the chances were slightly better than even that she would. But to think that his fate would be decided by some biddy working in Alice's publishing house! Probably not Claude, the wife of the *pénaliste*, at whose St. Cloud house she'd been on the "sleepover" that had caused Schmidt so much grief. If she were the trusted advice-dispensing friend, wouldn't Alice have named her? It had to be someone else, and although the friend was French he thought he knew the kind, knew it intimately. Enough of them had come to dinner or lunch or drinks and God knows what else while Mary was still alive. Widowed, divorced, or lesbian, all permanently soured on men for one reason or another. Ugh! The thing to do was to go out and clear his head before it burst. As the chances of her coming to the apartment in the afternoon were close to zero, proper unpacking could wait.

The sun had come out from behind some very high clouds. Walking quickly, he crossed the square and then the Seine at the Pont de la Concorde. He knew where he was going: to that spot in the Tuileries where he now knew that final chapter of his life, his rebirth under the sign of Alice, had begun. He found a green metal folding chair near the *bassin*. If it had been a Wednesday afternoon, when schools were closed all day, a flock of children would have been there taking advantage of this glorious October afternoon. They'd be launching their model sailboats and motorboats under the supervision of mothers, nannies, or retired grandfathers, all of them hovering just behind their charges, ready to restrain a child who was leaning too far over the water. Long ago he had dreamed of bringing a grandchild and the fancy sailboat that was a present from Grandpa Schmidtie to the pond in Central Park. Watching other people's grandchildren was the best he could aspire to now. If he was still around on Saturday and the weather held, he could have his fill of children at this *bassin* or at the one in the Luxembourg Gardens, at the pony and donkey rides, at the carousel where they tilted at the brass ring, or at the remarkably well-appointed Luxembourg playground that charged admission. That was a practice that had never ceased to shock Schmidt: paying for the right to play in a public park! For that matter, if the grandparents were feeling flush in the midst of a financial crisis that could turn into a second Great Depression, they would perhaps be at the atrociously expensive aquarium at the Trocadéro. The day before, the Dow had closed at around 8,500, a dispiriting decline considering that a year earlier it had stood above 14,000. Not that Schmidt was worried. He still had more than enough money. No, as Mike Mansour had been fond of saying before the spectacle of Schmidt's misery made the inquiry seem cruel, the question was: Did Schmidt have anything to spend his money on or anyone to spend it with? Did he have a life or only an estate plan? The answer to these unanswered questions now depended on Alice. Alice seeking lunchtime counsel from some feminist fossil who was surely one of Serge's allies; Alice at her office, where everything, perhaps even a photograph on her desk, must remind her of Serge; Alice recalling the humiliation to which Schmidt subjected her in London.

The dozen or so boats in the water were all piloted by elderly types—in Schmidt's opinion, retired postal clerks, shopkeepers, and café owners, if café owners who did not retire to their native hamlets in Auvergne existed—hunched over their control consoles. A regatta, complicated by a puffy breeze, was in progress. The lead boat, which had been barreling wing and wing toward a notional buoy, its location fixed by a mysterious agreement of the owners, rounded it, jibing noisily, and continued, close hauled, on a port tack. Moments later, the other boats also cleared the marker, and the entire armada was beating toward the far shore. They still had a ways to go when Schmidt's attention to the race slackened. The afternoon might be mild, but he was shivering. He knew the reason: nerves and fatigue. He should have worn a sweater under his heavy tweed jacket.

What's done cannot be undone. By him or by others. For instance: just then, coming about at the next buoy, the lead boat pinched its sails. In irons, the mainsail luffing helplessly, it lost precious seconds that Schmidt didn't think could be made up. What had remained of his interest in the race vanished. The damage done in London, he suddenly concluded, was likewise beyond repair. He was insane to have come to Paris to plead his case. His reward would be a fiasco followed by the start of a new cycle of sorrow and remorse.

He checked the cell phone in his jacket pocket and shrugged: it was turned on, the battery was fully charged; Alice was still at lunch confessing to the feminist director of conscience. Following the familiar route to Alice's apartment, he left the Tuileries through a side entrance and walked along rue de Rivoli toward the gray vastness of the place de la Concorde. His reflection in the window of Hilditch & Key, before which he stopped because of the display of shirts and neckties on sale, frightened him. Red nose and bloodshot eyes, lips pursed up tight over the shame of stained and uneven front teeth, an expression so lugubrious, so pained, that it resisted his effort to smile. The features could not be rearranged; the mouth continued to droop. His mop of hair, once red and now discolored and streaked with gray, stood on end and stuck out over his ears. He knew who he looked like: the man, the monstrous chemistry teacher become a hobo reeking of carrion, Mr. Wilson, who had deflowered and would have, but for the strength of her character, perverted the fourteen-year-old Carrie! He had run over and killed Mr. Wilson in heavy fog on a Bridgehampton road. And now he had turned into the image of the man! Twinned with Mr. Wilson. Twinned with him in misery and disgrace.

Should he run away, leave Paris without seeing Alice? Turn off his cell phone, let the phone in the apartment ring unanswered, run before she can grant him an audience or deny it. He could pick up his kit, head for Roissy, and take a plane for most any place on the globe. What good was having an American passport and money if not for just such an escape? Once he got wherever he had decided to go, he would sit and think and send her a postcard if he found one he liked. After all, people change their plans all the time, on a moment's notice. Hadn't Alice just done so herself? He had never stood up anyone before, but why let that stop him? Alice wouldn't be shocked or disappointed. She would be relieved, her view of him as a cad royally confirmed. A childish wish formed in his head: he wanted to call Carrie and ask her what to do. But even he, stupid though he was in his panicked state, knew that would be a dumb move.

In fact, the idea of running away was absurd. He did have to think, but he could think right here in Paris, and think fast, before it was too late. The first order of business was to brush his hair and then wash his face and hands in real hot water. It would help to have a drink too, something warm, a toddy, or even a cup of hot chocolate. Logically, he should jump into a taxi—if he retraced his steps he could find one at the stand on rue de Castiglione—and go home. But what had logic to do with how he felt? Here he was in Alice's neighborhood, a circumstance that he found comforting and fitting, consistent with his status as a supplicant pilgrim. Besides, he wasn't sure he could face the unpacked suitcase and the edgy elegance of his apartment, the good pieces of furniture, the stately velvet curtains framing the windows, the sheen of the parquet floor. His present needs could be satisfied just as easily at the Meurice, three blocks away on rue de Rivoli, going in the wrong direction. He had never stayed there, but since it had been good enough to serve as command headquarters for the Wehrmacht all through the war, it would probably suffice as a place for him to pee. The old Continental was nearer but in his opinion was déclassé, having been renamed after it was bought by some midwestern chain; he'd have to make do there with paper towels in the washroom. He had reached the Meurice when a thought struck him. Eye drops! Is it Murine or Visine that gets the red out? Backtracking, he found both at the English pharmacy in the middle of the first block of rue de Castiglione and bought one of each. His spirits lifted.

Nor did the *toilettes* at the Meurice disappoint him: huge mirrors and overhead lights muted to be flattering. His most urgent business done, he examined his face more closely. The furrows left by his habitual scowl were what they were, and he would not pay to have them erased. Besides, would anyone recognize him without them? The same went for the bags under his eyes, although he knew that shrinking them was a simple enough matter. Gil Blackman had had a polo-playing doctor on the Upper East Side, renowned for eye work, fix him up, but Schmidt did not direct big-budget films and unlike Gil at the time had no DT to look younger for. He would do without Hollywood-style improvements. His teeth were another matter. Gil had also had his front teeth capped, a procedure that was possible if, despite wretched appearance, they were still soundly rooted. Gil's natural teeth were filed down and then covered with individual caps so cunningly fashioned from tinted porcelain that no one could guess they were an orthodontist's handiwork. A major financial transaction would doubtless be required, especially in view of the dentist's confession to Gil that he had been ripped off by Madoff. It stood to reason that the dentist would try to recoup from his patients by slapping a surcharge on his bills. So be it! Why skimp on the upkeep of his mouth while not questioning the need to stain the house or paint the trim whenever Bryan, his self-appointed cat sitter, handyman, and majordomo, told him that time had come again? He would let Gil's dentist fix his teeth and still manage to cross the ocean anytime Alice beckoned and to be in Paris as long and as often as she liked, if only he could persuade her to take him back. Not that Schmidt expected to be making those trips and burning through his money for very long. The ten years' estimate he had given Gil was 100 percent sincere. Albert and his little sister and any brothers and sisters to come would still receive the legacy he had promised Carrie and Jason, and there would be plenty left over for Alice if only . . .

The toilet attendant, a smiling brown-skinned gentleman—nothing wrong with that man's teeth!—filled the basin with warm water. Schmidt asked to have it hotter, slowly washed his hands and face, dried them with a good linen towel tendered him on a salver, and put a drop of Visine in each eye. It stung, but the effect was satisfying. A two-euro coin deposited on the same salver discreetly tendered again elicited a broader smile with lots of teeth. Two more attempts to smile at himself in the mirror, and Schmidt was ready to sally forth. Call Alice? No way. He would wait for her to make a move. Tea and drinks were served in the hotel lobby. He found an armchair in the corner, hesitated between a bourbon and hot chocolate, and chose the latter. The tea sandwiches looked good. It turned out they were. Ravenously hungry—he had eaten a yogurt on the airplane, refusing the rest of the breakfast—he kept reordering until a benign warmth spread through his body. At last he began to feel calm.

More than an hour later, when he was back at the apartment, she did call. He had unpacked and reestablished order among the photographs on the desk in the living room and on the chest of drawers in the bedroom: Mary, Charlotte during her last year at Brearley, Carrie during their first year together, Carrie and little Albert, and Alice, this last presumably forgotten by her, else she would have asked him to return it. Ten years old, she stood on the beach in Deauville, shirtless in a little boy's short pants, behind her the flat sea.

Well, vulture man, she said, are you too tired to have dinner tonight?

No, yes, I mean yes, I would like to have dinner tonight. Where? When?

Eight o'clock? You said your apartment is on the place du Palais Bourbon. There is a good restaurant on the right-hand side of rue de Bourgogne, in the last block, the block between rue de Grenelle and rue de Varenne. It's number fifty-something. I'll make the reservation and meet you there.

It was one of those restaurants without a vestibule: one walked in directly from the street past a heavy red velvet curtain concealing the first of two rooms where diners were seated. Pulling the curtain aside and greeting Schmidt was a young man in a suit, the manager or the owner, who also took his raincoat and handed it to a young woman summoned from somewhere in the back. When Schmidt said that he was meeting Madame Verplanck, the young man was all smiles and led Schmidt to a table in the first room from which he could see people enter. The restaurant was pleasantly full; the low pitch of the French chatter was pleasant as well. It was ten to eight. That too was well. He had wanted to be the first to arrive. Since the young man assured him that he could make a dry gin martini, Schmidt ordered one and was not disappointed. Then he saw her walk through the door. She wore a light brown overcoat that hugged her figure. Time and recent grief—Popov!—had traced new fine lines in the corners of her mouth and caused her eyes to retreat deeper into their sockets. There was more gray in her hair, more than he would have thought likely for dark blond hair. He thought she resembled Michèle Morgan and was more beautiful than she had been thirteen years earlier, quite simply the loveliest woman he had ever seen. He rose and reached her before the young man had helped her out of her coat. A scent enveloped her that was a mixture of a perfume he didn't know, her body warmed by a long walk—he was sure she had walked, he would have seen her taxi if one had pulled up—and of the fresh evening air. It overwhelmed him. He had not made a mistake: he loved her. She pulled off her long dark red suede gloves and held out her hand, palm down and bent slightly at the wrist. He knew it was a sign that she expected to have her hand kissed, but he feared doing it awkwardly, like an American. Instead he took her hand—a marvelously warm large hand with long fingers that had traveled over every inch of his body—and shook it.

He waited until her glass of champagne was served and she had drunk from it to tell her about Charlotte. At some point, perhaps when he spoke about his visits to Sunset Hill, she put her hand over his and left it there until he had finished.

So now you know, he said. You had to know. The wound isn't one that can heal, but I've learned to live with it. That is a given. It's very strange, I wouldn't have believed it myself, but now that I'm with you, I am more certain than ever before, more certain than when we were in each other's arms, that I love you. That is assuming *"love"* is the correct term for the experience of great happiness due to the other person's presence and the astonishing need, like the need to get enough air into your lungs, to make the other person happy, to protect her, to surround her by a mountain range of goodness. That is also a given. There is yet another given, which is my age. I will be seventy-eight next month. I am in excellent health, that's nothing new, I've never missed a day of work. Still, something tells me I have only ten years to live. Actually, that's the most favorable hypothesis, assuming that during those ten years my physical condition, my vigor, and my energy can remain undiminished. I sense that they will. Beyond? It's anyone's guess. I tend to think that the worst outcomes are most likely. Considering these facts, if I were your father or your brother . . .

My father died, she broke in, his girlfriend too. I have no brother.

I am so very sorry, Schmidt persisted, but if your father were alive and you sought his advice he would surely tell you I'm not a horse you should bet on. So let me fill in a few details of what I am proposing, and my reasons, and why I believe I am at least entitled to plead my case.

Oh, Schmidtie. She sighed. What a lot of words.

Yes, I'm ashamed to run on like this, but do hear me out. It's been such a long time since we were last together, there is so much to say, and this concerns the most important business of my life.

Schmidtie, she said, if I must go on listening I shall, but do order another glass of champagne.

Done, he said.

They were silent while they waited for their drinks, and Schmidt, without thinking, permitted himself an extraordinary liberty. He took her hand and caressed it and then brought it to his lips.

As soon as she had taken a sip, he continued. He was in a hurry to say it all; he couldn't help himself.

You remember that I proposed marriage. That offer stands. You would make me happiest by accepting it. Our life together would have a simple, clear structure. But it doesn't have to be marriage. Live with me, on such terms and on such conditions as you like. In sin! Wherever you wish. Bridgehampton and New York City, they are my home; I know how to live there. The house in Bridgehampton is one that I know you'd like. But I can live most of the year here in Paris. Or anyplace else.

I've inherited my father's beautiful house in Antibes, she whispered.

All right, I've never been to Antibes, but I've always wanted to know the Côte d'Azur. Just a few more words, beautiful Alice, a few more words about you and me. I loved our sex. I can still do it. I can't imagine I'll be getting better, but who knows? Little father's helper pills have been invented that didn't exist back then. I haven't tried them, but I'm told they're good, and I'm ready to use them. Now, why do I dare to speak to you like this? First, because I love you. Second, because you seemed to like me. Third, because I am so very lonely, and I know my life would be transformed, made joyous, if I lived with you. Fourth, because I reason that, unless you have someone else—and if you do, please tell me, and I'll stop at once—you might also be lonely. Life with me might be an improvement for you too.

She whispered again: I have no one. And I am lonely. My son, Tommy, is my only family. He's a professor of mathematics at the University of Melbourne and living with a psychologist who is almost six feet tall. She is teaching him to surf. I went to see them last August. It didn't go well.

That's very hard, he said. Alice, I know that we would do well together, making love, keeping each other company, making sure neither of us feels lonely, cut off from life. Will you risk it? Will you give me a second chance?

I gave you a first chance, she said, and look what happened.

But Alice, you gave it to me without setting down the rules, disclosing all the terms. I thought that there was no one else then either. I made a fool of myself thinking that, babbling away about marriage and so forth. If I had known about Serge, I wouldn't have behaved that way. I'm certain of it.

He knew that his answer was disingenuous. It was impossible for him to know that he would have been willing to share Alice. What he really meant was that, had he known, their first afternoon together would likely have ended when they rose from the lunch table. He did not think that he would have competed for Alice with Serge.

I know, she said. It was stupid of me. Perhaps wicked. I wanted you to think I was better than I was. I kept on meaning to explain it to you, and then I couldn't. So I was wrong. I was at fault. But Schmidtie, you showed me another side of yourself, one that was angry and mean. How am I to know that you'll be able to keep it in check? That you will be able to look at me, touch me, make love to me, live with me, without thinking, This is Serge's girl. Or whatever horrible way you might put it.

There is only my assurance. I understand that may not be enough. There is the fact that I have been through a lot since that time. It may sound stupid, but it's true: I've grown up. I'm different now. I can step back from things instead of going off on a tear. A nasty tear it was, I know.

I see, she said.

I don't think I've convinced you. I have an idea: why don't you try me out? Satisfaction guaranteed or your money back. Alice, give me that chance. Come away with me—to Venice, to Vienna, to Barcelona. Please, Alice!

You're such a baby, Schmidtie! I'm a working girl with

responsibilities. Even if I were ready to say I want to, I couldn't fly off with you just like that, on some trial honeymoon.

Then come to see me in Bridgehampton! Come for a nice long visit. Or part New York and part Bridgehampton. At Christmas!

She became very serious. I think I will give you that chance. Not at Christmas, but I could come to Bridgehampton on New Year's Eve. And I might stay for a week.

She laughed. If you give satisfaction. But there are two conditions: you leave me alone, you let me think until then without being harangued, and you agree that I may change my mind.

You mean you might not come?

Yes, that is what I mean. But I'll let you know, one way or the other.

They ate almost in silence. When they finished, she said, I'm going to ask them to call a taxi. It's too late for us to walk. She let him hold her hand. When they were on rue St. Honoré, outside her building, she offered him first one and then the other cheek to kiss. Since she wasn't turning to punch in the code that would open the door, he took her in his arms and kissed her on the lips, insistently, until she opened her mouth and her tongue joined his. It was a long kiss, her mouth abandoned to him and her body pressed against his.

I wanted it so badly, she gasped, it's the only reason I might perhaps give you that second chance. But it's a bad reason.

Alice, he answered, it's the best reason. Please, may I come upstairs?

No, she answered, not tonight. Wait till I come to see you on *la St. Sylvestre*, New Year's Eve. If I do decide to come. Oh, Schmidtie, please go away!

XXV

Thursday, January 1, 2009, nine o'clock in the morning. The outdoor thermometer on Schmidt's front porch showed sixteen degrees. It would warm up later in the day, but not much. The predicted high of twenty-five still seemed a good bet. He picked up the newspaper from the beginning of his driveway and brought it into the kitchen. Sy and Pi were sitting next to their dishes looking alert and expectant, Pi as always silent, Sy making guttural observations that Schmidt knew how to translate—Hurry up, stupid, we're hungry, and other sentiments to that effect.

Good morning, cats, replied Schmidt, and Happy New Year! Keep your shirts on. It's coming.

He meant their daily portion of a half can of cat food each and, in addition, out of deference to the bargain struck between the Cat that walked by itself and the Woman, for each a bowl of milk with a small spoonful of the Swiss yogurt that was Schmidt's favorite.

Because of the holiday, Sonia wouldn't be coming. It was just as well; he had looked forward to preparing breakfast for Alice and himself, with croissants he'd bought the day before at Sesame as the *plat de résistance*. He found they didn't need

to be heated and so set them out on a plate, got butter out of
the fridge, and from the cupboard local honey from a farmer
in Water Mill and, as a special treat, bitter orange marmalade
that was distinctly not local. The next step was to make coffee in the push-through device and to heat milk. He took his
coffee black, but Alice might want café au lait, so it was best
to be ready. The truth was that he didn't recall ever having
had breakfast with her. All his preparations were a shot in the
dark. But if it turned out that she wanted eggs sunny side up
with bacon, she wouldn't be disappointed. He was ready to
display his talents as a short-order cook. It would have given
him wonderful pleasure to take a tray up to her, but she had
made a point of telling him when she awoke that she wanted
to have her breakfast in the kitchen, exactly the way he did
every day.

Although they had gone to bed late—after Mike Mansour's
party, there had been necking and toasting the New Year at
home—she had awakened early because of the change in time
zones, and when she began to stir, he woke up too. Then he
remembered: contrary to Alice's injunction that she would
sleep in his bed but they would only cuddle—a restriction for
which he, fearful of being put to the test, had been grateful—
they had in fact made love. She made it clear she wanted it.
They had gone to bed naked; he was lying on his back, drifting
into the vague space that separates sleep from waking, when
he felt her buttocks on his thigh. She was rubbing against him,
warm and moist and, he had no doubt, open. How to respond
without spooking her? Making her think that he had forgotten
that only cuddling was allowed? Was this perhaps only a more
advanced form of cuddling? The refrain of a Frank Sinatra song
rose up from wherever sixty-year-old memories are stored:

Easy does it, yes easy does it every time. He began to respond to the rhythm of her pressure but very mildly, staying, he thought, within the vast land of the cuddle, joyous to find her movements and her breathing accelerating and the flow of moisture confirming that she was ready. But was he? He thought so. A discreet movement of his right hand reassured him. And then he felt, heard her come! Sweetie, he asked, would you like to? The question was fair; he had learned that her first rapid climax was most often only a prelude. She turned and pulled him toward her until he was between her legs. At once she raised her knees. Almost unbearable happiness, he thought, intense, profound pleasure that was a homecoming.

The cats had licked their dishes and bowls clean and now, like a vaudeville team, sat before the door leading to the garden. Right away, Schmidt said, at your service, but remember it's cold. If you don't like it, come back quick. The kitty door is open. He held the screen door while they sniffed and surveyed the situation. No rush, Schmidt told them, I like to freeze. Then they were out. Schmidt watched them, Sy limping slightly, Pi way ahead. Arthritis, that was what the vet had told him. He's a senior cat. That was the truth: he might live happily another five years, half the time Schmidt envisaged remaining for himself. Left behind, Pi would be disconsolate. If it turned out that Alice liked cats—No, you idiot, Schmidt reproved himself, the question is whether it turns out that she likes you—all right, if Alice likes him, and likes cats, Pi might get to bring up an Abyssinian or Siamese kitten as carefully as he had been brought up by Sy. Everything depended on Alice.

The water in the electric kettle was boiling; the milk was hot; he was ready to argue his case, with hope of prevailing in the capital affair of his life. He heard her footsteps on the uncarpeted back stairs that led directly to the kitchen. That she should descend them, as though the house were hers, that she should be barefoot, enchanted him. Had he developed a foot fetish? Once more he noticed with great emotion the bright red she always painted her toenails. His gaze traveled up to take in the celadon peignoir, white nightgown embroidered with tiny red and green flowers, the hair loose, the lips, the body that had lately clung to his.

Bonne année, mon Schmidtie.

She put her arms around his neck and kissed him on the eyes and then on the lips. A long, gentle kiss, unlike the kisses that had taken command of his mouth, probing for something deep inside him.

What a beautiful breakfast!

Yes, she liked both honey and marmalade, and did take milk.

Having drunk her cup of coffee, she said: I have a statement to make. I am definitely keeping you. But are you ready to be kept on my terms? I won't marry you; not now, perhaps never, though perhaps after a while. I won't leave Paris until I am obliged to retire. That won't be for another year. If I'm allowed to stay on as some sort of consultant, I'll probably want to. It wouldn't be for long. It will be better for us if I continue working. My conversation will be more entertaining. But I'll spend as much time with you as you like, and as work permits. Here, if you prefer. But I'd be very happy if you spent a lot of time with me in Paris. And one thing more: I will be faithful to you, Schmidtie, because I love you. What do you think? Is it a deal? With these terms, will you have me?

Was this the modern form of the marriage vows?

I do, Schmidt replied, I do, I will.

A NOTE ON THE TYPE

The text of this book was set in Van Dijck, a modern revival of a typeface attributed to the Dutch master punchcutter Christoffel van Dyck (c. 1606–1669).

Typeset by Scribe, Philadelphia, Pennsylvania
Printed and bound by RR Donnelley,
Harrisonburg, Virginia
Designed by Peter A. Andersen